SEX, GODS AND ROCK & ROLL

A trilogy – Legend One

CURSE OF THE JUJU BIRD GODS

DENNIS CONLON

Published in 2014 by FeedARead.com Publishing

Copyright © The author as named on the book cover.

First Edition

The author has asserted their moral right under the
Copyright, Designs and Patents Act, 1988, to be identified
as the author of this work.

All Rights reserved. No part of this publication may be reproduced, copied, stored in a retrieval system, or transmitted, in any form or by any means, without the prior written consent of the copyright holder, nor be otherwise circulated in any form of binding or cover other than that in which it is published and without a similar condition being imposed on the subsequent purchaser.

A CIP catalogue record for this title is available from the British Library.

Phoenix Book Designs

Acknowledgements

What can I say but THANK YOU for all the support received in writing this book: to the members of the many writing and editing groups I've passed through. All at FFG, my Editor in Chief, Mark Leyland, my guru, Michael J Hunt, Mary Berry, Janet Green, Vic Hanson of Trebuchet. All at SWC, especially my inspirational muse, Dorothy. Apart from the book there is also the audio version, for my Dragon's Den submission. All at Scriptshop, especially, my script writing guru, Julie McKiernan. To Darryl Clark, Andy Cryer and Northern Broadsides for the actors and musicians who did the recording. Of course, Roy Johnson for his production and kind use of his studio and without whom this whole project wouldn't exist. And finally, my beautiful children: Katrina, Dominic, Sean, Charlotte and John, for keeping me happy and putting up with me, (though I'm hoping they don't read the naughty bits). And to John for his wonderful designs. Love you all.

THE AUTHOR

Better known as an actor with extensive credits in television, film and theatre, played The Chief in Channel 4's Shameless, ran Mr Patel's corner shop in BBC's Waterloo Road and was Dennis Waterman's landlord, Clive, in YTV's Stay lucky: appearances in over a hundred productions, including all the usual soaps, Coronation Street, Casualty, The Bill etc. Films include: Rita, Sue & Bob Too. As a writer, the play "Tadpoles" was performed by M6 Theatre on tour throughout the Northwest and also in the BC Buds Festival in Vancouver. Whilst doing Shameless, was invited to get involved on their Shadow Writing Scheme: also took part in a scheme, the BAME Initiative, to write storylines for the soap Emmerdale. Prior to becoming an actor was a prog rock musician, playing throughout the world: Jan Dukes De Grey had three albums released. Worked alongside Simon Cowell when son, Sean, was a minor in the Boy Band, Five.

PROLOGUE - LEGEND ONE

London – 2019.

"Bloody hell, woman, the Yorkshire Ripper's hammer had more brains on it than you've got in your stupid head."

Jeannie broke from their clinch. "Adam Fogerty, you've come out with some horrible things in your time but that's got to be the most disgusting thing you've ever said." She pushed him away. "Ripper's bloody hammer? Have you any idea what it was like for us women in those days? Especially in Leeds."

Adam crossed to the window of the plush hotel. Below, the Knightsbridge traffic had come to a standstill. "I'm sorry, Jeannie, love. It's your fault. You provoked me."

"Provoked you? How did I provoke you, you warped old get."

"You suggested we get married. I mean, why would I want to get married? I'm seventy-years-old."

"You're seventy-one." She sat on the bed. "And, I didn't suggest we get married. I asked what you thought about marriage. Why would I want to marry a disgusting old bastard like you? I don't know how I've put up with you for the past fifteen years."

He ignored her scowl and went to the mirror for a quick touch up of his eyeliner. The scowl became a snigger. He ignored this too. This was something he'd done since they'd been in a band together, when they'd actually first met, forty years before.

She shook her head. "You're revolting."

"I've said I'm sorry, haven't I? I can't help it. I just say these things that come into my head. It's like Tourette's."

"Tourette's my arse; you're just a twisted old man. Adam, I was only being practical. They're making an STV series out of your book. You'll make a fortune."

"STV: don't know why they couldn't just make an ordinary film, like *we* used to go and see."

"Never mind what we used to bloody see. Fact is: Surround Vision is going to make you rich. If anything happened to you, I could be left with nothing, once all your kids start coming out of the woodwork."

"All what kids? I've only got two."

"That we know about."

"I'll make a bloody will, if that's all that's bothering you, better than getting bloody married." He went to the wardrobe and took out his overcoat. "Anyway, when did you develop this mercenary attitude about money?" He struggled trying to get his arm into the sleeve. "What's happened to your 'Women's Lib' philosophy? You've always been dead against marriage."

She got up, took the coat and held it for him. "Maybe I've decided I need a sugar-daddy. I mean it wouldn't be for long, would it? You've only got a few more years."

He turned to face her. "Sugar-daddy? You saucy mare, you'll be seventy yourself, soon."

"Thanks for reminding me." She checked herself in the mirror. He'd always liked her curls, though they were no longer blond. She smiled her impish grin. "Your Evie said to me: hey, you'll be a September-geranium like Granddad."

"Cheeky little minx, acts more like twenty-six than six."

"Yeah, I wonder where she gets it from." She gripped his chin and pulled his face toward her. "Look, I wasn't talking about getting married to prove anything to your daughters, if that's what you think. What's between us is between us. So long as we love each other, that's all that matters."

He pulled away. "Love? What the frigging hell has love got to do with owt, at our age?"

"Probably very little, seeing as you've never once said 'I love you' in all the time I've known you."

He checked his watch. "Bloody hell, look at the time. I'm late."

"Never mind, bloody late." She tugged on his coat lapels. "Adam, don't you dare mess things up. This is important. It's for us." She straightened his tie. "Good luck. Let's hope they've made a decent job of it."

"What can they get wrong? It's just a story about a handsome, young, George Best look-alike pop star."

She laughed. "You don't look anything like a dilapidated, fifty-year-old alkie."

"Cheeky bugger." He checked himself in the mirror. He still looked good. "What are you going to do while I'm at the studio?"

"I'm going shopping; spend some of this fortune you'll be getting. It's years since I've been down here, in London."

He looked around the faces in the studio viewing room, mostly techies. He didn't recognise anyone apart from Marshall. Marshall was his agent but in terms of the most useless articles on the planet such as chocolate fireguards, the Pope's tits or a one-legged man at an arse kicking party, this tosser was right up there. *Wish I'd got rid of the spot-squeezing pillock while I had the chance.* The kid should've been on his paper round, that's if they still had paper rounds. *Bollocks, here he comes.*

Marshall picked a white speck off his purple Armani sleeve. "Yo, Adam, my senior player. Have you signed?"

"No."

"No? Adam, it's central for you to sign that contract. There's a lot of Jane Austens at stake, here. I saw a screening yesterday and our Power Kitten has done a fat job."

I'd like to give him a fat lip.

Another pick at the Armani sleeve. "It'll make you purr."

"Well, *I* haven't seen it have I? I want to see what she's done with the pilot before I agree to a series."

They were standing in front a row of cinema seats, strange headgear visors on each arm. Marshall picked up one. "Surround Vision is going to be colossal."

"I think I'm being ripped off. It says I won't get the money for the series until it's finished. I'm sixty-five-frigging-years-old."

"The man's not trying to filch your payment. You'll get your money when the treatment's finished. Listen old man, I've invested a lot of clock rotations on this one. I don't want you mashing things."

Adam thought about a fist rotation coming up under Marshall's chin but the 'Power Kitten' came into the room. Carmel Verity was the 'Producer'. Actually, she was producer, director, screenwriter, and probably if you stuck a brush up her arse, she'd sweep the floor while doing the editing. She'd adapted Adam's book for the screen.

She sashayed over to him. Her skirt was definitely too short for a woman in her late forties. "Ah Adam my sweetie, you're here." She tapped his cheek. "You're late. Okay, everyone take your seats." She tapped Adam's cheek, again. "You can sit next to me, my sweetie." She picked up a visor then called over her shoulder. "Okay, Charlon, roll SVT."

Adam copied Carmel and put on his visor. He was immediately in the midst of a group of African natives, chanting and performing a slow ritual shuffle. Drums played. What the hell was happening? What did this have to do with his book? He looked out over the savannah landscape. A title scrolled across the clouds: 'SEX, GODS AND ROCK & ROLL'. *Gods?* – The silly cow had got the title wrong. His book was called 'Sex And *Drugs* And Rock And Roll'. The natives continued chanting. Compelled to shuffle along, Adam marched with them into a clearing where four African women, tied to posts, faced a spear firing squad.

He was about to take off his visor when the sonorous voice of a narrator came in: "Nine hundred years ago in the Mashonalands, the Great Zimbabwe Kingdom was under the tyrannical rule of Chief Mwana Mutapa." Adam looked up to a stand to see the Chief looking down on the women. "Four of the Chief's five spouses had displeased their husband and were dealt with according to tradition." The Chief gave a signal. The women screamed and Adam instinctively ducked as spears whooshed through the air.

He lifted his visor but everyone else seemed engrossed. When he put it back down, he was inside a rectangular straw hut. A woman knelt. The rampaging Chief grabbed a shield off the wall and threw it at the woman. It missed and bounced off one of the wooden pillars supporting the roof, landing at Adam's feet.

Bloody hell, everything was so real.

The narrator continued: "One night, without reason; the Chief attacked his remaining wife, Lobengalu." Adam jumped out of the way as the Chief hurled Lobengalu across the dirt floor. Then, from the corners of the hut, four spirits appeared. Each had the body of a woman and the head of a bird. They spoke, or rather screeched with women's voices. Adam backed away; sweat dripping down the inside of his visor. The Chief cowered before the Bird Spirits. They smothered him and then disappeared. Everything went quiet, the screeching and the drums underscoring the scene stopped. Adam checked the Chief's body. He was dead, his face mutilated. Lobengalu sobbed.

Adam took off his visor again and called to the gantry. "Miss, can you stop the film a minute?" No response. "Hello? Can anybody tell me what's going on?" Everyone kept their visors down. Adam again lowered his to a group of chanting women, carrying Lobengalu on their shoulders.

"The Elders did not believe Lobengalu's story," the narrator said. "She was sentenced to execution. But the women of the tribe rose against the Elders. Lobengalu was not only spared but made Queen."

The scene changed. Women were all around. From one side, a tribeswoman, dressed in animal skins, handed over four statues to what looked like her daughter: from another, a woman dressed in traditional dress, handed over to a modern African woman. "The Queen decreed that all women keep four carved fetishes as protection against their male partners."

Adam was then surrounded by four statues, exactly like the frigging ones Theresa Bone used to have. That was enough. He took off his visor, stood before Carmel and knocked on hers.

Carmel took it off and raised her index finger to the control box.

"What's going on?" Adam asked.

The other viewers took off theirs. Carmel gave a calming wave to the room then turned back to Adam. "What's the problem, sweetie?"

"Never mind frigging sweetie. What's this crap? It's supposed to be a story about a drummer and you're showing me all this rubbish about those frigging statues."

"This is only the intro. We then jump to the US base in Germany, Nineteen-Seventy-Six and tell your story, just as you told us in your book."

"My book's not about no African Chief and it's definitely not about them frigging statues. It's supposed to be about me."

She took his arm and sat him back in his seat. "Please, watch the rest and then see what you think?" It wasn't only her skirt that was showing too much. The brazen hussy flaunted her deep cleavage under his nose. She gave a caustic smile. "Incidentally, sweetie, my face is up here."

"What? No, I wasn't …"

"Don't forget, I know all about your antics."

Marshall stepped forward. "I'm truly sorry, Carmel. He has no bad intentions. The grey matter gets a little cloudy when you're nearing the final whistle."

Adam rose from his seat. "Final frigging whistle? Who rattled your cage, Master-frigging-Bates?"

Carmel found another caustic smile. "I'm astonished he still has it in him."

"It's unlikely he has." Marshall gave his usual stupid laugh. "Look, guys, why don't we all chillax? Adam, you need to request Carmel's forgiveness and then I suggest we all watch the rest of the movie?"

"I'm not 'requesting forgiveness' from anybody. I've done nowt wrong."

"Holy gonzos, Adam, can't you just hang it on the rack for once? I'm working for you here."

"I don't need you to work for me. I can speak for myself, thank you very much."

"You need to listen to Marshall, Adam. Over forty years and you appear to have learnt nothing." She sat. "Women don't laugh things off these days."

Marshall wagged his finger. "No they do not." Another stupid laugh. "Acceptability denied, Mr Fogerty. These days, they sue your arse first and then kick you in the gonads."

"I'll kick *you* in the gonads you, you pizza faced pillock. If this is your way of resigning, it's worked. You can stuff your Jane Austens. Accept that."

"Hey, sorry to set off this spoiler alert, Granddad, but I never thought you and me were destined to live happily ever after."

"Go play with your crayons, I'm out of here." Adam walked toward the door.

"Suits me, I've had enough of trying to turn geriatrics into commodities."

"Piss off. I hope your next shit's a hedgehog."

Marshall pulled a face as though the hedgehog was on its way out.

Adam walked down the corridor, imagining thousands of 'Jane Austens' disappearing out of the window. Jeannie's warning echoed. "Don't mess this up, Adam. It's for us."

Bugger, what have you done, Fogerty?

Behind him, he heard the clicking of heels. He turned.

Carmel folded her arms and gave him a stern look. "How old are you, Adam?"

"Sixty-five."

"No, you are not. You're seventy-one and it's time you started acting like it."

"I wasn't looking down your dress. I'm not some sex mad perv."

"Adam, I've read your book, remember. And I know what you musicians are like, even retired seventy-one-year-olds."

"Whatever you've read, it doesn't mean we all go round trying to jump on thirty-nine-year-old producers."

"It doesn't mean you wouldn't like to try. And you can drop the flattery. As you probably know, I'm forty-eight."

"Are you really? You look great."

"My God, you can't help yourself, can you?"

"Sorry." He laughed. "Can't blame me for trying."

She also laughed. "So what exactly is your problem with my movie?"

"I just wasn't expecting that African stuff. I wrote the book so that my grandkids would know something about me."

"Look, sweetie, it's my job to take the raw material and interpret it for the market. Books are one thing but Surround Vision is new. It needs something special. We felt it important to start with a bang, with the legend. And we also wanted to tell the story of some of the other band members." She put a hand on his shoulder. "Come back and watch the rest of the pilot and if you're still unhappy, I'll talk to Fatima about making some edits."

"I don't trust Marshall. He winds me up. I haven't signed for your series."

"I know. He told me. Don't worry about that now. Let's sort the pilot first, shall we? Marshall's merely young and ambitious but it *was* him that got you this deal. In fact, he's invested in the production. It's up to you, of course, if you wish to change agents but without him, we can't go ahead. I don't think any of us wants that, do we?"

"I suppose I was a bit hasty."

"Give me a couple of minutes. Let me go talk to him."

Back in the studio, Marshall had gone.

Carmel called to the back. "Okay, Charlon."

Adam put on his visor and was immediately surrounded by the four bird-women statues. The deep voice of the narrator said: "Beware vengeful Deities."

1 Adam's Sexploits: Garmisch. Sept 1976:
Why Y'all Play No ZZ Top?

Lock up your frauleins, Fogerty's here. Adam's purple loon pants slipped further down his legs as he thrust into the young German bending over his dressing table. *Cop a load o' this, you Kraut cutie.* The intensity of the frolicking sent his hairspray can, rattling to the floor. Adam had already forgotten 'Kraut Cutie's name. After all, he'd only met her twenty minutes before when he'd enticed her into his 'dressing cupboard', the dilapidated room next to the stage where visiting bands prepared for their performance. She was merely one of the local *madchens*, eager to fraternise with the exciting English pop musicians that graced her country. Although several bulbs surrounding the mirrors were missing, enough light enabled the handsome stud to admire his technique from his many reflected images adorning the tiny space. In the lottery of good looks, he knew he'd 'dropped-on'. His flowing dark mane afforded him a comparison to the footballer Georgie Best, enhancing his image of a "likeable rogue".

Oh, this feels so good, man.

The *fraulein* echoed Adam's moans as the pace quickened. His grip slipped down from her waist and dug into her shapely buttocks.

"Go on, Adam lad, give it some wellie." Without interruption in rhythm, he preened his jet-black hair and continued pounding until the raucous foghorn thundered into the dressing room.

"Fogerty, get your arse on this pissing stage, now."

Tossburgers, frigging Colin, our illustrious bandleader!

The activity across the dressing table increased, sending more items clattering to the floor, accompanied by Adam's yelp of satisfaction. This was the prelude to his real performance on stage. He withdrew, wiped himself on her miniskirt, leaned across and whispered in her ear: "*Danke.*"

"*Es macht nicht.*"

"Sorry babe got to run." He patted her bottom, pulled up his trousers and zipped from the dressing room, leaving her prostrate.

"About bloody time." On stage, Colin had that glower that melded his Neanderthal eyebrows. "We're up here twiddling our thumbs while you're getting your rocks off with some tart."

"Do I detect a modicum of jealousy?"

"Cool it, you two, there's punters listening." Steve Langton, the Peruvian/Scouse road manager stuck out his bushy head from behind a bass bin speaker.

"What the hell have you come as?" Adam asked. "You look like you've just stepped out of a poster for 'Hair'. Come on you old hippy, give us a song." Adam performed a mock Sixties dance, scrolling two fingers across his eyes while singing: "This is the dawning of the Age of Aquarius."

Steve displayed his kaftan "This, my friend, is called style."

"Well, I'm sorry, you just don't happen. You're not going to pull so much as a Christmas cracker, dressed like that."

"Fogerty, stop bloody rabbitting and get your kit set up." Colin nodded toward the dressing room. "He's a dog, Steve, just been bonking some Kraut tart."

"Merely sampling the delights of the local culture." Adam's hand swept the air.

"Local culture?" Colin said. "Looked to me like you were having a quickie with the local bike. Where'd you dig her up from anyway? We've only been in Germany five seconds."

"She came in for an autograph."

"Autograph? Bloody tart."

Centre stage, a dumpy girl clutched a microphone. It was Theresa, the vocalist, Colin's better half. That was typical of the guitarist, slagging off a piece of fit German crumpet, when his wife would be lucky to win second prize at Crufts.

The lights dropped and a khaki-clad American MC jumped up on stage and swept a chubby hand across his blond crew-cut. "Ladies and Gentlemen, direct from London, England, on their first night in West Germany, put your left hand to your right hand and give a big Garmisch welcome to 'Images'."

"We're from Yorkshire, you fat twat." Unfortunately, Colin's aside was a little too near the microphone.

The G.I. host raised a middle finger to thank him for his kind correction. A trickle of applause almost made it to the stage.

Adam sat behind his drum-kit, flexing his biceps. *Cop a load o' this, you Yankee bastards.* His sticks tapped together above his head. "A one, two, three, four."

Six bars later, Theresa was belting out the classic 'Proud Mary'. Known as T, she modelled her style on her favourite singer, Elkie Brooks. Unfortunately for T, other than the same black wavy hair, she bore absolutely no other physical resemblance to her heroine. "Left a good job in the city; working for the man, every night and day."

Despite his scathing of her looks, he had to admit she had a cracker of a voice.

By the time she was "Rolling down the river", Adam's adrenaline was pumping. The twenty-minute stint in the dressing room was simply one of life's bonuses. This is what it was really about – the gig - the playing - the music.

What a crock of shit!

Best thing about being a pop star? The birds: German girls decorated the G.I. audience. During each number, Adam perused his female admirers seated around the front tables, a salamander eyeing the potential of its next meal, availability the main factor. Instead of a tongue, he shot out predatory glances in the hope of making that all-important eye contact that said: "I am ready and willing for a casual shag".

The rear vantage of a drummer didn't make T look any better. Voice apart, whoever had the idea of putting her on stage in front of a horde of pissed up yanks, must've been sharing a laugh with her costume designer. But with or without the spindly heels, she'd surely have done better in life had she not been saddled with husband, Colin and his 'hilarious' patter.

"I thank you. This next number is entitled: She was only a petrol pump attendant's daughter, but she liked the smell of Benzole."

Colin and his mousy mullet could easily have played a thug in *The Sweeney*. On the few pre-tour English gigs, the big oaf had antagonised the audience more than once. He showed pride in the fact that, in previous groups, fights had often been caused due to something he'd said or because he felt someone had looked the wrong way at "The wife". The others were embarking on this venture with a serious concern over the bruiser's reputation.

After the set, Adam pumped more money into the phone-box. All the coins going into the slot were English shillings, the same size as *Deutschmarks*. He was calling England to give his brother a progress report and to check that his flat hadn't burnt down or his dog, Ralph, hadn't eloped with one of the Queen's corgis.

He returned to the dressing room and closed the door. "A musician of my experience shouldn't be taking orders from someone who used the last of his brain cells learning to walk upright." Colin and T had gone to the bar; leaving the other two band members.

Jimmy McCann, the young bass player, returned to the mirror for the fourth time to continue the fight with the strand of hair that had come adrift from its blond setting. "What key did you start 'Dr Hook' in, Jeannie?" he asked, without so much as a glance at the keyboard player.

Jeannie adjusted her overflowing boob tube. "Oh yeah, sorry about that."

Adam stopped sorting through his change. "Excuse me, did I just hear right? Was that an apology from Ms Germaine Greer?" Ms Hay was on the short side, though her well-endowed figure was in proportion. "You know why she cocked up her playing, Jimmy? Too busy making eyes at that fat MC. She'll shag owt, has a ready-made mattress, strapped to her back."

"You're only jealous because I'm better at pulling than you are." Cropped, curly, blond hair framed Jeannie's impish grin.

"You can't compete with me at anything, sweetheart. There's not many can equal me when it—"

"I didn't say equal, I said better."

"It's time you learned your place, girl."

"Oh yeah, and what place would that be, *boy*?"

"A woman's place is in the oven." It wasn't only their oil on water relationship that irritated Adam; her refusal to be feminine spoiled her. This wasn't merely his opinion; most blokes would agree. "Why can't you be like a normal bird?"

"A normal *bird*? You know why they call us birds, Jimmy? It's 'cos we go round picking up worms." She gave Jimmy a wink and went to the door. "I might need you lads to vacate the dressing room, later. I'm feeling a bit lucky tonight."

Jimmy laughed as she left the room. "It's obvious, you two fancy each other."

"Well I wouldn't climb over her to get to you, Jimmy lad."

"I think she's great."

"Oh aye?" Adam's scornful reflection hid an inward smile.

"I mean she's a great keyboard player."

"Not bad for a bird. And she'll definitely be a bit useful in front of all them American squaddies, compensate for T."

"T? What's wrong with T?" Jimmy abandoned his cuticles. "T's brilliant."

"Yeah she's a belting singer, but you wouldn't say she was pretty, would you?"

"No, I suppose not."

"Dead right you suppose not. God gave her the ugliest face in the world, then he hit it with a shovel."

The soldier MC had managed to get some things right. Garmisch was the first stop on a tour of American Army bases in Bavaria. This was a big change from the last time Adam had worked in West Germany. Then he'd been climbing the pop circuit ladder, representing his record company on a mammoth support tour. Now he was back, so far down the ladder that he was not only playing US bases but playing cover records of the band he'd been supporting on the previous tour. This was an itch in the groin of enjoyment now that he was back. However, next year would be his Big Three O. For all he knew, this might be his last raid on the Fatherland. Might as well make the best of it.

Back behind his drum-kit he slipped once more into salamander mode. The Kraut cutie from the dressing room sent a smile. He ignored her. The casual-sex food source was plentiful. Adam never had to work at seducing women, it just happened. He knew that when a bird came to a gig she was hoping for a good time. When she walked into a club, she was playing by different rules. She wasn't looking for romance. In the presence of a shoal of desirable females, with faultless patience, he relentlessly watched, waited and tugged at the line until the float disappeared. Once the catch was on the hook, he was very good at keeping it there but even Adam had no idea what he used for bait. He put it down to playing in a band. Plus, of course his amazing good looks and magnetism. And then there was his dynamic personality and not forgetting his sexual prowess. Whatever the attraction, duty done, it was then naturally okay to throw her back into the water just as easily as he'd fished her out. The catch from the dressing room had paired up with an American soldier.

"Frigging slag," Adam said.

The following night, Adam glowered at the empty pickled gherkin jar at the side of the stage. The bands in America, who were less than successful, didn't appear to carry the same kudos as their British counterparts. Playing in pubs and bars, they were little more than servants with a receptacle for tips like waiters or barmen. Much to Adam's disgust, this demeaning custom had transferred across the Atlantic and plonked itself on his hallowed rostrum, bringing home just how far down the ladder he'd slid.

The US bases operated entirely on dollars. Apart from gambling machines and the telephone, although in West Germany, it was impossible to spend any other currency on what was considered United States soil. As on mainland America, 'green backs' ruled. The band was paid in them. So it appeared outside the understanding of the average G.I. Joe that anyone could be affronted by the tips jar.

Audience showed appreciation, by putting a tip in the jar, a bit extra if accompanied by a request. This could either go in the jar or be made in person. As the final set started, one such personal touch came from a couple of young drunkards who'd broken from a known group of exuberant Texans. They approached the stage.

"Nice music, man, but why y'all play no zeezee top?" the short one asked.

"Pardon?" Colin said.

The soldier tried again. "Why y'all play no zeezee top?"

Colin turned to the band. "What's he on about?"

"'Tifarno," Adam said.

"Fucked if I know, either," Colin said.

The Texans repeated the phrase several times.

"Can anybody tell me what these drunken buggers are saying?" Colin asked over the microphone. Several members of the audience were keen to translate. 'ZZ Top' was the latest band to come out of Texas. Enlightened, Colin apologised and explained that their fame hadn't yet reached the shores of Britain. "Maybe if you stuck ten dollars in the jar instead of all this shrapnel, we might learn one at the next rehearsal." His attempt at humour appeared to get lost in translation.

The delay to the music had gone on long enough. At the end of T's rendition of 'Nut Bush City Limits', the audience were duly appreciative with several more coins filling the coffers. The taller of the Texans came back, waving a ten-dollar bill. He beckoned Colin down to eye level.

The soldier put the ten-dollar bill to his mouth, licked it and planted it firmly in the middle of Colin's forehead. "Now play some ZZ Top."

Colin obliged the request with a 'Glasgow-kiss'. Head and ten-dollar bill connected with a distinct crack on the bridge of the soldier's nose. The place erupted. First, the short Texan rallied to the aid of his friend. Colin duly despatched him with a right hook. The rest of the audience responded with a shower of miscellaneous missiles.

Crouched behind his bass drum, Adam watched an ashtray hurtle toward Jimmy's head. The lad would've definitely had to re-comb his coiffure, had T not used her microphone to deflect the projectile with a Geoffrey Boycott style cut to the gully. The heroine then offered herself as a human shield as more flying items tried to embody themselves into the bass player. Jeannie jumped on the back of one of the Texans, who was writhing about on the floor like a tortoise with a rogue shell, as she tried to pull his nostrils up over his head. Steve came to the soldier's rescue by extracting the keyboard player from her victim. She still managed to kick another in the 'orchestra stalls' while being carried to the safety of the dressing room.

When a bottle bounced off Adam's tom-tom onto his crash cymbal, he decided it was time to go pack his flight case.

Sorry Colin you'll have to sort out all remaining requests on your own.

The final set was never completed. Fortunately, the group wasn't immediately shipped out of Garmisch to the greyness of East Germany, as Adam feared. Nor did they have any money docked from their wages for this unfinished symphony, the only financial loss being the tips jar, tossed into the audience by Colin during the affray. Still, they hadn't got off on their best foot.

Gherkin jars aside; Garmisch was a cracking start to the tour. Under the shadow of the Zugspitze, the whole area was beautiful, full of colour and excitement. Adam easily imagined himself as one of the rich jet setters, taking a winter break in any of the picture postcard retreats. The various ski centres were busying themselves in readiness for the coming winter months.

"Have you seen the talent flooding into this place?" Steve asked Adam. They were sitting outside a café in the Garmisch Partenkirchen city centre.

"You're not kidding, almost makes the job worthwhile."

As the tour was a low-budget affair, the six members had to share three rooms. Adam had known Steve for over twelve years, so they naturally went in together. This left 'the married couple' in one room and Jimmy and Jeannie in the other. These arrangements suited Adam.

"So how come you haven't jumped on Jeannie, yet?" Steve asked.

"Are you kidding?" Adam took in the panoramic view then zoomed in on two chicks at the far side of the café. "Do you think I'm about to lumber myself with someone in the band with all this foreign crumpet around?"

"Yeah, right on: good thinking, man."

"I wonder if our friends over there fancy some horizontal refreshment." Adam finished his cappuccino and manoeuvred across. "Excuse me, ladies, would it be okay for me and my *compadre* to sit here and chat you up?"

"*Comment?*" The prettier of the two brunettes answered.

"Do you speak English?"

"Yes, we can speak English. *Est ce que vouz parlez Francais*?"

"Oh, you're French are you? Here for the skiing?"

The sarky cow looked from her friend to the skis at the side of the table then made a show of checking for her goggles on her head. The friend giggled.

He liked the giggle. "I'm Adam. This is my buddy, Steve."

Steve saluted. "Hi."

"*Ciao*, Steve. Simone."

"I am called Monique."

Adam moved around the table from the prettier girl to shake hands with the more friendly. "Hi Monique, would you like to see Steve's willy?"

"*Pardon*?"

"It's a very nice willy. He's put talcum powder on it. Isn't that right, Steve?"

"Thanks, Adam." Naturally, they'd played this 'dumb cop, clever cop' chat up routine before.

Monique had a totally bemused expression. "*Qu'est ce qu'il dit*?"

"*Il veux que tu regardes sa bite.*"

Simone's apparent translation made Monique giggle again. "You are a crazy man."

"I know; I'm just being silly. I get a bit flustered in the presence of beauty, makes me say daft things. What about you, Simone? I bet you'd like to see Steve's willy."

"Please go away."

Adam mimicked Simone's giggle free frown. "Not even with talcum powder on it?"

Simone turned to Steve. "At what hour must you return your friend to the hospital?"

Steve laughed. "If I don't get him back in time for his tablets, he starts flashing his own willy." He did a mime of exposing himself.

Simone laughed. "Oh my God, then you must take him away, quickly."

"Very funny." Adam didn't laugh. "You two should be on the stage. There's one leaving in about twenty minutes." Steve appeared to have forgotten the routine. "Speaking of being on stage, we're in a band. Or to be more precise, I'm in a band. Steve's just a roadie."

"Hey, less of the 'just', if you don't mind." Steve and Simone shared a smile. "Adam's one of these people who hangs around with musicians. He's a drummer."

"Bastard." Adam scowled and shifted his chair. "You know what, Monique? *You* could come and see us play. We're on just up the road, tonight."

Simone held up a hand. "We are not staying in Garmisch. We are only visiting." She was proving a difficult adversary.

"That's a shame." Adam was getting a little snowed under with all this negativity.

"But we return on Thursday to stay for a week," Monique said.

"Perfect." Adam gave Monique's arm a stroke as though welcoming a Saint Bernard dog that'd come to his rescue. He picked up a beer mat from the table and wrote on it. "That's the number at our digs." He presented the beer mat. "We're playing at Mr D's next Friday. It's on the army base but it's the best club in Garmisch. Call us if you're not going to make it."

Monique took the beer mat. "Perhaps."

He took hold of her hand and kissed the back of it. He then lifted it to his cheek and stroked down to his neck. "Oh, dear, you've touched my necklace. Do you know what that means where we come from? If you touch a man's necklace in Yorkshire, it means you have to make love to him."

Simone snatched Monique's hand and yanked it over to the giggle free zone. "We must go, Monique."

It mattered not to Adam. The adversary had nothing in her armoury to match the lady-killer smile. A final kiss on the cheek should secure it. "Right then, Monique, I'll see you next Friday at Mr D's."

"Perhaps."

Simone pulled Monique to her feet. "It was good to talk with you, Steve. *Ciao*."

Steve gave her another smile and they left.

Adam looked at Steve. "Hangs about with musicians? Scouse git, shouldn't you be out nicking hubcaps, or something?"

One of the perks of playing in Garmisch was the free access to the skiing facilities on their days off. On their second Sunday, after a pleasant time on the *piste*, Adam and Jeannie returned the equipment to the plush hotel, where they hoped for an even more pleasant *Apres-Ski*.

"I can see why it's called The 'Grand' Sonnenbichi," Adam said. Secluded among the forest, the historical hotel was right up his *strasse*. They sauntered through the lobby to the accompaniment of 'The Girl From Ipanema'. "That Herp Albert, he's a right bighead, don't you think?"

"Yeah, he's always blowing his own trumpet."

"Bastard."

She grinned. They carried on sauntering. "Don't you feel the ambience of these Art Nouveau style furnishings just permeates your bones?"

Pretentious bitch.

They settled in the expansive bar. "I wish we was staying in places like this," Adam said, between sips of his Singapore Sling. He cocked a Noel Coward style pinkie and put on his best posh voice. "Do you think they'll mind if we take our drinks on to the terrace, Ms Hay?"

"How many rooms do you reckon this place has?" She asked.

"'Kinundreds." It was a reasonable estimate.

"I'm gonna take a shower in one of them."

"How are you going to manage that?"

"Are you coming or not?"

Adam followed her to the reception trying to appear nonchalant.

"Excuse me." She smiled at the maroon uniformed boy behind the counter. "I'm with the pop band 'Images'. We're working on the American bases. Mr Keinhorst said it would be okay for us to get changed in one of your rooms."

"I'm sorry madam; Herr Keinhorst is not in today." The youth picked up the telephone. "I will try to get someone else for you."

"He did say we could come in whenever we wished," she said. A telephone rang in the distance. "He's arranged it with Sergeant Gabbitas from the base; said we could use any equipment we liked." She flashed him the pass card that allowed them the use of the nearby slope and ski hire.

The boy replaced the receiver. "I think it will be okay." He handed her the key to room 302.

She winked at Adam. He'd have to keep watch on Ms Hay's talents.

Room 302 was every bit as luxurious as expected. Adam was about to comment on the nifty way the bedside lights actually slotted into the headboard of the bed— "Christ dancing a polka."

Jeannie's bra landed on his shoulder. He stopped admiring the décor and stood agog, staring at her pert firm cheeks flaunting into the bathroom. The shower splashed into his imagination. "Come on then," she called.

Bloody hell, there was something not quite right here. Even by his own standards, this was 'pulling' of the highest order. Of course there was the risk of being 'lumbered with a band member' but he'd be stupid to pass this up.

Jeannie's scattered garments lay at his feet.

Bugger the 'nifty lights'.

His own clothes soon mingled with hers and he rushed into the bathroom but stopped short in wonder at the cascading water. *God, aren't tits great?*

"Gold taps," Jeannie said.

"Not many, Benny."

"Go on, admit it. I can see from your friend, you're dying to turn them on."

"Not many, Benny."

He stepped into the shower, took the soap from its gold dish, pressed it into Jeannie's hand and circled a ring of lather around her navel. His lips welcomed hers as she guided the soap downwards. He worked enough lather to both excite her and still have some left to cover her breasts, giving them that silky feeling he liked. The soap fell and bounced about their feet.

Adam and Jimmy exchanged rooms.

2 T's Adventures: Garmisch. Sept '76:
Long Tall Sally.

Jeannie stubbed her cigarette and threw it on T's potato peelings. "He's the most arrogant, male chauvinist arsehole I've ever met in my whole life."

T continued peeling. "I thought you were getting on great together? He's just moved in with you, hasn't he?"

"That was before he told me about his hot date."

"Hot date? What hot date?"

"Him and Steve are only meeting up with two French poodles at Mr D's, tomorrow night. Do you know when he told me this piece of wonderful news?"

T shook her head.

"When we were in bed. He says: 'I didn't think you'd mind, you're just like one of the lads.' Bastard." Jeannie lit another cigarette.

"I didn't think Adam was like that. He's always been quite respectful with me."

"T, where the hell have you been for the past six weeks? Adam respectful? Don't make me laugh. His perfect woman would have a flat head for him to stand his pint on, then after he'd given her one, she'd turn into a meat pie."

T laughed so much she had to hold on to the sink. It was possibly an over reaction. "You crack me up, Jeannie; you really do."

Including the present group 'Images', Colin had put together four bands, one a year since T's audition. So far, working in Garmisch was her favourite time. Through the kitchen window, the sun bounced off the snow-capped hills and into her concentration, a pleasing bonus to the preparation of Colin's dinner. "I love this place." She scratched her left calf with her right foot. Her flip-flop slipped to the floor.

"What are you doing wearing *them* with tights?"

T tried to squeeze the rubber back between her toes. "Bloody things, I haven't brought much casual stuff."

Jeannie checked the saucepan of potatoes. "When you've finished that, I think we need to go and sort through your stuff."

From the moment Theresa Morgan signed the marriage certificate to become Mrs. Bone; she acquired her nickname of 'T'. At their first meeting, after answering his advert for a singer, she decided she was going to marry Colin. She knew immediately that life with him would be both adventurous and difficult but worth it. T loved her nickname. They were now three years into the marriage, though it felt like his snoring had announced the dawn forever. Nasal peculiarities aside, she would've said: three blissful years but there was one thing missing.

"We're going to have lots of kids, one day; aren't we, Col?" T showed Jeannie into her bedroom. She had, of course, mentioned this before to her friend but she wasn't going to miss the chance of raising the subject in the presence of her husband. "Did you hear me, Col? I'm just telling Jeannie, we're going to have lots of kids, one day."

"Bloody hell, woman, put another record on, will you?" Colin got off the bed. "I just wanted five minutes' peace. Is that too much to ask?"

"I was just saying; that's all."

"When are you gonna get it into that thick skull of yours? The last thing we need right now is the pitter-patter of tiny money gannets." He thumped the door on his exit.

Jeannie's eyes wandered around the room.

T tried to mask her embarrassment with a broad grin. "Sorry about that." She hadn't realised Colin would be in the bedroom when she'd invited Jeannie in to help sort her wardrobe.

Jeannie took Colin's place on the bed. "Why do you let him talk to you like that?"

"It's my own fault. I'm always winding him up about having kids."

Jeannie pointed at the innocent door that'd taken the brunt of Colin's frustration. "I thought that door was going to be *you*, for a minute."

T let slip a slight giggle at Jeannie's ridiculous notion. Colin had never hit her. He could hardly be described as 'gentle' but she'd always envisaged being married to a 'man's man'. And he was no more forceful in bed than she ever wanted. She kept the defence of her husband inside her head and carried it to the full-length mirror of the wardrobe. A five-foot-two image, dressed in underwear stared back. She was only thirty-one but had felt for some time that she was hurtling toward mid-life at the speed of a Freddie Trueman full toss, a phrase she'd cherished from her cricket-loving dad.

"You'd think it'd be easy to find a pair of tights to fit a short arse like me." She pulled up the waistband over her breasts yet still the gusset hung down somewhere in the region of her knees.

"You know, you've got gorgeous hair, T."

T noted the tact. Modesty prevented her from telling Jeannie how proud she was of what Colin called 'her best physical feature'. And besides, when anyone complimented her hair it brought to mind the person at school who once said her face was best seen from the back.

"You should have kicked him in the bollocks," Jeannie said.

"It was a girl." The same cow had also described their family as having 'more chins between them than a Chinese phone book'. She pulled up the tights yet further to reach the plural chins. Now, she really did look ridiculous. She turned to show Jeannie. "Ta-dah."

Both laughed.

Jeannie bounded off the bed and joined her. "Come on; let's see what we've got."

T opened the wardrobe and ran a hand along the clothes rail. Nothing in here did her any favours. She pulled out a Polyester, turquoise trouser-suit. "I forgot I'd packed this."

"T, that's hideous."

T had bought the suit for her nephew's wedding. "Everyone said I looked the bee's knees in this."

"You might've done in the glass vestry door of St Philips on the bloody Marsh but it's not exactly Suzie Quatro, is it? We need to do some serious shopping."

Prior to auditioning for Colin, T had only been semi-professional, singing on the Working Men's Club circuit whilst working as an auxiliary nurse. Playing in a pop band on the Continent was a million pints and bedpans from either of her two previous jobs. She'd known since her teens that she had a good voice but portraying herself as a sex object was always going to be an obstacle to her change of direction. Colin's belief in her had steered her around this obstacle, taking in love on the way. However backhanded the compliments, no one had ever shown her this kind of faith. "It doesn't matter how plain you think you are; with a voice like yours, you're the sexiest thing on two legs."

At her audition, she'd sung Little Richard's "Long Tall Sally" but she was unsure if it was the best choice. Apart from it being a man's song, she was neither 'long' nor 'tall'. Colin had put her at ease.

"You've got a dead gutsy voice. It's like a Harley Davidson starting up." Colin helped her gain the confidence she needed to step into the world of 'raunch' where her unique vocals belonged. The rest of her may not have fitted in this pop world, but her Harley Davidson voice had bought her a ticket on the ride of 'Rock & Roll'. She loved it, even if she did only experience it from the pillion seat.

She put the last of the clothes back in the wardrobe and dressed in the turquoise Polyester trouser-suit. "Not that bad."

"Horrendous," Jeannie said. "Do you fancy a trip to Innsbruck, tomorrow?"

"Where's that?"

"Austria."

"Austria? We can't go to Austria. We've got work."

"We'll be back in plenty of time; it's only just across the border, about twenty-five miles away; just like going to York from Leeds."

"That's a fab idea. I like York."

Exhilaration spilled into T's gravy boat at the thought of this spree. Jeannie gave a thumbs-up but stayed by the kitchen door.

"No, no, you can't, no!" Colin said, through a mouthful of lovingly prepared mashed potato. "You can't just bugger off to Austria for a day's shopping." His objections made some sort of sense, as 'Images' were about to play in their favourite of the four Garmisch clubs and Colin had ordered them to get in early for a rehearsal. "My reputation's at stake here." He mopped up some gravy. "We're already in trouble for that dust-up with the Texans, last time we played at Mr D's."

"That wasn't my fault." T looked to Jeannie for support.

"It doesn't matter whose fault it was." He pointed with his fork. "I happen to like it round here. I don't want moving on to some shit-hole." He got up from the table. "And those spuds were lumpy."

"Sod you, you bastard," T said. Of course, he'd left the kitchen, out of earshot. "What time do we leave?"

"What? Are we back on?" Jeannie's eyes widened. "We'll have to get away early, eight o'clock."

"Let's make it half seven. He won't even know I've got out of bed." T surprised herself.

Jeannie slapped T's shoulder. "Right on, let's hear it for the Sisters' Rebellion."

The name above the door read "*Nyabinghi*". T liked shopping. Foreign shopping was even more fun, especially in a shop like this. Patchouli oil caressed her nostrils as she entered. "You just wouldn't find owt like this in Leeds," she said.

"You might in York." T knew Jeannie was taking the Mick but it didn't bother her.

The shop bulged with African knick-knacks and mystical trinkets. Incense burners hung from the ceiling. "It's like Aladdin's cave," T said. "Happen, you could be Jeannie of the Lamp."

Jeannie picked up a tacky ornament. "God, its ethnicity is so genuine."

T's enthusiasm wasn't to be dampened. The shop was fab. Even the shopkeeper was alluring. Heavily bejewelled with earrings, necklaces, bangles and bracelets, he wore a pillbox hat and a gold tooth that glittered when he smiled. His dress looked African but he wasn't really Coloured. Jeannie said he was probably Greek or Turkish and only dressed like that for the tourists.

"He's like an Arabian Nights' storyteller." T's eyes feasted on beads, masks, rugs and wall hangings made from antelope, zebra and something called an 'Okapi', of which she'd never heard. She sniffed at the mustiness of the skins. Everything enchanted, as any rubies, pearls or emeralds from the Dark Continent. Choice seemed impossible, until she came across the most captivating treasure in the shop: four, small black figurines, each with the head of a bird on the naked body of a woman.

"T? Hello, T?" Jeannie waved a hand across T's face.

T heard Jeannie speak but couldn't pull her eyes away from the carvings.

"T, what have you found?"

"I love these." She picked up one of the ornaments and fondled it. A shiver went across her shoulders.

"You were in another world, then."

The figure nestled in T's hand. It was heavier than expected. "Is this ebony?"

Two pinches from an elliptical rococo snuffbox, placed on the back of his hand then sniffed with great vigour up each nostril, and the storyteller's head looked like it was going to spin off, earrings jangling and eyes blinking. "Not ebony, soapstone, very lucky, especially for ladies." His gold tooth flashed through his sales pitch. "Almost one thousand years old, discovered in the Land of Ophir, made by the Shona women who worshipped them as gods, plundered by the Portuguese, centuries ago." So much history, culture and mystique: "As you can see, lady, they are in very good condition. I believe they once belonged to King Solomon, himself." The storyteller stamped the base of his fist into his palm like an auctioneer's gavel.

T read the price tag. "They're a bit expensive. Could I just buy one of them?"

"No lady, no." The shopkeeper snatched the statue from her. "Very unlucky to split them. Very important, they must stay together. Very, very unlucky to split them."

"Oh bugger it, I don't care how much, I'm having them," T said.

This brought another slap to her shoulder from Jeannie "Good for you, lass."

On the way to the railway station, T lagged behind. "Hang on, Jeannie, what's the big rush?"

"You're the one who wanted to get back to get Colin's tea on." Jeannie's pace quickened. "Come on, that train leaves in ten minutes."

"Sod Colin's tea, I'll end up dropping all my stuff, at this rate." They reached the station with only three minutes to go.

"Which platform is it please?" Jeannie asked the ticket puncher.

"*Gleis nummer zwei. Schnell, schnell, machen Sie schnell.*" He pointed in the general direction of some steps. They broke into a canter.

"What platform did he say?" T asked.

"Number three." Jeannie checked as they boarded the carriage. "Does this train go to Germany?"

"*Bitte*?" the elderly guard asked.

"Ger-man-ee?"

"*Ja, ja, Deutschland*." The man ushered them on to the train and closed the door.

T settled back and looked at the booty of figurines captured on her sortie across the border. The Arabian Nights' storyteller had also provided a beautiful hessian covered box to keep them. T gave a little snigger. "Colin will do his nut when he finds out how much I paid for these."

"Well, you didn't get them for Colin. It's your money as well as his, you know."

As though they'd a will of their own, T's fingers stroked the carvings and she felt a strange surge of defiance. "Yeah, you're right. Sod him." The train pulled out of Innsbruck. She felt good.

Jeannie checked her watch. "We needn't have hurried; it's ten minutes late, not exactly German efficiency."

Soon enough, fields flicked by as the train sped through the countryside, unaware of the activity in its carriages. The statues looked so comfortable in their hessian box. The storyteller was right; they were in good condition. "Do you think they're genuine?" T asked.

"Don't be ridiculous. Do you really think you'd find thousand-year-old statues in a knick-knack shop? They're probably churned out in Stoke or somewhere."

"Don't care, I still like them."

"I like the sound of those Shona women with their female gods."

T tried to match Jeannie's joke capacity. "Yeah, you know, God is a female. Who else could've made the world in six days and managed a day of rest to do the ironing?" Both laughed.

"Adam says God must be a woman 'cos she put men's bollocks on the outside." Jeannie trumped T's attempt yet again. "She should've put their todgers on the end of their noses, then we'd always know what they were up to."

T was helpless. "Oh no, I just had this vivid picture of Colin with his todger on the end of his nose." She laughed so much she slipped off her seat, again possibly over the top.

Jeannie pointed out the Zugspitze in the distance: "The biggest mountain in Germany." The scenery was beautiful.

The journey to Innsbruck had taken thirty minutes. Garmisch Partenkirchen was just across the border but they'd crossed into West Germany an hour ago and the Zugspitze was now behind them. "That's not right," Jeannie said. They discounted the possibility they were taking a slower paced longer route, since the train was breaking the sound barrier and hadn't stopped once. Jeannie's attempts at breaking the language barrier had failed, so they were unable to discover anything from the other passengers as they ran frantically along the compartments.

T rocketed Jeannie's panic by saying: "I'm sure we've just sheened through a station with a sign saying Munchen something or other."

"Please God, no," Jeannie said.

But the ticket inspector confirmed it. They'd passed beyond Munich and what's more, they wouldn't be stopping until they reached Nurnberg.

"But we're on stage in two hours," Jeannie said.

The inspector couldn't help them, nor apparently even understand them.

"I knew you'd got the wrong platform," T said.

"Well if you're so clever, why didn't you say something?"

"I'm just saying; you're the one who's supposed to speak German."

They reached Nurnberg with fifty minutes to spare before they were due on stage. It wouldn't have helped had there been an hour and fifty; there wasn't another train back to Garmisch until the following morning. They had to find a hotel. Jeannie called the club with the cheerful news.

T's prediction proved correct. Colin did "go ape-shit."

"They're having to make do with guitar, bass and drums," Jeannie told her. "He says Steve will have to come out of retirement and sing a few blues numbers. And he wanted to know why you didn't ring him yourself."

"Now you've got the number, I might try later, see how they got on. Happen he'll calm down a bit once the gig's over."

This time the prediction wasn't so correct.

"Well?" Jeannie asked.

"I spoke to Jimmy. They didn't go down too well. There was a riot."

"There was a what?"

T recounted Jimmy's tale.

"I'll break their bloody necks," Colin had said, following the third set of jeers. Also, Adam and Steve's "poodles" were refused entry into the club, it being unsafe for civilians. So having missed out on their night of French cuisine, *they* weren't very happy, either.

"That's not the worst bit." T slumped on her bed. "We're being kicked out of Garmisch."

On the early morning train journey back, there was no mention of female gods, todgers or anything else to make the girls forget their glumness. The inquisition waited in T's bedroom.

"Is this it?" Colin exhibited one of the statues to the three lads. "Is this what you disobeyed me and trailed halfway across Europe for, this lump of wood?"

"Not to mention ruining mine and Steve's love life," Adam said.

"It's not wood, it's soapstone," T said. "They're supposed to be lucky."

"Lucky?" T thought about putting her fingers in her ears to block out the anticipated bellowing but decided against it. "Pissing lucky? They weren't very lucky for us lads, were they? We were standing up on that stage like four pillocks." Colin thumped the statue down on the bedside cabinet. T picked it up and checked for damage. Colin's volume knob turned a notch. "Are you listening to me?"

"I heard you. You were like four pillocks."

Jeannie giggled. T struggled to stem the snigger trickling from her mouth. She looked across the bed at Jeannie for support. Jeannie gestured a penis on the end of her nose. The trickle became a gush. T's floodgates opened into hysterics. Colin discontinued the cross-examination and stomped from the room. The Three Stooges followed.

Sod 'em.

3 Adam's Sexploits: Werneck. Oct '76:
Play That Funky Music White Boy.

Hatred glared from the villagers' faces at the white Transit van entering Werneck, suggesting outsiders were not welcome in this little Bavarian hamlet. Having been dismissed from the ski resort with a damaged reputation, the band's new accommodation was some fifteen miles away from the next venue.

"Why can't we stay in Schweinfurt? That's where most of the gigs are." Jeannie was sitting in the front seat, between driver Colin and his disobedient wife.

"Because it's too bloody expensive," Colin said. "I've told you all this once, if you'd taken the trouble to listen."

Two rows of English eyes endured the villagers' scowls. "There must be somewhere better than this. Look at them." The traffic lights changed. Jeannie stuck out her tongue at their new neighbours. "Anyone would think we'd arrived from a leper colony."

T turned to the lads in the back row seats. "What did this club manager say, Adam?"

"Apparently, one of the incumbent American cannon fodder got pissed one night. He then decided it would be a good idea to take a tank from the barracks for a test drive. Problem was: he didn't notice when he ran over a parked Volkswagen."

The van crept through the Hans Christian Anderson type village square, past the naked Maypole and past the shrine to the courting couple killed in the VW. The *Rathous* was in darkness but the local Mayor and his town councillors were probably inside, plotting what to do to the British invaders in the white van with the strange initials written on the side.

"*Das Alt Dorf Gasthous.*" Jimmy spotted the hotel. It was as it read on the sign: 'The Old Village Guesthouse'.

The grumpy proprietor, who was as it read on *his* sign, showed them around their new home. A great deal of English giggling erupted when he introduced himself. "Do I say something to amuse you?"

"Sorry, Herr Kutz." Adam and he exchanged looks of mutual disdain when the German host laid down the very strict 'House Rules'.

"There will be no eating in the rooms, no drinking in the rooms, no loud music in the rooms and most important, no visitors to the rooms after darkness."

Adam whispered to Steve: "Why is it that all little Krauts sound like they're planning to take over the world?"

Herr Kutz hitched his grubby trousers and glowered at the Englishmen. Enough starch ran through the irritable little man, no shirt collar necessary.

Frau Kutz's fit little body squeezed snugly into her functional dress. She was a good fifteen years younger than her cranky husband. Adam whispered again. "What's a cracker like her doing with a little despot like him? Steve?" Steve wasn't listening. He was exchanging smiles with the cracker.

After settling into the hotel, Colin called the band together to visit the base "for a recce".

Debbie Latham's bouffant hair did a little dance around her cheeks as she entered the office at the club. She introduced herself as the "Liaison Officer", working on Daddy's base. Daddy was the General. One of her duties was to show the band their new place of work. Bulky clothing was obviously intended to hide the bit of excess weight but the chunky jumper wasn't quite doing its job.

Steve gave Adam a nod of approval, obviously in recognition of the chunky jumper. Adam surreptitiously returned a lewd gesture, indicating the top-heavy proportions. Whoops, obviously not surreptitious enough.

"Is there something wrong with your hands, Adam?" Debbie asked.

Adam quickly put the offending hands behind his back. "Sorry, little touch of arthritis."

She gave him a knowing smile. "I'm also the one who brought y'all here. I hope you're not going to let me down."

"Oh, I don't think you'll feel let down," Adam said.

"Good. Me and my husband Bobby are going to take y'all out on the town tonight."

"Husband? I didn't realise you were married."

"Well, you do now. We'll pick y'all up at eight." She blew a voluptuous kiss from the office door. Her lips wouldn't have looked out-of-place on a Black woman. "Don't worry. We're gonna have a great *tahm*."

After she'd left, Adam gave another gesture with his arthritic hands.

Debbie arrived for the night-out wearing a different weight-concealing pullover. Her big hair was on the prowl, still on the lookout for a corsage as escort to the old school prom. Her family originated from Georgia though she and husband, Bobby, had moved to West Germany from Fort Wayne, Indiana. Evening hors d'oeuvre was dancing at the local *bier keller*. The Georgian Peach was true to her word, they were "having a great *tahm*". Bobby's insistence on paying for the whole evening made it all the greater. The group had no qualms about accepting any of this, particularly Colin: "Seeing as how the flash bastards had turned up in a Mustang." The car was an apt appendage for the thoroughbred Bobby.

"I'd have said it's more of an extension," Jeannie said.

"You would," Adam said.

A long dark perm softened Bobby's angular features. Debbie described this as a "shag style", initiating the expected, childish tittering from the Englishmen.

"I thought Adam was the only one got a shag from his hairdresser," Colin said.

Bobby looked more a male model than a mechanic yet his job seemed to entail fleecing the US Army motor pool. He hated soldiers.

The American hosts shared their dancing skills among the whole group, though Adam and Jeannie received most attention.

Cavorting along to Wild Cherry's 'Play That Funky Music', sweat poured from the surprisingly athletic Debbie. The heat of the dance floor and the thick clothing didn't seem to slow her down any. Nor did the pullover inhibit any movement of its inflated contents. As The Doobie Brothers played the introduction to 'China Grove', Adam instinctively undid his choker, wiped the back of his neck and put the choker back on.

The belle interrupted her go-go display to stroke Adam across the chest. "That's a nice looking necklace you got there, honey." She had to shout.

Attraction of the necklace measured how much a girl might fancy him. She'd tweaked his sexual barometer. He leaned in closer, voice pitched high enough above the Doobies for the intended listener only. "If you touch that, it means I have to make love to you." The routine and his answer were more habitual responses than any real attempt at seducing the forward American.

"Oh my, I better watch where I'm putting my hands, then." She allowed them to linger.

Normally, he would've welcomed a tilt at what she was hiding under her bulky jumper but a look across to Bobby who was giving some sort of martial arts demonstration made him stop and think again. "Maybe we should sit down," he said. They arrived back at the table. "What's going on here?" Adam asked.

"Bobby's been telling us how he beat the living crap out of three soldiers," Colin said. Using a cocktail menu, Bobby had explained how he'd disciplined the recruits.

"They call him The Karate King," Debbie told them. He'd won various trophies for it. The only thing Adam had ever won was the egg and spoon race at Clapgate Juniors' Sports Day. Even then he'd cheated. The pulverised plastic sprinkled more than a touch of bromide over Adam's lusty thirst. Any desire he might've had for the karate expert's wife was well doused.

Following the Bavarian disco, the main course of the evening was an Italian meal. When the party reached the restaurant, Debbie was still doing the organising. "*La Tavola*" was like any other Italian restaurant in Leeds, with Chianti bottles serving as candleholders. Imitation vines crawled across the ceiling, clinging to faded, yellow trellising, which clashed with the red and green décor. Each waiter, immaculate in black-and-white attire, greeted the Lathams personally: "All genuine Neapolitans," Debbie told the group.

Two tables were quickly put together to accommodate the large gathering. Each of the 'Images' party sat where told. Like the good hosts they were, Bobby and Debbie split to either end. Adam found himself in a female sandwich, T on his right and Debbie on his left.

"What do you like to drink?" Debbie asked him.

"Not sure. What do you suggest?" Adam was still having 'a great time'.
"Something sweet."

"Something sweet? I know just the thing." Instead of calling over the waiter, she reached in her handbag and brought out a bottle of rosé wine. "Try that."

"Oh boy, watch out, man," Bobby shouted down the table. "Here comes the Strawberry Hill."

T indicated the bag from which the wine had come. "I like your purse. It's nice and big."

"Hey up T, when did you learn to speak American?"

Debbie showed no appreciation of Adam's wit. "It's more a shoulder bag than a purse."

"I like a big bag." T produced her own gigantic repository as confirmation that she was speaking the truth. "I keep absolutely everything in here." She delved into the bag for more evidence. Out came a couple of the African statues.

"How come you're humping those things around with you?" Adam picked up one. "Ooh look, a parrot with tits."

"If you don't mind, I love 'em." T recounted the history of the figurines. "They're lucky, especially for women."

"Is that a fact?" Debbie picked up the other. "I'd like to get me some of that." She held it aloft. "You hear that, Bobby? This little sucker says I'm gonna get lucky tonight." She kissed it.

"Pass it down here," Bobby said. "I wouldn't mind getting lucky myself."

T took the statues from both Adam and Debbie. "When you've all finished taking the Mick out of my lucky mascots." She put them back in her bag.

"Some lucky mascots," Colin said. "You missed the bleeding gig, you gloit. Got us kicked out of Garmisch. Two riots in three weeks."

"You can't blame my birds for that."

Christ on a trampoline!

"What's up Adam?" Jimmy asked. "Are you okay?"

"Eh? Yeah." Adam took a large gulp of Strawberry Hill. "Bit o' pizza went down wrong hole." *Bit o' pizza, my arse*! The wide-eyed contortion on Adam's face that'd prompted Jimmy's concern had nothing to do with pepperoni. Under the table, Debbie's right hand had undone Adam's trouser zip and was now groping into his underpants. Another sip of his drink washed down some pizza to help with his choking ruse. The conversation at the table turned back to the subject of Bobby's karate prowess. Adam took several more swigs of Strawberry Hill. Debbie refilled his glass with her left hand. After an age, the meal ended.

Thank God that's over. Next time I want something sweet I'll stick to the cassata.

As they walked across the car park, Debbie tried to link arms with her prey.

"What the hell are you doing?" Adam pulled away. "Are you trying to get me killed?"

"Don't worry about Bobby. It's all arranged, Bobby's sweet on Jeannie. He wants her and I want you."

"Oh do you?" He looked around for a set of blond curls. "And does Jeannie know about this?" To Adam's surprise the blond curls were disappearing into the bottle green Mustang.

"I told ya." Debbie ran a finger down his spine. "Don't worry baby. Bobby can be real persuasive when he has to be. I'll come back with you." She'd climbed into the van before Adam could protest.

Adam was unsure what to make of Jeannie and Bobby being in the hotel bar together when he got back. Bobby immediately leapt up to order from Frau Kutz, serving behind the bar: "drinks for everyone."

"Hey you, come here." Adam pounced on Jeannie to see if she was into the arrangement made by the American swingers.

"Adam, do you really think I'm going to fall for your little sordid ploy to get me into an orgy? Tell Bobby he can sod right off with clogs on."

"Come on, Jeannie, do I look like somebody who wants a romp with a mad yank mechanic?"

She said nothing, merely raised an eyebrow.

"Look, I don't want any orgy but if you take care of hubby, I can think about giving his Mrs the benefit of my expertise."

"I've probably got some spare clogs for you, as well."

"Don't drop me in it. I thought you were a team player."

"Team player? Is that like 'one of the lads'?"

"Frigging hell, we're not back to that, are we? I didn't even get to sample any crêpe Monique thanks to you two."

"I'm off to bed."

"Jeannie?" Adam was left to erase any confusion her sudden disappearance might've sketched on the situation.

The bar was an enclosure of dark wood. Dark wooden benches set at dark wooden tables on a dark wooden floor, surrounded by dark wooden walls with even darker overhead beams. Adam sat with a dark wooden grin.

Bobby returned with the drinks. "Hey man, where'd Jeannie go?"

Adam rubbed at the sketch. "She's just nipped up to get something from her room."

Debbie returned from the toilet and sidled up close to Adam. He edged away. He'd already been unclear about the rules of this foreign game before Jeannie's departure. He didn't want to make any dangerous moves now that one of the main players was missing from the opposing team. Maybe he should try to enlist Steve.

I might need a half time substitute.

Steve seemed involved in a game of his own, deep in conversation with the snug fitting Frau Kutz, at that moment snugly slotted into a dark wooden corner of the bar.

Now that could bring the game into disrepute. Oh shit!

This reminder of Dammen und Herren Kutz momentarily diverted Adam, giving rise to the other problem, the 'House Rules', in particular the strict instructions: "No nightly visitors allowed in the rooms".

Jeannie obviously wasn't coming back and Bobby's recently purchased bottle of tequila was taking effect. It seemed all the impetus he needed to go in search of her.

Debbie grabbed Adam's arm. "Okay baby, let's go." She whipped him away from his team selecting talk with Jimmy.

"Where are we going?"

"To your room."

"Thought so."

Adam's room was upstairs, second along the corridor. They had to pass Jeannie's on the way. He was in luck. Bobby was nowhere in sight. Perhaps he was already inside, sharing the remains of the smuggled tequila with the cantankerous blonde.

The clandestine couple crept into Adam's room. He locked the door. They kissed.

She broke the clinch and sauntered around the small room, running her fingers over the Teutonic furniture, like she was checking for dust. "Very German." She unfastened the belt buckle of her corduroy jeans and yanked the belt through the loops. "Can you guess what this room reminds me of?" She folded the belt and strapped it across her palm. He backed against the Teutonic dresser. She strapped into her palm again. "It reminds me of a strict German mistress and men who do exactly as they're told."

"Really? Reminds me of Pinocchio."

"Say what?"

"Pinocchio: film when I was a kid, wooden puppet, lived in a room like this."

The belt lowered. "Pinocchio?"

"Do you want to hear a joke?"

"Do I what?"

"A girl sits on Pinocchio's face and says: okay, you little wooden bastard, tell another lie."

She whelped him across the thigh.

He jumped. "Oy, bugger off, stop it."

"Strip."

"Sod off, I'm not into owt kinky."

She struck him again. "I said take off your clothes."

"Okay, okay, just stop it with the belt. I hate pain." He grabbed the hand holding the belt, pulled her to him and kissed her. "You have to ask, nicely." He seized the belt, threw it into a corner and then took off his shirt.

Debbie pulled back the quilt. "Get in."

"Nicely?"

"Please."

He finished undressing, got into bed, lay back and watched as this strange intruder into his fairytale land performed an exotic song and dance.

"Play That Funky Music White Boy . . ." She undid the buttons on her corduroys then teasingly wriggled out of them. Adam's excitement grew; especially aroused by the discovery that she hadn't been wearing any pants under her jeans.

She removed her pullover and bra in one deft movement. That's when he saw the sight that would make him forget belts, even karate. As though he'd received a visit from the Holy Ghost, he was ready to face anything and anyone without fear. These exhibits should've had first place rosettes pinned on them. He stared at the dark brown pigment encircling her protruding nipples, mentally measuring the ashtray on the sideboard against the aureole in front of him. The ashtray took the runners-up award. Not wanting to appear too keen, he moved to flip on his side.

Too late: she stroked a hand over the contour his ardour had shaped in the quilt. "Theresa's statues said I was going to get lucky tonight, seems they were right." She joined him in the bed. He buried his head into the prize-winning breasts, but a distant knocking halted his advances. He lifted his head from its mammary pillow to improve audibility and heard a male American voice coming from somewhere down the hall.

"Come on honey, open the door. I know this is your room; Colin just told me."

"Piss off." The reply from the next room was Yorkshire and female.

"Open the goddamn door," Bobby said.

Jeannie vehemently repeated her first retort. The pair in the Teutonic room waited and listened in silence.

"There's nothing to worry about," Debbie said after another minute.

"How do you work that one out?" Adam's Holy Ghost had donned his hat and coat and deserted the scene.

"Come on, honey, he's gone." She kissed him. "He's gone. What are you waiting for?"

He waited a bit longer. *Hey, come on:* Cyclops said from between his legs. *What's going on? You're being stupid.* Of course, they were right. Bobby appeared to have given up his quest. It was safe to return to the matter in hand, or rather the matter in both hands. Despite the interruption, Cyclops was still sufficiently aroused not to be put off. In fact, his excitement was such that he felt it best to dispense with the foreplay, lest it dispense with him. He climbed on top, manoeuvring into entry position, ready to strike home.

Cop a load o' *this you Georgian cutie.*

This was where he discovered the button that would set off Debbie's nuclear reactor. Suddenly, from apparently nowhere, she began thrashing about and screaming at the top of her Southern twanged voice.

"*Aarghh*! Fuck me Big Boy, fuck me hard." Having started the reactor Adam looked around for the button or lever that would both shut it down and shut her up.

"Shush!" His plea was of no avail, onward screeched the machine.

"You call that fucking? Do it to me now, you limey bastard."

Fearing that Herr Kutz and the whole of his hotel clientele would be outside the room in a matter of minutes, Adam grabbed the pillow and tried stuffing it into Debbie's thick-lipped mouth. Even with her face covered, the reactor screeched on. Then came the inevitable knock. Adam had a brief worry that the door would burst open and he'd be caught trying to smother her.

"Is that you honey?" Bobby's voice drilled from the other side of the door. "Hey, come on you guys, let me in." The machine ground to a halt.

Debbie pulled the covers over her breasts. "Go away Bobby. You're not wanted."

Yeah, go away. Too bloody true, you're not wanted.

"Aw, come on, man:" Bobby said. Debbie moved to get out of bed.

He knew it was illogical but he kept his voice low in the hope Bobby might not realise he was there. "Don't you dare let him in." She stayed where she was.

"Hey honey, is he doing it to ya?" Strange thumping accompanied Bobby's moans. "Oh yeah go on babe, ride that sucker."

"What's he doing?" Adam asked. "

"Jerking off," Debbie said. '

"Oh my God." Adam pulled his hands away from the vicinity of his genitals, lest they be implicated in this obscenity. "Shut him up before he gets us all thrown out." Debbie jumped from the bed. "No!" He made an attempted grab for her arm. "Don't let him in. Just tell him to stop and go away." Too late. She'd unlocked the door and Bobby was inside.

Adam remained in the bed trying to persuade the adjoining wall to provide an escape hatch. Bobby wriggled out of his leather trousers. A leer accompanied his invitation: "Hey everybody, keep cool, we're just gonna have some fun. Isn't that right honey?"

Honey didn't seem too sure and stayed by the door. "Come on, Bobby, calm down. You're getting too worked up."

Bobby, eager to start the fun, got into bed with Adam.

"Er, perhaps not." Adam sprang from the bed and joined Debbie.

She grabbed him around the neck and pinned his back against the door. "Don't go I won't let him hurt you."

Bobby leapt from the bed and grabbed Debbie, sandwiching her between him and Adam. "Hold him there, honey."

It was time for Adam's substitution but the subs' bench was empty. He was trapped.

The Georgian harpy clung about him, her head buried in his shoulder, the bouffant hair wrapped around his face. Her mad husband locked on and began thrusting. Adam was only inches away from the frenzied grin on Bobby's face. "Come on Adam, loosen up. Enjoy the fun."

"Okay, baby, give it to me good and hard." Debbie grabbed Adam's crutch. "Let's go Big Boy."

Bobby started giving it to her good and hard. Adam's head banged against the door, repeatedly, swirling him into oblivion until the entangled team members collapsed in a heap. Adam saw his chance. He jumped up and was out of the room quicker than anyone could say 'you're next, my son'. However, his immediate sense of relief was short-lived. "Shit!" Stranded and naked in the chill of the corridor, he scuttled along and knocked on Jeannie's door." Jeannie, please, please, let me in."

Back along the corridor, the naked Bobby emerged. "Hey, great idea, man." He called back into Adam's room. "He ain't run off, honey, He's gone to get Jeannie."

Adam hammered on the door. "For fuck's sake, Jeannie."

"Say you're sorry."

"What?" What the hell was the dizzy blonde talking about? "Jeannie, it's me, Adam."

"Say, I'm sorry for wanting to shag that French poodle."

"Jeannie, stop messing about."

"Say it."

"Alright; I'm sorry. I'm very, very sorry. Please, Jeannie." Liberation, she unlocked the door. "Thanks a lot." He pushed past her. "You nearly got me stuffed."

The t-shirt clad Jeannie tittered. "Very fetching."

The naked Adam scurried to Jeannie's bed. "It's not funny."

"It is a bit funny." She got in beside him.

"They're mad. They're both as nutty as each other. God knows what they'd have done to me."

"Serves you right." She lit a cigarette.

"Come on, Jeannie, give us a break."

"That's your punishment for being a twat to me." She blew a puff of smoke at him.

"Jeannie, we didn't even get to meet up with those French birds."

"If you'd had your way, you'd have done more than meet up with 'em."

Before he could go on with any defence, from his room came the sound of the nuclear reactor starting again. "*Aarghh*! Fuck me, Big Boy . . ."

Jeannie stubbed out her cigarette and exchanged the same shock expression across the pillow with Adam. For the next five minutes they said nothing, merely listened and waited for the reactor to subside.

"Thank God for that." Adam turned to face the wall. "Now, maybe we can all get some sleep." He plotted a route up the pattern on the bedroom wall, in the hope the ordinance survey map might lead to slumber-land. "Night Jeannie."

She nudged him between the shoulder blades. "Adam?"

He turned back "What?"

"Fancy a shag?" She'd straddled him without negotiation. Nose to nose, they shared the moment's humour with a joint chuckle.

Oh well, in for a *pfennig*.

The following morning, Adam returned to the playing field of the previous night's bizarre game. He found his bedroom door open and his American opponents gone. They'd either left in the middle of the night or it'd all been a nightmare. He pulled back the straightened quilt and checked the sheets for evidence, nothing. Perhaps he'd gone sleepwalking into Jeannie's room. He went to the dresser for his clothes. A note prevented him opening the drawer.

Thanks for a great night: Debbie and Bobby. We sure got lucky, xxx.

He dressed with a sense of relief. "Absolute nutters, the pair of them."

The nightmare theory dissolved when he got downstairs into the hotel bar. "You must all collect together your things and vacate your rooms today." Herr Kutz had his hands placed on his waist in a Hitler like pose. "This behaviour is not acceptable."

"But . . ." Adam's feeble attempt at an apology didn't even make it to the crease before he was given 'caught out at silly-mid-off'.

"But that's not fair," Jimmy took up the batting. "Just because *he* can't keep his trousers on for more than two minutes, shouldn't mean we all have to suffer."

"The boy is right, Gerhard." Herr Kutz didn't see the smile his wife sent in Steve's direction. "They should not all have to leave."

"*Naturlich liebling*." Herr Kutz pointed at Adam and Colin. "You and you, vacate your rooms, please." Obvious culprit was Adam, most noise coming from his room. Colin had to go because he was in charge and therefore responsible. Poor old T just happened to share the same room as Colin.

When the trio arrived downstairs with their luggage, Herr Kutz met them. "Your keys, please."

T emptied the contents of her bag on the bar. Colin drummed his fingers on the back of a chair. "Bloody hell woman, what have you got in there?" Herr Kutz waited. Out came a couple of the African statues. Colin and Adam shook their heads.

Adam picked up one. "Do me a favour, T. Next time we meet that Debbie, keep these bloody things away from her. I don't think I can handle any more good luck."

T found the keys.

Given that all the cheap hotels in the Schweinfurt area were full, and following the crushing of the Volkswagen, Herr Kutz's hotel was the only affordable digs around that didn't have a phobia of *auslanders*. They agreed the best course was for Jimmy, Steve and Jeannie to take advantage of Herr Kutz's leniency and stay in the Alt Dorf. The outcasts would have to search for alternative accommodation.

"Thanks for the solidarity, brother," Adam said. "You don't fool me, Steve; you're just trying to get your end away with Eva Braun."

Colin threw his suitcase into the van. "Shut up, Fogerty, this is all down to you."

Plenty of vacant rooms littered Bad Kissengen but as well as being slightly outside travelling range, all were way above the band's price limit. Short of time, Colin suggested they go back and accept the least expensive of the batch.

"We'll take *zwei zimmer*," Colin said, to the manager of the new hotel. "*Ein dopple und ein single.*"

Bloody show off. Adam pocketed his unopened phrase book.

"Have you identification?" The manager asked, in perfect English. Colin appeared unimpressed. T searched through her overfilled handbag for the passports. Again, out came the two statues.

Adam pointed an accusing finger. "There's definitely something about these little juju bastards."

"Give over, Adam." T found the passports at the bottom of the bag and handed them to the manager. "For a minute I thought I'd left them at the other hotel in *Ooer*neck." She'd never quite grasped that 'W' was pronounced 'V' in German.

"Do you mean *Wer*neck?" the manager said.

Adam didn't like the way he corrected T's pronunciation or the way he scrutinised the passports. "Sorry mate, she's not too good with names."

"Do you mind? I'm not stupid." T put the statues and other contents back in her bag. "Yes, we stayed in *Wer*neck last night, at the Alt Dorf Hotel."

"The Alt Dorf Hotel? I see. One moment please." The manager tapped the passports together on the counter then took them into his office.

"Hey, what ya doing?" Colin's scowl went unnoticed by the manager who was immediately on the telephone gabbling in German. When he returned, he handed back the passports to Colin.

"I am very sorry sir. Herr Kutz is a personal friend of mine. I cannot allow you to stay in my hotel."

Out in the street, Colin snarled at T. "Great. Good move mentioning the Alt Dorf."

"Kraut bastards," Adam said. "T, are you sure that bloke said your juju birds are supposed to bring you *good* luck? 'Cos every time they're around--"

"I'm gonna ring that twat up." Colin punched his fist into his palm. "I'll give him a bloody haircut."

"Then, nobody will have anywhere to stay," T said.

"So what do we do now?" Adam asked.

Colin drummed his fingers on his skull and cross-bone belt buckle. "We'll just have to drive further a field."

"What; like Poland?"

"Shut up, Fogerty. You're not helping. It's too late to do anything now. We need to get back. I'll ask the club manager to ring round for us, while we're on stage."

When Colin picked up the others, on the way to the club, Steve got in the van alongside T and greeted them with a big grin. "How did you get on?"

"No luck," Colin answered.

"Well, I've got some good news and some not so good news. I got Frau Kutz to work on her hubby. Result is, Colin and T, you can have your old room back." Steve dangled a key in his right hand. In his left hand, he dangled nothing. "I'm afraid he wouldn't budge for you, Adam."

"Frigging Nora, that can't be right," Adam said. "That's not fair. What am *I* supposed to do?"

T broke from hugging Steve and turned to the rear seats. "Happen you could stay tonight in that nice hotel we looked at – the place with the stables, and then look for somewhere else tomorrow."

"The Postplatz? Are you kidding? I'm not paying for that, not even for one night. I'd rather kip in here."

"You can't do that; it's middle of bloody winter," T said. "You'll freeze."

"Oh, well worked out, Einstein. Have you ever thought of starting your own pub-quiz team? Your area of expertise could be the frigging obvious."

"I was only trying to be helpful."

Farther down the road, Jeannie spoke up from the back. "Adam could stay in the van and we could smuggle him out a spare duvet and stuff." She gave an exaggerated wink.

"What's that supposed to mean?" he asked.

She snuggled up to him. "Give it half an hour in the back of the van and I'll sneak down and let you in. You can stay in my room."

"Right, we're here:" Colin said. "Come on, we need to get to it."

"Good, I'm bursting for the loo." Jeannie jumped up. She was out of the van and gone before Adam could discuss the plan in more detail.

On the base, the Liaison Officer was nowhere around. A sigh accompanied Adam's smile. The club manager, William Carter, a large, jolly Afro/American welcomed them instead. The sign on his office door assured he was a *bona-fide* Sergeant but the parrots, canoes and palm trees on his Hawaiian shirt suggested he wasn't too fond of army issue. His brow lifted and his eyes widened with every beam of his chubby cheeked smile, which seemed to happen at the end of every sentence. Sometimes a reflexive chortle would accompany a particular phrase or when it was something he obviously found amusing, a full-blown guffaw would escape his rotund shiny face.

"Aw, Miss Debbie is a little bit weird:" Carter said, when Adam asked of her whereabouts. This only merited a chuckle on the laughter scale.

"Really?" Adam said. "I hadn't noticed."

During the Bellamy Brothers, third number of the first set, Adam looked up from his drums to see a brunette bouffant of 'Farrah-Fawcet' hair arrive at the front table.

Cosmic! This is obviously my lucky day.

With a smirk, he tried to convey 'you've got a bloody nerve coming here'. Debbie smiled and gave a cheeky little wave. In front of her was a cardboard box, almost the size of the table.

"Hey Ace, that nutter's here," Steve said, when Adam came off stage.

"I know. I've seen her."

"She's got something for you. I had to carry it in for her."

Everyone accompanied Adam to Debbie's table.

"How ya'll doing?" The Georgian flashed a grin, giving no indication that the events of the previous night had taken place. "What about *you*, Adam?"

Adam turned to Steve. "How am I doing? She asks."

Steve grinned. "Yep, that's what she asked, man. How exactly *are* you doing, Ace?"

"Well, thanks to you, Debbie love, I've been kicked out of the hotel and I'm spending the night in the freezing cold, in the frigging van."

"Sorry." She opened the box. "I brought you a present."

Adam counted twelve bottles of Strawberry Hill. "If they'd been twelve blankets, they might've been more use."

"I thought you'd like them."

"Did you?"

"Come on, honey, I came all the way down here to make up for last night, dropping you in it like that with my naughty husband. Man, when he hits that tequila."

Adam shied his gaze away from the tittering faces around the table. He took out one of the bottles. "Yeah, right, well thanks. I'm sure these will go down a treat."

"That's better, honey." She pinched his cheek and kissed him. "Come on honey, open it."

Adam screwed off the bottle cap.

"The way to a man's heart is through his stomach," Jimmy said. "The way to Adam's is obviously through his liver."

"Through his groin." Jeannie shook her head and scowled.

Maybe she was right. Why wasn't he getting as far from this nutter as common sense advised?

Before going back on for the second set, Adam explained to Debbie what'd happened over the hotels. He secretly hoped she might suggest paying for a room at the Postplatz; given that Daddy was a minted General. All that booze could've paid for a luxury suite.

"Gee I'm sorry about what happened. I suppose I could square it with Bobby for you to come home and stay at our apartment." She obviously had no talent as a mind reader.

"I'd rather not bother Bobby."

"You don't need to worry about him. He's fine about you. It was Bobby who dropped me off here."

"I'm not worried about him. Look, it's probably not that bad in the van. I'm quite looking forward to it." When he'd said it to T, he hadn't meant sleeping in the van as a serious suggestion, but with plenty of spare covers, plus of course there was Jeannie's wink. Besides, any idea was better than a night fighting off a tequila infused naughty Bobby."

"Hey, why don't I stay in the van with you? It'll be cool," Debbie said.

"Cool," Steve said. "It'll be freezing."

"Are you nuts?" Adam asked. She didn't need to answer.

Steve shared another headshake with Jeannie. "It's not only *her* sanity that's in question."

Maybe they were right. Adam was, after all, considering spending a night with a lunatic. It's not as if he needed the sex. Then again, he tapped the box of booze. "At least we've got these for company. You know what they say: A bird in the van is worth twelve bottles of Strawberry Hill."

"Or it could be worth a kick in the knackers." Jeannie scowled again as they went back on stage.

By the time Steve had packed away the equipment at the end of the night, the second bottle of Strawberry Hill was three-quarters empty. They were well into the third bottle by the time the rest of the group were entering the Alt Dorf, abandoning Adam and Debbie in the hotel car park. October was colder in West Germany than in England. This didn't prevent the pair being naked, probably just as the other band members were gathering around the log fire in the hotel bar. At least things couldn't be as weird or frenetic as the previous evening. Nevertheless, there was a slight variation on the nuclear reactor theme when Adam's attempt at oral sex was accompanied by: "*Aarghh*! Eat me, you limey bastard."

Shortly after Adam opened the fourth bottle of what he'd christened "nectar", the van was bouncing in time with Debbie's breasts. It might've been this or the fact that he'd drunk well in excess of his body's nectar capacity that caused Adam to vomit. "Sorry love." Through the fuzz in his head he suddenly remembered Jeannie's wink. He closed the van window and began dressing but only got as far as his underpants. Then confusion hit when he tried to distinguish the armhole from the neck of his sweater. The nectar was terrible at making decisions. He gave up and got out of the van.

"What are you doing?" Debbie asked.

"What's it look like? I'm going to get in through Jeannie's window, then I'll let you in." The plan didn't get the best start. He slid back down the drainpipe. A squall of laughter came from Debbie at the van window. What the hell was so funny? He'd only slipped, for God's sake. It wasn't cool when a bird laughed at you. With a supreme effort, he collected his senses and managed to shin up all the way to Jeannie's window.

Well done my son. Give yourself a pat on the pack. Whoops, best not do that or you'll fall. Hee, hee, that's so bloody funny.

He stretched across and knocked on the window. Jeannie would be so impressed.

The window opened. "Are you right in your bloody head?" she asked.

"This was your idea. You said I could stay in your room. Let me in, I'll go down and open the front door for Debbie."

"Funny enough, I was thinking more on the lines of just you and me; you pissed up, insensitive bastard. What do you propose doing with Sweet Georgia Brown?"

"What do you mean?"

"Where's *she* going to sleep?"

"I can't leave her in the van, can I?"

"Tell her to go home."

"How does she do that; get Herr Kutz to call a taxi? Let me in, it's freezing out here."

She leaned out and looked down the drainpipe. "Course it's bloody freezing, you wazzock, you're only wearing your undercrackers."

"Come on, it wasn't easy climbing up here."

"You've got a bloody nerve." She shook her head and took an inviting step back from the window. He put his weight on the drainpipe mountings and grabbed for the window ledge. *Oh shit*! The mountings came away from the wall. Adam let go of the window ledge and swung back to the safety of the drainpipe. *Bad move, man.* The guttering was now only holding the top section of the pipe, which certainly couldn't support his full body weight. Guttering, drainpipe and Adam plummeted into the metal dustbins.

A jolt of pain shot through his spine and forced the air from his lungs making it difficult to speak. "You bastards. I've broken my frigging back."

Debbie was now out of the van, gripping her sides.

Three lights snapped on inside the hotel in quick succession followed by Herr Kutz's appearance at the door. The irate proprietor shouted something but Adam couldn't understand.

"Fuck off, you Kraut bastard." Not Adam's most scintillating attempt at wit and repartee but he didn't care.

"This is not acceptable," Herr Kutz said.

"Piss off. I hope your next shit's a hedgehog." Adam clambered from the dustbins and limped back to the van. The hotel door slammed shut and the three lights snapped out in reverse order. Jeannie had closed her window.

"I guess you're in real trouble now." Debbie struggled to contain her laughter.

"Bollocks to him. What more can he do to me?" As he went to climb back in the van, he slipped on the vomit. Debbie exploded.

The following day, no amount of apologies from Adam could prevent the exodus of suitcases with the eviction of the remaining band members.

Jeannie beckoned. "Can I just make something clear between us? I'm not one of the lads. From now on, we just work together, okay? I think you're a twat."

"Jeannie, I didn't—"

"Shove it."

Adam waited until they were in the van. "Look, guys—"

"Just don't say another bleeding word." Colin was at the wheel, driving toward Schweinfurt. "This is gonna cost us all a pissing fortune. That's if we're lucky enough to even find any new digs."

Adam sat in the back of the van and remained *schtum*. "Sorry" was the only 'bleeding word' he'd tried saying, anyway. He felt bad; not only because of a sore back and the hellish hangover he was nursing but the situation in which he'd placed his mates. He wasn't too clear what Jeannie's problem was but from now on, he was giving up drink, especially Strawberry frigging Hill.

4 T's Adventures: Schweinfurt. Oct '76:
Sweet Home Alibami.

When Sergeant Carter heard of the band's predicament, without hesitation he came up with a solution. "No problem, man," he said. "I got plenny a room at my place, enough for ya'll. You guys were bad last night."

"It wasn't all of us." T pointed at Adam. "Just him."

"Silly bugger, T." Jeannie laughed. "He's not talking about what happened at the Alt Dorf, that's what Americans say when they think something's good. He liked our playing."

"Especially, you lady." He pointed at T. "You got one hell of a voice."

Everyone agreed that it would be an adventure to move in with the 'jolly fat man' until something else could be found.

Enquiries about Sergeant Carter from the soldiers on the base revealed him as a family man with odd-coloured children on whom he 'lavished much love'. Sharing this love was his wife, Kim, not quite as fat but an equally jolly Vietnamese woman he'd met during the war. They did indeed have plenty of room. For the next six weeks, the three Carter kids would be away visiting Grandmother in the 'States'.

The room allocation included yet another roster, this time for the downstairs couch. T and Colin were exempt.

"No, we can't take this. This is your bedroom," T said.

"When you are guests, you must stay in here." Kim was shorter than T, yet she didn't appear blimpish. "We move into my son's room."

"No, we wouldn't feel comfortable doing that; would we Col?"

"If that's what Kim wants, don't want to be rude."

After a respectable amount of refusals and objections, T and Colin moved into their host's bedroom. A comfortable space, it much resembled their own, brightly coloured, with fitted wardrobes, shag pile carpet, plus two bedside cabinets and lights. A variation to the clock radio that T kept by her bed, the Carters had a cassette player built into the purple and lilac studded headboard. T pressed the play button. Percy Sledge joined them to give Colin some tips on: "When a Man Loves a Woman".

This will do nicely.

T looked forward to a pleasurable stay in Schweinfurt, secretly hoping the digs situation wouldn't be resolved too soon before the Carter children returned.

As with the bedroom, the Carters' living room was not too dissimilar to the Bones', other than there wasn't a bloody great horrible bar in the middle. Another shag pile, burgundy and more sedate, covered the downstairs, complimenting the white and dark red of the walls. Kim drew open the vertical white linen blinds allowing T and Jeannie to see out to the main street. Light filled the spacious room.

Kim never showed her legs. Dresses always reached the floor and all her trousers were over baggy. She seemed not to take steps but shuffled everywhere. She picked up the photographs of their Negroid/Oriental boys and ran it over her sleeve. "I miss them when they away."

"They're so cute, so beautiful. They look just like their daddy." T became suddenly aware of Jeannie's mischievous grin.

"I go make dinner." Kim shuffled to the kitchen.

Jeannie was still grinning.

"What?" T asked.

"They're so beautiful," Jeannie said in a silly teasing voice. "Just like their daddy!"

"I didn't say that."

"You fancy Carter, don't you?"

"Don't be ridiculous. He's a happily married man. And I'm a happily married woman, if you don't mind."

"Not sure about happily. But it don't worry me. Fill your boots, I say."

T went and sat on the roster couch. "Anyway, what's happening with you and Adam?"

"Me and Adam? What's that arsehole got to do with anything?"

"You can't fool me, Jeannie Hay. It's obvious you're nuts about him."

"Now who's being ridiculous?"

"Don't blame you for being mad at him, going with that Debbie."

"They're just about right for each other. She's welcome to him."

T looked away. "Sorry."

"What have *you* got to be sorry about?"

"Dunno. I just feel a bit responsible. She said it was my statues brought her good luck."

Jeannie was staring out on the street. "It doesn't need statues to get Adam to drop his trousers."

"It is a bit strange though. There's been some weird things going on."

Jeannie turned back into the room. "What's a bit strange?"

"I've been thinking a lot about this. It's like something's been guiding us here. I'm sure it has something to do with my statues."

"Have you been at Kim's cooking sherry?" Jeannie sat in the armchair alongside T's couch.

"Seriously, if we hadn't gone to Austria to get them, we wouldn't have missed the gig, then we wouldn't have had to leave Garmisch." T leaned across and gripped her friend's wrist. "And then, when we went to book in at that other hotel in BK, it was only after I got the statues out of my bag that he refused to let us stay."

Jeannie made a spooky voice and hand wave to accompany her rendition of the 'Twilight Zone' theme. "Da-dee, da-da. Da-dee, da-da."

"Wazhappening, ladies?" Carter had come in. He was rarely seen without a smile.

"Sit here, Carter." Jeannie went back to the window. "Hey T, why don't you show Carter your magic statues?"

T glared. *And you can wipe that smirk off your face Missy.*

"Magic statues?" Carter took Jeannie's seat.

"Go on. T, show him." Jeannie kept facing the street but it wasn't hard to imagine her goading expression. "I mean; if it wasn't for them, we might not be here."

"Shurrup," T said.

Carter finally shifted his attention from Jeannie's rear, back to T. "So what's the story?"

"T's got these African statues and they've got supernatural powers."

"Powers? What kinda powers?"

Jeannie was obviously having fun. "Strange things happen when they're around."

Strange things will happen to you, if you don't shut it.

Jeannie's spooky voice was back. "It's the African juju."

"African?" Carter said. "Sounds interesting."

"Take no notice of her." T made a show of speaking through clenched teeth. "She's just being stupid."

"No, go on," Jeannie said. "You'd love to see them, wouldn't you, Carter?"

"Sure would."

T skipped off to fetch the birds. When she returned she wasn't disappointed with Carter's reaction.

"Oh my, I love them. You know, my momma had a statue much like one of these." Carter carried the figurines to the dresser and took them from the box. "Why don't you keep them down here during your stay? They'll remind me of home." He kicked off his shoes, sat back in his chair and gave a nod of approval at the statues. He unbuttoned the top button of his shirt.

"See? What did I tell you," Jeannie said.

"What did you tell me about what?" T had no idea why the mischievous blonde flaunted a triumphant sneer.

"He's only been in the room with them for ten seconds and already he's doing a striptease."

"I'm going to make a brew." T needed to hide her embarrassment at the imagined vision of Carter, twirling his tassels. "Anybody want one?" There were no takers. She escaped to the kitchen. On her way, she checked over her shoulder at the statues, in their new setting.

Oh yes, this will do very nicely, indeed.

Later that day, when T came into the living room, Kim was examining one of the statues. "What these are?"

"They're from Africa. They're very lucky. Carter told me to put them on there. He likes them."

"Yes I like them, also, very much."

"You do? Oh good. Kim, I can't thank you enough for letting us stay here. I don't know how we can repay you."

"Thank you. I like very much."

Carter came in. "Wazhappening?"

Kim showed Carter the statue. "Theresa give gift for us."

T's tongue refused to object. "Eh?"

Carter's eyes widened. "Hell, really? My, oh my! Remember, Kim, Momma had one of these? Why thank you, Theresa. I know these meant something to you."

"No, no, I didn't …"

"No, we really do appreciate them."

A manic smile was all T could manage.

Three days and T still hadn't managed to explain the misunderstanding over the statues. She was enjoying her stay too much and didn't want to risk spoiling it. She chopped the onions and mixed them into the mince.

Carter looked on. He didn't have much hair but what he did have contained no grey. He also had a neat little moustache, which he often preened between the thumb and forefinger of his left hand. "I sure do like a woman who can cook." Ebony skin stretched over his body with a permanent sheen.

"I'm probably nowhere near as good as your Kim but I do like cooking."

"My Kim got to be the best in the world."

Better just to bide her time with the statues. Happen when she and Kim were in the kitchen alone, together. "She showed me how to do this." Kim's version of the American meatloaf was the band's favourite. "The lads love it."

"You guys been together long?"

"Nearly three months." She stirred the mince.

"Something I been meaning to ask you."

"What's that?"

"You guys are called 'Images', right?"

"Course."

"So how come you got something else written on your truck?"

"Oh, TBM-mobile, it stands for the Tetley Bitter Men."

"The what men?"

"Tetley Bitter, it's a beer from Yorkshire." She adjusted the strings of her apron. "TBM-mobile, it's what Colin calls his van. It's his pride and joy. He thinks more of that than he does of me."

"Well I don't understand that, any more than I do about the name."

It'd been T who'd thought up the band's name of 'Images'. Colin didn't actually agree with her choice; he thought it was 'drippy' but "The Tetley Bitter Men" wouldn't have sold very well to the US bases.

T was giving another stir to the contents of the pan when Kim returned from her trip to the commissary. Carter relieved his wife of the shopping bags. T sprinkled some cayenne pepper into the pan. "I hope you don't mind, I made a start."

Kim looked in the pan. "You are guest. No need to cook. Kim cook."

"Sorry, I was just browning the meat."

Kim picked up the hem of T's apron then looked at Carter.

"Oh yeah, I gave her one of your aprons, babe."

"Not to keep." T laughed. "Just to borrow." She took off the apron.

Carter took it from her and handed it to Kim. "Theresa been telling me all about her band's old truck."

"You better not let Colin hear you calling his precious baby an old truck." T laughed again and picked up a jar of oyster paste. Her fingers were slippy so she handed it to Carter.

Kim snatched it from him and turned the lid. It opened with a fearsome pop. "Kim cook."

The Carters were a good ten years older than the Bones.

T sat up in bed watching Colin undress. "It's just the odd occasion, I'm not sure if she likes me but then most of the time it's like having an older sister."

"Soppy cow." Colin's attempt at masking his own fondness for the Carters didn't fool her for an instant.

She put down her book. "I don't know how to tell them. They think I've given them the statues as a present."

He climbed into bed. "What is it with you and them things?"

"It's no different to you and that bloody TBM-mobile." She snuggled into his bare chest. "Do you want me to talk dirty to you?"

"You what?"

She ran her hand down his chest and into his Y fronts. "Carburettor! Oily spark plugs! Revving pistons!"

"Come here, you mad bugger. I'll show you a revving piston."

Joey Proudfoot was definitely not vegetarian. He looked like he'd been fed on meat since leaving the womb, probably raw buffalo. He and his five Native American Navajo friends had chosen the army rather than the bleak life back home on reservations. It'd been young Jimmy who'd first met the Navajo and introduced them to Colin and T. Colin's immediate reaction was to say: "What, you mean you're real live Red-skins?" He'd then put two fingers up behind his head to signify feathers, whilst placing his other hand in front of his mouth to make the sound a child makes when imitating a Red Indian. Big Joey had taken offence at this insult and a minor scuffle had broken out. Colin had taken on all six renegades and the minor scuffle had wrecked the Bad Kissengen club. Images were no longer allowed to play there.

"If he gets us thrown out of Schweinfurt, I'll swing for him," T told Jeannie and Carter.

Jeannie was back looking out of Carter's living room window. "Where is he, anyway?"

"Where is he?" T was back on the couch. "Believe it or not, he's round at their place."

"Round at whose place?"

"The bloody Red Indians: suddenly they're all bosom buddies."

Carter was sitting in his armchair, preening his moustache. "Colin's the first man ever to stand up to Big Joey. I can see why the Indians invited him to join their club."

T sipped her brew. "He's been there every night this week."

"What happens at these pow-wow gatherings?" Jeannie asked.

"They drink and play country & western, what else?" Carter said.

Colin's explanation for his newfound Indian friendship was simple. He liked them because they were different. They told him interesting things, such as:

'throughout the whole North and South Continents, the Aboriginal Native Americans, were unable to grow facial or body hair.'

"I mean; have you ever seen a Red Indian with a beard?" Colin said.

"What, not even under their arms?" T asked.

"Who has a beard under their arm?"

"No, you silly bugger, I mean, don't they even grow hair under their arms?"

"Not even pubes." However, four of the Indian group had ignored this biological fact and had grown spurious moustaches in their vain attempts to look like the White Man. The whole tribe of soldiers wore cowboy hats and had their 'country & western' evenings in the pursuit of 'Civilisation'.

Also banned from Bad Kissingen, the tribe had taken to visiting Schweinfurt. Colin was spending more and more time with them, even during the band's set breaks. To avoid becoming a Navajo widow, T decided to go with him but Mr Proudfoot didn't exactly make her feel welcome.

"Say woman, when are you going to learn some real music instead of all this rock shit you sing?"

"What do you call real music?"

"I mean Emmylou Harris, man. Now, she's a real singer. She's got everything. Ain't that right, Colin?"

"She sure has," Colin said.

"Has she really, Colin?" T nipped his thigh under the table.

"Ouch!" Colin cleared his throat. "Well course, she can sing okay but she's a bit of a shovel compared to you."

"Shovel?" T swirled her drink around the glass. "Sorry, Mr Proudfoot, I don't like country & western. It makes me want to vomit."

"Hey, Colin, my man," Joey said. "I think you need to put your squaw on the right path."

"The only path he's putting me on is the warpath." She swirled her drink again, downed it and left.

Working at Carter's club allowed the girls a rare luxury, a dressing room of their own. T took advantage of the privacy to ask Jeannie about something that'd been bothering her for some weeks. "You know when the lads call a girl 'a bit of a shovel', what do they mean?"

"Eh? Erm, it's just a band thing, really."

"I guessed that but what do they mean?"

Jeannie's floundering feet betrayed her discomfort. "You know, just a bit of group parlance, as they say." T folded her arms. Jeannie cleared her throat. "Well, erm, you know Adam's joke about unattractive girls?"

"No."

"Yes you do. He says, God gave her the ugliest face in the world, then he hit it with a shovel." T didn't laugh. "So now, if they see a girl that's a grot-bag, then she's a bit of a shovel. If she's really ugly, she's two-shovels."

"I bet they think I'm a bit of a shovel, don't they?"

"What? No, don't talk daft."

"I'm not talking daft. Even Colin says it."

"There you are, then. He wouldn't do that if he thought they were talking about *you*, would he?" The feet shifted again.

"Nice try, Jeannie, I'm off to the kitchen, see how many chips I can 'shovel' in my ugly gob. Just a bit of group parlance, as they say."

Indians aside, Schweinfurt had turned out even better than Garmisch. After some friendly persuasion from Carter, Kim's kitchen had become T's playground. Kim allowed her to open the odd jar and had even taught her a few recipes from the East. Since being "put on the right path" by Big Joey, T had spent a few singing breaks visiting the club kitchen, where Carter had some recipes of his own. His work at the club usually had him either cooking or supervising the menu.

"Hi Carter, what's cooking?"

"Today we got a big choice. We got Country Fried Chicken, we got Hawaiian Chicken or we got my favourite Alibami Surprise."

"What's Alibami Surprise?"

"A chicken dish from Alabama." Carter's laugh rattled off the pots and pans.

"You're a daft bugger, Carter."

"Theresa, please: call me William."

"Okay William."

"You a mighty fine-looking woman, Theresa."

"I beg your pardon." She scanned the kitchen, making sure they were alone.

"Yeah, a mighty fine-looking woman."

"What me?" It suddenly didn't matter who thought she was a 'shovel'. Here she was with a man who, though he was no oil painting himself, had just called her 'a beautiful looking woman' or words to that effect. "Even my husband thinks I'm plain," she said. "My nose is a bit flat."

"Your nose is fine." The Oil Painting took hold of her hand in his own clammy palms and squeezed her fingers. She didn't resist "You shouldn't let your man treat you like he do. I wouldn't hurt my Kim for anything in the world."

"No, neither would I."

He let go of her hand and took her around the waist. Her heart pumped. She took deeper breaths, though again she didn't resist.

"I love my Kim. We got a good thing going. But if I didn't have her, if I had a fine lady like you, I'd treat her good." He pulled her close and kissed her. Was this really happening? Had she just been kissed? There wasn't even time to close her eyes. Is this right? Still, she didn't resist. She'd never kissed a Coloured man before. The lips actually were different, softer, spongier. She liked it, a lot but these lips belonged to someone else. Should she put a stop to it?

Give over, you silly woman. It's only a bit of harmless flirting.

Carter stepped away and took back hold of her wrist. "Mighty fine indeed."

Suddenly, bloody Steve came into the kitchen. T snatched back her hand and wiped it on her trousers in case any sweaty evidence might give her away.

"Hey T, you're on girl." Steve turned and left the kitchen. If he'd seen anything, he was being discreet but Steve was like that.

Oh, who cares?

T pilfered a kiss from Carter's cheek and skipped back to the stage.

That night, the Harley Davidson sang its little engine heart out.

Later, T got into bed. "Col, I think we should learn that Lynyrd Skynyrd song."

"What Lynyrd Skynyrd song? What do you know about Lynyrd Skynyrd?"

"Sweet Home Alabama, one of the young squaddies asked for it."

"I didn't know you talked to any squaddies." He switched off his bedside light and settled down. "Tonight's the best I've heard you sing for ages." Although the pillow muffled his voice, the compliment was clear enough, with no backhanded element.

T switched off her own light. "Yeah, I felt bloody good tonight."

5 Adam's Sexploits: Schweinfurt. Oct '76:
The First Time Ever I Saw Your Face.

"Frigging hell Steve, there's an alien coming down the street." Adam didn't manage to panic the scouser into getting off the couch. The 3 ft 6 in, extraterrestrial figure ambling through the off base married quarters was on its way to the gridiron football field. Adam checked, first the child, in his padded equipment, then the American, street name. "Do you think the Krauts know about this place?"

"The yanks probably don't know they're in West Germany," Steve said. "They probably jumped on a plane and thought they were coming to another State, like Hawaii. Then again maybe the whole of Carter's apartment block has been miraculously transported back to the United States. Maybe we're—"

"Bloody hell, Steve, I wasn't asking for your thesis on the subject."

Steve Langton was an outsider in all respects, and not just because he was the only Black member of the group. His unusual origins came from his father, a Peruvian sailor; Langton was his mother's name. The bohemian had never quite accepted the roadie role, maybe because he'd once been a vocalist. However, for reasons he preferred to keep from the other four, he'd given up singing. He believed that outside forces controlled all life. In his case, he blamed a Peruvian God for taking him in certain directions he'd rather not have—

"She's here." Adam abandoned the window and thoughts of Steve's Inca God. He shot to the door. The girl he'd been waiting for was coming along the street, carrying the familiar brown paper bags that told him she was on her way back from the commissary. She was Emma Virgilio, a tanned, tall, slender, Italian with long dark hair, who lived in the apartment above. "Emma Virgilio." Adam enjoyed saying her name. The au pair supplemented her income by working weekends and odd nights in Carter's kitchen.

Adam greeted her from Carter's doorway with a nod and a huge grin. He watched and waited but she merely eased past him, no response from her exquisite mouth. She made her way upstairs. He called after her. "Don't forget tonight." Her reply was merely a delicate smile thrown back over her shoulder but it had the power of a defibrillator.

When Adam returned, Steve still lounged on the couch. He sang: "When the moon hits your eye like a big pizza pie, that's Amore."

"There's something not quite right about a stunner like that being up to her elbows in greasy dishwater. What do you think?"

"What do I think? I think if that Debbie catches you, she'll chop your bollocks off and graft them on your ear'oles. That's what I think."

"Possessive bitch, where does she get off telling me she don't want me shagging anyone else? She's frigging married, for fuck's sake."

"You're talking about a chick and logic, man. Those two just don't belong together."

"We're not frigging betrothed. I only stayed at her place 'cos he wasn't there. Bitch! I was going to ditch her, anyway."

"Really? You're going to ditch her? That sounds like an event not to be missed. Are you selling tickets? I imagine Hell hath no fury like a nutter dumped." Steve sat up. "You should never have got involved."

"Oh yeah, man, like, you wouldn't have? Your God of Destiny would've said, 'Get in there my son' and you'd have been up Debbie like a rat up a drainpipe."

"My God of Destiny, as you call him would've probably been in there before either of us but that's not the point."

"What is the point?"

"The point is: she might send us packing. She is responsible for the bookings; remember?"

"Shit, I never thought of that. Perhaps I should put off the ditching for a bit, wait 'til she gets fed up of me. Anyway, I'm not sure where I stand, yet, with Emma."

"I know where you'll stand with Colin, if you get us thrown out of another gig."

Adam had recently met the au pair when she'd come to clean Carter's flat. Usually, Emma also did the childminding for the Carters but as the children were away, Kim had generously suggested the cleaning to make up her money. Not that Carter's apartment needed cleaning with Kim around. It was spotless but they obviously thought a lot about the girl.

One drawback came with Emma; she hardly spoke any English and understood even less.

"Have you got a fella at home in Italy?" Adam had asked her. She'd been dusting T's statues at the time. Her hair had fallen across one eye, reminding him of an American film star whose name he couldn't remember.

"I am living in Milano."

"No I meant . . . Oh nowt. It doesn't matter." He'd aborted other attempts at striking up a conversation, but earlier that morning, before she'd gone to the commissary, he was sure she'd agreed to go for a drink with him after work.

Kim returned with provisions and checked her meatloaf in the oven.

"Smells delicious," Steve said.

"Where is evibody else?" Kim still struggled with English consonants.

The clock confirmed it was nearing the time to get ready for work. "They'll be back soon," Adam said.

Almost on cue, Jeannie came in. She sniffed. "Oh good, meatloaf, I haven't eaten all day. Been running round like a blue-arse fly."

"Why? Where've you been?" Steve asked.

"Been out with Bobby all day."

"Bobby?" Adam tried to process what she'd said. "As in Debbie and her tequila monster, Bobby?"

"I've been seeing him for a bit now. He's lovely."

"Lovely? What the hell are you talking about? He's a sex maniac."

"I wouldn't say he's a maniac but he could definitely show some of the blokes I've been with a few tricks."

"Where's all this come from?"

"All what? A bit jealous, are we?"

"Piss off, jealous."

"You know what this means?" Steve was grinning.

Adam wasn't. "What?"

"If Bobby's having his fun, Debbie's going to be expecting you to provide hers."

"Bollocks, you're right. That's all I need" Adam turned to Jeannie. "I just don't believe you sometimes." He opened his arms to Steve. "See what I mean? She'll shag owt." Steve's self-righteous eyebrow lifted. "What's that look supposed to mean, Steve?"

"I think the words 'kettle' and 'black' seem to be in order."

"You're not the only one who can pick and choose, you know, Adam." There was something evil in Jeannie's smirk.

Adam ignored the stench of smugness. Jeannie's antics had given him something else to think about. He stroked his earlobes, imagining what he'd look like with his testicles hanging from them.

That night Adam kept a watchful eye from the stage, on the lookout for any signs of would-be liaison officers bearing gifts of Strawberry Hill or grafting tools. At the end of the first nectar free set, he popped into the kitchen to confirm his date for later.

"You, me, drink, tonight?" He mimed the drink.

Emma's smile assured her understanding. "We go taxi?" At the end of the night, she was waiting with her coat draped across her shoulders. They got into the taxi without saying a word. They got out of the taxi, still not having spoken. Adam had told the driver to take him to the only place he knew in Schweinfurt: "*La Tavola*", the Italian restaurant Debbie had taken them to on that first night.

"Do you want something to eat?" He knew it was a stupid question given they were standing outside a restaurant. He pointed into his mouth. It was an even more stupid gesture. Someone like the warped minded Debbie might've thought he was suggesting a lewd appetiser.

Emma gave the response of an innocent. "*Si, mangiare.*"

She was obviously more at home in the restaurant, chatting with the Neapolitan waiters. The familiar vines across the ceiling, the Chianti candleholder bottles and the red and green serviettes became Adam's friends. The pace of communication improved, though most of this consisted of swapping the meaning of English and Italian words. He thought about the last time he'd been in the restaurant and tried to imagine Emma's hand going to the same place that Debbie's had. His thoughts would have to remain in fantasyland. Emma was not Debbie. Nor was he drinking Strawberry Hill. He topped up her glass, albeit with House red. However, wine was only a minor contributor to his light-headedness. Her smile, her beauty and her mere presence was enough to create an air of intoxication.

"How do you say 'dog'?" he asked.

"Yes, I like dogs very much."

"I knew you'd be a dog lover. I've got a dog. His name's Ralph."

"Ralph?"

"Yeah, I called him that because he said that was his name."

"*Scusi?*"

"I asked him his name and he barked: '*Ralph*'."

Emma laughed. He liked her laugh. You could easily fall in love with a laugh like hers. Only once before had Adam been in love: really and properly in love, that is. He freely admitted that when he was drunk he fell in love with chairs but his only long-term relationship had been June Roundhill. June had rescued Ralph from being 'put to sleep'.

"You remind me of a girl I used to know."

"She look like me?"

"Not really, no." June's hair was Pre-Raphaelite red. "But she was beautiful and sexy, like you." June Roundhill, the only time in his life he didn't want or need to 'shag around'. Unfortunately, she hadn't been of the same mind. She'd run off with the sax player of a rival band.

"She was girlfriend?"

"Yeah, she left me. Walked out, left a note on the telly saying: 'I'm leaving you, it's not working.' I couldn't understand it. I plugged the bugger in and there was nothing wrong with it." He cut short his lonely laugh.

"*Scusi?*"

Though he often joked about it, June Roundhill had broken his heart. The exact reason for the break up had expunged from his playboy memory, the details buried beneath sordid reminiscences of gang-bang exploits, back street 'knee-tremblers' and one-night-stands. He preferred the bachelor life, though there'd been odd moments of regret when he found himself missing June Roundhill. But tonight wasn't one of them

It'd proved quite an enjoyable evening without a hint of sex between them. They hadn't even kissed. So it stayed throughout the long walk home. Together with the diamante earrings, she wore the moonlight as though it'd been created for her alone. Their mutual vocabulary exhausted, they arrived at the door of Emma's apartment. Without speaking she indicated, with a shake of the head and the flat of her palm, he couldn't come in.

Bugger, I knew it was too much to hope for.

But then she cupped her delicate hands around his face and kissed his sulking lips.

Oh, okay, maybe all is not lost.

Their lips parted. "*Tchuess,*" she said, then went inside and closed the door.

The word "Bollocks" came out in a deep sigh and he stared at the closed-door for at least ten seconds before abandoning it.

Before he reached Carter's door, a voice fluttered down the stairs and tapped him on the shoulder: "Adam." It was Emma. Each step back upstairs became a trampoline. "*Alles ist klar.*" She grabbed his waistband, pulled him inside and led him into the darkened living room. They kissed and she unfastened the buttons of his satin shirt.

Frigging hell, she's beautiful.

The undressing didn't stop there. She motioned him on to the sheepskin rug and deftly slid his velvet trousers from under him before straddling him to make sensuous love in the firelight.

Alright God, I owe you one, unless you didn't send her. Maybe she's sneaked out of heaven without you noticing.

No, Emma was definitely not Debbie. This time there was no nuclear reactor; merely some gentle Latin moans accompanying the swish of her long dark hair across his face. Without interrupting the flow, she managed to flick the switch of the cassette player. Roberta Flack whispered into the room: "The First Time, Ever I Saw Your Face."

He looked up at the closed eyes of his lover. "Emma Virgilio," he said, underscoring the symphony in his head. *I think I'm in love*, he added, so far down the mix that no one else heard. Not another word of Italian or English was spoken throughout the whole activity.

Adam returned from Emma's sheepskin rug to find Steve taking his turn on the couch. A black thicket of hair poked from under the continental quilt. "Alright, Ace? You've got the silly grin on."

"I have that."

"You've been making the beast with two backs."

"I have that."

"I heard you."

"No, you didn't." Adam's eyes flicked toward the ceiling. "Must be Colin and T you heard. Emma was as quiet as a mouse."

"I heard you come in. And I knew you weren't up there all this time playing tiddlywinks."

"This is definitely the one. I'm never shagging anyone else."

"Oh, here we go again." The thicket sat up. "Had a few sherbets have we?"

"But that's just it, I've hardly had a drink all night. Okay, I've had a couple, but she's really got me. I haven't felt like this since June."

"Why, what happened in June?"

"Not June, you daft bugger: June Roundhill."

"June Roundhill? Let's hope she doesn't shit on you, like her then."

"She won't shit on me. She's an angel. Angels don't shit."

Emma took some extra nights' kitchen work to coincide with 'Images' appearances in Carter's club. Living in the same apartment block, she came back in the van each night with the band. Something was definitely developing and Adam was happy with the development. The angel symphony was growing louder and stronger and the sheepskin rug was wearing thinner and thinner. However, the ditching of Debbie ceremony hadn't yet taken place, so the sobering fear that she may turn up and catch him with his Italian was still prominent. Equally, of course, he didn't want Emma finding out about Debbie. In terms of female qualities Emma could match up to anyone but there were two areas he wouldn't have pitted her against Debbie, breasts and fighting. Hence, if the Georgian combatant did turn up, his angel would be flying around with clipped wings and he'd probably have a Strawberry Hill bottle inserted into his anus. His bottom puffed relief at the end of each evening to find that Debbie hadn't arrived.

    On his fourth night, Jeannie came into the boys' dressing room waving a large pin before his bubble. "Steve, did you bring my bag in? Ah, there it is." She took out a sequinned top and began changing. "I'm going to stay in Wurzburg tonight. Bobby's taking me to a posh hotel. Debbie's supposed to be picking you up, Adam, to take you back to the house." Not even Jeannie's exposed chapel hat-pegs could distract from the impending threat.

    "Bloody hell, Jeannie, whose idea was that? Couldn't you have stopped her?"

    "I didn't realise you wanted me to stop her." Jeannie snapped her bra strap over her shoulder.

    Hope remained. Debbie hadn't yet arrived. "Jimmy, what are you doing?" Adam asked.

    "Washing my hair."

    "Can't you do that when we get back? Come on, guys. Help me out here." Grafted testicles loomed large.

    T was making a polite inquiry of Colin. "Why don't you get bloody Joey Proudfoot to iron your blue shirt?"

    Adam was equally polite. "For fuck's sake, you two."

    Colin stopped scowling at his wife for a second. "Alright, Adam, keep your Y-fronts on, we're coming."

    "Well, we're not moving with the sense of urgency one associates with being alive."

    "What's the bloody rush?" Colin asked.

    "It's a matter of life and death. Okay, maybe not, but definitely a matter of ears and bollocks."

At last, everyone was in the van, Emma sandwiched between Adam and Jimmy on the back seat. Unfortunately, before Colin got behind the wheel, the Mustang pulled up in front of them. Debbie got out of the driving seat. Her head poked inside. "Hi babe! We gotta drop Bobby and Jeannie off at the railway station, then I'm gonna take you back to my place."

"Well actually, love, I'm knackered." Adam managed a yawn. "I'm just gonna go home and get an early night, if you don't mind."

"Oh, I see." Debbie's eyes fixed on the Italian delicacy in the English sandwich. "I see what's happening here. And who is this bitch?"

"Who? Oh Emma? This is Emma." The Italian smiled at the mention of her name.

"Oh yeah, and who exactly is Em-ma?" Though Debbie had split the syllables, Emma smiled again.

"She's Jimmy's girlfriend. Isn't that right Jimmy?" Adam said.

"Eh? Oh yeah!" The flustered Jimmy sneaked his arm around Emma's shoulder, trying to make it look like it'd been there all week.

"You lying bastard," Debbie said. "I hope you and Emma rot in hell." Adam prepared for the onslaught but none was forthcoming. She jumped back into the Mustang and sped toward the barracks gate, throwing the incumbent Jeannie across the rear window.

Excellent result! Debbie had gone and Emma hadn't understood a word.

Adam smugly escorted Emma upstairs to her apartment. She stopped at the door as she'd done on their first date.

"Adam, I see you no more."

"What?"

"This girl? She is girlfriend, yes?"

"Which girl? Oh Debbie, no, she's Jimmy's girlfriend."

"Goodbye Adam." She went inside and closed the door. He stood there in the dark. "Emma, please!" His forlorn plea couldn't penetrate the door. The

Development Bubble that'd floated into his life had gone. Some bitch had come along and . . . pop!

He sloped downstairs. This time there was no voice fluttering down to tap him on the shoulder. Instead, all he got was a "See ya", from Jimmy, exiting Carter's apartment with Colin.

He ignored them and entered the living room to find Steve on the couch. "She's chucked me, all because of that bastard, Debbie."

Steve didn't even turn his head. "You'll be getting back on the shagging wagon then?"

"Silly me, I was expecting sympathy." Adam crossed to the window and looked through the blinds. Colin and Jimmy were rounding the end of the street. "Where are them two going?"

"Colin's taken young Jimmy round to Big Joey Proudfoot's."

"Over by the hospital? How come they haven't taken the van?"

"Cos they're going to be getting pissed."

"Since when did Colin worry about driving pissed?"

"He's not. Jimmy threw up the other night. He's not allowed in the van when he's had a drink. Colin and T have had another row."

"What about?"

"Probably because he keeps going round to Big Joey Proudfoot's to get pissed."

"Frigging women, eh?" Adam threw his suede jacket, intending it for the back of the couch. The jacket overshot, knocking two of T's statues to the floor.

"Don't damage them buggers, else she'll be after *you*."

"Bollocks to her. Shit, what am I saying? As if I haven't had enough bad luck for one life." Adam picked them up and spoke to one directly. "Sorry, I didn't mean that. T's alright." He replaced them. "I'd rather fight her than shag her, though."

Steve produced a bottle of whiskey from the side of the couch. "Do you want to get yourself a glass?"

"Why not?" He went to the kitchen. *I'd rather fight her than shag her, that's quite funny.* "How much to shag T?" he called. He got himself a mug and returned. "Would you do it for ten grand?"

"I'd shag Colin for ten grand." Both laughed.

"Yeah, I probably would, an' all."

Steve poured some whiskey into Adam's mug. "Why do you do that?"

"Do what?"

"Why do you have a go at people that have done nothing to *you*? T's never done you no harm, man."

"Give over; I was only having a laugh. I'm not hurting her, am I? She's not here. She can't hear me."

"She could've. She could've popped down for a drink, just as you shouted from the kitchen. You shouldn't do that, man. She doesn't deserve it."

"Frigging hell, man, alright, I get the message." He got up and went back to the statues. "Hey up, you little buggers, I'm very, very, sorry, okay?" He came and sat back down. "See, no bolts of lightning."

"You can be a right arsehole, sometimes. No wonder June Roundhill dumped you." Steve sipped his whiskey. "I saw her, you know, just before we came away."

"You did what?"

"June, I just bumped into her."

"Why didn't you tell me?"

"Didn't think you'd be interested."

"You didn't think I'd be interested? Steve this is the love of my life you're talking about, here."

"How can she be the love of your life? She buggered off with that tit out of the Dawnbreakers."

"Where did you just 'bump into her'?"

"Beckets Park, she's moved in to her mum and dad's new place. I was up seeing Jamie Peacock."

"What did she say?"

"What did she say about what?"

"What did she say about *me*? Did she say: I've really missed Adam? Or did she say: thank God I got rid of that tosser?" Adam put down his whiskey.

"We just chatted. Didn't say much about anything, really. Why?" Steve frowned. "You wouldn't want to get back with her, would you?"

"Are you kidding? I'd give my left bollock to get back with her."

"Then you should look her up when we get home."

"I can't. I've completely lost track. I don't have her address, any more."

"I've just told you her address. She lives four doors down from Jamie Peacock. You could write to her."

"You what? Hey that's a brilliant idea, man. That's what I'll do. I'll write to her. Thanks for that."

"Good, does this mean you're over Emma? Wow, time's such a great healer."

"Very funny. No, seriously, Steve, I've got to stop messing things up. You were right about June. Every time I get something good, I mess up and it turns to mush. I need something steady in my life. You too, man, you should think about finding yourself a nice filly."

"It'd have to be the right filly, man."

"Remember that bird you had in Tangier?" They'd first worked together there in the mid sixties.

"Ayise? That was a lifetime ago."

Adam refilled his cup. "You shouldn't have packed in singing, man."

"I had to get off the beach before the tide came in. I got too old for all that malarkey."

"Steve, you're a freak." He only aged three out of every four years. "You look the same age as Jimmy."

"But I'm not the same age as Jimmy; I'm thirty-five."

"Thirty-five's not old. It hasn't stopped you shagging." They drank and reminisced throughout the next hour, until something brought their ladish recollections to an abrupt halt. An almighty crash of glass outside the apartment sent them rushing to the window.

Steve got there first and pulled the blinds. "It's that nutter."

Adam arrived to see broken Strawberry Hill bottles lying next to Colin's van. Debbie held up another. "Come out you cheating bastard." Luckily, the street was deserted. "Come out or this goes through your truck window, man."

"Oh God, no." Adam said. *Why didn't Colin just take the van?* "You better go shut her up."

"Me?"

"She'll kill *me*." Adam stepped back from the window in case his presence should antagonise her. "I shouldn't need to tell you, the prospect of Colin coming home to find a bottle of Strawberry Hill sitting in the driving seat of his van is not good."

"Neither is going out to face a screaming banshee." Steve grabbed the van keys from the hook by the door. "I'll move it. You owe me one for this, man."

Adam went and sat on the couch and waited five minutes.

Good old Steve. Looks like he's sorted it.

He edged back to the window and peeped. Where had they gone? Must've taken her for a walk. Yeah good idea, get her away from the van *and* the house. He relaxed back on the couch. After another fifteen minutes, curiosity drew him back to the window. The TBM lettering was rocking to and fro. "What the fu . . .?" He opened the window. Faint but familiar strains met his ear.

"*Aarghh*, fuck me, you damned Inca. Fuck me hard."

"You black bastard." Adam closed the window. "And you *are* frigging old."

One of the Bird God statues he'd knocked over earlier fell to the floor.

6 T's Adventures: Schweinfurt. Oct '76:

Young Hearts Run Free.

Sex with a Coloured man must be just the same as sex with anyone else. T allowed her imagination to go for a little stroll across the club kitchen to where William was chopping potatoes into chips. He turned toward her, put two of the chips in his mouth to simulate fangs then started a monster-like walk around the table. She screamed and ran, eager to take part in the game, which of course meant allowing herself to be caught.

When he'd stopped tickling, he took the chips from his mouth and kissed her. "I sure gonna miss you coming to my kitchen after tomorrow night."

The reason she was saying goodbye to Schweinfurt clubs and kitchen rendezvous with William, thanks to bloody Adam, this was the band's penultimate day in the venue. The thwarted Debbie had pulled the plug on the gig so they were moving on to Frankfurt.

The following day, T stared at the Bird Gods on the dresser. It was crunch time. She had to either, speak up and say she hadn't intended them as a gift, or she'd have to go on to Frankfurt without them. Then again, happen losing them was a small price to pay for their time in Schweinfurt and for all the attention William had lavished on her. They'd be a fitting memento. Happen he'd think of her every time he looked at them.

The rows between T and Colin were becoming more frequent yet neither he nor the other male group members appeared to suspect anything of her friendship with William. Of course, sex with a Coloured man hadn't taken place nor had it ever been suggested. It wasn't what T wanted. Nevertheless, she not only enjoyed his attention but also the fantasy. The odd snog was far enough. After all, there was Kim to consider.

T went to join the Vietnamese genius, dishing up a special recipe for the band's final meal with the Carters. "How do you say it, again?" she asked.

"*Ayam,*" Kim said.

"Mm, garlic, ginger: ooh, what's that other smell? Is it aniseed? It's so exotic."

"This only chicken noodle soup."

"Eh? Oh right. Yeah, course it's chicken, why else would it be one of Carter's favourites?" She sneaked a stir of the pot while Kim's back was turned. "You've been so good to us. I'm going to miss you two."

"Is good that you go."

"Pardon?"

"I know abough you an William." Kim checked the rice. T took a moment to register. She didn't respond. "He say he rike you a rot." The mispronounced consonants didn't obscure the clarity of what Kim was saying.

T felt physically sick. "I don't know what to say." She couldn't read Kim's smile. It didn't make sense there was any smile at all. "You must hate me? You've taken us into your home and I've paid you back by messing with your man."

"You very bad woman."

"I promise you, nothing has happened. He wouldn't hurt you for anything. Neither would I."

"How you know what hurt me? How you rike I tell your husband?"

"Kim please!" T cleared her vision with the cuff of her sleeve.

"You bad woman."

"Nothing has happened, Kim. And nothing will happen. We'll be gone, tomorrow."

"Yes, is good that you go."

T could think of nothing to say that would help. She inadvertently picked up the ladle.

"No." Kim took the ladle from her. "No cook, you must go."

"Sorry, yeah, I'll go finish my packing." T escaped. She carried the weight in the pit of her stomach, up to the bedroom that'd so selflessly been given up for them.

What have you done, Morgan?

She threw the suitcases on the bed, began packing and tried to disentangle her confused feelings. It'd only been a bit of flirting, hadn't it? No, if Colin had snogged another woman she'd be devastated. Why had she done it? What was the reason for her despicable behaviour toward the saint she'd left in the kitchen? What'd led her to seek comfort from someone else's man? As usual, the needle of the culpability compass indicated Colin. Their relationship was at the root of this.

As if conjured by her thoughts, Colin appeared. Without any sort of greeting he moved the suitcases off the bed and flopped in their place.

"Do you mind?" she said. "I've just started packing them."

The grunt could've been an apology but she wasn't in an accepting mood.

"Where've you been, anyway?"

"You know where I've been. It was the last chance for a blow-out with Joey and the lads. We'll be gone, tomorrow."

"So you've been getting pissed with your Indian mates?"

"What the hell's got up your nose?" Colin almost lifted his head off the pillow.

"Colin, I want a baby."

"What, now?" He not only lifted his head but opened his eyes and checked his watch. "We haven't time. Kim's making us a special dinner. It's just about ready."

"I'm not joking, Colin. I've had enough of traipsing round Europe singing to pissed-up squaddies. I want a family."

"We're in the middle of a tour, you silly bugger. We can't just pack it in because you've got a bit broody. Thanks to bloody lover boy, we could all be going home to nothing but we're not." He sat up. "We've been given another chance in Frankfurt. Besides, I've told you before, we're not ready to be tied down with a sprog."

"Well, when will you be ready?"

"Look, we're not having any kids, right?" He threw back his head on the pillow. "Why are we having this stupid conversation? We've got a gig to do tonight."

T didn't visit the kitchen that night. Instead she sat morosely in the dressing room. She couldn't face William.

After the final set, while the other band members were packing up and having a last drink in the bar, William crossed the threshold of the girls' dressing room and faced *her*. "Thought you might like to try one of these." He put down his tray of chicken wings and spare ribs. "You didn't come down for dinner."

"I feel awful, William. We did a bad thing."

"We didn't do nothing, babe." He sat in front of her and began tucking into the wings. "I keep telling you, I'd never do anything to hurt my Kim." T no longer wanted to hear that. She didn't understand what it meant. It didn't help her and it didn't deal with all the feelings that'd passed through her head since Kim's revelation. The day's events had left her with many thoughts to sift.

"I don't belong in this place." This had been one of the thoughts she'd been sifting. "I don't want to be trailing round a foreign country, singing ditties to American yobs."

"Those American yobs love you, babe."

"No they don't. They don't want to listen to me. They'd rather be at home. And you know what? I'd rather be at home, as well. In fact, that's what I'm going to do. I'm going to leave the band."

"You're *what*?" He fumbled with the wing about to enter his mouth. "You can't do that. What would they do without you? Man, you got more soul in your voice than some Black singers. When you sing Lorraine Ellison, babe, I get a tingle down my spine." He stood to give his rendition. "Stay With Me Baby." His attempt to lighten the mood wasn't working though this was as good a compliment as she'd ever received and more pleasing coming from William. Nevertheless, she'd have no choice.

"I'm going home and it probably means I'll have to leave Colin." She wanted to explain. If only she could be more articulate. She didn't want William to think she was doing this on account of him. If Colin wasn't such a pig, this would never have happened. If Colin wasn't such a selfish sod, she'd never have sought affection from the first person to show her some kindness.

"Hell babe, you sure you know what you're doing?"

"I wanted a baby. I've been kidding myself all these years." The explanation felt valid. "Colin doesn't really want kids. He never has." She almost added that their marriage had been fruitless and pointless but that was going too far. William had abandoned the chicken by now. Her stare rose from the tray into his deep sepia eyes. "I'm glad I met you, William."

"I'm glad I met you, babe." This would've been the ideal parting couplet had Colin not come in at that point and doused the sunset.

"What's up wi *you*? Why are you sulking around in your dressing room; you mawky cow?" He moved Jeannie's jeans on to the dressing table to sit. "Have you seen the state of her? She's had a face on her like a wet Whit Monday all day. It's your fault, you know, Carter. You've made it too good, here. She doesn't want to leave." T's mind filled with screams but she kept the irony to herself.

William shook his head and walked to the door. He took a last look around the dressing room. "I brought you guys some wings, figured you might be hungry." He looked at Colin. "The ribs are for you. I knowed you don't eat chicken." He gave a final nod to T and left.

Colin picked up a rib. "What a star."

"I'm not coming to Frankfurt; I'm going back to England."

There I've said it.

"What are you talking about, you soppy mare?" Colin's response gave the impetus she needed.

"*That*! That's what I'm talking about. I'm not a soppy mare, or a mawky cow or thick or stupid."

"Alright, alright, keep your Tupperware dry."

"I'm not your slave, either. I'm not putting up with it any more: neglect, aggression, always putting me down, I'm finished. Not that you're likely to notice whether I'm here or not." Her articulation surprised her. Her only concern now was, having let loose with the first onslaught, she had to prepare for the comeback. She made ready for the outburst.

"You're right, I'm sorry." Instead, his composure remained steady and collected. "I'm sorry for calling you mawky. Course I'd notice if you weren't here. Where would I ever find a singer to replace you?"

"Singer?" She picked up one of the wings and threw it him. "What about replacing me as a sodding wife, you bastard." She reckoned that in the list of Colin's most prized possessions, she figured somewhere between his TBM-mobile and his guitar.

"I didn't mean it like that. I meant it's not just me that needs you. We all do, the whole group."

She picked up the chicken missile and threw it in the bin. "Jeannie and Steve can take over."

"Don't talk wet." Jeannie's jeans that he'd put on the edge of the dressing table dropped to the floor. He got to them first. "And even if we did have time to rehearse them in, there isn't anybody could hold a candle to you."

And you can stuff your compliments.

She took the jeans from him and draped them over a chair. He came up behind and took her around the waist. "Come here, you soppy mare. Come on give us a snog, you stupid bugger."

She shrugged him off. "Colin, stop calling me stupid."

"Well stop acting bloody stupid. How can you leave the band? How will you get home? Are you gonna bloody hitch-hike?"

"Forget it, Colin, I'm going."

"Really? Do you mean to tell me you could just walk out on your friends?"

He was pacing. *Damn, here comes the outburst.*

"What are they gonna live on? You're putting the whole lot of 'em out of work, not to mention that I'll probably get sued for cancelling the tour." He paused, long enough to look at her directly. "If you want to bugger off home and fuck it up for everybody, that's up to you but you'll have to tell 'em yourself, I'm not. I'm off to get a pint. See? We can all be selfish twats." He picked up a handful of spare ribs on his way out.

Shit, what happened there?

She felt worse now than before. As a tactic in guilt transference, something had badly gone skew whiff. Was that all it was, just a way of blaming Colin for what she'd done to Kim? Happen she should be blaming William. Did she really want to leave the band? Was it only an idle threat? The dressing room door burst into her mingled thoughts. In came Jeannie, Jimmy, Adam, Steve and Candi Staton's voice.

"Colin says you're leaving the band." Jeannie was the spokesperson. So much for him not telling the others. The door closed, shutting out Candi's singing. T checked the concerned faces. She knew her bravado was not securely tied.

Well, that's put a stop to that little idea. Sorry Candi, this Young Heart's not going to be Running Free. "Er, no," T said. "We just had a row that's all."

Adam gripped her hand. "Frigging hell, you had us worried, then."

More self-reproach rained in, as each member sought confirmation that she wasn't going. Compliments showered over her, making her feel worse. Even Adam said she'd one of the best voices he'd ever heard. Her confidence set off, running down the hill, rope trailing behind.

You're not going anywhere tomorrow, girl, other than Frankfurt.

When T entered Colin was sitting up in bed. She'd no idea what the look on his face meant, nor did she care. She took no notice of his sigh, and crossed to the packed suitcases. She foraged through the case for a pair of tracksuit bottoms then collected his toiletries from the bathroom. "Here, it's your turn on the couch."

He ignored the items. "You what?"

"You haven't had a turn. You can't ask the others to sleep down there if *you're* not willing to do it."

"What are you on, woman? Adam's on the couch, isn't he? You're not wanting him to take my place in here, are you?" He gave a laugh that had no humour whatsoever. "I wouldn't put it past that randy bastard to suggest it."

"Adam's swapped with Jeannie. She's taking your place. You're on the couch. And she didn't suggest it, I did." She thrust the toiletries and tracksuit bottoms at him. He didn't move. "Come on, Jeannie's waiting to come to bed."

"T, what the fuck are you playing at?"

"I'm not playing, Colin. I've agreed to finish the tour but that's as far as it goes. I'm not sleeping in same bed as you. From now on, we have separate rooms. That's the deal, take it, or leave it."

He said nothing, grabbed the tracksuit bottoms and swung his legs out of bed and into the trousers. Just as deftly he stood, whilst pulling the bottoms over his blue and grey paisley Y-fronts. He pulled on a sweater, slipped his feet into his shoes, picked up his jacket from the floor and left the room, disregarding the toiletries. She pictured the scowl he'd give to Jeannie waiting downstairs. "I expect this is one of your Women's Lib ideas?" she heard him shout.

The downstairs front door slammed. Jeannie came into the bedroom and gave an accusing look. T snapped a welcome that lasted a little over a nanosecond. "What?" she said.

"Nothing."

T slammed down the suitcase lid.

Next day, whilst the others were downstairs giving thanks to Kim and William for their stay, T sat on the bed, in her lap, the hessian box. There was no point packing it to take to Frankfurt, empty. She was waiting to hear the others say their goodbyes.

Colin's voice came from the bottom of the stairs. "How long does it take to check a fucking bedroom? Come on, we're three hours late. It's going to be dark when we hit Frankfurt as it is."

She waited until he'd gone out of the door before going downstairs. She avoided Kim's eyes and carried her box to the dresser: "Is it okay if I take these?" She picked up one of the Bird Gods.

William looked at Kim and then back to T. "Sure, if that's what you want."

Kim stepped forward and snatched the statue from her. "No, not take. Kim's statues."

"Sorry, you don't understand. I never meant for you to keep them." She was speaking to Kim but her appeal was more to William.

William picked up the other three statues from the dresser and handed them to T before turning to Kim. "Kim, give her the statue."

"No, Kim's statues."

He went to her and tried to take it from her.

She screamed and hung on grimly. "No, Kim's statues." Her eyes bulged. "She is bad woman, very bad woman."

William pointed a finger. "Kim, stop it. Give Theresa the statue and apologise."

"No, no apologise."

"It's alright William, let her keep it."

"No, goddamn it. Kim, what's wrong with you, man?" He grabbed the statue. Kim wrestled, refusing to give it up. She dug her teeth into his hand. He yelped and let go. "You goddamn bitch."

"Stop it; stop it, you two." T sobbed. "Please, keep the bloody thing. It doesn't matter."

Kim's eyes filled with tears but the anger still showed.

William sucked the blood from his hand "It do matter, Theresa." He turned back to Kim. "Woman, you better apologise."

"William, she doesn't need to apologise." T put the other three statues in the box. "I don't blame you, Kim. Sorry, I didn't mean to hurt you."

"You ain't hurt no one." He turned to Kim. "I keep telling you, we ain't done nothing wrong."

There was a knock at the front door. William went to answer it. Colin's voice filtered through to the living room. "What's she doing? We're all sat in the van, like prannocks."

T tried a last attempt to convey her regret but she was never going to get past Kim's venomous glare. "I'd better go." She picked up her box and pushed past William on the doorstep without looking at him.

So it was that the emotionally befuddled Mrs Bone said good-bye to Schweinfurt and with her unwanted feelings stuffed in the suitcase alongside the three bird statues, she set off for their new venue.

Frankfurt Am Main was: "a metropolis, over three times the size of Bonn, the capital". T didn't give a stuff. She just wanted to get out of the van and the tense atmosphere between her and Colin. The TBM-mobile arrived, just as the silhouette of the commercial sector buildings was joining forces with the ultramarine skyline to complete the evening horizon. The red and yellow of a West German tricolour fluttered against the black oncoming picture of night, reminding her that she was hundreds of miles away from home. It would be easy for the party of Brits to blend anonymously with the thousands of Americans swarming the city. Everything was big, much bigger than T expected. She was glad they weren't staying in the city but in Hanau, a sprawling town on Frankfurt's outskirts. The hotel was a functional, two-floor hostelry with a nice little bar and lobby taking up most of the ground floor. The band occupied the upstairs.

"I stayed in a place just like this in Ambleside," Jimmy said.

"I'm very pleased for you," T said.

Jimmy's bottom lip pouted.

Bloody hell, Theresa, is there anybody else you want to hurt? "Sorry Jimmy." She shouldn't be taking it out on him but Colin's scowls, on top of the squabble she'd had with Kim were too much to deal with. She'd had to contain her sobs for hours. *Why didn't I just let her keep the bloody statues?* She needed to get to her single room, let go of the sobs and do more thought sifting.

Over the following two weeks, Images quietly eased into their new surroundings. Colin had actually tried for reconciliation but she blocked all attempts at bridging the chasm. For now, she was content simply doing her singing and returning to her room after the gig to read. Jeannie whooped at the idea of getting a new "pulling partner" but T was reluctant to embrace life as a single woman; and anyway, she'd no way of keeping up with the loose blonde.

Bobby was still frequently visiting Jeannie, making the fifty-mile trip up from Schweinfurt. However, this didn't prevent the keyboard player from demonstrating her dexterity to as many Americans as she could meet. Bobby wasn't even Jeannie's only regular. Much to T's disapproval, she was now also seeing Lincoln, a Coloured captain in the US Army. T's annoyance was not due to Lincoln's colour, though there was a certain amount of envy following her friendship with William. The main irritation stemmed from the way Jeannie juggled them all, like a circus performer keeping a row of spinning plates up on their poles.

Throughout the whole Frankfurt and Hanau legions, Lincoln was the only Coloured man to have attained his rank. Obviously he had to have some special quality to achieve this. There was no difficulty in accepting that besides his soldiering, he was also working for a doctorate. Jeannie hadn't made it too clear exactly what Lincoln's work was but it had something to do with his 'Haleyan Roots', whatever that meant.

Jeannie showed her the Alex Haley book. "It's about where all the Black people in America originally came from in Africa. That's what he's studying. I'm helping him."

The quirky couple would spend four hours at a time in the library, following a night of rampant sex.

While Jeannie was out studying, Colin was grasping an opportunity for some bridge building.

"So where is she?" He swanked across the room to T's bed, propped up the pillow and sat with his back against it. He stroked a hand along the single quilt. "Who is it today, the Karate Mustang or the Smart Arse Jungle Bunny?"

"She's gone into Frankfurt with Lincoln."

"She's unbelievable. No wonder you've gone funny. It's her, filling your head with all this 'Women's Lib' rubbish. I wish I'd never taken her on."

"The reason I'm on my own's got nothing to do with Jeannie. It's you."

"Course it's got something to do with Jeannie, you thick cow. All this started when she talked you into going off to Austria together. She got us kicked out of Garmisch."

"Colin, if you ever call me a 'thick cow' again, I'm straight out o' that door and on the first train home. And get your arse off my bed."

He stood, not exactly to attention but quick enough to suggest he knew she was serious. "T, please, I'm sorry. It's not you I'm mad at; it's Jeannie. Please come back to my room."

"I'm not coming anywhere, 'til you learn to behave yourself. This has nothing to do with Jeannie." She laid the pillow back in its place. "Anyway, what do you need me for? You've got your precious TBM-mobile, haven't you?"

"I've only been spending time on her, 'cos I've had nowt else." His head drooped. "Okay you're right, I'm sorry. Listen babe, I've been thinking about what you said in Schweinfurt. I thought maybe we could talk about starting a family when this tour's finished."

"This wouldn't be Mr Desperation talking would it?"

"No, I mean it." He came to her and clasped her waist. "T, please—"

Jeannie burst in with Lincoln in tow. Although she'd rapped on the open door, her entrance was still a surprise. The embarrassment at being caught *in flagranté* with Colin made T break away.

"Oh, sorry," Jeannie said. "T, we've seen your birds. We've seen your birds in a book at the library."

Bloody hell, Jeannie, I had him just where I wanted, then.

"What birds?" Colin asked.

"T's African statues, the ones we bought in Innsbruck." She picked up one from the table. "They were in this book that Lincoln was looking at for his research."

Lincoln explained that in search of his roots, he'd traced his lineage to the slaves captured from the present day Rhodesia. His family tree included the Ndebele tribe, through to the indigenous population of the Mashonalands, the Shona people and even beyond to the Kingdom of Zimbabwe. The Austrian shopkeeper, T's Arabian Nights' storyteller, had been almost accurate in his account of the birds' origin. What he'd omitted from his tale was the real legend of these Goddesses.

"This African Chief." Jeannie took over the narration. "He was a right bastard. He had five wives and he treated 'em like shit. Then one day, he gets so pissed off, he has four of 'em executed."

"What for?" T asked.

"It doesn't matter what for. For nowt. I told you he was a misogynist bastard. Anyway, the one that's left is called Lobengalu."

"Lob on who?" Colin asked.

"Lobengalu. So one night he attacks Lobengalu and suddenly, these four bird spirits appear, just like these." Jeannie brandished the statue. "They were the spirits of the murdered wives."

"Go on," T said.

"They killed the bastard." Jeannie put the statue she was holding back with her sisters.

"Killed him?" T looked at the statues and then at Colin. *You wish, Morgan.*

"Anyway, the leaders of the tribe didn't believe her."

Lincoln put a hand on Jeannie's shoulder. "The Elders."

"Eh? Alright then, the Elders, they were still all men and they didn't believe her. They tried to execute her." Jeannie put one foot on the bed and raised a Britannia like fist. "But the women of the tribe rose up against 'em, saved her and she became Queen." She relaxed the pose. "From then on, statues were kept as protection against male chauvinist arseholes."

Lincoln nodded his approval "The four Bird Goddesses not only represent the wives, but are also protective spirits against four aspects of male dominance."

Jeannie indicated the individual carvings on each statue to support the text given by the knowledgeable American "See? 'Four aspects of male dominance': Arrogance, Aggression, Disrespect and the biggest bastard of all, the Phallus, which must be the one you left in Schweinfurt."

T gulped at the mention of the missing statue. She'd told Jeannie it'd simply been forgotten.

Jeannie stroked the Disrespect statue. "T, the guy in the shop was actually right. It says: if they're split up, it really is bad luck."

The silt of remorse stirred in the pit of T's stomach but Lincoln pushed thoughts of Kim aside. "The protective magic is supposed to work as a deterrent." He read the printout to conclude the legend. "Every man knew that if they offended the spirits while in their vicinity, the Gods would take revenge." During the recounting, Colin had been examining the figurines. He picked up one as Lincoln said the word "revenge".

"Right that's it. I've heard enough," he said. "I want these out of here, now." He held aloft 'Exhibit A'. "Seriously, T, you need to get rid."

"They aren't going anywhere, you soft bugger," she said.

"You heard Lincoln." Colin threw the statue on the bed and almost cowered. "Disaster follows them around wherever they go."

"Don't be such a superstitious idiot," T said. "You're being ridiculous. Lincoln didn't say anything of the sort."

"Colin's right Theresa." Lincoln picked up Colin's discarded Goddess and pointed it at her. "These Spirits do have a mighty powerful magic. They got some wild happenings in Africa, man. I seen all kind o' strange things in my looking."

T took the bird from him and placed it back on the table. "I don't care what they've got in Africa. These are just ornaments, my ornaments."

"Come on love, you have to admit we've had some pretty bad luck since you got these things," Colin said. "Think about it." T started packing the figurines back into their box, trying to ignore the barracking. "Bloody hell, we've been kicked out of every single place we've been, since they turned up. You were that unhappy, you almost left the band."

"That'd nowt to do with these." T closed the box lid. "I was gonna leave the band 'cos you were treating me like shit, getting pissed every night with your Red Indian mates."

"Alright, let's not get carried away. All I'm saying is, they're not lucky like you thought they were." Colin tried putting his arm around her.

T pulled away. "And all I'm saying is, get stuffed. Go molly coddle your van."

Colin turned on Jeannie who'd been sitting innocently on the bed up to this point.

"This is your fault. She'd just agreed to move back in with me before you came in with your mumbo jumbo." He left the room, punching the door on his exit.

"Sorry," Jeannie said.

"Don't worry," T said. "We weren't moving back in together. He's dreaming."

7 Adam's Sexploits: Hanau. Nov '76:

By The Rivers Of Babylon.

Propped up by his pool cue, Adam inclined his head to get a better peep down Heike Schenklar's deep bra-less cleavage. The German blonde leaned across the green baize and took careful aim at the eight-ball over the corner pocket. The black sphere dropped into the hole, leaving the three 'stripes' on the table.

The Kraut bitch had won again. His only consolation for being beaten four frames out of five was that he could ogle down her jumper or up her very short miniskirt while she lined up her shots. Not exactly a face to launch a thousand ships across the Aegean but he knew enough lads to fill a few dredgers if they thought they'd a chance to get at that 'Page Three' candidate's body. He'd been having regular pool and sex sessions with Heike since reaching Frankfurt. She was equally proficient at both.

The vanquished Brit escorted his conqueror into the other bar. "What do you want?"

"I do not wish more to drink. Put again 'Boney M' on." He slotted an English shilling into the jukebox. "What does 'meditation of our hearts' mean?" she asked.

"I haven't a bloody clue." He was fighting to keep his voice above 'the Rivers of Babylon'. He yielded against the torrent, finished his drink, then leaned over and shouted in Heike's ear. "Let's go back and meditate in the hotel before I go to work."

Following the Transcendental session, Adam sat up in bed. Heike's bare swinging, disembodied breasts crossed the room. The miniskirt zipped and the bags of delight snapped from sight as the jumper compressed them. "You've got some cracking bazoomers." Her smile appeared to accept the compliment though Adam was pretty sure 'bazoomers' wasn't in the German dictionary. "You know, you could be a model, Heike. You're gorgeous and by God, you're sexy."

She came to him and gently kissed his cheek. "*Danke*."

That's what he liked about her, the way she gratefully snapped any titbit of a compliment out of the air, a bit like Ralph his dog. "It's my day off tomorrow," he said. "What do you want to do?"

"If you would like, you can come to my home for dinner."

He had the seasoned nose of a musician; so with the smell of a free meal in the air, he didn't need any coaxing. "Abso-bloody-lutely."

"Then you can meet my family."

"Yeah, I'd like that."

"I must warn you, mein papa is sometimes a strong speaker."

"Are there any more grown up sisters at home like you?"

"No, I have two brothers, eleven and thirteen."

"Eleven and Thirteen? Couldn't your parents think up better names than that?"

The joke soared across the ceiling above her. When he'd finished watching her dress, he threw back the covers and leaped athletically from the bed.

"You have a very good body, Adam."

He posed. "Just call me Adonis."

"*Bitte*?"

The door of the adjoining room burst open to Adam's full frontal. "Steve!" Adam instinctively covered his manhood.

"Sorry, I didn't know you had anybody in here."

"I thought that door was locked."

"The lock doesn't work. Anyway, Colin sent me up for you. He's having an eppy. You're late." Steve left. Adam had one last snog and fondle of Heike's breasts before dressing.

"What the fuck are you playing at Fogerty?" Colin was in a jovial mood when Adam finally appeared in the hotel foyer. "Now just see if you can all stay in one place while I go and get the van."

"What's up wi' him?" Adam asked.

"He's seen his arse," Jimmy said.

"I guessed that much."

"I've no idea why. He doesn't need a reason, does he? He's just seen his arse."

"What does he mean?" Heike asked.

Adam explained that should someone see their own backside, this would probably be a very upsetting experience and make them annoyed. Therefore, to 'see your arse' means to have a show of anger.

Heike still wore a confused frown. "Why is he angry?"

Adam shouted across the foyer. "Oy Jeannie, what's up with Colin?"

"He's seen his arse."

"Frigging hell, this is like pulling teeth." Adam turned to Heike. "Don't ask."

Jeannie came over and recounted the history and legend of the Bird Gods and how it'd affected Colin's relationship with T.

"I said there was something suspect about those juju bastards." Adam took Heike outside just as Colin drew up in the van. "Hey up Col, I've just been hearing all about this legend and what those statues are going to do to you if you don't start treating T a bit better."

"I know what I'll do to you if you don't shut it." Colin helped Steve load the suit bags into the van.

Jeannie came alongside Adam. "You should be more worried about yourself. If anyone's a prime candidate for a kick in the bollocks from the Bird Spirits, it's you."

"If they come anywhere near me," he gestured with a raised forearm, "I'll give them a bit of this juju."

"Typical," Jeannie said. "Hey, Heike, I hope you don't think all Englishmen are like him."

"Take no notice of her, Heike." Adam eased her away from Jeannie. "She's jealous. She knows better than anyone how perfect I am."

Steve broke off loading. "Except when he's pissing off ball-breakers and getting us kicked out of gigs."

Adam followed Steve to the van. "Maybe it was you that got us kicked out of the gig."

"What?"

"Maybe you couldn't live up to what the ball-breaker was used to. That's what pissed her off."

"If you mean I haven't got your knack of shitting on chicks, you could be right." Steve threw in the last of the bags and slammed the van door.

Colin rushed around to the rear. "Oy, stop slamming her door." He went back to the front. "Now, are you lot getting in this van or are we going to stand here all day fighting about statues?"

The dressing room that night buzzed with cheerfulness.

"I don't get it, Jeannie." Adam applied his eyeliner. "Why would Lincoln go to the library to look for his boots?"

"You stupid wassock." Jeannie gave him a friendly push. "He was searching for his roots."

"Oh sorry, thought he was going to give these Goddesses a kick in the slats."

"I'm warning you, Adam," Steve said. "You don't want to go upsetting T's Bird Gods or you really will be sorry."

"Bog off, you daft pillock. You don't scare me with your bits of wood."

Jimmy broke off from his nightly hair routine. "I bet you five bucks you daren't sleep with them in your room for the night.

"For five bucks, I'll sleep with them up me arse."

Colin thumped a fist down on the dressing table. "For Christ's sake will you lot give it a rest with them statues? I'm sick of hearing about them." He turned on Jeannie. "Tell that jungle bunny boyfriend of yours, he can stick his roots up his arse."

Jeannie stopped applying her eye make-up. "Do you mind, Colin? That's way out-of-order." She went back to the mirror. "For one thing, you shouldn't be saying stuff like that in front of Steve."

Steve shook his head and went to the dressing room door. "Don't worry about it, Jeannie. I've been called worse." He slammed the door as he left.

"Don't they have bloody doors in the jungle?" Heads turned toward Colin but no one voiced disapproval.

Jimmy released a slightly hysterical giggle. "So, it's a bet then. Is that okay, T? You take the statues round to Adam's bedroom after tonight's gig?"

Adam nodded toward the dresser in his room. "Don't fret, T, I'll take good care of them."

T put down the statues. "You better had."

"Oh yeah, thank Jimmy for the five bucks." He was still chuckling to himself when he locked the bedroom door. Twenty minutes later, in only his underpants, he emerged from the bathroom and approached the statues. "Cop a load o' this." He simulated the act of masturbation over them. Still laughing, he got into bed, switched off the light and within minutes was dozing . . .

'Boney M' played on the jukebox. Heike was shooting pool with Colin.
Oh no, I hope she hasn't invited that bastard to dinner.

Wait a minute; something didn't look right. "Are you alright Colin? You don't look too good." Adam was trying to fathom why Colin's head was on back to front.

"Do not be concerned," Heike said. "He is trying to see in his arse."

"Why, what's he angry about?"

"Every time he tries to take his shot, there is a strange rattle coming from under the pool table."

The reverse-headed Colin was having trouble lining up his shot. Adam listened. Sure enough, there it was: a strange rattle.

Adam half-opened his eyes and tried to make sense of the dream. The rattling had been so vivid. He settled back into sleep. *Rattle! Rattle!* He snapped open his eyes again and tuned his antennae. From the other side of the room came scratching, followed by a faint, almost inaudible moan. He switched on the light and scanned the room.

"Hello?" He was either imagining things while still half asleep or the water pipes were being mischievous. *You silly bugger, Fogerty.* There was nothing. He switched off the light and settled again. Soon the noises were back, first the scratching from the left-hand side of the bed, then the rattle from the end of the bed. He didn't switch on the light but listened intently.

This time there was no moan but a girl's voice in a cod African accent said: "Dis am de ghost of Lobengalu."

"So am dis," another voice said.

Adam clicked on the light to see Steve and T, equipped with maracas and cabasa, laughter spilling them from the wardrobe. Then the equally helpless, giggling pair of Jimmy and Jeannie, crawled from under the bed.

"You set o' bastards." Adam got out of bed and checked his door. It was locked. "How did you get in?"

"Through Steve's room," T said.

"That one doesn't lock, remember." Steve opened the adjoining door to demonstrate.

"How? When? I didn't hear you."

Jimmy was still laughing. "We came in when you were in the bathroom."

"What, you were in here all the time?" Adam tried to find the humour.

"I don't know how we kept quiet," T said.

"Especially when he said 'cop a load of this'." Jeannie gave another twist of the percussion instrument. In turn, she, T and Jimmy collapsed on Adam's bed in one giggling heap.

Steve shook his maracas at the statues. "Cop a load of this, darling." He keeled over on the others.

Adam stood apart. "Alright, you've had your fun. And who said you could use my things?" He snatched the cabasa and maracas. "Now, would you all mind getting off my bed?"

Steve sat up. "You better watch out, Adam. If you think that ball-breaker, Debbie was bad news; those Bird Gods will really give you what for." There was more laughing.

There was no laughing from Adam. "Course, you would believe in all that voodoo, shite. Like Colin says, you're a jungle bunny."

The frolicking on the bed stopped. "Time to go, I think." Steve climbed off. He and Jimmy made their way out.

Jeannie followed. "You're such a wazzock, Adam."

Adam went to the door and called after them. "Steve? Steve, I'm sorry. I didn't mean it to come out like that."

T gathered her statues. "Yep, she's right. You're an idiot."

The following day was Sunday, Adam's day off. He looked out of his hotel window to find several more inches of snow had fallen. The conditions caused some concern; Heike might have to break her promise to take him home for his free meal. However, six trips to the window later, there she was. He threw on his new leather jacket, purchased earlier that week in Frankfurt, and went to meet her. He drove the orange Volkswagen the twenty miles to Heike's home in Kloppenheim, a small village to the north of the big city. The landscape of the village was difficult to judge on account of the snow but the uniform grey pebble dashed apartment blocks were common to any West German village.

Herr Schenklar, a small wiry man with a wizened face, twanged his black and grey bracer strap against his grubby collarless shirt before welcoming Adam. Frau Schenklar, the type Adam described as 'pleasantly plump', wiped her chubby, cake making hands on her Bavarian apron before doing the same. Heike introduced her two younger brothers.

"Ah, you must be Eleven and Thirteen." Both lads took after their mother with mouths that looked permanently stuffed with hamburger. Adam gave them proper names: 'Tweedle Dum and Tweedle Dee'. The family was okay, considering they were Germans. Adam judged a race by their toilet habits. German toilets had an inspection-shelf built into the bowl, a revealing insight into the Kraut psyche. "Never trust a nation that shits on a shelf," he would espouse. Other than this, and the bombing of English chip-shops, there was no special reason for his dislike of Germans.

Frau Schenklar had made a *Jaegerschnitzel*, veal done in breadcrumbs and covered in a mushroom sauce, very nice.

"Would you like more to eat?" Heike asked.

"No thanks," Adam said. "I've had an elegant sufficiency of every little delicacy."

"*Bitte*?"

"I'm stuffed."

"*Bitte*?"

After dinner, Herr Schenklar was keen to give his views on such subjects as: "The laziness of the English" and "How useless the British Army was during the war". Adam was equal to it. He enjoyed the banter and it was a small price to pay for such a delicious meal. Besides which, much of the conversation between the adversaries needed translation by Heike because Herr Schenklar's English was not up to scratch. This took some of the sting out of the argument. But with the hock flowing, it was proving an enjoyable evening and gave Adam an opportunity to meet real Germans in their lair.

"Papa does not like English football hooligans. He says they should all be put into prison."

"Hey watch it, Fritz, I come from Leeds. I take it you've heard of Leeds United?"

Papa almost spat. "Leeds United? *Scheisse!*"

"Well yeah, I can understand why you might not be too keen on Leeds, all their board members being 'teapot lids'. I've got nowt against 'teapots' myself but I know you Germans are a bit funny about 'em."

"*Was hat er gesagt?*" Papa asked.

"*Ich weiss nicht,*" Heike said.

Papa might not have been too keen on Leeds United's Jewish board members but it appeared deep down Herr Schenklar must've actually liked Adam because to prove the point, he brought out the fatted calf in the shape of an ancient, yet virgin bottle of his homemade schnapps.

Heike interpreted for Papa. "We must drink all in one night."

"Sounds good to me." Adam had floated past the tipsy stage some time ago. "Bring on the dancing-girls." Papa poured a generous measure and indicated that Adam should knock it back in one drink. The potency of the old schnapps hit Adam's gullet like a blowtorch. He grabbed his croaking throat. "This stuff's like rocket fuel." Both Papa and Mama Schenklar laughed proudly at the effect their drink was having on the Englishman. Tweedle Dum and Tweedle Dee huddled in front of the television, sniggering as though they'd seen this happen before.

"*Noch einmal.*" Papa didn't wait for Adam's consent but filled his glass once more.

Adam pushed the glass away. "*Nein, nicht, Ich bin kaput.* No, thank you."

"Ah, ah. English!" Papa said. "Not real man. No good English." This swipe at Adam's patriotic manhood struck home. He grabbed the glass. He was doing this for Queen and Country, English chip-shops and Leeds United.

"Okay Fritz, light the blue touch-paper and stand well back." Adam swigged back the rocket fuel. The effect was no less devastating for him having been prepared. He wheezed around the room as though suddenly struck by an asthmatic gene, using the furniture to prevent himself from falling. The Schenklar family showed their delight in his performance by applauding. The brothers continued sniggering in front of the television. Adam imagined that it was Heike's job to go out and entrap men by use of her inviting breasts and bring them home for the family's entertainment.

"*Gut* man," Papa Schenklar said, with a hefty pat on Adam's back. Adam didn't feel good. He could barely stand. He went and sat at the table. Papa refilled his own glass, then Adam's.

"*Prosit*!" Papa handed Adam Rocket Fuel, Number Three.

"No, definitely no more. Bollocks to the Queen's chip-shop."

"*Kommen sie, trinken.*"

"Hey who do you think you're ordering about? We're not in Nazi Germany, now, you know."

"*Was?*"

"Oh right, yeah, I suppose we are." Adam chuckled. "Okay Fritz, I'll tell you what. I'll drink but you've got to meet me half way. We've got to drink to the teapot lid board members of Leeds United. Agreed?" Adam raised his glass. "To the Jews!"

"*Ist er ein Juden?*" Papa asked.

Adam's head was spinning. "Come on, you miserable bugger, drink. Let bygones be bygones. To the Jews!" He threw the drink toward his mouth but most of it went down the front of his shirt.

Heike had stopped translating and appeared unable to move. It was difficult for Adam to focus but he managed to meld the four brothers into two. "Hey, *you*, Brothers Grimm, tell your dad to stop being a bigot and drink." Both brothers stopped sniggering and looked at him. "Come on you *kleine* fat gets, tell him, Leeds United's board members. I knew it. You're all Nazis."

Frau Schenklar gathered her Hitler Youths into her apron.

Papa hurled a tirade of what Adam assumed to be German abuse at Heike. Adam picked out the bits he understood "*Ficken, scheisse* and *bloeder Hund*": all swear words. His Enigma Code Breaker translated the rest for himself. 'How dare you bring this man to my house, to eat my food and drink my schnapps? And have you actually screwed this Jew lover?'

"Yes, she bloody well has, you Nazi racist. My dad should o' shot you while he had the chance. You're all bigoted arseholes." Adam would've continued his appraisal of the Schenklar family but for Papa's fist connecting with his nose. Ouch! Right on the button! He felt dizzy, and then his pain left him.

When Adam came to, he was in the hallway of Heike's apartment block, the clothes he'd been wearing at the time of the punch, his shirt and his jeans, soaked in schnapps. Bloodstains on his white shirt confirmed the throbbing in his nose. His new leather jacket was on the wrong side of the door. He knocked. No reply. He knocked again.

"Heike!" He tried the locked door. "Heike let me in."

Her voice came through the door. "Go away!"

"Heike you've got my jacket."

"Go away or Papa will telephone the Police."

"Open the door, you big titted freak." A door opened down the hallway. "What do *you* want, you bald-headed get?" Adam's polite enquiry went unanswered and the door closed.

Adam, again, tried Heike's doorknob. She wasn't going to let him in. He'd have to forfeit his jacket and brave the trip back without it.

Outside, Adam's drunkenness met the cold head on. This, and his bloody nose, helped him focus. Walking was his only option. Freshly fallen snow waited for his footprints. He'd done it again. Why couldn't he learn to keep his big mouth shut? What was it he'd called Heike - a big titted freak? *Why do I do that?* "Jungle bunny?" *For Christ's sake, Adam, why would you insult your best mate like that?* Maybe Steve was right. This was payback from them statues. *Wise up, Adam, they're just bits of wood.* So how come he was waltzing around in the middle of nowhere, pissed soaked through in booze? And his nose was killing, might even be broken. The snow became heavier, causing drips of remorse to fall from his hair onto his face. "Jungle bunny?" Why was he thinking about that, now? It would've made sense had it been a pleasant thought like being wrapped in the arms of Emma Virgilio on the sheepskin rug in front of her cosy fire. He did that thing he often did; trying to retrace the root of his thought but the origin was as intangible as the solution to his predicament.

He needed a plan of action. Emma Virgilio wasn't going to appear round the corner carrying a mug of hot Bovril. It was 1:00am so public transport was out, have to be a taxi. "Aw frigging hell, no! My money's in my jacket. Frigging Heike, you big titted freak." He had to get that coat, however much grovelling it took. He tried backtracking. "Bloody hell, whoever made these footprints must've been pissed out of their brains." He reached a point at which he'd detoured along an ice-covered mound. "Bollocks." The tracks disappeared. He was lost. "Christ on a sledge, I'm as cold as a penguin's chuff. If I don't get indoors soon, I'll die." Perhaps if he found a taxi, Colin could 'sub' him the money at the other end. He broke off his search for a taxi rank when he came across an oasis. There was no blue light so it wasn't 'Dixon Of Dock Green' but '*Polizei*' definitely meant police station. This gave him another idea.

"I've been mugged," Adam said.

"*Bitte?*" The desk sergeant failed to understand him.

"I'm English and I've been mugged." Adam exhibited his nose and the blood on his shirt. "They've taken my coat and my money." The officer showed him to an interview room.

Another officer came to take some details. "Where have you been? Where did the attack take place? Why are you soaked in alcohol? How much have you had to drink? Where did you get it? What are you doing in West Germany?"

Pretending he was drunker than he was, Adam managed to avoid answering most of the questions. Had the officer even known who Heike was, telling him about her would only bring worse trouble. What had seemed a good idea out in the snow, now threatened a night in a cell.

"Listen, I'm sorry," Adam said. "If there's nothing you can do, I'll be on my way."

"*Nein*," the officer said. "You must give a description of your three attackers and of your stolen property. You will stay here now and we will contact your employer in Hanau."

It was six in the morning when Colin arrived at the police station, a tad unhappy. The TBM-mobile had burst a hose on the way, losing its water and antifreeze. Colin had patched up the damage. Adam was now heading toward soberness but he felt it prudent to continue the mugging charade, both for the police and for the fuming Colin. He said he'd got very drunk in Frankfurt. He didn't know how he'd ended up in Kloppenheim but he remembered three men jumping on him and stealing his jacket.

"I thought you were supposed to be going to Lifebelt Lil's for your dinner, yesterday?" Colin said, on the way back to Hanau.

"Heike? She didn't show up. I went into Frankfurt on my own."

When they got back to Hanau, Steve and Jimmy were up having breakfast. Adam joined them. "Listen, Steve, I'm really, really sorry for what I said, Saturday night."

"Why, what did you say?"

"You know what I said. I'm sorry. I don't know why I do that."

"Forget it. Have some coffee." Steve poured Adam a cup. "So what's been happening to *you*?"

Adam re-spun his tale of woe about getting mugged.

"I thought you were going for dinner with Heike?" Steve said.

"Kraut bitch, she stood me up."

"Really? I'm amazed," Jimmy said. "You're not having much luck with your women."

"You're not kidding, Jimmy lad," Adam said. "If I fell in a barrel o' tits, I'd come up sucking my thumb."

"See? It's all that voodoo shite." Steve said. "I told you to watch out for those Juju Birds."

Adam came out of the barrel sucking his thumb again, later that day when the police came to take him back to Kloppenheim. Someone had handed in a jacket, with a report about a crazed drunken Englishman going berserk in their apartment block.

"You were violent and abusive to a Herr Schenklar and his family," the officer said.

"Me violent and abusive? He punched me on the nose, knocked me out." Adam indicated his still glowing hooter.

"You were also abusive to a Herr Schwarzenbecker."

"Herr bloody who? You're making these names up, man."

"Herr Schwarzenbecker is the neighbour of Herr Schenklar and they are both willing to testify that you were indeed violent and abusive."

"Oh, do you mean that baldy fella? He was just sticking his nose in where it wasn't wanted." Adam watched the officer writing into a file. "Hey, what do you mean, testify?"

"This is a very serious situation, Herr Fogerty. You could be deported."

"Hang on a minute. I just got a bit pissed and called him a few names."

He was not deported but let off with a caution for wasting police time. He did, however, miss the gig that night. 'Images' were moved on, yet again and Adam was to blame, yet again. He also felt an uncomfortable sense of embarrassment with the others at being caught out in a lie.

8 T's Adventures: Wildflecken. Dec '76:

Wipe Out.

The TBM-mobile skidded on toward the new venue, Wildflecken. Inside the van, T pulled up her scarf around her chin. What was it they called it in Catherine Cookson books when the weather matched the mood of the characters? 'Pathetic-fallacy': very apt. Windscreen wipers, set on the fastest setting, couldn't cope with the onslaught of hurtling flakes. Black ice beneath the tyres meant steering would've been impossible without an expert at the wheel, or so Colin said. Making things more difficult were winding treacherous roads with precipices that could've ended the tour at any turn. As for Wildflecken itself, the blizzard could've been one of its children. The mountainous region leading into the bleak outpost made T think they might be entering an outlaws' hideout. The inaccessibility of the little West German village served a good purpose, the appeal being its strategic military position, overseeing the East German border.

T and Steve sat in the front, alongside Colin. Besides the doom-laden atmosphere of their new venue, there was another reason for the dejection in the van.

"Now that's what I call pretty good going," Jeannie said, from the rear tier of the cabin. "A hundred and thirty miles and it's only taken us four hours."

"Listen, Moaner Lisa." Colin looked into his rear-view mirror despite it only showing as far back as the equipment partition. "It's taken us four hours 'cos we've got a dodgy water hose. While you've been kipping, I've had to keep refilling the radiator. If anybody thinks they can do any better, they're welcome to try."

"Is this contraption supposed to get us back to England?" Adam asked.

"You shut it, Fogerty," Colin said. "It's your shenanigans with Lifebelt Lil that caused this to happen in the first place."

T sent an apologetic smile into the back. Adam 'shut it' and switched off the interior light.

"They've got a point though, Colin. You can't pull your National Breakdown trick out here." The first band that she and Colin had been in together four years earlier, in those days, when called out, the National Breakdown didn't attempt roadside assistance. So, Colin would use this loophole when he worked a particularly long distance from Leeds, for example, Plymouth. He would immobilise his van by removing the rotor arm from the distributor, then call out the National Breakdown. The transporter driver would then turn up just in time to see the last of the equipment going into the motionless van. A couple of turns of the ignition would confirm the van was defective and needed relaying home, thus saving Colin three hundred miles worth of fuel.

"And you never got caught?" Jimmy asked.

"Nope," Colin said. "I saved a few bob and gave the Old Girl a rest."

"It's a female then?" Steve said. "Funny, I never saw it as a chick. The Tetley Bitter Men makes you think of it as one of the lads."

"No," Colin said. "She's a fine lady, here to serve the Tetley Bitter Men."

"I hope you treat her better than you do other women," Jeannie said.

"I know how I'd like to treat you."

"Hey, you need to watch yourself, Col." Steve winked at T. "You might fall foul of the curse."

"What curse?" Colin asked.

"You know: The Curse of the Juju Bird Gods."

"Oh, we're back on that again, are we?" Colin changed down a gear.

T's elbow dug into Steve's ribs.

The gear crashed. "Bollocks." Colin yanked at the guilty gear stick. "I know one thing, if we do break down on the way home, those black juju

124

bastards 'll be firewood." Before he and the TBM-mobile engine boiled over yet again, Colin had found Bahnhof Strasse, *funf-und-dreizig*, the digs.

Bahnhof Strasse was, as its name suggested, the street of the railway station. They'd arrived too late for twilight but the snow gave the scene weird early morning brightness. Number thirty-five was a spacious house with four upstairs bedrooms. In the kitchen, T quickly forgot the elements and delighted at the rows and rows of cupboards and modern appliances. Every utensil imaginable filled the drawers of the green kitchen units and lined the gleaming yellow tiled walls. "Hey listen," she said. "If it's okay with everybody, this kitchen is mine. And I don't mind taking charge of the cooking, while we're here."

There were many interchanged shrugs and nods. Adam appeared to speak for the group. "All those who want to fight T to be chief cook, raise your hands." All hands stayed firmly by their sides.

In the large living room, to the right of the hallway, a round, six-seater dining table ruled. After parking the van, Colin came in with an armful of logs. "There's a bunker out back with enough of these to last 'til summer." He threw them down into the hearth of the open fire. "I'll light this when we get in, after the gig."

T took off her scarf and imagined the burning logs. *This will do nicely.*

There were two single and two double bedrooms to fight over. Jimmy had 'bagsed' one of the singles, because later that month, his girlfriend, Marie, was coming out to spend Christmas. Adam and Steve took the double room at the top of the stairs, leaving T in a quandary. Jeannie had made it clear that she still intended juggling between Lincoln, Bobby and anyone else she could fit into her sex life calendar. "Obviously, I might need some privacy, every now and then," Jeannie said. "But don't do anything on my behalf." T neither relished playing gooseberry in a double room with Jeannie, or letting her wanton friend have the other single, as this would mean having to share with a husband expectant of his conjugal rights.

Colin stepped into T's kitchen while the others explored the house. "I've really missed you, you know."

"Have you?"

"Course I bloody have. I'm going nuts on my own. For one thing, I haven't had a jump for yonks."

Good God, how did I ever resist such a smooth talking charmer?

He carried on with his seduction. "How long are you going to keep this up?"

"Keep what up?"

His index finger traced across the table as though he was working out an invisible strategy on imaginary notepaper. "I mean, when we get back home, we'll be back together then, right?"

"I don't know what I'll be doing when I get home. I might stay in the spare room." She inwardly chuckled at his frown. "I might even move out."

"Move out?" He massaged the turning cogs inside his temples. "How are you going to have a baby if you move out?"

"What baby?"

"That's what you want when we get home, isn't it?"

"You know it is."

"Well then, we might as well move back in together now, now that we're in new digs."

"It's such a tempting offer, Colin, but no thanks." She went upstairs.

In the bedroom, Jeannie was sitting on the double bed chatting on the bedside telephone. She hung up when T came in. T got started on her unpacking.

Jeannie coughed. "T, you know what we were talking about, before? I've just had Bobby on the phone. He's coming up Sunday. Is that alright?"

"Not really, no."

"I've already said he can come, now. That's why I mentioned it. You should've said if there was going to be a problem."

"Where am I supposed to sleep?"

"What do you mean, where are you supposed to sleep? In here, of course."

"What, with you and Bobby? I'm not taking part in one of your threesomes."

"Don't be bloody stupid. Bobby will sleep downstairs. You just might have to give us a bit of space, every now and again."

"Like every bloody waking minute, if I know you and Bobby." T left the room and went back downstairs to where Colin was still at the kitchen table, his head propped up against one hand, his other still drawing on the imaginary notepaper. She went and sat alongside. "I'll think about taking you back, on one condition."

He sat up. "What sort of condition?"

"I want a solemn promise. We start trying for a baby as soon as this tour is finished."

He searched her face. "Seriously, you're not taking the piss?"

"Are you serious about the baby? You didn't just say it because you haven't had a jump for yonks?"

"No I mean it. If that's what you want, that's what we'll do."

"Okay, you promise and we've got a deal."

"Way hey!" He grabbed her, plonked a smacker on her lips and then bounded upstairs, calling all the way. "Jeannie, you're in the single room. Me and T are having this one."

Had she given ground too easy? Would she regret it? Truth was: she was in need of some conjugals herself.

"Right, come on you lot." It was good to see him so excited. "You can finish unpacking when we get back. We'll be lucky if we've got time for a sound-check."

The US Army barracks was only a mile or so from Bahnhof Strasse, albeit at the top of a high mountain. Any soldier being sent there must've thought they'd arrived at the Russian Front. And that night, the weather did make it feel like Siberia.

Following the arduous journey, 'Images' were ready to let rip. Even Steve got in on the act, though not in his former role as vocalist. No, Steve was a virtuoso on the silver kazoo that lived at the bottom off his green leather Head-bag. When a group of exiled Californians requested the old surfing number 'Wipe Out', it was outside the band's repertoire. So, Steve played it on his trusty kazoo, augmenting the instrumental into Adam's drum solo. The Californians went wild. The rest of the audience, obviously starved of good entertainment, gave a kind welcome to their new band. 'Images' took their warm reception home and wallowed in the pleasure of being indoors, in front of a sweltering log fire, leaving Siberia outside.

The Bones' new bedroom looked over a very non-German front garden and picket fence. They'd no balcony as Adam and Steve's back bedroom had but T didn't mind given that it was the middle of winter. Sparse furniture paid no heed to the lonely bedside rug. T missed the shag pile, not only from home but the one she'd got used to a month earlier at the Carter's. There was no upstairs log fire but the central heating was more than adequate. Having filled the limited wardrobe space with their clothes, she unpacked her hessian box and placed the three Bird Gods on the chest of drawers.

"Come on T, play the White Man." Colin stopped undressing. "Not them again."

"And why not?" A fight wouldn't have been the most unwelcome thing at this point, if only to test Colin's resolve. The Bird Gods stayed where they were. The victory added flavour to the sexual reconciliation. Not that their coming back together needed much spice after a month apart.

Morning arrived. The snow was up to the top of the picket fence. Colin joined T at the bedroom window. He put an arm around her and kissed her neck. "We'll have to get some o' those chains for the Old Girl's wheels. They all have 'em round here. I'm just going out to check her over, then I'll try and find some more antifreeze."

She left him overdressing with several layers of clothing and went to the bathroom. He'd gone when she came out. She joined the others downstairs in the living room where the three lads were sitting around the large dining table, playing cards.

"Where did Col go?" Jimmy asked.

"He went out to see to his sweetheart."

Adam threw a quarter into the pot. "Now that Col and T are back together, poor old Tranny van's been kicked out of bed and has to kip in the car park."

Jimmy checked his cards. "He better hurry up." He threw in his hand. "We're waiting to take his money, here."

T went to the window but the station car park was out of view. "He must've gone for more antifreeze."

The card school played on.

Jeannie was lounging on the floor in a corner, reading a travel book. T sat in the armchair next to her. Jeannie sat up. "Remember what we talked about in Frankfurt, T?"

"No, what?"

"You said you were going to start being adventurous now that you're a single woman."

"Did I? Well I'm not single anymore, am I? Me and Col are back together, just like you wanted, a bit of privacy, remember?"

"Don't start blaming me."

"No, like you didn't want the single room all along."

"Anyway, I didn't mean that sort of adventurous." Jeannie indicated a page in her book. "There's a place near here called Kreuzberg. We're gonna go skiing every Sunday if we can. I thought you could come with us one week."

T thought about offering up one of her usual pretexts: 'I can't ski', 'not my sort of thing', 'you don't want somebody like me along', but she put off her excuses. "Who's us?" she asked.

"I told you: Bobby's going to be coming up every week."

"Every week? Doesn't his wife have something to say about that?"

"As a matter of fact, she doesn't."

"Are you and him serious, then?"

"Don't be silly, T, it's just sex. It's okay; you won't be in the way. Steve says he's going to come sometime."

"Jeannie, can you really see me on a pair of skis?" She returned to the window. Where the hell had he gone for this antifreeze? "He's here now." She rushed to open the door.

The look on Colin's face brought the card school to a halt.

"I think the block is cracked." He strode upstairs, his tearful eyes beckoning her to follow. In the bedroom he slumped on the bed. "She's gone." T put her arm across his shoulder, unsure of what to say. The wrong thing would only provoke an unintended volatile reaction, so she said nothing. "How am I gonna get everybody home?" he said.

"Can't it be fixed?" As the seeming innocuous words were leaving her lips, she wished she could swallow her disobedient tongue. Too late!

"Fixed?" He shrugged her arm from his shoulder. "There's a whopping great crack across the engine, you stupid cow. How am I supposed to fix it, eh? Put some sticking plaster on it?"

"I only thought." Again she cursed her inability to keep quiet in these situations.

"Oh, you only thought, did you?" He was now on his feet and pacing. "The water - around the engine block - has frozen - and forced a massive crack in it, okay?"

"Okay."

"It's fucked, knackered. Right?"

"Fucked, knackered."

His pacing took him past the Bird Gods. He gathered them in his clumsy arms. "See these? They're going in the bin, where they belong."

She stepped into his path. "Aw no Col, please, don't!"

"I hate the bastards." He brushed her aside. T followed him downstairs. The activities around the card table stopped. T scuttled behind, through the living room and into the kitchen. Colin pressed open the pedal bin and hurled the statues, one by one, into the rubbish. "Right, I don't want to hear any more about statues."

T gripped his arm. "Colin, please, I'll keep them out of the way."

He pulled away. "What have I just said?"

The others had gathered in the entrance to the kitchen, Jimmy at the front. "What's wrong with the TBM-Mobile?"

"It's knackered." Colin pushed past them and went back upstairs.

"What does he mean, knackered?" Jimmy asked.

T sat at the kitchen table and relayed the technical jargon of 'knackered'.

"Can't it be fixed?" Jeannie asked.

"Apparently, not." T felt too weary to go into the 'sticking plaster' explanation.

"We should be able to get another engine from a scrappers," Steve said.

"Yeah," Adam said, "there must o' been hundreds of English bands passing through here. Surely a scrap-yard 'd have an old Tranny or two?"

"Go up and tell *him* that," T said.

"Yeah, bound to have. No dramas T, I'll sort Colin out." Adam gave T's shoulder a friendly pat then he and Steve went upstairs.

Jeannie took the three Bird Gods from the pedal bin and carefully wiped off the mashed potato and gravy. "I'll keep these in my bedroom for you."

"Thanks," T said.

Colin calmed over the next couple of days yet he still managed to send some accusations in T's direction for the demise of the TBM-mobile. She visited Jeannie in her single room and tried to explain the reasoning behind this.

"What, and you agree with him?" Jeannie said." I don't believe you. You're acting like it was your fault."

"I might've pushed him too far. Happen I should've taken him back in Frankfurt."

"What's that got to do with anything? It wasn't your fault his van broke down."

"It could've been, in a way. He says it was worrying about our relationship that made him neglect her."

"Her? It's not a her, it's a pissing van and it broke down 'cos he forgot to put antifreeze in it when he knew we were coming to the Arctic."

"He didn't forget. He put some in but it pissed out again 'cos the water hose burst."

"There you go, then. It was Adam's fault. Nothing new there." Jeannie opened her door as though inviting T to leave. "If Lover Boy hadn't gone off shagging, Colin wouldn't have had to go get him and the hose wouldn't have burst. Tell Colin to take it out on Adam."

T stopped at the door. "Can you hang on to my Bird Gods; at least 'til after he's found a scrap-yard?"

"Don't worry about them." Jeannie opened her wardrobe to show them nestled in the bottom. "See? Safe and sound for as long as you want."

T turned from the wardrobe to see Colin in the open doorway. *Shit*!

"What did you do with my grey jumper?"

"Erm, grey jumper? Oh, I had to put it back in the wash. It had a gravy stain on it."

"Bollocks, I wanted to wear that." He scowled at Jeannie as T ushered him back to their room. Had he noticed the Bird Gods?

The hunt for a scrap-yard proved simpler than expected. The soldiers told them there was actually one in Wildflecken. Heartened by this news, Colin finally had a good gig and determined to go the following day to find a transplant for his baby.

It was in everyone's interest; Colin had said. "So everyone's gotta come."

Jeannie complied with the summons to the winter junk heap but couldn't see any point in raking through rust ridden cars over laden with three feet of snow. "Why do *we* have to be here? We're just girls, aren't we? We're not supposed to know our axles from our elbows."

"It's for everybody's benefit," T said. "Just look round, like he told us to."

Jeannie pulled down her woollen hat over her ears. "Just because you want to do your penance, shouldn't mean we all have to suffer."

Jimmy said that when he died and had to go to hell, this is where it would be, a Wildflecken scrap-yard. The Devil would hand him the wrong sized spanner and he'd have to spend eternity trying to unscrew the bolts off a rusted manifold. Colin said that this was his idea of heaven. T didn't want to admit it but she was in Jimmy's camp. Great arms of rusted metal jutted from the snow like lost souls trying to claw their way out of Hades. Underfoot, although the ice was at least six inches deep, a black gunge had worked its way to the surface from the river of oil beneath: vehicles, dropped haphazardly on top of other vehicles, covered in snow then more vehicles dropped on them with another covering of snow, a giant rust lasagne.

"*Was wollen Sie?*" The proprietor asked.

Colin and Steve struggled to make themselves understood. However, they did discover, under all that snow were hidden three Transit vans. On establishing this, the group abandoned trying to converse with the proprietor and commenced digging through the snow. Sure enough they uncovered all three vans within a fifty-yard radius. The painted names of 'The Playboys' and 'Black Scabbards' were on two of the vans; fur-lined upholstery covered the cabin interior of the other. This, and the right-hand-drives was enough evidence to show that all three vans had belonged to British bands.

Colin deduced that 'The Scabbards' was definitely a heavy-metal band, and had probably: "Thrashed the arse out of their engine." 'The Playboys' sounded like "nice lads", so he deemed that theirs would be the best engine to replace the TBM-mobile's. After a couple of exploratory prods with the spanners and screwdrivers to confirm his choice, Colin set off to barter.

Jeannie peered from under her hat. "Can us girls go now? I think we've done our duty."

T scampered alongside. "Yeah, I need to get tea on."

"Go on then, and take him with you." Colin pointed at Jimmy "He's as much use as a one-legged man at an arse kicking party."

The tea was in the oven by the time two of the grease monkeys returned from the scrap-yard. "Where's Colin?" T asked.

"He's saying goodbye to his van," Adam said.

"What?"

The subdued duo explained that the engine in 'The Playboys' van had met with the same fate as the TBM-mobile's. Indeed, all three vans had frozen something or other due to the intense cold of the area. The English bands had all arrived as equally unprepared for Wildflecken as 'Images' had.

When Colin did eventually come in, he said nothing but went straight upstairs. T followed. He did his familiar slump on the bed, his ashen-face hinting that it was another of those 'keep your mouth shut girl' occasions. But as usual, she couldn't. "There must be plenty of other scrap-yards, mustn't there?"

"There might be, but there won't be any English vans in them. Transits aren't exactly common around here."

"There were three in one scrap yard."

"That's 'cos they belonged to the bands that played here, on the base."

"You won't know unless you look."

His scowl told her she'd said enough. "I shouldn't have neglected her. I was too busy with all that other shite."

She hesitated before speaking. "All what other shite?"

"What?"

"All what other shite?" She stood over him. "Do you mean me?"

"Eh? No, I don't mean you."

"Colin, that's so unfair. It's not my fault your van broke down."

"I didn't say it was your fault."

"What did you mean then, too busy thinking about all that other shite?"

"I don't know. I just meant I had other things on my mind, instead of sorting out the antifreeze."

"Yeah, what other things did you have on your mind?"

"Eh? Well, that first night here, for instance."

"What about it?"

"Well, I was more worried about the gig than I was about her, more worried about a group of Californian squaddies than I was about my own van. 'Wipe Out'? Fucking hell, they weren't fucking kidding."

"Utter bollocks Colin. That's not what you said the other day, is it? You blamed me. You said it was my fault for not taking you back in Frankfurt."

"Yeah, well, you've probably got a point there. If it hadn't been for you and your blackmailing, I might've been able to think straight."

"Blackmailing? Did you just say sodding blackmailing?"

135

"What else would you call it? You threatened to leave the band unless I promised to have kids. That's not only blackmailing me, it's blackmailing those poor buggers downstairs."

She took a controlled breath while she considered her options. Grabbing the chair and smashing it over the back of his head was immediately ruled out. And, although they were next door to the railway station, it was a hell of a way back to Leeds. Besides, she'd tried that once and hadn't got beyond the first plea from the others to stay. Colin was right; it wasn't their fault. She got the said chair to reach the empty suitcase on top of the wardrobe.

"Oh, here we go again. Is this it, then?" He got up from the bed and began pacing. "Every time we don't get our own way, we threaten to leave the band?"

She opened the case. "This isn't for me, it's for you. You're moving. Start packing." She went downstairs. "Jeannie, you need to swap rooms with Colin." All eyes at the living room table looked in her direction.

Jeannie and Steve followed her into the kitchen. "Are you okay?" Steve put a hand on her arm.

"Do I look okay?" She pulled her arm away. "Did you hear me, Jeannie? You need to put your stuff in the double room. Colin's moving in to yours."

"T, you can't ask me to do that. I'm not swapping back, now."

"Aren't you? Are you taking over as singer, then? 'Cos there's no way I'm staying with this band while me and him are sharing a bedroom."

"Pissing hell, Colin, you wazzock." Jeannie went upstairs.

Steve's hand was back on her arm. "You need to calm down, girl. It's not worth getting yourself into this state."

She yanked away her arm. "Don't tell me to bloody calm down." She went back upstairs.

Jeannie came out of her bedroom with an armful of clothes. "Where do you want me to put these?"

"I'll make some room for you." T went in her bedroom. Colin had left. The suitcase was still on the bed. She grabbed as many of his clothes as she could carry from the wardrobe. "Put your things in there. I'll come back for that other stuff." She carried the clothes into the single room. He was lying on the bed. She dumped them on the floor and opened Jeannie's wardrobe with the intention of piling them in the bottom but stopped when she noticed a vacant space. She ran back to her bedroom where Jeannie was sorting her things. "Jeannie, what did you do with my Bird Gods?"

"Your Bird Gods? Oh shit! They're still in the bottom of the wardrobe."

T ran into the single room. "What have you done with my bloody statues?"

"What statues are they?" Colin, still lying on the bed, put his hands behind his head.

"You know what bloody statues. What have you done with them?"

"You know what I did with 'em. I threw 'em in the bin."

"Stop pissing about, Colin. Where are they?"

"They're gone. I got rid."

"What do you mean, you got rid? You got rid where?"

"I burnt them."

"You did what?"

"You must think I'm a right numpty."

"What do you mean, you burnt them?"

"Yesterday, chucked them on the fire. They went up like a good 'un, box and all. Did you really think I wouldn't find 'em?"

So he had noticed. "You bastard!"

"I told you what I'd do with 'em if my van broke down."

"You fucking, sodding bastard!"

"So what you gonna do?" He sat up. "Aren't you leaving? 'Cos you know what, I don't give a fuck what you do. And that includes when we get home, move out or don't move out, makes no odds to me 'cos as far as I'm concerned, you've blackmailed me for the last time. You can forget about having kids, ever."

Tears welling, she ran from the room.

Jeannie waited by the door of their bedroom. "I heard all that. What are you going to do?"

"What do you think I'm going to do? I'm going home."

"Please, T can't we discuss it?"

"What's to discuss?" She started to pack.

"T, you can't just go. You need to wait a couple of days. You've got to sort out train times and things. You need to think about what you're doing."

T stopped packing. "Bastard!" Of course Jeannie was right. She couldn't simply jump on the '57' bus to Leeds. But she knew that if she didn't go now, she probably wouldn't go at all. She shouldn't take it out on the others. It wasn't their— What was that smell? She ran downstairs, into the kitchen and opened the oven door. "Sodding hell!" Smoke filled the room. "Are you lot stupid or what?" Steve, Adam and Jimmy came in. T took the billowing tray from the oven.

Adam looked into the tray. "What was it?"

She got five plates from the cupboard and scraped out the charred remains. "Enjoy your lasagne."

9 Adam's Sexploits: Wildflecken. Dec '76:
Let There Be Drums.

"I'm sick of that fat bastard blaming me for everything," Adam said across the four-foot divide from his bed to Steve's.

Steve looked up from his crossword. "He's not blaming you. It's poor old T, he's taking it out on." Once again, the other band members had needed to plead with T to get her to stay.

"Excisely, he's an arsehole. Thanks to him, we could've lost our singer. Job 'd be right up the spout if she'd buggered off home."

Steve scribbled another clue. "The course of true love never did run smooth."

"And it's rubbish without no van." Having tried all available scrap-yards, Colin had decided their best course was to manage without transport for their remaining couple of months. "It's crap schlepping up that hill every night. Why can't he hire one now? Why do we have to wait 'til the end of the tour?"

"We can't afford it."

"Talk about confined to barracks, it's like being in prison. They don't let foreigners on the base. We can't get out of Wildflecken without transport. Ergo, we can't get a shag without a van. We need to get to Fulda."

"Fulda? It's over thirty miles away."

"Presactly."

"There's plenty of yank birds on the base."

"Steve, are you blind or daft? The only women on that base are either dyke soldiers, or they live in the married quarters."

A couple of days later, one of those American ladies approached Adam. Jodie was petite, coming up no higher than the silver clasp fastening of his shirt. Her prettiness compensated for her lack of breasts. He'd just come off stage following his 'Cozy Powell' drum solo, which had gone down particularly well that evening.

Jodie twisted a lock of her chestnut hair around her index finger. "Hi, so you're from England?"

"That's right."

"Don't suppose you'd know a Mrs Gunney from Rochdale, England, would you?"

"I'm not sure. What does she look like?"

She placed the chestnut strand behind her ear. "She's my Great Aunt Sophie."

"Is she a little old lady with grey hair and a Lancashire accent?"

"I don't know; I've never seen her. Hey, you don't really know her do you?"

"No, I was mixing her up with Gracie Fields."

"Say again?" Her expression showed confusion.

"You're not very big for a soldier."

"I ain't a soldier, I'm married to one."

"Thought so." Despite her being off-limits, Adam instinctively went into his necklace routine. "It's a nuisance. The clasp of this thing always ends up at the front."

When he'd adjusted it, she pointed. "Is it real gold?"

"Don't touch that." He took hold of her hand and lifted it toward his neck. "If you touch that, it means I have to make love to you." Jodie had an unflinching stare. He waited for the tension in her wrist to tell him she was trying to pull away. It didn't come and the stare continued. He directed her hand up to his throat and guided her fingers along the choker. The stare bloomed into a cheeky smile. The barometer forecast a tornado.

Jodie visited the club on the next three nights. She loved the drums; especially drum solos, though she'd never heard of the British musician, Cozy Powell. She was married to Merle, 'the Tattooed Corporal', fifteen years her senior. Adam hadn't actually seen the tattoos but Jodie had described the cobra on his chest. Merle was frightening. Only an inch or two taller than Adam and not particularly well-built but sinewy; you just knew he was a dirty fighter.

Jodie nodded. "Yep, sometimes he can be real evil." Jodie and Merle both came from Iowa. "Unless you know pigs, Iowa can be the most tiresome place on Earth." The marriage had happened five years previously, in the week of her seventeenth birthday. Since leaving Papa's farm, she'd never had a job other than looking after her husband. Merle had joined the Army two years after their marriage to escape Iowa and the pigs. They'd been in West Germany for almost two years. "But if I used to think it was boring at home, this place got me bored shitless. I hate it." The other wives were much older than Jodie. So she spent her days lounging around the house. "Merle says I should appreciate all the nice things he's bought for me."

"What sort of nice things?"

"Well, we got a waterbed."

"Sounds lovely."

Merle was not bored. He'd prospered well since coming to Wildflecken. He'd disappear for days on end, following his 'outside interests'.

"Do you think he's shagging around?"

"Sorry?"

"You know, going with other birds, other women."

"Hell no, I just meant he has a lot of what he calls 'business activities', and he has the love of his life, his car."

"His car?"

"Yep, a Nineteen-Fifty-Eight Oldsmobile, he treats it better than he treats me."

"Sounds like somebody else I know. Oh hello Colin, I was just talking about you."

"Don't expect it was owt complimentary."

"Oh, you wound me, Colin." Adam took hold of Jodie's arm and guided her away. "Come on, let's go somewhere more private."

Adam backed up Jodie so that her bottom rested against the dressing room table.

"What have we come in here for?" She asked.

"I thought it might be better if we were on our own."

"Hey, I ain't no easy lay. And I certainly ain't gonna get anything on in here."

"We'll just have to find somewhere else then."

"That ain't gonna happen, Adam. Besides, Merle would skin us both alive just for thinking it."

He released her from the dressing table. "Ah yes, good point. In that case, I suggest we postpone the shagging until after your divorce. Then again, from what you've told me about Elvis, I still wouldn't be safe."

"Elvis?"

"Those sideburns make him look a bit like Elvis Presley."

"Man, he's gonna love you when I tell him that. He thinks he is Elvis."

"Whoa, whoa, whoa, just back up there, sweetheart. Why would you be telling your crazy husband, with a penchant for skinning people alive, that you've been chatted up by an English drummer?"

"I told him all about you."

"Why?"

"We just don't have much else to talk about."

He checked his watch. "God, look at that. How time flies when you're having fun."

Jodie brushed out the creases of her skirt as they left the dressing room.

Adam tried his best to stay out of Merle's way. However, one night after he'd come off stage and gone to the bar, there was a tap on his shoulder. It wasn't Elvis.

"Hey man, you're Adam right?" Merle's sideburns twitched when he tried to smile. "How ya doing? I'll get these." A wink and ten dollars were given to the bartender. "Give me a whiskey, man, and keep the change." Adam checked around but Jodie was nowhere. She hadn't been in the club all evening. Despite never having been near her sexually, Adam still had a sense of danger. He picked up his tray, thanked Merle for the drinks and tried to behave sociably while edging away from the bar. He crossed the room, heading for the safety of the other band members. Merle followed.

"This is Merle. He bought these."

"Thanks Merle, I'm Jimmy." He leaned across to shake hands. The others introduced themselves.

"What's your bag then?" Colin asked.

"Well Colin," Merle said, "I'm into country & western music, for my sins."

"Hey, I'm a 'C & W' man myself."

"Have you heard of my namesake, Merle Haggard?"

"Have I?" Colin slapped his thigh like a demented cowboy. "You bloody bet I have."

Merle having found a soul mate in Colin meant that Adam didn't need to speak to the tattooed monster. Now that the danger of being skinned alive had passed, Adam left them to each other's company and delivered the drinks to Steve, Jeannie and T at the next table.

Relief was short-lived. In the middle of the country & western conversation, Colin asked Merle: "How do you come to know Adam?"

Merle gave a little laugh. "Oh, he just happens to be screwing my wife."

"Oh, oh," Steve said. Both tables fell into a hush as everyone's attention turned to the country & western table. Merle still had a smile on his face; Adam didn't.

He straightened his flamboyant lapels and taking notice of Colin's clenched fist, thought he should try to defuse the ensuing brawl. "I haven't touched your wife or anybody else's wife for that matter."

"Hey everybody, it's cool. I ain't looking for trouble." Merle displayed his hands, as though showing he wasn't carrying a gun. "In fact I was hoping to have a quiet word about something that might be of interest to both you and to Jodie, a little proposition."

Adam wondered if this little proposition was going to end up on the point of his recently mended nose. He tried to remain calm in the knowledge that Colin would prevent Merle inflicting any serious damage. Nonetheless, he didn't relish being hit, not even if he'd been guilty, let alone for something he hadn't yet done. "What sort of proposition?" he asked.

Merle looked at the faces staring at him from around the tables. He took a second look at the two girls and said to Adam: "Can we go somewhere more private?"

Colin's fist tightened. "That doesn't sound like a very good idea."

"No it doesn't." Adam didn't fancy a more private punch on the nose, any more than a public one.

"I ain't gonna hurt him," Merle said to Colin. "Anyway, it concerns you too, man."

"Me? Okay, come into the dressing room," Colin said. The three men went to the compact room behind the stage.

Merle took advantage of the mirror by running a comb through his hair and sideburns. He then dumped his hairy arse against the same dressing table that Jodie's petite bottom had rested. "I'm looking for a private house, off base, where I can throw some parties. Your little station house would be ideal."

Colin's face betrayed a glimmer of interest. "What sort of parties?"

"Hey man, you know, some girls, some booze, some dope."

"I see," Colin said. "You want somewhere to sell your drugs?"

"I'll supply all the drinks and organise things. Hey, I'll even throw in some weed for the band, for free."

"You're taking a bit of a risk, coming in here offering us drugs, aren't you?" Colin said. "How do you know we won't report you?"

"You ain't been here too long, have you? You don't know me, else you wouldn't even suggest that." Merle gave his sideburns another quick comb. "Why don't you put it to the others?"

"You obviously don't know me very well, either." Colin ran his fingers, quickly through his mullet. "The others will do what I tell 'em."

Merle gave Colin a pat on the shoulder. "Sounds good, man."

Adam kept Colin between himself and Merle. "Glad you two are getting to know each other but what's all this got to do with me?"

Merle manoeuvred so he could give Adam's shoulder the same pat he'd given Colin. "Hey, you like my wife don't you?"

"We just have a few friendly chats, now and then. I've never touched her."

"I bet you'd sure like to." Another pat. "She'd sure like to screw you. Never stops talking about ya, man." Adam wasn't going to step into the trap set by Merle, even if the bait sounded pretty tempting.

"I don't think she'd rat on you with anybody." Adam wanted to state the obvious, that 'she'd be too frightened' but Adam, himself, was too frightened to say it.

"Hey man, we don't need no bullshit here. Here's the pitch. I need Jodie out of the way when I'm having these parties. She ain't gonna stand for other chicks being around, if you know what I'm saying? Anyway, she don't hold none with drugs."

"I still don't see what that's got to do with me."

"You keep my wife occupied while I'm round at your place and she's all yours. You can do what you want with her."

"What if she doesn't want me to keep her occupied?" This was obviously too good to be true but with the slight possibility that it might be for real; Adam wanted to cover all the small print of the contract.

"Man, you don't know Jodie." Merle finally removed his hand. "I tell ya, she's got the hots for *you*."

"Well, I suppose we could go for a drink or something." Adam tried a nonchalant laugh.

"Yeah sure. You take her for a drink or something. Listen man, I don't care what you do with her, just keep the bitch out o' my face."

When they left the dressing room, Adam did a quick mind-check of the date. "No, it's definitely not April the first." This was a long way from being skinned alive, by Elvis or anyone else.

The following day Adam and Jimmy sat together tucking into their American style sauerkraut and French-fries. Since the burnt lasagne episode, T had relinquished her position as chief cook. So, they'd taken to eating on the base because the army subsidised the refectories and it saved them having to do their own cooking.

"You mean he's just gonna let you shag his wife?" Jimmy said.

"That's what he says."

"I wish I was as jammy with women as you are."

"It's not jam; it's style." Adam gave Jimmy a friendly slap to his chin. "That's something you'd know very little about." Just then, as though to illustrate the point, two butch-looking female soldiers passed by and without any apparent reason, one smiled at Adam. The legs of her uniform, tight around her squat inner thighs, chafed together as she waddled across and sat at an adjacent table. The stocky little prize-fighter beamed another smile from her round ball of a face.

"Who's that?" Jimmy asked.

"I haven't a clue. But she's a two-shovels, if ever I saw one." Adam plopped more ketchup on his plate and mixed it into the sauerkraut attempting to ignore the distraction of the smiling dumpling. "So what does Marie think of this wonderful Wildflecken?"

Jimmy's girlfriend had arrived a few day's earlier, from England. "She hates the place," Jimmy said. "Wanted to go back home on the first day."

"Who put you up to it? That's what I have to ask."

"Put me up to what?"

"Marie, she must be all of six foot. Don't you feel a bit of a dick walking round with a bird six inches taller than you?"

"She's five foot, ten. She's only one inch taller than me."

"Yeah, if you're stood on a box. I mean, she don't need to take the pill. You can practise the biscuit tin method of contraception."

"What?"

"Yeah, you stand on your biscuit tin and when she sees your eyes go funny, she kicks the tin away."

Jimmy copied Adam's gourmet speciality with the ketchup. "I'll get her drunk at this Christmas party next week. Maybe then she'll start to cheer up a bit." He dipped a chip in the ketchup and ate it. "She's getting on well with Jeannie though. They've really hit it off."

"I'm not surprised she's pissed off. I wouldn't volunteer to spend Christmas in this dump for nowt, not even with Raquel Welch. She must be keen."

"She is. So am I. We're really into each other."

"Soppy get," Adam said. After all, Jimmy had only known Marie for eleven months and almost four of those he'd spent here in West Germany. Most of their relationship had taken place through the post or, occasionally, over the telephone.

At that point, Adam lost interest in the subject of Marie. Another smile from the butch soldier nipped in like a pickpocket and snatched his concentration.

"What is she playing at?" Jimmy asked.

"She probably just wants shagging."

"I thought all the female soldiers were supposed to be lesbians?"

"Even dykes need a proper shagging from time to time." Adam reinforced his view with the point of his fork. "It's too high off the ground to eat grass."

"Well rather you than me, she's bloody horrible."

"You're spot on there, Jimmy lad. I've seen better faces hanging from a witchdoctor's belt but I didn't say I wanted to shag her, I said she wanted shagging." Adam mopped up the remaining sauerkraut with his last chip. "Look, if I was to go up to her and say 'I suppose a Donald Duck's out o' the question darling', she'd probably give me a smack round the kisser." He wiped the said kisser with a napkin. "But if I sweet talked her a bit, said she was beautiful, well then, her legs'd be akimbo in no time at all."

"I'll take your word for it."

They left the table. As they passed the soldier, she grabbed Jimmy's arm. "Excuse me, you're in that band, ain't you?"

"Eh? Oh yeah, we both are," Jimmy said.

"Yeah?" She skimmed over Adam. "Well I never noticed him but I remember you from last night. What's your name?"

"Come on Jimmy, we're late." Adam pulled Jimmy toward the exit.

"I'll catch you later Jimmy," she called after them.

"Frigging lesbians," Adam said.

10 T's Adventures: Kreuzberg. Dec '76:
Down Town on the Piste.

You silly fat cow, Morgan! Why couldn't you just say, 'sorry I don't know how to ski'? As usual, Mrs Bone used her maiden name to reprimand herself.

During the month T had spent in Garmisch, she'd never taken advantage of the free facilities to go skiing. She wasn't sure why she'd agreed to make up the foursome on the trip to Kreuzberg. There'd been talk of 'trying it out' in Garmisch but Colin had told her: "It wasn't their sort of thing. Skiing's for thin people." He was probably right. They'd have looked out of place. Nevertheless, this time, she'd decided to see what it was all about and go on Jeannie's trip.

The other band members had found alternatives for their free time. Jimmy's girlfriend, Marie, having arrived from England to spend Christmas with him, the young lovers had a lot of catching up to do. Adam wouldn't come near any place that Bobby was and as for Colin, apart from still sulking over the loss of the TBM-mobile, she'd no idea what Colin was doing for the day. Did she care? Absolutely not. Since the row, work had become barely tolerable. On stage, Colin and T didn't even look at each other never mind communicate. At the digs, she simply kept out of his way. What would happen at the end of the tour? She'd no idea; mainly because she didn't know what she wanted to happen. He'd apologised for all the "bad things" he'd said but she still waited an apology for the burning of the Bird Gods.

So, happen the skiing trip wasn't such a bad idea. It'd be a relief to get away. The fear of being the gooseberry had gone because Steve would also be there.

Jeannie leaned against the kitchen sink. "You'll be able to touch him up while you two are squashed in the back of the Mustang."

"Don't be so disgusting." T turned the dial of the washing machine to spin.

"Bet you wouldn't say that if it was Carter."

"Give over, Jeannie." That was another drawback to the room sharing. Apart from having to sleep on the couch every time Bobby stayed, it was too easy to let slip the odd secret fantasy during their girly chats.

"Don't give me that Little Miss Innocent look." Jeannie's impish grin suggested a bombardment.

They had to shout over the racket of the spinning washing machine. "I don't know what you mean."

"I think you do."

"Look, me and Colin might not be together, right now but I'm still a married woman."

"I'm not sure about still married but I do know he's still a wazzock. You deserve better. Anyway, the odd fantasy about Carter's not going to harm anyone, is it?"

"Happen not. It's not like I'm ever going to see him again." The washing machine reached a louder spinning cycle. They moved into the living room.

"I bet you have wild dreams about his cooking." Jeannie gave one of her winks. "Wouldn't you fancy a bit of Alabami Surprise?"

T grinned. "Actually, I wouldn't mind being casseroled by him."

"Casseroled? I don't get it. Do you mean caressed?"

"No casseroled, look it up. To be done slowly over four hours." T laughed out loud at her own joke, proud that she'd topped Jeannie's.

"Now, you're talking, girl." Jeannie joined in with the laughter.

"That's just a joke, Jeannie. The only casseroling Carter's going to be doing is with Mrs Carter." The spinning finished, she returned to the kitchen to unload the washing. "I feel bad enough as it is about the way we left it with Kim."

"What do you mean?"

"Well, we didn't leave under the best of terms, did we?" T had never told Jeannie about the falling-out with Kim over the statues and she'd certainly never mentioned snogging William or that Kim had known about this. And now that the statues were gone, the tussle over them had all been for nothing.

"I didn't realise there'd been a problem with Kim. Did you two have a row? You've never said owt."

"What? No we didn't have a row. It's just that—"

"What the hell are you doing, T?"

"What?"

"Why are you still doing Colin's laundry?"

T looked at the shirt she was about to hang on the clotheshorse. "I'm not sure, just habit."

"You've got to stop this, T."

"Stop what?"

"He treats you like shit. He's burnt your statues and you're still washing his pissing smalls. You've got to break this grip he has on you." She took the shirt from the clotheshorse and threw it back in the laundry basket.

T put it back on the clotheshorse. "What time did Bobby say he was getting here?"

Jeannie shook her head. "I give up." She checked her hair in the kitchen mirror. "While I remember, Lincoln's coming to the party so don't mention it to Bobby."

"Lincoln? Is he still serious about getting a transfer up from Hanau? He must be nuts about you to come to a place like Wildflecken. We're only going to be here for a couple of months."

"I didn't ask him to do it. It's embarrassing."

"But you must be flattered."

Jeannie was still juggling around her men. Lincoln had joined Bobby as two of her most favourite 'spinning plates'.

Room sharing wasn't all bad. Jeannie was T's only contact with Womankind, so happen the skiing trip could be fun. It'd been such a long time since she'd had a laugh. She got into the back seat of the Mustang alongside Steve.

He squashed himself along to make room. "Come on, girl. It's a bit of a squeeze but at least we'll be cosy."

She dismissed the obligatory wink from Jeannie. There'd be a few more coming if she didn't choose her words carefully. Don't make it too obvious. "Hey Bobby, how's Debbie?"

Jeannie turned and scowled at T. Whoops; happen it wasn't such a harmless idea mentioning Bobby's wife. And the attempt at initiating a discussion about William failed to reach the track. The news that Bobby and Debbie were getting a divorce tripped-up the plan in the starting block. Debbie was to leave West Germany and return to the family ranch in Georgia. Bobby was staying to work for the army motor pool until they'd sold the apartment. He'd then return to Indiana.

T got back in lane. "Will she still be looking after the bands at William's club until she goes?"

Jeannie's scowl had now become a smirk. "You're not fooling anybody, T. You're not interested in Debbie. What she's really asking, Bobby, is how's Carter and has he cooked any good casseroles, lately?"

"Jeannie!" T avoided Bobby's smile.

"Old Carter's fine. He's always asking about ya, Theresa."

"Is he? You never said, Jeannie."

The smirk got bigger. "I didn't think you'd be interested, you being a married woman and all that."

"Very funny."

Jeannie turned and rested her chin on the back of her seat. "What were you saying this morning about having a row with Kim before we left Schweinfurt?"

"I didn't say we had a row. I just felt I didn't get a chance to thank her properly for all she'd done for us."

"Oh, I see." Jeannie turned back to the front but a few seconds later her chin was back. "Maybe, after Christmas, when I go down to Schweinfurt, you could come with us. That'd be alright, wouldn't it Bobby?"

"Hell sure."

"I'm sure they'd both love to see you," Jeannie said.

"I don't know. I'll have to see." Of course, seeing William once more wouldn't be the worst thing in the world but T wasn't desperate to face Kim, even if there was a chance to make things right between them. Happen best change the subject. Among the other topics raised was the Bird Gods.

"Are these your 'lucky' statues?" Bobby asked.

"Maybe they weren't as lucky as I thought they were." T explained about the legend and the curse.

"Sounds like they may be worth something."

"They're not worth owt now, are they? They've gone."

"I wouldn't have thought soapstone 'd burn that easily," Steve said.

"Happen they were made of wood, after all," T said. "He did say they went up like a good 'un."

"He's a cheeky bastard, sneaking into my room to get 'em," Jeannie said.

"He must've seen you showing me where they were."

"What I don't understand is: when did he do it? I'm sure I saw that box still in the wardrobe that morning."

"You obviously didn't," T said.

"So how did you discover this legend?" Bobby asked.

"Lincoln," T said.

"Lincoln? Who's Lincoln?"

"Er, Lincoln's just some old Black guy, T met in Hanau. Isn't that right, T?" T eventually nodded. "He's studying African ancestry." Jeannie's panicked expression made it clear she didn't want any plates knocked off their poles.

Beautiful as it was, secreted away in the Vogel Mountain Range, Kreuzberg was a very different set-up to the ski resorts of Garmisch. Garmisch mainly catered for the rich Austrian and German jet setters. It had several slopes. Kreuzberg, on the other hand was a monastery at the top of a mountain. More castle than monastery, Bobby thought it might've been some sort of medieval fortress before the monks had taken it over. He also mentioned the Order to which the monks belonged but T didn't care enough to listen. All that was important was, these monks, whatever their name, brewed their own beer, a thick, black and very strong brew, called 'Bock Bier', that she had heard. Nevertheless, this didn't give enough incentive for going up that big mountain.

"I think I'll wait down here in the car."

"Don't be daft, we'll be hours," Jeannie said.

"No, Colin was right. I don't think skiing's for me."

"Aw come on, you're not scared, are you?" Jeannie scowled. "There's nothing to be scared of. It's only a bit of snow."

"I didn't say I was scared and it might only be a bit of snow but it's up there."

"Listen, T, you've got to prove to Colin he hasn't won. You have to break that grip. You need to show him you're just as confident without the statues as you were before."

"Statues? What have my statues got to do with it?"

"That's why Colin hated them. He was terrified of the confidence those Goddesses gave you."

"Jeannie, I'm not twelve. Your child psychology isn't going to make me do something I don't want to do."

Bobby came round to T's side of the car. "You'll be missing out on a great view, Theresa."

"I can see the mountain from down here, thank you." T grinned at him. "You can't really miss it."

"What about the drink? It's worth the visit just for that."

"He's got a point, there, girl." Steve joined the assault. "I can't wait to get stuck in to some of that gear, myself."

"And if you don't like the Bock Bier, then they got Mosel Wein," Bobby said.

"Why are you all so determined to get me on top of that mountain?" T got comfortable in her seat.

Jeannie attacked again. "I don't know about beer and wine, you'd soon be out of that car if Old Carter was up there with his casserole."

"Will you shut up about bloody casseroles?" It seemed the mountain wasn't all Jeannie was eager to get T on top of.

"Go on, admit it, if Carter—"

"Alright, alright, if it'll shut you all up, where's the cable car?" T got out of the Mustang.

A proper cable car, like those in Garmisch would've been scary enough but to reach the top of this mountain there was only a chairlift, or rather a line of continuous moving planks of wood, each like a child's extended swing. You had to wait for the swing to come along then jump on it whilst it was moving.

"No, don't even think about it." Before T had time to change her mind, Jeannie pulled down the safety bar, the only device to keep them from falling into the snow-covered mountain trees. "I promise; it's safe."

Bobby was right. Kreuzberg was a picturesque setting. Acres upon acres of fir trees covered the surrounding area. The highest in a cluster of mountains in the Hessischer Nature Park, its only slope was the "steep, steep" incline.

T climbed off the swing at the summit. "Bloody hell, I'm not looking forward to going back down on that thing."

"Ah, there's something else I forgot to mention."

As a fortress, it must've been very successful. It was impossible to get out of the place, never mind get in. The chair lift didn't take skiers back down the mountain. The idea was to ride up to the monastery, then get out of your skull on the monk's Bock Bier. This would then give you the nerve to ski back down the slope.

"You bugger. So what do I do now? I told you. I can't ski."

Although T hadn't tried it, she'd learned that Garmisch had trained instructors who'd make sure you wouldn't hurtle down any ridiculously dangerous mountains until you were well and truly ready. Here there were no instructors or any other coaching facility.

"*We'll* teach you." Steve doled out the hire equipment.

T was sure that although the boots fitted her, they hadn't given her the right size skis for someone of her weight. Surely she wasn't expected to "go down that big slope on those two little sticks." The chairlift was terrifying enough. "I might need one or two of those Bock Biers before I do anything," She said. They went to the bar.

After twenty minutes, Jeannie got up from the table. "Are we skiing or what?"

T poured the rest of her Bock Bier into her glass. "Look, why don't you lot go off and enjoy yourselves. I'll be alright here, for a bit."

Jeannie pulled down her goggles and picked up her poles. "I give up."

"Do you want another of those Mosel Weins before we go, T?" Steve asked. He brought the drink, then left her to it and went off to hit the slope with the others.

Eventually, it was time for everyone to squeeze back into the Mustang to go home, but the Mustang was at the bottom of the mountain.

Steve took hold of T's arm. "Come on girl, I'll show you what to do."

"Get your hands off me; I'm not that sort of girl."

"Bloody hell, she's arseholed," Jeannie said.

"I told you it was mighty strong stuff," Bobby said.

T picked up an empty Mosel Wein bottle and sang into it. "Sugar in the morning, sugar in the evening, sugar at supper tyeem." She attempted a bow but slipped forward. "Whoops, sorry Bobby." She steadied herself on the American. "You don't mind, do you? I've heard all about you, you randy bugger. I don't want any of that hanky-panky if I do come to Schweinfurt."

"Have you had a good day, Theresa?" he asked.

I've had a brilliant day." She wanted to repay him. "I know; why don't you come to our Chrishmas party?"

"What Christmas party?" he asked.

"We're having a big party," she said. "It's gonna be great, loads of free booze." She checked around. "And *drugs*."

Bobby looked at Jeannie. "You never said nothing about no party."

Oh bugger!

"Take no notice of her, she's arseholed." Jeannie shook T by the shoulders. "Look here, you; get those skis on and stop pissing about." There was a ten-minute pantomime with everyone falling over in the snow.

Steve handed Jeannie the skis. "You get these on, I'll hold her." T was held down with her legs in the air while Jeannie and Bobby clipped her boots into the skis.

T tried to disentangle herself from the mêlée. "Get off, you randy sods."

Skis on. Steve managed to get T to her feet. "T, I'm only trying to help you down the mountain."

"I'm not going anywhere." She flopped over, back into the snow.

Jeannie stood over her. "T, we've got to go home. You can't stay here all night."

"I can. I like it here. It's nice. I don't want to do that skiing thing."

Jeannie folded her arms in that way she did when she disapproved. "See, what did I tell you? You *have* turned back into a wimp."

"Wimp? Who's a bloody wimp?"

"You are." Jeannie brandished T's ski poles. "Before he burnt them statues, you'd have whizzed down this mountain without a second thought."

"Get out of my way." T stood and grabbed the poles. Steve took hold of her. She shook him off. "Just show me what to do. I don't need holding. I'm not a wimp."

Steve backed away. "Okay, take it real steady."

So, armed with a little tuition from the others and the Spirit of Bock, T pushed down the slope. As she felt herself accelerating, the sudden rush of cold wind in her face worried her. Best just to go a few feet at a time. She wondered if it might be easier to stop by sitting. She didn't stop. Nor did she fall but accelerated down the mountain, using the skis as a sledge. She reached the bottom, exhilarated.

Jeannie and the others arrived to find her on her back, skis in the air. "How the hell did she manage that? Are you okay, T?"

"I want to do it again."

"Not a good idea, girl." Steve and the team quickly got her out of the ski boots. The equipment returned; they bundled her into the Mustang.

Off the autobahn, in twilight they could've been anywhere in England, on the Scarborough road, even. "When you're alone and life is making you lonely, you can always go, Down Town." T's melodious hiccups bounced around the car. "Come on you miserable buggers, shing up." Steve helped by augmenting the happiness, harmonising on his kazoo. It reminded her of childhood with her two brothers on the way home from the seaside in the back seat of dad's car, singing like Petula Clarke. By the time the kazoo had blown its last bit of enjoyment, the rear seat had an overhead glow.

"So Theresa, you going to be singing at this party you were talking about?" Bobby asked.

T giggled and whispered to Steve. "Happen he'll be able to have one of them threesomes with Lincoln."

Bobby frowned. "What did she say?"

"Ignore her, Bobby. It's not a party. Adam has met this psychopathic soldier, who's persuaded him to let him sell drugs from our place." Jeannie ran to the farthest spinning plate before it crashed to the floor.

Very impressive.

Jeannie turned to the back. "Steve, can you just sit on her head?"

T hoped she hadn't spoiled things with her gigging sister. "Whoops, sorry Jeannie, I forgot. Don't mention the party to Bobby."

"What does she mean?" Bobby asked

Jeannie continued spinning. "I told her not to mention the party to you 'cos it'll be full of soldiers. You hate soldiers. I don't think I'll be going myself."

"Yeah you're right, I sure do hate soldiers," Bobby said. So they arrived back in Wildflecken, T and Jeannie still friends and with all Jeannie's plates intact and on their poles.

11 Adam's Sexploits: Wildflecken. Dec '76:
Blue Suede Shoes.

When did shagging get so complicated?

It was left to Adam to plan how he was going to keep Jodie away from Merle's party. Merle had told his wife that he was going out of town on army business. He'd even suggested that she might throw a dinner party for some of the other wives and their partners. And perhaps she could include Adam among the guests. Adam had laughed when Jodie told him this. It was probably a shrewd move on Merle's part but Adam was unsure of the corporal's motives. Perhaps he'd suggested this to give Adam the opportunity to seize the moment. Then again, perhaps not. More likely, Merle had thought up the dinner party, with lots of guests, so that Adam wouldn't get a chance of any lone-time with his wife.

"What about Jodie?" Steve asked Adam. "Is she up for it?"

"Why wouldn't she be?"

"Well for one thing, she's got this monster for a husband." Steve leaned up in bed. "I can't imagine she'll walk very well with your severed head stuck up her arse."

"She's been giving me the come-on since we got here."

"You need to ask yourself why." Steve lay back again. "She might be just trying to make Merle jealous."

"Could be, I suppose." Adam got out of bed and began dressing. "I'll suggest ditching the other guests. If she says yes, then it's on."

Jodie turned up at the gig, to make 'arrangements', a curl of chestnut hair twirled around her finger.

"Why don't we just have our own private dinner party?" Adam said.

Jodie beamed. "Okay."

Well, that was easy. Maybe Merle was right. Maybe she has got the hots for me.

The apartment was more luxurious than expected, not your average squaddie's digs. Other than the few tacky Elvis photos littering the room, Adam rated the décor and furniture as stylish and classy. After dinner, they settled back on the large, cream leather divan, while the orange blob slowly made its way to the top of the lava lamp.

"Tell you what, Jodie, those prime ribs were lovely. I've been eating crap for the past week in that refectory. I'm really looking forward to dessert."

"I ain't made no dessert."

"I'm not talking about apple pie. I mean the other sort of afters."

Jodie giggled and poked him in the chest. "You're so crazy."

"Is that a good crazy or a bad crazy?"

"It's good. Adam, I ain't had no fun in years. You make me laugh."

"Hey look, if it's laughs you want, I'll paint my face and stick a cherry on my nose if it's going to lead to horizontal refreshment."

She giggled again, this time without the poke in the chest. She initiated a preliminary round of kissing.

From a corner of the room, the black and chrome hi-fi system had assisted the Isley Brothers and Chicago, obviously from Jodie's collection, in providing the music through dinner. The orange blob settled on the bottom of the lamp. Soft lighting created an ambience suitable for more kissing and a bit of fumbling. Primed and ready to go, or so he thought but when he pulled down the zip of her trousers, she pulled it back up again. She obviously needed more laughs. "Do you know, Jodie? My willy's gruesome."

"Say what?"

He took her hand and stroked it over his groin. "Whoops, it just grew some more." It seemed to do the job. The kissing became more passionate and she allowed him to fondle her breasts, albeit outside her shirt. Oblivious to the blizzard on the other side of the ethnic cane window blinds, he wafted along on the 'Summer Breeze' created by the Isleys. He surfaced for air. "When are you going to show me your famous waterbed?"

"It ain't my waterbed, it's Merle's."

"Course it's yours, you sleep in it, don't you?"

"Actually I don't. I sleep mostly on here." She looked forlornly at the cream leather divan. "Merle can't sleep with no one in his bed."

"Don't tell me, his willy's so big he can reach you from the bedroom."

"You're crazy." This phrase appeared to need a poke to the chest to give it emphasis. She sat back. "Merle ain't touched me in months, other than the odd time he gets drunk and needs to get off real quick."

"How romantic!" *No wonder she's got the hots for me.* So why was she playing so hard to get? Maybe it was some sort of teasing game. But Adam wasn't the sort for games. He stood. "I need to use your loo."

In the hallway, there was only one room other than the bathroom. Merle did indeed love Elvis. No subtlety here. 'The King's memorabilia littered the bedroom. Forget the photos in the living room; this was tacky. Blue suede shoes probably filled the wardrobe. Stretching down the centre of the room was Merle's folly, covered with a leopard-skin eiderdown. A prod at the foot sent a wave up the bed. Adam shouted toward the living room. "Hey Jodie, I've found your waterbed." Overhead, an imitation shell light-shade gave an offensive pink hue to everything, a definite clash with the leopard skin.

Jodie came in. "Adam, what are you doing in here?"

He strummed his fingers over a small china guitar. "Very nice." Ornaments decorated an array of shelves.

"Folk bring him this stuff from all over the place, some of it even from Graceland." Jodie switched off the master light and replaced it with a more pleasing bedside, plain beige affair, throwing interesting shadows across the room.

Adam fell backwards on the bed, undulating up and down as anticipated. "Oh yes." He laughed at the ebbing water under his body. "Come here."

"No, come on; let's go back in the other room."

"Okay, give me a lift up." He held out a hand but when she took it he pulled her on the bed. She laughed as they bounced around. He kissed her, hard. She responded. He unbuttoned her shirt and cupped his hand inside her bra. She didn't resist. Although the breast was smaller than he'd have preferred his arousal caught up with where it'd been on the cream leather. Cyclops sent a wink of approval. "I've been looking forward to this." There was nothing new or particularly exciting about the fondling sensation but it was pleasant enough. "I've never done it on a waterbed before."

"And you ain't gonna do it on this one." Jodie removed his hand from its nestling place.

"Aw don't be like that."

She got off the bed, the movement causing the water to splash around under his frustrated frame. The motion stopped. She re-fastened the buttons on her shirt. Good God, this was hard work. Small though the breast was, he didn't take too kindly to having it snatched away.

"I can't do this, Adam. I thought maybe I could but I can't."

"We might not get another chance like this."

"I ain't never cheated on Merle before and I ain't gonna start with you."

"But he cheats on you all the time, you said so yourself."

"Well that don't mean you get to sleep with me. I told you before. I ain't no easy lay. I just wanted a bit of fun, is all."

"He hasn't touched you in months. You shouldn't have to put up with that."

"What happens between me and Merle is between me and Merle, ain't got nothing to do with you."

"So why did you tell me, then?" This wasn't part of the deal at all. He'd kept his end of the bargain. Now Merle's business partner was reneging on their part of the contract. What was she playing at?

She sat on a chair in front of the dressing table. "Sorry."

"Jodie, why did you tell Merle about me?"

"What do you mean?" She opened a drawer in the dressing table and took out a brush.

"Were you trying to make him jealous?"

"Jealous? Hell no." She bit the end of the brush. "I just thought that if he knew someone else was interested in me, he might pay a bit more attention." She turned her back on Adam and began brushing her hair in the mirror. "If he ever finds out you've even been in his bedroom, he'll skin you alive."

Now, she was simply trying to frighten him with silly threats. Adam's agitation grew, given that he'd taken so much trouble to check the small print. "No, he won't skin me alive. That's what you said last time. You know as well I do, he's probably expecting me to be here."

Jodie laughed and shook her head. "And why would he be doing that?"

"Look, if you're trying to make him jealous, then you might as well go for it. He's going to think you did whether you do or you don't."

"I ain't trying to make him jealous."

"Oh, so you're just a prick-tease then, are you?"

"I ain't no tease; just wanted a bit of fun. I think you should go now, Adam." The brush stroked through the chestnut, again.

"Jodie, what do you think your rat of a husband's doing right at this minute?"

"How would I know what he's doing right at this minute?"

He propped himself up on the leopard-skin pattern pillows. "I'll tell you what he's doing. At this very moment, he's round at my place shagging himself silly."

"Merle's away on Army business." A frown suggested she was trying to dismiss her doubt.

"He's not. He's round at our house, shagging. That's screwing in your language."

"Adam, do you really think I'm that stupid? Do you think telling me this is going to make me jump into bed with you?"

"I'm not lying. Look, we made a deal."

She turned back to the mirror. "I ain't made no deal."

"No, me and Merle made a deal. He said I could make love to you in exchange for using our place to sell his drugs."

"You and Merle made a deal about me?"

"He told me: 'just keep the bitch out of my way.' I know he's shagging, it's obvious."

Jodie's reflection took a moment to register. "He said what?"

"How else would I know he was selling his drugs?"

"Bitch? I'll show him who's a bitch." She was now shouting.

"He said you agreed. He said you had the hots for me."

"You want to see hot? I'll show you fucking hot." She exploded around the room, each smashed ornament receiving a high level expletive. "Fucking Snake! You think I'm gonna sit here, while you screw around?"

He'd hoped telling her what Merle was up to might convince her to have revengeful sex. And yet, something in her demeanour suggested she wasn't wholly in tune with this plan. The hairbrush smashed against the defenceless Elvis clock. "Let's see you fix that, you goddamn, fucking, two timing bastard."

She punctuated the attack on the clock by hurling the hairbrush at Adam's head. Fortunately for him, it missed, bounced off the black leather headboard and knocked two more pieces of *objet d' art* off the bedside cabinet. She stormed from the bedroom. Adam sat there wondering how he was going to get this genie back in the bottle. The genie re-entered, brandishing a Norman Bates type carving knife.

Adam drew up his legs and tried to back through the leather headboard. "Now come on love, let's not get silly." She tossed away a corner of the leopard cover to lay bare the blue rubber skin of the waterbed. Holding the knife with two hands, she plunged several frenzied thrusts, into the bed. Small jets of water spurted up on the quilt. The rubber ripped and water gushed from its wound. The bed gave way under his weight, lowering him to the frame. The soaked Jodie collapsed, crying at the foot of the waterless bed. Droplets of water dripped from her freshly brushed hair onto her already wet face. Only the handle of the abandoned knife was visible: the blade, buried in leopard-skin and rubber.

Maybe we should forget the sex.

"Bastard!" She slapped a hand on the floor, causing more water to splash up in her face.

Oh, is it that time already?

Perhaps he should go and see how the party was progressing. He slid off the bed frame and edged his way, through the puddles, past the sobbing Jodie to the bedroom door. "I'll be getting off then. Don't do anything daft with that knife, will you?" He retrieved his coat from the hallway. "Thanks for dinner. It was lovely," he called. "Merry Christmas and all that." He escaped into the cold night air.

He'd gone to Jodie's prepared for the cold walk home, bringing out of mothballs his old fur coat. However, he hadn't anticipated going home with drenched under-garments, shivering and soaked to his skin. And this was no ordinary winter cold. This was freezing to the bone marrow cold, hardly able to move for fear of snapping a femur cold. Inside his Chelsea boots, water had seeped down into his socks and sent out an invitation to Frostbite to come and join the shindig. Coat or no coat, this was colder than the night he'd been thrown out of Heike's. Fortunately he was much nearer home. The Chelsea boots squelched the mile and a half down the hill to Bahnhof Strasse. Moonlight glistened off the snow-covered roofs of the deserted streets. He briefly considered avoiding the party because Merle was there, but he needed to get out of his wet clothes before he died. Besides, the limited options gave him no choice. Three days before Christmas, yet the only festivities on offer were back at the house.

The trudge at least gave him an opportunity to plan what to say if anyone was to ask how he'd got himself in such a state. He'd say that the snow had turned to sleet. He'd tell Merle that the dinner party had been a boring failure and most of the guests, including him, had departed early. Adam was fairly sure that when Jodie had calmed, she'd never divulge having him alone in the apartment. This would be like scheming behind Merle's back. He hadn't a clue what excuses she was likely to invent about the bed or the ornaments but that'd be her problem. Onward to the party.

A realisation seeped into his sodden mind. Steve shouldn't be in that house with all those drugs. Adam had been so wrapped up in the Jodie thing he'd neglected to consider his friend's history. During their time in Morocco, Steve had developed a problem. For the first three years after leaving Tangier, he'd been a heroin addict, culminating in an overdose and then a six-month stay in rehab, paid for by his mother. He'd been clean since but there was a limit to temptation.

A thumping bass met Adam halfway down the street and escorted him to the party. Maybe the evening wasn't going to end in disaster. Maybe Merle had brought along a few spare birds. There was probably a couple waiting there, now, pining for his body. However, they'd first have to chisel the frozen trousers from his legs.

"You Ain't Seen Nothing Yet." Bachman Turner was very much in Overdrive when Adam got in the house. However, spare birds there weren't. Lots of high and drunken soldiers, none of whom were chicks, were dancing with each other. Adam's attention drew towards a muscular man, naked from the waist up. The bright light of the living room shimmered off a completely, shaven head, a pair of plastic devil-horns fixed on with rubber suckers. Eyebrows betrayed the man had once been blond. Around his neck he carried an ice-cream tray, the contents of which appeared to be every type of illegal substance imaginable.

The man was strolling around selling his wares with the flair of an American circus ringmaster. "Roll up, roll up. We got blueys. We got dex. We got purple hearts. We got grass …" The list was endless. Adam felt as if he'd walked from his own nightmare into someone else's, hopefully not Steve's.

Adam's search for his buddy led him into the kitchen. "Where's Steve?"

"Hey, my main man," Colin said, in an American accent.

"Which bit of Birmingham are you supposed to be from?" Adam asked. "Where's Steve?"

"I'm here, why?"

Adam checked the dilation of Steve's eyes. "Are you okay?" The pupils seemed to suggest his earlier fears were unfounded.

"Why wouldn't I be okay?" Steve slumped onto a kitchen chair "I thought you were out making the beast."

"I don't want to talk about that," Adam said. "Where are the others?"

"Jeannie and Jimmy are in their rooms," Steve said. "They're both off their heads."

"But what about Merle? Where's Merle?"

"Ah yes, your mate Merle," Steve said.

"He's awright, your mate Merle." Colin was slurring his words. "I won't hear a word aginn 'im"

"Your mate Merle is upstairs in our chuffing room, shagging two birds."

"Oh brilliant." Adam knew that Steve's objections to Merle having two women were not prudish but more likely rooted in jealousy. He had a few objections of his own. "That means I can't get frigging changed. I'm sodden. I'm going up to have a shower. That's if I can get anywhere near the bathroom."

The bathroom was empty. Adam locked the door. He tried to ignore the vomit around the toilet bowl and washed some of it down into the water with his urine. A brief sigh accompanied the last of his wet clothing into the washing basket.

The shower felt good and the running hot water blocked out the sound of the distant fairground attractions happening beyond the bathroom door.

When Adam switched off the shower taps, the bass thudding had stopped. So had the "Roll up, roll up" of the demon, ice-cream drug-peddler. In its place was a nearer and more chaotic noise. He stood in the bath and tried to disentangle the various sounds, which seemed to come from right outside the bathroom.

This bloody nightmare's following me.

Breaking into his aural decoding, came a loud rap on the glass door. "Adam, get out here quick." It was Steve.

"I'm in the shower."

"Never mind that, just get out here."

"Steve, I'm in the nackety."

"If you don't open this chuffing door now, I'm gonna kick it in."

"For fuck's sake." Adam peered around the door. "This better be good."

"Oh it is pal."

To Adam's amazement, the landing was full of soldiers.

"That nutty wife of your mate Merle has turned up. They're locked in our bedroom and it sounds like he's killing her." The gravity of Steve's words took a moment to sink in, then plunged to the centre of Adam's brain.

"What?" He grabbed a towel and ran, dripping.

"You don't half pick 'em," Steve said, in Adam's wake.

Party revellers assembled outside the closed-door of Steve and Adam's bedroom.

"She's done something to the Boss," the drug-peddling devil said when Adam and Steve had pushed their way through to the front of the gatherers. From the other side of the door came whimpering.

"What the frigging hell's happened?" Adam was still dripping wet, though he'd by now covered his lower half with the towel.

"As far as I can make out, she just turned up and asked to see her husband," Steve said. "It was T who answered the door."

T arrived and took over. "She said it was urgent. I knocked on the door. He let her in. Two seconds later, all hell let loose."

Adam turned the door handle.

"Don't you think I tried that?" Steve said. "It's bolted."

Adam knocked. "Merle? Merle, it's me Adam. Is everything alright?"

"The bastard's dead." It was Jodie. "If you come in here, I'll kill you too."

The crying hit a crescendo, two voices, none of which sounded like Jodie.

"For fuck's sake, what's happening?" Adam said. "What has she done?" It was difficult to imagine exactly what she *had* done. Merle was a good deal bigger than her. Nut-case though she was, she was unlikely to have won in any sort of fight. Yet it was her voice coming back from the bedroom, her voice saying she'd killed *him*, no sound from Merle; and this crying?

"Come on girl, open up." Steve banged on the door. "Nobody's going to hurt you." The anonymous crying subsided. Jodie said nothing. Steve tried again. "Whatever you've done, we'll make it alright."

"Do you think she's serious?" Adam asked.

"We better break the door in." Steve readied himself.

"I don't think that's wise." Adam held up a hand. "You heard what she said."

"Don't be such a soft get," Steve said. "She's only seven-stone, wet through."

"You haven't just spent an evening with her."

T shook her head. "My God, I might've known this had something to do with your lady-killing charms."

"I haven't done anything," Adam said.

Ignoring Adam, Steve spread his arms to create room among the party revellers. He kicked the door and the fragile bolt easily separated from the doorframe to reveal two naked girls huddled together at the top of Adam's bed. Exposed, crying from both girls took an upsurge. By the time Adam had followed Steve and ventured into the bedroom, Jodie was just disappearing out of the window onto the narrow balcony that joined the rear of No: 35 with No: 36.

"Go away and leave me alone," she said. Any brief idea of following her, disappeared with the sight of Merle's corpse slumped, half off, half on the side of Steve's bed. The cobra, tattooed on his chest, was choking on the blood oozing from a wound in his neck. From the other side of the room, the whimpering girls, splashed with blood, remained huddled together on Adam's pillow. At their feet lay a blood stained carving knife. It was the same 'Norman Bates' type knife Adam had last seen buried in Merle's waterbed. And now, there it was again, obviously having been buried in Merle's jugular. Bloody garments of mixed gender lay strewn at the feet of the dead corporal. There was a warm smell of blood that covered everything, the rug, both of the beds, the furniture and especially the magnolia walls. Naked skin tones completed a carnage of flesh and blood.

T removed the knife from the bed and placed it on the bedroom dresser. She picked up Adam's blood-spattered quilt, wrapped it around the naked shoulders of the two, jabbering German girls and weaved her duvet sandwich through the crowded bedroom to the stairs.

Steve was leaning out of the window. "Come on girl, it's freezing out here." It was too. Jodie edged along the lip of the balcony, almost reaching No: 36. She was having none of it. Adam put some distance between himself and the window.

Following the absence of the duvet-clad girls, the flesh tone substitutes of Jeannie and Lincoln arrived, quickly followed by the tottering pair of Jimmy and Long, Tall Marie, obviously under the influence of too many funny cigarettes.

"What the fuck's going on, man?" Jeannie surprisingly, looked the most lucid of the newcomers. "Fucking hell, has anybody called an ambulance?"

No one answered but Adam indicated Merle's cobra and gave a brief synopsis. "No use calling an ambulance, she's killed him. We need to sort this place out before we call anybody. There's drugs everywhere."

Steve came in from the window. "No dice, man, she's a nutter."

"Are you just going to leave her out there?" Jeannie asked.

"You're welcome to have a go."

Jeannie indicated that she was wearing only a camisole. "That's very gallant of you, Steve." She pushed him aside and climbed out on the ledge.

"Chuffing hell." Steve went back to the window.

In admiration of his colleagues' tenacity, Adam poked his head out of the window at the same time as the next-door neighbour.

"What is happening here?" the man from No: 36 asked.

"Go away," Jodie said to him.

Steve leaned forward. "Sorry mate, she's a bit upset."

"Go away, all of you. I'm warning you." Jodie peered down into the street.

Jeannie held out a hand. "Come on love, come inside and talk about it."

Steve pulled at Jeannie's shoulder. "Careful, she was threatening to jump, before."

"Then for *Gott's* sake let her jump and we can all get some sleep." The neighbour slammed shut his window.

Adam agreed with the neighbour. He turned back into the room to the sight of Jimmy trying to hold up his giggling girlfriend. All the usually staid Marie had said since entering the room was "Jesus, Mary and Joseph, will you look at this mess?" Merle's corpse appeared unfazed by the surroundings.

Jimmy eased Marie away. "Is he really dead?"

"It's days like this makes me glad I didn't become a plumber." A short hysterical laugh escaped Adam. "Is he really dead? Well he's not looking a picture of health, is he? On his plus side though, have you noticed how the tail of that snake gives his dick a reptilian extension? Course he's frigging dead."

Jimmy edged Marie toward the door. "Then shouldn't we do something or call somebody?"

"I already have." T had returned. "I've phoned an ambulance. It'll be here in a bit."

"Oh bollocks!" Adam said. "What did you do that for, you silly mare? They'll send for the police as soon as they see this frigging mess."

"Don't call me a silly mare," T said. "Someone's been stabbed, you stupid bugger. We should've called the ambulance ten minutes ago."

"Christ on a dog-track!" Adam threw up his arms. "Am I the only one who can see the seriousness of this situation? We've got a dead body, a houseful of drugs, some idiot has called an ambulance and the cops will be right behind them." The drugs-devil was standing over Merle, with his ice-cream tray still about his neck. "Oy, Mr Whippy, might I suggest you get rid of that lot?" Adam went to the window. "For fuck's sake, Jeannie what are you doing out here in your vest? Forget about her, she's got her coat on. Come on, Steve, we've got to start clearing up downstairs."

Jodie was left to freeze on the balcony. The word 'cops' seemed to trigger a decision en block among the party revellers not to help with the clearing up. Collecting the various over-garments from around the house, in a matter of moments they'd gone.

Adam was wrong about the ambulance men sending for the police. The next-door neighbour had already done so. When they arrived, the clearing up was almost complete, all traces of drugs being burnt on the fire or flushed down the toilet. There was little time for anything else, including the putting on of clothing.

The four policemen organised everyone to sit where they could around the living room. Adam regarded the officer in charge. With his peaked cap pulled over his eyes, making his face invisible, he was little more than a uniform. Adam labelled him: *ah, ah, an SS Storm Trooper*. He checked to see if the SS Man was wearing jack-boots, he wasn't. The officer took his brogues upstairs to inspect the murder scene and presumably have a go at getting the forsaken Jodie back in the fray. Whatever he said proved successful. Five minutes later he came downstairs, steering the subdued mad knife-woman with one hand, while carrying in the other, a forensic bag containing the Norman Bates weapon.

"I don't believe it!" Steve said.

"Ve haf vays of making you come in off ze vindow ledge," Adam said for Steve's ears only.

The two girls, still wrapped in Adam's quilt, had stopped crying and presumably, as the chief witnesses, were giving their version of events to the police. Adam had no idea what they were saying. Amongst the pandemonium of broken English interrogation, various efforts of translation and garbled police radio messages, the SS Man established Jodie responsible for the knife attack. She snarled at Adam on the way out. Adding to the chaos, the ambulance arrived. One of the policemen led out the two German girls. Adam's quilt went with them.

Shouting came from upstairs. It was the ambulance men attending to Merle. The SS Man translated that the tattooed body was still alive. A flurry of activity broke out in transporting it downstairs and into the ambulance. The devil insisted that he should accompany his boss to hospital. Strangely enough the police allowed him.

Adam listened to the siren of the ambulance taking away the main protagonists. This left only the witnesses, the police, the mess upstairs and what Adam suddenly realised, somewhere in the house was a cache of drugs. Before the devil had departed, he'd not only abandoned his red stick-on horns but was also without his ice-cream tray.

Shit!

It was obvious that the SS Man and his compatriots were well out of their depth. They'd answered a call from a nosy neighbour and had come out expecting to deal with a rowdy party. Instead they were confronting a potential murder case. The unsuitability of the local police to the task was confirmed by the arrival of the Major League players, in the shape of three plain clothed policemen, accompanied by a couple more of the green uniformed brigade. This lot were even more sinister than the SS team.

"Hey up, the Gestapo's arrived," Adam said, again from the side of his mouth. The Gestapo ignored the people in the room and went straight upstairs, taking their measuring and photographic equipment with them.

This had to be the most exciting Christmas Wildflecken had ever seen. Then things really got going. The Military Police arrived, two of them. All British eyes steered toward Captain Thomas, who appeared to get lighter in complexion. Dressed only in his underpants, apart from his hair length, there was no reason Lincoln shouldn't be taken for a band member.

All questions concerning the activities at the time of the knifing, received short shrift. "We were in the kitchen" or "We were in our own bedroom". The MPs left.

The plain clothed Gestapo members came downstairs. The Chief smoothed a hand across his temple, careful not to disturb his blond, combed like a ploughed field, hair. He gave a swish of his long black raincoat and adjusted his small horn-rimmed glasses to give an officious stare at the group.

"That coat and them glasses makes him look like Himmler," Adam whispered to Steve.

"Himmler wasn't blond. Do you mean Goebbels?"

"Yeah that's him, Grimmballs."

The story of Merle gate-crashing with two girls and his vengeful wife turning up was retold for the sake of Herr Grimmballs. He approached Adam. "Why is your hair wet?"

"I was in the shower when it happened."

"You took a shower in the middle of the party? And why are you all without clothing?"

"I've told you, I was in the shower; them four were in their bedrooms."

"Their bedrooms? My colleague tells me there were others here, also without clothing."

Of course they were without clothing you, you stupid Kraut. "They were humping, you know, having sex. That's why his wife stabbed him."

Herr Grimmballs touched Adam's hair. "*Al-zoh*, that is why you are wet. This is a sex ritual, perhaps? And the knife is part of *diese* ritual, also, perhaps?"

Steve stepped forward. "What, you think all this is part of some bizarre orgy?"

Colin chuckled. "Maybe they're just jealous 'cos they weren't invited."

"Shut up Col," Steve said. "Look officer, we've told you what happened."

Herr Grimmballs glared at Steve.

One of the Green-uniform brigade was looking around the room, examining and sniffing the ashtrays. He said something to the SS Man. Everyone had to stand. Given most of the witnesses were scantily clad; the searching process was an easy one.

Visual evidence alone should've indicated that at least three of the party had been smoking something other than German Woodbine. There was still a strange smell coming from the burning logs. However the only police action was to tell the witnesses to sit again. Even the unsteady Colin was given the benefit of the doubt. All the witnesses were pronounced clean. All that is, apart from the black trouble-making roadie, whom they forced to stand on one side for special frisking.

Herr Grimmballs continued the interrogation. "*Was ist das*?" he asked, when handed Steve's kazoo.

"It's a kazoo," Steve answered.

Herr Grimmballs sniffed it. "*Es ist eine pfeife, ja*?" He sniffed it again. "*Fur* smoking drugs?"

An ironic headshake passed from Adam to Steve, who didn't even smoke cigarettes, these days.

"I abhor drugs," Steve said. "It's a kazoo, *musiker*." He reinforced his explanation with a little dance. The man had a puzzled look on his face. "Give it here." Steve started to cross toward Herr Grimmballs but stopped when two of the green policemen simultaneously went for their guns. The other witnesses all held their breath until Herr Grimmballs motioned to his underlings that it was okay. He handed the kazoo to Steve who put the instrument in his mouth and played a refrain of '*Deutschland, Deutschland Uber Alles*'. A stern look from the SS Man told the green uniformed section of the audience to close their gaping mouths. Sniggering petered from the witnesses, except Colin.

"Cool it Col," Steve said.

But Colin couldn't cool it. He took up the chorus of the German National Anthem. "Krautland, Krautland up your arse hole. Stick your Krautland up your arse." A bout of helpless laughter followed. Herr Grimmballs nodded at the green uniforms, indication enough for two of them to bundle the uproarious Colin out of the door. The big idiot was too helpless to put up any resistance.

"*Diese* inquiries will continue at the police station. Please put some clothing on." Everyone that needed to returned to their bedrooms to follow the affronted policeman's instructions.

One of the green uniforms accompanied Adam to his bedroom, presumably in case he disturbed the evidence around the scene of Merle's attack. The room looked a shambles. Adam glanced momentarily at the blood-spattered walls and Steve's blood soaked quilt but the empty ice cream tray lying on his own bare mattress grabbed his main focus. He scanned the room. Perhaps Devil Ringmaster had hidden the drugs in the drawers. He searched through each drawer on the pretence of looking for some clean socks. He found nothing, though what he would've done had he come across a stash of heroin, cocaine or whatever else was on the tray, he didn't know.

The officer came over and looked in the drawer. Adam quickly edged him aside, brought out his lost socks, finished dressing and set off to join the others downstairs. On the landing, the officer still tailing, Adam met Lincoln and Jimmy. Adam raised an eyebrow at Lincoln, dressed in some of Jimmy's clothes. Lincoln winked. The short arms and legs were obviously an alternative to his army uniform.

They joined the others in the living room. Herr Grimmballs and the SS man had gone. Ushered outside to an awaiting Green Maria with the words "*Polizei*" written in white on the side, the party filed into the back seats. Inside, Colin was no longer singing.

When the van doors locked on the eight members, Colin pulled up a sleeve to display a forming bruise. "One of them Kraut bastards has just walloped me with his truncheon."

T turned to Jeannie. "Should've been over his head."

"He hit me for nowt." It seemed unlikely that Colin hadn't deserved the walloping but deserved or not, Colin's treatment indicated the police were not to be taken lightly. The mood in the van became serious.

Marie sobbed. "My brothers will swing for you when they find out what you've done to me," she said to Jimmy. "You've drugged me. I've been molested by a smelly German policeman, and now I'm being carted off to prison like a common criminal."

"Well you can't say Jimmy doesn't know how to show a girl a good time," Adam said.

"Piss off Adam." Jeannie put her arms around the distraught Marie, giving solace to her newfound friend.

Jimmy sat apart, incapable of offering any comfort to his girlfriend. "We shouldn't have stayed," he said. "She hates anything to do with drugs."

"She could've fooled me," Adam said. "She's stoned out of her head." He ignored another glare sent from Jeannie. "Listen, if she really wants something to worry about, I think that baldy bugger might've stashed his gear somewhere in our house. If he has and the coppers find that lot, we'll *all* be for the high jump."

Wildflecken police were obviously incapable of dealing with crimes of such magnitude as homicide. The green van took the group the thirty miles to the much larger Fulda. Inside the police station, separated from the girls, the five men sat around an oblong, Formica covered table, in an otherwise empty room. There was little to look at but the mustard painted walls, every blemish made prominent under the bright fluorescent light.

"Anybody got any cards?" Adam asked.

Lincoln crossed his legs and grabbed his crotch. "Man, I need the john."

"My bloody arm's killing me." Colin exhibited his bruise again.

"What do you think they'll do to us?" Jimmy asked.

"Well I imagine Cold Tits is aptly named at this time of year," Adam said, pleased at coming up with such a clever joke at ten minutes to three in the morning. The cleverness was lost on the others. "Don't you get it? Colditz, Cold Tits?"

"And I thought I was going to miss the Two Ronnies' Christmas Show," Steve said. Adam gave up. It'd been a far too exhausting and eventful night to start defending his sense of humour.

Lincoln came and sat next to him. "What was it you were saying on the way here about the drugs?"

"That bald fella with the devil's horns, I found his empty ice cream tray on my bed."

"So you think the drugs are still somewhere in the house?"

"I looked everywhere but couldn't find 'em."

Steve was sitting next to Adam. "It's my guess he smuggled them out in Merle's ambulance."

"I guess maybe he could've." Lincoln got up and went to the door. "Man, do I need to go to the john?" He knocked.

"Piss in the corner." It was unclear how serious Colin's suggestion was.

Steve went and also knocked on the door. A green uniformed officer opened it. "My friend wants to go to the toilet." Steve performed a mime of urination.

"Yes I do, I need the toilet quite badly."

Adam sniggered at Lincoln's attempt at a posh English accent. Fortunately, the Kraut didn't distinguish it from Yorkshire. He took Lincoln out.

Twenty minutes later, the officer returned without Lincoln. "Adam Fogerty?"

Adam stood. "That'll be me, then."

"*Kommen Sie mit.*"

In the interview room, Herr Grimmballs was waiting for Adam. The underling stayed by the door.

A stroke of the ploughed blond hair accompanied the officious stare. "Please explain to me further what happened last night?"

Adam regurgitated his tale of a private party and a gate-crashing couple getting into a fight.

"And you do not know Frau Stoop?"

"Frau who? Never heard of her."

"Herr Fogerty, I should explain to you that Frau Stoop has given a statement saying that she spent the evening with you." Herr Grimmballs checked his notes. "And that you had an *arrangement* together. You were having an affair, perhaps. Was this *arrangement* to kill her husband?"

Oh shit.

"I didn't realise you meant Jodie. I didn't know she was called Stoop."

"Then you do know her?"

"Yeah, but I didn't know she'd come to the party. I was in the shower."

"And what was this arrangement that you had between you?"

"I didn't make any arrangement with her. The bird's off her chump. Her lift doesn't go all the way to the top, if you know what I mean?"

The policeman removed a white speck from the sleeve of his black coat. "No Herr Fogerty, I do not know what you mean. Please tell to me what you mean."

Adam decided to come clean. "Look, I didn't have any arrangement with Jodie; I had an arrangement with Merle, her husband."

"*Al-zoh*, Herr Stoop, the husband, who you also said you did not know."

Adam was squirming a little under his bravado. "Well okay, yes I know them both."

"And what was the arrangement between yourself and Herr Stoop? To kill Frau Stoop?"

"No, I didn't arrange to kill anybody." Adam momentarily closed his eyes, silently pleading to be believed. He decided to come cleaner. "Merle asked me to keep his wife out of the way because he had another girlfriend. Surely you can understand that?"

"And you obliged him, yes?"

"Well yeah, course I did."

Herr Grimmballs checked his notes. "For what reason?"

"Eh? What do you mean for what reason?"

"For what reason would you oblige Herr Stoop in keeping his wife occupied?"

Is this bloke stupid or what? Well, I was hoping to shag her. Perhaps not.

Adam quickly weighed up the consequences of becoming even cleaner. He did have the option of becoming squeaky clean by telling all about the drugs, but he thought he'd wait until the officer chose to mention them first.

"Well, Herr Fogerty? What did you get from Herr Stoop?"

"I didn't get anything. She was just a friend that's all."

Herr Grimmballs' index finger ran up and down the notes, several times. This was looking bad. Jodie could've tried to drop Merle in it by confessing anything into those papers. The officer surfaced and looked over his horn-rimmed glasses that'd fallen down over his nose. "How long have you been in Deutschland, Herr Fogerty?"

"About four months."

"And which places have you wisited during your time here?"

"Wisited?"

Herr Grimmballs scowled.

"Erm, I've been to Garmisch, Schweinfurt, Hanau and now Wildflecken." Adam was trying to work out the line of questioning.

"Have you been to a willage of Kloppenheim?"

"I don't think so." Adam answered truthfully and without correction.

"I have from our records that someone with your name and your description, has terrorised a neighbourhood there. And that you were in police custody before for this." Adam tried to decipher the information. "It would not be too difficult to check your identity." Herr Grimmballs pushed his glasses up on the bridge of his nose.

Shit, the night at Heike's.

"I didn't terrorise anybody. I just had a fight with a girlfriend's father."

"Ah, so you were violent on that occasion also?"

"*I* wasn't violent. *He* beat *me* up."

"You were given a deportation warning, yes?"

"Please, I haven't done anything wrong."

The door opened and another officer's head appeared.

"Excuse me one moment, Herr Fogerty." Herr Grimmballs collected his notes and they went, leaving Adam alone with the underling guarding the door. He sent a half-hearted smile over to the officer. The man in green parried with a stern stare.

The black raincoat swished back through the door. "Herr Fogerty, I will now be going from my duty. But before I go, do you have anything to add about the arrangement you had with Herr Stoop? Did he offer you payment, perhaps?"

"No, he didn't offer me anything." Adam's concern deepened with his confusion. "Is Merle okay? Is he dead or what?"

"No, he is not dead but he is serious. He has lost much blood. Are you anxious from this?" Herr Grimmballs made some further entries to his dreaded notes. Adam felt the veneer of his bravado being rubbed away to reveal him squirming in the chair.

"No, I'm not anxious. Can I go back and join my friends, now?"

"I'm sorry you must wait further. Your friends have been released."

"What! They've gone?" Concern deepened further.

"Yes, they have gone. They have been taken back to Wildflecken. I have a colleague who wishes to speak with you later. I suggest you sleep now." Herr Grimmballs patted the tabletop, as though suggesting it as a pillow.

"Oh cosmic. Donkey shite." The words slipped from Adam's mouth out of habit.

"*Bitte?*" The man did not appreciate the pun.

Adam thanked him correctly. "*Danke shon.*" The two officers left him to his timber resting-place.

Adam awoke later to the sound of his own snoring. He adjusted the crick in his neck and was trying to get back to sleep when he sensed he was no longer alone in the interview room. He sat up to face three men. His focus pulled toward one with a blond crew cut. The man, early forties, sporting an unbuttoned, blue double-breasted suit and gaudy tie, came to sit at the table and smiled.

"Mr Fogerty, I'm Lieutenant Lance Robinson and this is my colleague, Herr Director Vogel." He indicated the prospective bank manager over by the door. The third man, who was not introduced, was obviously just an ordinary policeman. Adam hastily tried to re-assemble his faculties. His first problem, after remembering his whereabouts, was to work out why the man he was now facing in this German police station was speaking with an American accent. The man solved it. "I'm from the US base at Wildflecken. I work for the Military Police."

"Hiya," Adam said.

"We understand you may be able to help us with a 'domestic argument' concerning one of my soldiers." The man visually indicated quotation marks around the words domestic argument by raising the two fingers of each hand, as if miming rabbit ears. Adam couldn't help seeing the man wearing these ears as he retold yet again his story of the private party. This time he admitted knowing Merle and Jodie.

"So what time did you arrive back at your house?" the lieutenant asked.

"I don't know, somewhere between ten and eleven."

Herr Vogel stepped forward. "Have you ever been in trouble with the Police?" The immaculate 'bank manager', also in his early forties, was German. Adam followed the line of the pinstripe down to his polished black shoes.

"I wasn't in trouble with the Police. I just had an argument with a girl's father." He carefully avoided the word 'fight'.

"I am talking about in England. Have you ever been in trouble with the Police in England?"

"No," Adam said. "Please, what is it that you think I've done? Why am I here?"

"Well, we know you ain't no Bader Meinhoff." The lieutenant gave a hearty laugh but Adam didn't see anything funny. The lieutenant collected himself. "However, one of my men is dying in hospital and you seem to know all about it."

"I don't know any more than I've already told you," Adam said.

"Have you ever been involved with drugs, Mr Fogerty?" Vogel asked.

"Me? No." Adam felt secure in his lie as all previous contact with drugs was buried deep in his past. Surely they hadn't delved that far.

"Did you ever see Corporal Stoop with any drugs?" the lieutenant asked. Adam could've answered honestly that he'd never seen any drugs in Merle's possession but the words wouldn't come out of his mouth. He just shook his head.

"Did you see anyone else with drugs?" Vogel asked. "When you got back to the party, perhaps?"

The lieutenant raised a hand at his German colleague, suggesting the questioning be left to him. "People must've been smoking and drinking. Maybe a few joints were being passed around?"

Oh shit, they've found the contents of the ice-cream tray. The Voice of Reason appeared on his shoulder. *Well so what? They can't link that to you. You weren't even at the party*. Adam slapped a palm on the table. "Look, why don't you give me a blood test? Then you'll see that I haven't taken any drugs." *Well done*! The Voice on his shoulder pumped a fist.

"Mr Fogerty, we're not really interested in whether or not you've taken drugs," Lieutenant Robinson said. "But we do know that Corporal Stoop is the local drugs baron round here. I'm just trying to establish if this attack has anything to do with his narcotic activities."

"If you knew that Merle was involved with drugs, why haven't you arrested him?" Adam asked.

The lieutenant leaned forward. "If he doesn't die on me first, I intend to do just that." The coldness of his tone was enough to send the Voice on Adam's shoulder slinking off into a corner. The lieutenant stood up straight. "Meanwhile, we've got you. And we're sure if you try real hard, you could come up with something that will help us put a stop to Corporal Stoop and his organisation." He stepped aside.

Vogel took his place, like a bicycle team pursuit rider taking over the pacing. "You would not wish to find yourself being deported."

Adam had come as clean as he could. They already knew there were drugs in existence. He knew nothing of Merle's business activities. He had nothing to trade. Then he had an idea. "I don't know anything about Merle or his drugs, if I did, I'd definitely tell you. But if I tell you about something else, will you let me go?"

Lieutenant Robinson buttoned up his jacket. "Now that depends on what you have to tell us." He and Vogel sat opposite.

Adam hesitated before committing himself. He tried to read the American's face. "Well, you might be interested to know one of our group, which you brought in, isn't in the band. In fact he's not even English, he's American, one of your lot, an American soldier. He doesn't even look like he's in a band. He's got short, back and sides." At first there was no reaction from either the American or the German. Then they looked at each other, then back to Adam, as though seeking more information. Adam obliged. "He's called Lincoln, Lincoln D Thomas. He transferred here from Hanau. He's Black, for god's sake and he's a captain. That should make him easy to find. Can't be too many of them in Wildflecken, eh?" Adam's attempt at laughter shrank. Again there was no reaction from the interrogators. "Look, he was at the party. He's a soldier so he must know Merle better than I do. I'm just a musician and I've only been here for a few weeks. If anybody knows about the drugs, it's going to be Lincoln." Adam waited to see if his seeds had fallen on fertile ground. "Well, can I go?"

Suddenly, the seeds all sprouted at once. "Okay, you can go for now," Lieutenant Robinson said. The interrogators both rose from their seats in unison. There was no further discussion on the drugs subject. Adam didn't prompt any.

Despite having been stranded in Fulda, without money, thanks to some lucky hitch-hiking, Adam was back in Bahnhof Strasse by early morning, albeit with the threat of deportation still circling vulture-like over his head. He pushed open the broken door to his bedroom to find Steve asleep on a bare mattress. With no quilt himself, Adam had little choice but to do the same. He slumped on the bed, fully clothed. Neither the cold nor the bloody reminder of the red graphitised wall could prevent him from achieving a comatose state in a matter of minutes.

He was still tired when Steve shook him awake in the late afternoon but the interruption was a welcome relief. He'd been having a nightmare about Messrs Robinson and Vogel. The American and German interrogators had him hanging upside down outside his bedroom window, trying to extract the whereabouts of the narcotics. The lieutenant and the director had joined forces with the SS Man and Herr Grimmballs. All four of them turned into

T's Bird Gods. They were about to fly him to their nest when Steve's intrusion frightened the birds away. Adam had expected Steve to wake him in time for work later that evening but Steve's disturbance was for another reason.

"Ace, there's someone here to see you."

Adam checked his watch. "Who is it?"

"Come downstairs and see. You'll like it." Steve went to the door.

"Hey Steve, don't you want to know what happened to me, last night? I could be doing ten years hard labour."

"Stop being so melodramatic. Come on."

"Donkey shite to you too. Glad to see you're showing your usual concern. Where's Jeannie?"

"In bed."

"Is Lincoln with her?"

"No, he went to the toilet in the police station and never came back. We thought he must've been kept with you."

"He wasn't with me." Perhaps Lincoln had been in Fulda all night after all. The Voice of Reason came out of hiding. Adam had done the right thing grassing on Lincoln. The police must've known about him all along. There was no point in both of them carrying the can. Even Lincoln himself would understand that.

"Everyone's in bed," Steve said. "Come on, hurry up? Your surprise is waiting. Oh, I've got a couple more surprises, as well, later." He beamed a look, not quite the 'silly grin' but one that Adam recognised as excitement.

If Steve said Adam would like the surprise waiting for him downstairs, then it was definitely worth getting up for.

"This is Gabi." Steve introduced the tall auburn girl, standing in the middle of the kitchen. "She's brought your continental quilt back." Steve indicated the flowered bundle by the chair. The scouser was right, Adam did like his surprise. She was very tasty.

Adam assembled the jigsaw. *But of course*! It was one of Merle's naked German frolickers, last seen weeping off into the sunset. A black mini dress drew attention to her long shapely legs.

"Sorry, I didn't recognise you at first, with your clothes on." True or not, Adam's insensitive quip obviously embarrassed the girl, who didn't say anything but visibly blushed. "Whoops sorry, I wasn't thinking."

"I come to return to you your things," the red-faced girl said. "And to say thank you to the girl who helped us."

"T's fast asleep," Steve said. "I tried to wake her but she's dead to the world."

"Please tell to her thank you." Gabi stood for a moment, looking awkward.

Adam bounded toward the kettle. "Do you want a coffee or something?"

"Oh *ja*, for sure," she said.

Steve got three cups from the cupboard. Adam grabbed them and put in the coffee. "That was a hell of a night, last night."

"*Ja*, for sure."

"We don't really know what happened," Steve said.

"I don't know either. The girl comes into the bedroom and goes crazy." Gabi threw up her hands. "When Merle lets her into the room, he turns his back and she pushes the knife into his neck." Gabi gave a demonstration.

"She was his wife," Steve said.

"Yes I know that now but I did not know he was married when we meet." Gabi blushed. Steve's comment had obviously made her embarrassed, again.

Adam found it most endearing. "How do you come to know him?" he asked, though his curiosity wanted to ask what she was doing having a threesome with an American corporal. And more to the point, did she fancy another romp with a pair of British giggers?

"We only meet Merle since a short while ago," she said. "He invites us to the party. We smoke a lot of dope and before we know it, boom! We are in the middle of all this." Adam understood literally what she'd said but her phrase created a different mental picture of her 'being in the middle of all this'. "Can I perhaps collect our clothing? We are leaving them in the bedroom."

"I think the police have taken your clothes." Steve finished making his own coffee.

"Oh," she said. "Can I perhaps please use your bathroom?"

"Yeah, certainly." Steve's gushing was just too much. "It's upstairs, second on the right, but you probably know that already, don't you?"

Adam waited until she was out of earshot at the top of the stairs. "Would'ja?"

"Deffo."

"I'dje as well. Do you think she might like to see our bedroom, now that all the dead bodies have been cleared away?"

"You never know."

"She's left her coffee." Adam seized the cup of opportunity. "I'll take it up to her. Like you say, you never know."

"You're unbelievable."

Adam grabbed his quilt and took Gabi's coffee upstairs. However, his intention to lure his prey into the bedroom became redundant when he reached the top of the stairs. She was already in there. He peered round the broken door to see the German on her hands and knees, poking under Steve's bed. "Have you lost something?"

She jumped to her feet. "I erm, came in from curiosity." Her hesitation made her sound slightly suspicious. "I thought perhaps our clothing might be here." Adam looked to the bare floorboards where she'd been kneeling. "*Al-zoh*," she said. "I dropped my medication, you understand?"

"Oh right." He didn't understand at all why she'd be taking tablets in his bedroom. "Have you got a headache?"

"Oh no." She gave an embarrassing little giggle. "It is my medication for contraception."

"Oh right, your contraceptive pill."

Her eyes shot downward. She swooped and picked something from the floor. "I have it." She immediately put the pill in her mouth. He proffered the coffee, which she took without so much as a *danke* and took a gulp.

Adam checked his quilt and threw it on the bed.

"I have it cleaned but cannot take away the blood."

"Steve says the police have got your clothes." Maybe if he showed a touch of concern it might get his plan back on course. "What a night, eh? Were you and your friend alright?"

"My friend Ulrike and I are in the hospital since long time."

"Oh Ulrike, so that's your friend's name is it?" Adam looked at his bed, trying to remember the face of the naked blonde. "I've been in the police station all night."

"We are also talking with the police."

"Are you both from Wildflecken?"

"No, we are from Fulda."

"Oh, that's where we were taken."

She pushed her half empty cup back toward his chest. "I must go now."

"I thought you wanted to go to the bathroom?"

"*Ja*, I go already?"

He was sure she hadn't had time to use the toilet before he'd got upstairs but she was on her way before he'd time to query this. "Hey, why don't you and Ulrike come over and see us play?" He chased after her. "We're in the band who play up on the base."

"Really?" She became suddenly interested, on the bottom stair. "But I do not think we can come on the American base."

Shit, she was right. It was difficult for Germans to get on the base. Here was a girl who was daring enough to go for a threesome, she'd just taken her contraceptive pill and she was about to get away. "Well perhaps me and Steve could take you two out sometime?" He made a final attempt to keep hold of the slippery catch. She smiled. He felt the line go taut.

"*Ja* okay, for sure," the catch said. "I will talk with my friend Ulrike. Do you have something for writing? I will give you my number." He produced a pen and a piece of scrap paper quicker than a close up conjurer. He checked the number before folding it carefully then popping it into his breast pocket. He tapped his breast twice to confirm that the catch was safely in the keep-net. It was now okay to say their good-byes.

He waved her off and came back into the room. "Fit or what, Stevo? Gorgeous legs, all the bumps in the right places."

"Really? I didn't notice she had varicose veins."

"Daft bastard, I mean, you were right. She was a tasty surprise."

"I've got another one. I've found the bald fella's drugs."

"You've what?"

"Yep, all of them, everything on the ice-cream tray, I think."

"Where were they?"

"Under my bed. He stashed 'em in T's bird box."

"Bird box? What bird box? Why has T got a bird box under your bed?"

"Not that sort of bird box, not for feeding sparrows and shit. I'm talking about T's Juju Birds. Yeah, that's the other thing. I found T's statues. Colin didn't burn them. He buried 'em outside in the bunker, under the logs."

"Logs? What bloody logs?"

"You mustn't mention this to Colin or T. I haven't told her yet. I found them yesterday. I was trying to tell her at the party but her and Colin were fighting all night. Then he got stoned."

"Steve what are you on about?" Adam tried to rearrange the words 'juju', 'logs', 'bird box' and 'sparrow shit' into a well-known phrase or saying. "You're not making any sense."

"I found the statues but I didn't tell T. I was worried that if she found out what he'd done, they'd end up rowing and she'd threaten to leave the band again."

"What about the drugs? How come the cops didn't find them?"

"I think we've been lucky. They obviously missed them. I hid the statues under the bed. They'd been dumped on the floor. The box was pushed right to the back."

"I'd like to take issue with the word, 'lucky'. So let's do a quick bit of stocktaking, here. We've got you and we've got a cocktail of drugs. Why do I get the feeling this is all going to end in tears?"

"Look, Adam—"

"No, don't answer that. I don't want to hear any more about bird boxes or drugs. I need a clear head to think about all this. I'm off back to bed for a couple of hours. God, look at the state of this place."

With a head-clearing sleep and the prospect of taking out the two Germans, Adam had to admit that the vista looked brighter. It remained so until after the first set when a gust of inevitability blew three American soldiers over to the 'Images' tables.

"Excuse me," the bald spokesman said, "but I had to exit from your little get together in a bit of a hurry last night and I left something at your house." Although fully dressed and minus his horns, his baldpate was as distinct as his rich, ringmaster's voice. Except maybe to Colin; who was his usual genteel self.

"And who the fuck are you?"

"I'm a friend of Merle's. You may remember I was at your party, last night. I was just wondering if you'd found my property. If so it would be advisable for you to let me come by and collect it."

Colin stood, knocking over his chair. "And what fucking property would that be?"

"Hey cool it man, if you're looking to play hard-ball, we can play." The bald man indicated his two oversized compatriots. He picked up Colin's chair and smiled at him. "Look, in the middle of all that messy business with Merle's wife? I had to get rid of some things. I'm sure you know what I'm talking about. I put them in the box, under the bed."

"Box, what box?" Colin asked.

A moment of recollection passed through Adam's mind, mustn't tell Colin or T about the box, or was it the sparrow shit?

"We don't know owt about any fucking box," Colin said. One of the henchmen clenched a fist.

Steve was sitting in his usual place, on the next table with Adam, T and Jeannie. He stood. "It's okay Colin, I know what he wants." He approached the ear of the bald man. "Sorry pal, my friend was a bit wasted last night. He probably doesn't recognise you." He motioned Colin to sit. Colin did so. Steve took the arm of the bald man and edged him away from Colin's table. "Sorry, but if you're looking for your drugs, I'm afraid the cops have got them."

"Say what! Are you sure?" the bald man said.

"Yeah," Steve said. "We were all arrested and taken to Fulda."

The henchman unclenched his fist to grab the bald man by the arm. "So what do we do now, if the Kraut cops have got the merchandise?"

"Cool it Larry." The bald man plucked Larry's hand from his sleeve.

Adam decided to get in on the act. "It wasn't the Krauts. It's one of your lot. He's got your drugs. And I'm the one who's getting stuffed for it."

"What do you mean, one of my lot?" the bald man asked.

"I mean an American. He's had me locked up all night, quizzing me about your drugs. He's called Lieutenant Robinson."

"Do you mean Lance Robinson?" The name had obviously caused a decibel of recognition with the bald man.

"That's exactly who I mean, Lieutenant Lance Robinson, a right snidey bastard."

Larry grabbed the bald man's arm again. "Is he talking about Billy Whizz?" He turned to Adam. "Are you talking about Billy Whizz?"

Adam looked to the bald man. "Billy Who?"

The bald man held up a hand at Adam. "What did the lieutenant want?"

"He just wanted to know where the drugs came from. I didn't know anything. They let me go, eventually. I think he was just happy to confiscate the stuff." Adam shared a concealed smirk with Steve before turning back to the bald man. "Why do you call him Billy Whizz?"

"I'm real sorry to have bothered you folks. Come on boys. We'll let these people get on with their business."

Steve jumped in before the American party exited. "Sorry we couldn't help you. Was the stuff worth much?"

"Oh, only about five freaking grand," Larry said.

For a brief moment the bald man showed a glimmer of annoyance at Larry but he quickly readjusted. "If you'll excuse us, come on, Larry. Ladies!" The bald man's politeness was astounding.

Adam stifled a laugh and threw a wry smile across to Steve as the Americans walked away from the table.

Steve didn't contain his merriment any longer than they were out of earshot. "Five grand!"

"What the hell was all that about?" Colin asked.

"You've got the drugs, haven't you?" Jeannie said.

"Might have," Steve said. "Five grand!"

"What are you gonna do with 'em?" she asked.

"What I'm not going to do is give them back to that lot."

"I thought you said the cops had the drugs?" Jimmy said.

"Keep up, Jimmy, lad," Adam said.

T threw a solemn card on the deck of joviality. "I hope you two know what you're doing."

"It's their business. Leave them to it." Colin tried to engage T with his eyes. "We don't want to know nowt."

"T's right, you know, Steve. The fact those yanks know this Lieutenant Robinson, or Billy Whizz, or whatever they call him, it does confirm he's not the sort of bastard I'd want to piss off."

Steve laughed and gave Adam's cheek a couple of pats. "Stop worrying, Ace. This Billy Whizz doesn't know we've got the gear, does he?"

For the rest of the evening, Steve dispensed his soundman duties, wearing his excitement like a rosette. But after the gig, he was nowhere around. "Where is the Peruvian pillock?" Adam asked.

"He went to collect a spare duvet from the army stores," Jimmy said. "He's humped it back to the digs to catch up with some sleep."

Adam got back to the digs. Steve was not catching up with his sleep; he was sitting up in bed, staring at dozens of small packages laid out in front of him, littering his new quilt.

"There it is, five grand." Steve indicated the illicit substances. "I suppose that'll be dollars, won't it?" Adam was familiar with most of the assorted goodies that lay between Steve's legs, a variety of readily measured doses: bags containing pills, hemp, marijuana, bags of white crystals, and a few smaller bags of brown powder. He knew that the reformed junkie was even more of an expert.

Adam recognised the glazed expression in Steve's eyes. "I'm not sure this is a good idea. I don't think you should have anything to do with this shit. You don't want to start all that again, do you?"

Steve dismissed Adam's appraisal of the situation and picked up one of the bags of brown powder. "You don't need a reason to start, you need a reason not to, and I've got plenty."

"But Steve, you'll understand my concern. You're sitting there with a lapful of free drugs."

"The first hit is always free. I'm not gonna snort the stuff, or stick it in my arm, I'm gonna flog it for five grand."

Adam undressed for bed. "It's only worth five grand if you can find somebody to buy it for five grand."

"Well, we can get something for it."

"We?" Adam smirked. "The Lone Ranger sees thousands of Indians on the horizon and he says: 'We might be in a bit of trouble here, Tonto.' Tonto looks at him and says: 'What's this *we* shit?'" Adam left for the bathroom. While he was brushing his teeth he contemplated the state of affairs concerning his buddy and the drugs. Maybe the best way to remove temptation out of Steve's lap was to get the stuff sold as quickly as possible.

When Adam returned from his ablutions Steve was under his new quilt and the drugs were gone from the bed. "Okay Kemo Sabe, I'll help you get rid of the gear."

"That's awfully good of you." The quilt muffled Steve's reply. He brought his head from under the covers. "Listen, don't do me any favours."

"I'm not trying to do you a favour. You might be right. Why shouldn't we make a bit of money? It could be just like the old days: sex, drugs and rock & roll."

"Sex, drugs and rock & roll? You've got to be kidding haven't you? I've given up taking shit, I've given up singing and as for the other; I might as well have given that up for all the shagging I do these days."

Adam switched off the light and got into bed. "You're gonna be sorted on that front, any day soon, once you get stuck into that Ulrike." He heard Steve settle.

The new quilt rustled again. "Why am I getting stuck into Ulrike and not Gabi?"

Adam sat up and peered through the blackened room toward Steve's voice. "Because etiquette suggests that as I've done all the work, I get to choose."

"I thought you might say something like that. I don't even remember what this Ulrike looks like."

"You've seen her tits and her bare arse, what more do you need to see? It'll be just like a blind date, won't it?"

"Why don't we let the girls choose for themselves?"

"Because I've got the telephone number. Now get some frigging sleep, you ungrateful get."

12 T's Adventures: Wildflecken Dec '76.

I Wish It Could Be Christmas Every Day.

Although T had agreed to a festive truce with Colin, Christmas dinner in Wildflecken was proving a sorry affair. She wiped her greasy hands on her apron.

Adam sat at the dining table. "I'm not having a go at you, T; you know I absolutely love your cooking. I just thought we'd be having turkey for dinner."

"Adam, we all discussed this. Colin doesn't like poultry."

"I know and I agreed to have lamb but this is funny looking lamb."

The events leading up to Christmas Day had left little time for T to fit in her Yuletide shopping. By the time she discovered that eating lamb in southern Germany was the equivalent of eating horse in northern England, it was too late. A replacement dinner from the only two shops in the Wildflecken outpost had to be found. With only Christmas Eve to do this, they were sitting down to a meal of spare ribs done in Chinese sauce with mashed potatoes and sprouts. Steve and Colin joined the table for this gourmet feast, T allowing a kiss on the cheek from her estranged husband.

Jimmy, Marie and Jeannie had accepted Lincoln's invitation to Christmas dinner in the officer's mess. The captain hadn't been heard from since his mysterious disappearance into the Fulda police station toilet and as he'd made the invite before Merle's party, they'd set off not knowing whether or not they'd be welcome.

"Well, they haven't come back yet." Since they'd left, this was about the fifth or sixth time that Adam had suggested they might've been sent home.

"Who gives a stuff?" Colin held up an impaled sprout. "We weren't invited, so he can stick his officers' mess up his arse."

Aside from the situation between T and Colin, there was a lack of Christmas spirit around the dinner table. She hoped it wasn't the disappointment of the dinner.

Steve came to her rescue. "Those ribs were bloody gorgeous, girl." He picked the residue from his teeth. T smiled. Her efforts hadn't been in vain. Dinner wasn't such a disaster after all. She set about clearing the table, despite there being no particular rush. Although it was almost 3:00pm in England, it would need a television aerial with an immaculate reception to tune in to the Queen's Speech, which was T's usual Christmas Day practice. Having no television at all, they were in for a day of "ennui", to say the least. She would've said this to the lads but having only recently learnt the word from one of her books, she kept her pondering to herself for fear of being thought a clever-clogs. In the Queen's stead, Colin discarded John Denver and placed an Elton John album on the turntable. He obviously thought he was being considerate by not foisting the four-eyed whinger on everyone but the look on the other two faces suggested there wasn't much in it.

"Cosmic." Adam handed her his plate and then also began his teeth cleaning. "Thanks T. I take it all back; that was really tasty."

"Yer it was." Colin joined in with the dental exercise before adding a log to the already roaring fire.

She acknowledged his thanks, finished clearing away and segued into the washing-up and pondering. Of course, the real missing ingredient of Christmas had nothing to do with the Queen's Speech, it was children. As with every Christmas since her wedding day, she envisaged with relish the time when tidying mountains of wrapping paper might fill her Yuletide mornings. However, this was the first Christmas she'd had the words 'You can forget having kids, ever', reverberating inside her head. She dropped the thought into the bowl of dishwater and poured it down the sink. It was Christmas day, not worth spoiling it for the others. Anyway, having Steve and Adam was like having a couple of kids around the place. *What am I going to do to keep them occupied all day*? "Why don't you lads have a game of cards or something?" she called.

"Good idea," Steve said. "I've got half a bottle of whiskey upstairs. I don't mind donating it to the pot."

"I know where it is." She laughed to herself when she heard Adam knock over a dining chair in his eagerness. He was either desperate for a drink or frantically trying to get away from 'Crocodile Rock'.

She came from her kitchen, content to see the boys gathered around the dining-cum-card table. She settled back into a chair and dug into her Catherine Cookson. Adam poured a measure of whiskey, none of it having come her way.

Colin threw in a pair of fours. "Merry fucking Christmas."

"I thank you gentlemen." Steve scooped his winnings. The dollars flowed, keeping the children gleeful enough for her satisfaction. As it'd done over the previous couple of days, the conversation turned to Merle and the events surrounding the party.

"The bastard deserved it," Adam threw his cards on the table. "I'll stack my ace high."

Steve adjusted the order of his hand. "Ah well, if you treat women like he did, you can expect to get what you deserve."

"If you're bluffing again, *you'll* get what you deserve," Colin said. "I'll see you." Steve wasn't bluffing, he showed his flush. "Bloody Nora!" Colin flung his cards on the table.

"What does that shite mean?" Adam asked.

"What shite?" Steve collected his money.

"If you treat women like he did?" Adam said. "Is that another dig at me?"

"I just think it's ironic, he was a bastard to women and then Womankind dished out his punishment."

"Oh, we're not back on that voodoo bollocks again, are we?" Adam shuffled the cards. "Maybe it was that Lob On Goolie that stabbed Jodie's twat of a husband in the neck. I suppose it's your God of Destiny that's winning at cards. Tell the bastard, I want my money back."

"You're lucky she didn't stab you in the neck." Steve raised an eyebrow and gave the tilt of his head he did when trying to convey he was a man of mystique. "And listen, if you really think you're in complete control of what happens in your life, you need to wake up and smell the beans, man."

"Well, I don't think there's some silly Indian Chief, deciding what I should have for breakfast."

"What the hell are you two talking about?" Colin asked.

"Steve has this Peruvian Indian God." There was nothing unusual about Adam and Steve goading each other. "He's some ghost or sommat, isn't he? Goes around screwing things up for him."

"He's not a ghost," Steve said. "Look, just deal the chuffing cards."

"He thinks them juju statues crawled out from under his bed and told Jodie to stab Merle in the throat." Adam dealt.

Steve kicked Adam under the table. "Alright, you've made your point."

T stopped what little reading she was doing. *Under his bed?*

"Watch out, lads, it's the juju statues." Another kick. "Give over frigging kicking me, Steve."

T put down her book and glowered, first at Steve, then at Colin.

Steve got up from the table. "I'm really, really sorry T. I was going to tell you but I was waiting for the best chance."

Colin looked away at the logs in the fireplace.

She got up from her chair. "I don't understand. What's going on?"

Steve held out his hands in appeal. "Colin didn't burn your statues, did you Col? I've got 'em upstairs."

"You bastards," she said. "I wouldn't expect owt else from him, but I'm surprised at you, Steve. - 'Ooh, I wouldn't have expected soapstone to burn that well'. - I bet you bloody didn't."

"What no! I've only had 'em a couple of days. I found 'em. He hid 'em in the bunker, didn't you Col?" Colin was still looking into the fireplace. "Tell her, Colin. You were really upset, T. I didn't want to make things worse."

Colin glared at Steve. "Black twat!"

T approached Colin. "I suppose you think you're clever."

He drained the rest of the whiskey into his glass. "You started it."

"What do you mean, I started it? How the bloody hell did *I* start it?"

"You kicked me out, threatened to leave me, when you knew how upset I was."

"How bloody upset *you* were?"

"Are we playing cards or what?" Adam asked.

T spun around. "Why don't you just piss off?"

"Yeah, shut up, Adam," Steve said. "Your big mouth caused this, in the first place."

"Me? What have *I* done?"

She let go of a scream. "I don't bloody believe this. Christmas sodding Day and I'm spending it in a nut house with three selfish piss-heads." She picked up the empty whiskey bottle and brandished it at Steve. "Thanks for saving me a drink, by the way, after I made dinner." She grabbed her Catherine Cookson, went upstairs and threw herself on the bed. If she hadn't got out of Colin's way she might've done or said anything, yet she was still unsure what exactly she was most annoyed about. There was a knock on the bedroom door. It was Steve. "Here, the box is a bit grubby but they're okay."

She took out the statues and put them on the dresser. "Thanks."

"Sorry I didn't give them back to you straight away. I was waiting to catch you on your own."

"It don't matter."

"I couldn't really give them to you in front of Colin. I didn't want to—"

"Steve, it doesn't matter."

He came further into the room "T, I know Colin did a shit thing, lying to you like that but at least he didn't burn them."

"And your point is?"

"That means he must've intended giving them back at some point."

"Happen."

He went back to the doorway. "And I'm sorry about the whiskey, I hardly got any myself."

He left her sitting staring at her precious statues. She thought back to the day Colin said he'd burnt them. He obviously hadn't done it the day before, like he said. He must've had them with him in the bedroom all the time. Happen he hadn't overheard Jeannie. Oh well, she'd got them back now. Yet, as she tried to tap into her joy it seemed hollow. Funny thing is, after she'd thought she'd lost the three that Colin said he'd burnt, she'd thought instantly of Kim and wished she'd left them with her. Happen something was telling her she should have.

The telephone rang. "How you doing, babe? Merry Christmas."

She almost dropped the phone. "Good God, William! This is unbelievable."

"Bobby tells me you might be coming to Schweinfurt; that right, babe?"

"Er, I'm not too sure, yet. I can't believe you've just rung. It's uncanny. I was only thinking about you both, this very minute. William, I still feel bad about the way I left things with Kim."

"Listen babe, about Kim …"

T was staring at the Bird Gods. "You won't believe the trouble I've had with my statues since we left."

"You shouldn't bother none about all that."

"Happen they were right. Happen it was unlucky to split them up."

"About Kim—"

"Actually, you know what? I will come to Schweinfurt."

"You will?"

"If it's okay with Kim, I'd like to bring my statues. It was stupid taking them back. I want to make things right between us."

"Alright babe, if that's what you want to do."

"Can you ask her if that's okay?"

"Kim ain't here, right at this moment but I know she'd appreciate it."

There was a gap. "Right okay, I suppose I'll be seeing you soon then."

"Yeah, Bobby say he coming up to get Jeannie a week on Sunday."

"Okay." Another pause. *God, do you know what you're doing, Theresa*?

"So how's Christmas been for y'all?" he asked.

"I've had better."

"I was thinking about what I might like in my Christmas stocking and I thought, oh man, I wouldn't mind seeing you in stockings." He gave a laugh that could only be described as 'dirty'.

She checked her blushes in the mirror of the dresser. "Erm, right, I'll bring them down with Bobby."

"Yeah, I can't wait. You and me, we got unfinished business, right?"

"Sorry?"

A shadow cast across the door left open by Steve. It was Colin. "Is that your dad? Wish him Merry Christmas."

"Sorry, Kim, I've got to go. See you a week on Sunday." She hung up. *Sorry Kim? Why have I just said that*? "What do you want, Colin?"

"I came to say sorry."

"Sorry? It's a bit bloody late for sorry."

"I don't know what's got in to you, these days? You never used to be like this."

"What's got into *me*? Do you mean apart from all the shit I've had to put up with from *you*, all these years? I'll tell you what's got in to me. It's Christmas sodding Day. I should be at home, serving up stand-pie and Yule log, surrounded by kids and broken presents. Instead, I'm stuck in this godforsaken hole with a selfish piss-artist like you."

"Sorry, I didn't mean what I said about never having kids. I just meant we have to wait 'til we're ready, when we've got on our feet, a bit."

"Sod off Colin. You can't even stand up straight, never mind get on your feet." Colin gave a slight wobble as if to reinforce T's point. "Look, just bugger off back to your cards. I'm trying to read." She picked up her book.

"I'm doing my best, here, Theresa."

"Well, your best is shit, as usual."

"I think you need to calm down a bit, woman."

"Piss off." The mill girl on the front cover of Catherine Cookson thudded against the door, just as he staggered through it. T thumped both fists into the bed. It wasn't just that Colin's attempt at reconciliation was way off the mark. Even if it'd been a good attempt he'd be wasting his time. The anger just wouldn't go. She picked up the mill girl and threw her on the bedside cabinet, next to the telephone. That was another thing, what did William mean by "unfinished business"? Did he mean sex? No, he can't have. Why hadn't she mentioned that she and Colin were having problems? Maybe this trip to Schweinfurt wasn't such a good idea. She looked at the statues.

What the hell are you doing, Theresa? You've just given your Bird Gods away. You've only just got the buggers back.

It was too late for self-reproach. Besides, it was a chance to make things right with Kim.

A call from downstairs interrupted her tangled thoughts. It was Jimmy. "Come on Cinderella; get your glad rags on. You *shall* go to the ball."

The Christmas banquet was a huge success so Jimmy had been sent to fetch them; two cars waited. They were to come and join the evening festivities, namely, drinking the booze left over from the afternoon. "And there's shit loads of it," Jimmy said.

Adam came from the kitchen with a cup of coffee and sat in the armchair.

"What are you doing, Adam?" Steve asked. "Didn't you hear the lad? We're going to a party."

Adam remained where he was and sipped. "I think I'll give it a miss."

"Seriously, Adam, there's enough booze and grub to sink a battleship," Jimmy said.

"What about Lincoln? Is he there?"

"Course he's there," Jimmy said. "It was him who sent me down for you. Why, what's wrong with Lincoln?"

"Did you find out what happened to him, the other night at Fulda?" Adam asked.

"What other night?" Jimmy looked to the others. T shrugged.

The interrogation continued. "What about me, Jimmy? Did he say anything about me?"

"What like?"

"Like threatening to kill me, or anything?"

T looked from Adam to Jimmy but the lad merely returned her shrug. "No, he just said I should bring everybody up for a drink."

"Why would Lincoln want to kill you, Adam?" Steve asked.

"You heard; he doesn't," Adam said.

Steve hovered over Adam's chair. "You're up to something, Fogerty."

Adam ducked under Steve's curiosity and got up from the chair. "Right Colin, do you fancy getting stuck into this booze then?"

"Is a pig's arse pork?"

Adam offered a false smile to Steve then turned to T. "What about you, misery guts? Are you coming?"

"Course I am," she said. "It's bloody Christmas."

13 Adam's Sexploits: Wildflecken. Christmas '76:
Four Seasons.

"Merry Christmas, y'all." Lincoln greeted the group at the entrance to the officers' mess with handshakes. "What kind of a day y'all had?"

"Shit," T said." I haven't even had a drink yet."

Lincoln gave T's arm a stroke. "Let's see if we can make up for that here."

Jimmy proudly showed them into the Jackson Suite. One thing about officers, there always has to be exhibited extravagance in case of any mistake in distinguishing them from the rabble underneath. Flutes of champagne, plates of canapés and vol-au-vents floated around the large room above the medal clad, bottle green uniforms. In service of their betters, military underlings, spruced up for the occasion, wandered around supporting trays, with a variety of contents to supplement the feast, on which they'd gorged themselves earlier that day. Leftovers alone could've tabled another five banquets and Jimmy was right; there was 'shit loads' of booze.

Adam had evaded Steve's cross-examination about Lincoln. He'd enough unanswered questions of his own. Anxiety, over meeting up with the Black captain, was in a neck and neck race with Curiosity.

Given the way he'd welcomed them at the mess hall door, Anxiety faltered in the home straight. The convivial handshake suggested Lincoln was, after all, unaware he'd been 'grassed up'.

Steve stepped in. "What happened to you the other night?"

The panting Curiosity awaited Lincoln's answer.

"When was that?"

"The other night at the police station?" Steve grabbed a passing crabstick. "You didn't come back from the toilet."

"Oh, I get ya." Lincoln's eyes didn't even flicker in Adam's direction. "They just let me go. They wouldn't let me back in to see y'all."

Is that it? Have I been worrying myself sick over nothing? Except this didn't quite add up. A Black army captain comes to a drugs party. He evades arrest by masquerading as a British musician; yet it doesn't appear to interest the Military Police. Then why did they let Adam go in exchange for this information?

As the newcomers were settling into their drinks, Lincoln beckoned. "Hey Adam, please come with me. There's someone wants to meet you."

Anxiety and Curiosity were back on the racetrack. Lincoln took the bewildered Adam from the banqueting hall into a more select room. A dozen or so military hierarchy milled about. If the first was meant to indicate a separation between the wheat from the chaff, then this was obviously where they stored the premium barley. In here, the brass was shinier and the boundless wooden surfaces were more polished. The only two civilians were instantly recognisable as Jeannie and Marie, being chatted up by a couple of Top Brass. Adam ignored Jeannie's acknowledgement. He had other distractions. Where was Lincoln taking him?

Adam continued separating the faces from the uniforms as Lincoln led him across the parquet towards his goal. This time, coming up in the outside lane, Anxiety and Curiosity were overtaken as Fear pipped them to the post. The double-breasted suit and gaudy tie had been exchanged for a uniform but there was no mistaking. It was Lieutenant Robinson, alias Billy Whizz of the American Military Police Drug Enforcement.

"This is my friend, Lance," Lincoln said. "I believe you know each other."

"So, how you been since our last meeting?" The lieutenant straightened his already perfect tie.

"Hiya." Adam straightened his not so perfect worried brow. In his periphery vision, Jeannie confused the issue with a surreptitious shake of her head.

"Mr Fogerty? I asked how you've been."

"Eh? Oh yeah, okay, you know, Christmas and all that."

"Captain Thomas, would you excuse us? I'd like a private word with Mr Fogerty."

"Certainly." To Adam's surprise, the captain obeyed the lesser-ranked officer and went over to join Jeannie's group.

During his time in Frankfurt, Adam had attended a World Trade Fair. There, in the toy exhibition a Hungarian was trying to launch his new invention. It hadn't yet been seen in England, or anywhere else, as far as Adam knew. It was a little cube puzzle, the object being to line up the six sides of the cube with nine squares of the same colour on each side. Steve was the group member known for being good at puzzles but it'd been Adam who'd impressed his colleagues and the man by almost completing Rubik's brainteaser. Yet, maybe he needed the help of his buddy now because he couldn't fathom his position in this Lincoln/Lt. Robinson situation; there were too many missing colours.

"You were right Mr Fogerty; Captain Thomas was pretty easy to find." The lieutenant edged Adam away from the surrounding company and into a corner. "That is the same 'Captain Lincoln D Thomas' you mentioned, isn't it, the one who knows all about the drugs?"

There were a few possibilities. *It could be that Lt. Robinson has only befriended Lincoln because of my betrayal and now he wants me to confirm his guilt with a Judas kiss.* Or maybe it was nothing like that. Another colour turned into the wrong row in the Rubik's Cube.

"Have you found out any more information about Mr Stoop?" Lt. Robinson asked.

"How could I? He's still in hospital, isn't he? And I haven't seen Jodie. I don't know what's happened to her."

"I thought you had contact with Mr Stoop's friends? Didn't they pay you a visit?"

How could he possibly know that? Bloody hell, Lincoln.

"Yes, Mr Fogerty, I have my spies, everywhere. I believe a Mr Tait came to see you?"

"Do you mean the bald fella? He just wanted to know what happened at the police station."

"And what did you tell him?"

"I didn't know anything *to* tell him." The lieutenant's stare demanded more. "I told him that you knew all about their organisation."

"And what did he say about that?"

"He wasn't too happy about it. He knows you. He calls you Billy Whizz." Adam felt like he'd just snitched the class's nickname to a hated teacher.

The teacher ignored the snitching and placed a hand on Adam's shoulder. "Mr Fogerty, let me tell you what I want you to do for me."

Jesus, I hope this doesn't involve KY Jelly.

"Alan Tait, the bald man? I'd like you to make friends with him. I want you to infiltrate yourself into their drugs ring."

"That sounds a bit dangerous. Why on earth would I want to do something as daft as that?" The lieutenant merely smiled. Adam merely frowned. "You're going to tell me why, aren't you?"

"Same reason you informed on your friend, Mr Thomas; you wouldn't want my colleague, Mr Vogel, looking into your deportation order, would you?"

"Thought you might say something like that. I don't suppose I could get back to you on this?"

The lieutenant chuckled. "By the way, in case you were feeling bad about informing on your friend, Lincoln, I should tell you, Captain Thomas went to your party under my instructions. In fact, he came to Wildflecken under my instructions. He works for the Military Police."

Adam's mouth dropped open. The red, blue, yellow and orange squares fell into place. *Shit, Lincoln is a copper.* Adam looked over to Jeannie's group but no one was looking. "What is it you want me to do?" he asked.

"Tait's going to want to know why I'm interested in you. You tell him it's because you're a known English dealer. Enquire about buying some drugs. You will liaise with Captain Thomas and he will report your progress to me. Got that?"

"Think so."

"And I'm not gonna hang around waiting for you to make a deal, so don't get any funny ideas about stalling until it's time for you to go back to England."

"Course not."

"Okay, why don't you go and enjoy the party?" The lieutenant finally removed his hand from Adam's shoulder. Although free of his clutches, now that all the colours of the puzzle had been placed neatly in the right position, Adam wasn't in any party mood. He needed to get the hell out.

He avoided Lincoln and headed straight for the Jackson Suite. The number of guests had steadily built during his interrogation in the annex but he was able to find Steve within minutes. The daft Peruvian was performing a samba to Santana accompaniment, his partner, a bottle of green-coloured liqueur. "Get rid o' that," Adam said. "We've got to go."

An emerald dribble trailed from Steve's mouth down on his white sweatshirt. "Go where? I'm just starting to enjoy myself." He was oblivious to the stain on his mother's Christmas present.

Adam pulled him to one side. "I've just found out something about the drugs. If we don't get it sorted, we're in big trouble."

"Why, what have you found out?"

Adam checked over his shoulder then lowered his voice, trying to make the situation sound as grave as he felt it merited. "Lincoln is in the Military Police. They know we've got the drugs and we've got to get rid."

"Why, what has he said?" Steve took another green gulp.

"What has who said?"

"Lincoln?"

"Lincoln hasn't said anything but I've just been cornered by that Billy Whizz."

"Come on, Ace; it's Christmas chuffing Day. If he was going to do anything he'd have done it by now. He's just trying to scare you."

"Guess what; he's doing a grand job."

"He's not getting his hands on my five grand, I'll tell you that. Here, shurrup and have a drink." Steve forced his bottle up to Adam's mouth.

Adam took a swig without contemplating the contents. He coughed, splattering a green spray over the parquet floor. "What the frigging hell are you supping?"

"Crème de Menthe." Steve proudly displayed the bottle.

"You're frigging nuts." He left Steve dribbling on his mum's Christmas present and walked back to the digs alone.

Christmas Day was the only holiday for the group. Boxing Day evening would be back to work. The Christmas party at the officers' mess had revelled on until the early hours of the morning, so Adam had been asleep when the others arrived home. Everyone slept late. Steve, however, was already up and downstairs when Adam surfaced.

The scouser cupped his hands around his coffee. "I ain't half gorra throbbin' bobbin."

"I'm not surprised, with that shite you were drinking last night."

"You missed a knob-hot party. It was boss, man."

"In case you hadn't noticed, I'd just had my collar felt by Billy Whizz, the Laughing Policeman." Adam poured himself some coffee. "We've got to get rid of the drugs. He knows we've got them."

"He doesn't."

"Of course he does; that snidey bastard Lincoln was in the police van when I was explaining about the empty ice-cream tray. He even asked us about them in the cop shop."

"Yeah, but if you remember, I suggested the baldy bugger must've smuggled them out in Merle's ambulance."

"And?"

"According to Jeannie, Lincoln thinks that's what happened."

"According to Jeannie? Shit, Lincoln's not here now, is he?"

"No, Jeannie came home on her own. They had a Barney. She thought it was her irresistible charms that'd attracted him up from Hanau."

The week between Christmas and New Year passed quietly, by 'Images' standards. Steve and Jeannie had convinced Adam that neither the world nor his wife knew they had the drugs. Of course, this side issue was never going to prevent Adam from returning to his usual pastime. He'd telephoned Gabi. The number wasn't false, as Steve had predicted. So, the date was set for Saturday night, after the gig. Gabi and her friend, Ulrike had invited the British pair to a party at a club in Fulda. All other anxieties were placed in the drawer marked 'to be worried about later' in readiness for whatever the evening should bring.

A red leather mini-dress emphasised Gabi's height, when she stepped out of yet another orange Volkswagen to exchange seats at the gates of the US base. Adam obeyed his instructions and climbed in the back alongside the dress and Gabi's legs. Steve got in next to the blond driver. Gabi introduced her friend. Steve turned to the rear with a grin of approval, though Adam took it as a sign of smugness. Even through the darkness, Ulrike's pretty face radiated as she passed her smile across to the passenger seat. Adam ground his teeth. Even from the backs of their heads it was obvious, she and Steve had hit it off immediately. A plain leather coat and reserved hairstyle was in keeping with her conversation, unlike her stylish, auburn compatriot.

"*Al-zoh*, Steve, I am thinking: how are you now knowing Ulrike with her clothes on?" Gabi had the most raucous laugh.

"*Ruhig*, Gabi." Ulrike didn't appear to find it funny.

What had happened to the coy creature that brought back the quilt?

For just once in my life, why can't I find a nice girl? I'm not asking for a nun or even a librarian; just someone you wouldn't be ashamed to take home to your mother.

From inside his trousers, Cyclops made him consider otherwise. What the hell was he thinking? Gabi's revealing boldness was confirmation; this girl had been a willing participant in a triangular sex romp. Cyclops began to sense the possibilities of the night ahead.

Down boy, behave yourself. It's too early for that.

Adam shifted in his seat to make the one-eyed monster more comfortable. However, making the adjustment caused him to brush his hand along Gabi's naked thigh. Cyclops tried to poke his head through Adam's fly to see the flesh for himself. It was a relief to arrive in Fulda so the three of them could escape the cramped back seat.

The glitzy nightclub glared at them from the end of the street. Incongruous in its surroundings, the forefront of the club peeped out between a parade of shops and small offices. "What is this place?" Steve asked, as the foursome walked towards the lights.

"This is where we are both working," Gabi said.

"Oh, you work here, do you?" Adam momentarily pictured the pair in Bunny outfits, serving over priced cocktails.

Gabi, in high heels, sashayed along like a model, as opposed to Ulrike, who walked serenely in her flat shoes. "Yes, tonight is a *Weinachten* party for the employees." Ulrike was swinging Steve's arm.

"A staff party for Christmas?" Steve passed a nod back to Adam along with the interpretation.

"What do you do here, Ulrike?" Adam asked.

"I cook."

"You cook?" Adam's humourless laugh hit the octave of his voice. "What is it with this place? How come every fit bird in Germany ends up cooking in a nightclub?" The question was a rhetorical reference to Emma Virgilio. He turned to Gabi, who'd evaded taking his hand when they'd got out of the car. "Don't tell me; you're the glass collector." Gabi didn't have time to answer. They'd reached the club.

The pink neon sign read: *The Pussy Kat Klub*. The Englishness of the name hinted the club might be a haunt for American soldiers, enticing them the thirty miles or so up from the Wildflecken base. Two oversized penguin bookends guarded the entrance. One of the bouncers stepped forward.

A train-buffer palm pressed against Steve's chest. "*Entschuldigung, aber Sei koennen hier nicht rein.*"

"*Was ist los?*" Gabi asked. Although the conversation was in German, Adam could tell the irate protests of the two girls were having no effect on the immovable penguins.

"What's the problem?" he asked.

Gabi ushered the two boys away from the entrance. "He says it is a private party. You cannot come in."

"Well that's pissed on the fireworks," Adam said. "What happens now?"

He hoped she might say: never mind the party, let's go back to my place and touch belly buttons but she didn't. She merely said: "*Bloeder Hund*", and took Ulrike to one side to discuss tactics. Adam couldn't see the need for privacy considering they were speaking German. Gabi broke from the huddle and approached the buffer handed bouncer.

Ulrike came over to the boys and gave Adam's arm a stroke of reassurance. "She is going to reason with him. His name is Henri. He is not a nice man but he likes Gabi very much."

Shit, I hope he doesn't suggest fighting for her.

The reasoning appeared to be going well. Then the reasoning took an unexpected route when Gabi set off, hand in buffer, down the street with Henri.

"Where are they going?" Adam asked.

"I know not." Ulrike gave an uncomfortable smile. "Gabi is sometimes a crazy girl, don't you think?"

"I don't know what to think." Gabi became even more of a crazy girl when the eloping couple disappeared into a darkened alley between an estate agent's office and an optician's. "I don't get this." Adam craned his neck toward the alley. "Where the frigging hell is he taking her?"

Ulrike shrugged. Steve took hold of her. There was a two-minute spell of silence and snogging between the roadie and his cook.

The gooseberry perched himself on a rail surrounding the taxi rank. "What the bloody hell's going on?"

"Ulrike says they've gone to see the manager," Steve said.

"What? Tell Ulrike she's talking bollocks."

"Yes, I think so," Ulrike said. "She will ask him to let us in, perhaps." They resumed the snogging.

"Yeah perhaps," Adam said. *Perhaps she's giving the manager one as well.*

There was little to do but sulk. It was 1:00am and too far for a taxi ride to Bahnhof Strasse. He considered checking the alley but the thought of bumping into Mr Buffer Hands doing God knows what with Gabi kept him on his perch. It was quite simple, if they had gone to the manager's office, they'd come back through the main entrance.

Gabi and the dishevelled Henri emerged from the alley. The shivering girl wiped her mouth and approached the others. "It is good. We can go in now."

"I bet it was bloody good," Adam said. Henri's grin was as wide as the chest bulging under his penguin suit.

The inside of the venue was different to Adam's expectations. The neon *Pussy Kat* sign and the bouncers on the door led him to believe the club would be like one of the many Continental dives he'd played over the years, where your feet stick to the carpet. Contained in a homely ticket kiosk, a plump middle-aged woman chuckled a greeting to the girls.

"Who's that?" Adam asked. "Is that the Hun at the till?"

"*Bitte?*" Gabi said.

"Hun at the till? Attila The Hun, don't you get it? God, you Krauts have got no sense of humour."

From the tiny foyer, Gabi took them through a rabbit warren of dimly lit corridors, which led to a lively bar where, as expected, dancers crowded a corner disco floor. But not expected, around the room were private booths, each consisting of a red, velvet arced bench-seat surrounding a table. The most unusual aspect of the booths was their seclusion behind glass doors. "Summer Breeze makes me feel fine:" the Isley Brothers blew a spine shuddering reminder of Jodie's couch through the "Jasmine" of Adam's mind.

Dismissing the image of the knife wielding Jodie; Adam's eyes set upon a deep bra-less cleavage of an elegant, black evening gown, cut to the waist. The hostess ushered them toward a vacant booth. Adam ogled the wobbling breasts in the hope they might fight their way out of the dress. The teasing owner took the drinks order and closed Gabi's party into their seclusion, dampening most of the Isley Brothers.

Adam eased himself along the leather upholstery that backed the velvet bench-seat. From inside the booth, he could see that the seat was not a complete arc, but broken by a door space. He half expected a Roman Catholic priest to stick his head through and say: 'I've come to hear your confession, my son'. Not that he'd ever been in a confessional box but when June Roundhill, his one and only long-term sweetheart, used to mesmerise his early twenties with tales of Catholic redemption, the crimson velvet of the booth was how he imagined it. A sense of irony passed in the comparison between his life in those days and the one he currently led. He'd recently written to June in the hope of rekindling the stability of a steady relationship but so far there'd been no reply. June had met his mother many times.

I bet that Gabi's got a few things to confess.

Having discarded her leather coat, Ulrike displayed that she'd the body to match her face. The brown trouser-suit did her no favours but then she didn't need any. Under the red lights, she and Steve entwined. The chemistry between Adam and Gabi was obviously of a different mixture. He regretted the etiquette that'd granted him first choice of the licentious cow. "What was that business outside all about?"

"*Bitte?*"

"What were you doing with that doorman?"

"Ah Henri, I had to talk with him. I had to convince him to let us into the club."

"Talk to him? You must've done a lot of bloody talking. You were down that alley for ages."

"*Ja*, for sure," Gabi said. "He was very hard to convince."

"Hard? Yeah, he must've been."

The wobbling hostess arrived with the drinks. Adam's hopes for the popping out ceremony increased when she leaned across the table to hand him his lager.

It must be pure will power keeping them in there.

The intact hostess left, again closing them in behind the glass door. She hadn't asked for any money, nor had she written down the score on the beer mats, the way they usually did in such places. Adam shared a puzzled look with his buddy.

"Have you paid for these?" Steve asked Gabi.

"No, they are free. All drinks are free."

"Yo, bring on the dancing-girls." This was good news to Adam, who up to that point, feared the place looked a bit pricey.

"What's this door for?" Steve tried to open it but it was locked. Adam had been going to ask that very question prior to the distraction of the hostess.

Ulrike looked across at Gabi. Even beneath the red light her blushing was noticeable. "*Hast Du einen schluessel*?"

Gabi looked in her handbag and brought out a key as requested. "Would you like to see inside?"

"Why, what's in there?" Adam frowned at the girls, neither of which contained their childish tittering.

"Should I open it?" Gabi teased the key under Adam's nose.

"*Ja*, for sure," Ulrike said.

"*Entschuldige*." Gabi squeezed past Adam to get to the door. She opened it and switched on yet another red light. A silk covered bed dominated the tiny room. Adam looked across to Steve, whose eyebrows were stuck to the ceiling.

Adam's brow was in complete agreement. "Well, I don't have to ask what that's used for."

"No," Steve said. "But I'm dying to know who uses it."

"It is for the clients," Gabi said.

A suspicion began to grow in Adam that when Gabi had taken the bouncer into the alley, she'd only been doing what came naturally. "How come you've got a key to this room?" he asked her. "What did you say your job was?"

"Well I ain't no goddamn cook." Gabi said. Ulrike joined her in the subsequent raucousness. Adam tried to find a suitable reaction. His bemused smile didn't seem adequate. He considered himself broader minded than the average chap but the flagrant way in which Gabi had divulged her occupation had taken him aback.

"Oh, right then," was all he could muster in response.

"Does my work bother you?" Gabi asked.

"No, not at all. Live and let live, that's what I say." Adam tried a laugh to aid his attempt at nonchalance but that also fell short. *So much for taking her home to meet Mother.*

The wobbling hostess arrived and opened the door of the booth. She spoke in German to Gabi. Whatever she said made the young auburn extremely irate. Ulrike joined in, apparently giving support to her angry friend. After much gesticulating and swearing, Gabi thumped the table and stood in resignation.

"*Entschuldigt mich.*" She excused herself past Adam. "I must go and see the manager. Gudrun will take care of you." Gabi left the booth. Gudrun, the hostess, took another order for drinks.

"Where has she gone this time?" Adam asked, after Gudrun's breasts had left the table.

"She must go and see the manager," Ulrike said.

"Yeah, I got that bit."

"He wishes her to work."

"What sort of bloody work?" He looked toward the boudoir closet. "This is definitely out of order."

"Gabi does not want to do this," Ulrike said. "The manager knows we are at a private party but one of her favourite clients asks for her special."

"Bollocks to this." Gudrun eventually arrived with the drinks. Adam took his pint of lager. "Can you bring me a large whiskey, please?"

She noted his order. "For sure."

"Is that all anybody can say around here?"

"Does anyone else require another drink?" Gudrun asked.

Steve gave Adam a look of disapproval. "No thanks, we'll finish these first." Gudrun closed the door and left.

"What you looking at me like that for?" Adam asked.

"You're not starting on the silly stuff, are you? I don't want you falling off any drainpipes."

Adam didn't need reminding that his low capacity for alcohol had on more than one occasion been a cause of embarrassment. "Look Steve," he said. "I've missed-out in the shagging department; I may as well just get pissed, seeing as how it's free anyway."

"How do you know you've missed-out?" Steve asked.

"I know when I've shit-out and I'm telling you, I've shit-out, here."

Adam's whiskey arrived. He ordered another. When Gudrun brought the second whiskey, she said something in German to Ulrike.

"You two would look lovely in a pearl necklace." Adam said, to Gudrun's breasts.

"Ignore him," Steve said. "He flirts with the furniture when he gets drunk." Gudrun laughed and went away.

Ulrike stood. "Okay, we must go home now."

"Eh?" Adam said.

"What, to your place?" Steve's beam reflected his fantasies.

"Yes." Ulrike looked over to the bemused Adam. "Gabi will meet us there. She has sent a message with Gudrun. I must take you home to wait for her."

Adam tagged on behind the arm in arm couple and followed them out of the club. There was nothing else he could do, except go with the flow. He'd no other way of getting back to Wildflecken. Drink or no drink, he still had reservations about having anything to do with the wayward Gabi.

"See, Ace, I told you everything was cool, she wants you to wait for her." Steve and Ulrike were back to swinging arms.

"I'm not sure I want to wait for her. God knows where she's been or how many Krauts she's been with. Can you imagine what she's gonna be like when she gets in?" He grimaced. "Yuck, it'll be like shagging a bucket of wallpaper paste."

"Adam!" Steve indicated Ulrike.

"Yeah, sorry mate." Drink or no drink, Adam had little regard for Steve's German partner.

A sullen Adam sat in the back of Ulrike's Volkswagen on the way to the girls' apartment. The drink was reaching phase two, sending him into a doze, a welcome escape from the canoodling couple in the front of the car.

"Please say it to me again," Ulrike said.

Steve purred into the driver's ear. "*Du bist goldig, mein Liebling.*"

Ulrike shimmied her neck, intimating that a shiver had just run down her spine. "Ooh!"

Adam mentally wretched. Christ down the pit. '*You are golden, my darling?' I can't listen to much more of this. Where the hell did Steve learn all that guff? I didn't know* . . . Adam was asleep. He stayed that way until Steve's dulcet tones were coaxing him out of the car.

"Come on amigo, we're here." They'd arrived at the apartment. Adam was groggy and unhappy at the prospect of playing the spare part at the bedding of Steve and his 'golden *liebling*'.

They climbed the smartly decorated flight of stairs to the apartment.

"Who lives here with you?" Steve asked.

"Gabi, Gudrun and myself," Ulrike said. This at least assured Adam there were no hostile boyfriends waiting inside.

On the wall, aside the apartment door was a ten-by-eight inch square wooden board with a fixed paper pad.

"What's this for?" Adam asked.

"It is a message board." Ulrike unlocked the door.

"What? Do you mean for the milkman?" Adam looked around for the milk bottles. Ulrike ignored him; she and Steve were already heading for the sunset.

None of these Kraut bitches like me.

Adam picked up the marker pen hanging by string from the message board and wrote upon the pad: '*I Have Shit Out Here*'. He entered the apartment and followed the light source leading him to the living room where Steve and Ulrike were again locked in an embrace. Ignoring the lovesick couple, Adam scanned the Kandinsky prints on the wall and matched them with the chic furnishings.

Very tasty. Not what I expected.

Ulrike broke the clinch with Steve, took their coats and hung them in the hallway. "I will show you to the kitchen. You may help yourself." A quick sweep of her hand to display the kitchen appeared enough for Ulrike to feel she'd dispensed her duty. She took hold of Steve's hand and the pair disappeared down the hallway towards what Adam presumed to be the bedrooms. Left to fend for himself, he had a quick mooch through the cupboards and managed to make himself a cup of coffee. He returned to the living room and collapsed on the luxurious couch.

It was almost four o'clock on a Sunday morning so there was no way of getting back to Wildflecken other than Ulrike taking them home after she'd finished with Steve. Steve had never been known to rush when it came to 'making the beast with two backs'. *I don't know how he does it.* If he had Sandie Shaw and The Dagenham Girl Pipers in there working shifts, he'd still be hours. Adam knew he wasn't getting home until dawn. He lay back and let the coffee nullify what was left of the alcohol. Tiredness soon coaxed him into a deep sleep.

A strange tingling sensation entered his nether regions. Adam and Emma Virgilio were making love on the back of a great bird flying through the air. The black bird resembled one of T's statues. As the bird soared, so did Adam's excitement. When the bird swooped, his whole body went into spasm.

"*Ci sono quattro stagioni,*" he whispered into Emma's ear.

"Ooh, say it again please." Emma cupped a hand around Adam's cheek. "But please, please, say it this time in English." The bird soared again into the sky.

"Okay then, there are four seasons."

"*Ah si*." Emma gave the same neck-shimmy that Steve's '*goldig liebling*' had given. 'There are four seasons' was the only Italian phrase Adam knew. When Emma said it in Italian with her Sophia Loren accent, it sent shivers down his spine, so it was understandable that she should feel the same when he said it in English.

The giant bird went into its deepest plunge yet and the spasm caused Adam's eyes to pop open. The great bird had gone and he was back on Ulrike's couch. He looked down from where the tingling emanated. Blocking the sight path to the pleasure zone was a head of auburn hair. He tried to work out the identity of the Chinese dragon, breathing fire into his loins. He gripped the shoulder of the red silk embroidered dressing gown. Gabi raised her head and looked at him.

"*Hallo*." She wiped her hand across her mouth.

He pulled her head towards his and kissed her. "What a nice surprise."

She knelt back on her feet on the floor. "Come, I have a better surprise for you, for sure." She took him by the hand and pulled him to his feet.

"Oh goody, I like surprises." He fastened the top button of his loons lest they should drop where he was standing. She switched off the living room lamp and led him down the hallowed hallway into which Steve had disappeared. He was so aroused, he didn't care how many men she'd been with that night, or any other night. "Where are we going?"

"Paradise."

"Paradise?"

"*Ja*, for sure."

The first sight he saw when Gabi opened the bedroom door was Steve's black bushy hair and brown naked body. Adam would've more than welcomed a foursome alongside Gabi, Ulrike and his buddy but Paradise had gone one better. Steve was cavorting in some sexual antic, not only with the gorgeous Ulrike but also with the hostess with the mostest, Gudrun. Gudrun's long black waves of hair fluttered around her chubby face but Adam's eyes drew to her gigantic breasts, which had popped well and truly out and were bouncing with full vigour. The bedroom was as modish as the rest of the apartment but it was difficult to take in anything other than what was happening on the bed.

Gabi discarded the Chinese dragon dressing gown from her otherwise naked back and joined the others. Adam's eyes were running riot, from Gudrun's upper assets, to the pleasure-ridden grimace on Ulrike's beautiful face. "What the frigging hell am I doing with my clothes on?" He eradicated the matter within seconds and before his last sock hit the floor, Gabi had pulled him into the fray. The newcomers had a two-minute warm up session of their own before dovetailing into the activities of the other three.

Steve stopped for a breather. "I think I've died and gone to heaven."

"Not many, Benny. I can't believe this: six tits." Adam was fondling Gudrun but mentally playing with all six. This was more like it. In the old days, when he was a real pop star, he and Steve used to get into scenes like this all the time. "Yo, bring on the dancing-girls."

"*Es ist gut, ja?*" Gabi said.

Steve climbed on the back of Ulrike while grasping Gudrun's available breast. "*Es ist* bloody *gut.*" he said, with a strong German accent. "*Ja*, for sure." The laughs ricocheted around the bedroom once more.

It was Adam's intention to sample every pleasurable orifice or squashy bit he could get his hands or otherwise on. This he set about doing as the orgy became more serious.

"Oh God, I think it's prize giving time," Steve said, entwined with Ulrike. The contortions on the cook's face spurred Adam into a gallop. But then the elation froze into a weird-looking tableau at the sound of the front doorbell being rung several times.

Who the hell could that be? It was six o'clock in the frigging morning.

Gabi extracted herself from Adam and said something similar in German. She climbed off the bed, retrieved the red silk dressing gown and went to answer the door. Ulrike's contortions had stopped. Gudrun bounced across the room to listen at the door. Adam and Steve stayed on the bed, in the incomplete tableau. They heard Gabi opening the door.

Maybe it was an irate neighbour coming to complain about banging headboards or something. Two male, German voices filtered down the hallway as Gabi invited them into the flat.

"*Wir kommen zum fruehstueck*," one of them said.

"*Scheisse*!" Ulrike said. "*Es ist Henri.*"

Gudren grabbed her knickers and was dressing in a flurry of panic.

"Er, would that be Big *Grosse* Henri from the club?" Adam asked.

"Please, you must leave now." Gudren was collecting garments from the floor.

"Leave where?" Adam asked.

"Leave what?" Steve's prize-giving mood had drooped from sight.

Gudren explained that Big Henri and the other bouncer had turned up for 'breakfast', the reward promised to them in exchange for allowing Adam and Steve into the club.

"Frigging breakfast?" Adam pulled up his pants. "Wasn't his supper enough?"

"Please do not make such noise," Gudren said. "He will kill you, if he finds you here."

At the thought of 'Gross Henri' discovering that someone had already been nibbling his breakfast, Adam's belligerence joined Steve's prize-giving mood, hiding under the bed. "What are we going to do?" The button of his shirt cuff snapped off in his fingers. "Oh bollocks! Bollocks, bollocks, bollocks!"

"We'll hide in the wardrobe," Steve said.

"No, please, you must go." Gudren threw on a dressing gown. "Oh *mein Gott*."

Ulrike grabbed hold of her to stop her shaking. "*Beruhigen*, Gudren. *Alles in ordnung*." She turned to Steve. "I will bring your coats." She brought the coats, saying she'd managed to retrieve them without the two bouncers noticing but it was too risky for Adam and Steve to leave by the front.

"You must go through the window." Gudrun opened the said window and pointed.

Adam stepped on to the balcony and regarded the fifteen-foot drop. "Are you off your chump? We're two floors up."

"You must climb here."

Steve had joined Adam. "Chuffing hell. What was I saying before about falling off drainpipes?"

Steve stepped back into the room to kiss Ulrike. Laughter from the living room prompted Adam to pull the Peruvian pillock back to the balcony. The street below was deserted. "I don't frigging believe this."

Steve made the first climb. "It's not too bad a drop."

"From heaven to hell in two easy moves." Freezing air intensified the transfer down to join his bushy headed partner.

"*Tcheuss*," Ulrike leant 'Juliet' like over the balcony.

"*Du bist goldig*." Steve blew her a kiss.

"For fuck's sake." Adam dragged Steve off into the winter morning.

"Bollocks," Steve said. "Them bastards are gonna be shagging our six tits."

Adam pulled up his collar against the cold. "I'm getting too frigging old for this." The girls' apartment was on the outskirts of the town. They trudged the empty, desolate, Fulda streets. "And you, Steve, you're much too old.

This time of day, you should be patting your kids on the head and sending 'em off to prep school, not escaping from a couple of kraut gorillas."

"What's up with you, man? That was boss. Just like the old days, remember?"

"That is the last time I climb out of a bedroom window, trying to put my keks on at the same time."

"Come on, Ace, only last week you were saying: 'sex, drugs and rock & roll'. It doesn't get much better than this." A signpost indicated the way south. "Sex, drugs, rock & roll and six tits."

"No, man, you're wrong. There has to be more to it than climbing down drainpipes at half six in the morning." A lone passing car ignored Steve's thumb. Adam saluted. "And look at the state of me." He displayed his button-less, dangling shirt cuff.

Okay God, you win, got your message: time to find something better.

"I've got to find a nice girl and settle down, one that doesn't go off down alleys to blow on some giant penguin's trumpet. I mean, Gabi's a nice enough girl and all that but do me a favour, I deserve better."

Considering the hour, the boys were fortunate in their hitching venture. By 8:30am they'd reached Bahnhof Strasse. Adam instantly recognised the bottle green Mustang parked outside the house. "Cosmic."

T was at the kitchen table, finishing her breakfast. "Where've you two dirty stop-outs been all night?"

"T, I'm not in the mood to have the piss taken out of me, so don't even start." Adam checked around for Bobby.

"Right, just for that, I'm not gonna pass on your regards to your loved one when I see her this afternoon."

"What are you on about?"

"I'm going to Schweinfurt to visit Carter and Kim, today. I'll probably see your friend, Emma."

Adam halted his quest for the bedroom. "Emma? My Emma, Emma Virgilio?"

"Yes, that Emma." She got up from the table and went to the kettle. "It's just boiled. Anyone want a brew?"

"Not for me," Steve said. "I'm bushed. Gonna head up." He stopped at the hallway. "What are you doing with *them*?"

"What am I doing with what?" T asked.

He pointed back at the box on the kitchen top. "Them."

"I'm taking them for Kim."

"Really? Chuffing hell!" He carried on upstairs.

T called after him. "While you're up there, will you give Jeannie and Bobby a knock? Tell them I'm waiting to go."

Adam took the coffee she was offering. There was a brown splurge on the kitchen wall. He followed the stain down the yellow wall to a broken plate and a pile of spaghetti Bolognese.

"Don't ask," T said. "Me and Colin had a disagreement." She gave him a stern look. "Don't touch it. It's Colin's mess. He'll clean it up."

Adam sat at the table with his coffee. "I wasn't going to touch it."

"And tell Steve not to."

He sipped his coffee. "I didn't mean to be a dick when we came in. I'm a bit hung over, knackered, had no sleep. Are you really going to see Emma?"

"I'm going to Schweinfurt, so there's a chance."

"T, if you could make things right between me and her, I'd love you forever. Tell her: tell her I miss her to bits. Tell her I'm sorry. I'd crawl over broken glass to reach her if she'd give me another chance."

"Adam, it's alright saying all these things; you've got to mean it. You've got to stop all this gallivanting. It's not natural."

"I do mean it, T. You've got me all wrong. I'd love to stop gallivanting. I'd love to settle down with a nice girl."

"Would you buggery!"

"I would, honest. I've just been saying as much to Steve."

T continued throwing things into her handbag. "If I see her, I'll tell her what you said."

"How you doing, Adam?"

Shit, it was Bobby. Adam downed his coffee and rinsed his cup. "I'd best be getting to bed. I'm knacked."

Steve was already in bed. "Well, what do you think of that, amigo?" Adam said. "T's going to visit my angel. Maybe I should've sent a letter. What d'ya think?"

"For God's sake." Steve hid his head.

"What? You don't get it do you? I'm in love."

Steve came out from under the covers. "In love, my arse. Adam, not four hours ago you were ranting and raving with six tits in your hands. Then you were going on about June Roundhill. Who exactly are you in love with, now?"

"Emma."

"Emma? What happened to June?"

"Yeah, I still love June, as well. I've never stopped loving her. But I know she's never going to write back." Adam got into bed. "I can't wait forever, and if there's a chance with Emma."

"For God's sake, listen to yourself. There's only one person you're in love with and that's Adam chuffing Fogerty. Now please, I'm knackered out of my head. Can we for the love of Krishna, get some sleep?"

"Sorry." Adam pulled the covers up over his head. A few minutes lapsed and then he popped out again. "Steve?"

"What now?"

"Six tits! Bloody amazing, wasn't it?"

"*Ja*, for sure."

14 T's Adventures: Schweinfurt. Jan '77:
Can't Get Enough Of Your Love, Babe.

The Black Knight in shining chef outfit appeared over the horizon, the chicken emblem on his shield glinting in the winter sunlight. The mirage before T as she gazed through the mountainside was the latest fantasy of her jolly sergeant. The Mustang pulled out on the almost deserted autobahn. Keeping his pre-Christmas promise, Bobby was taking Jeannie and T to spend their Sunday off in Schweinfurt. There, T would meet up with William Carter in the flesh. Under different circumstances she may have left her husband for this man.

You silly mare, sometimes you do talk a load of rubbish.

Of course the relationship with William had been no more than a potential fling but her romantic dreams allowed her to see the Black Knight, riding his steed towards her, ready to rescue her from traipsing around the country and being insulted at every turn.

"You okay in the back there?" Bobby asked.

"She's miles away," Jeannie said. "Probably dreaming about Carter and his Alabami Surprise."

"What?" T turned from the window.

"Bobby was talking to you. You were miles away. I said you were probably—"

"I heard what you said."

"I could hardly blame you if you were. After what you've had to put up with all these years, you deserve someone like Carter, someone who'd treat you with a bit of respect."

"Don't you think Mrs Carter might have something to say about that?" T said.

Jeannie turned to T. "What was all that about last night?"

"It was just a row."

"A row? That wasn't a row; it was World War bloody Three. Did you see our kitchen wall, Bobby, spaghetti Bolognese all down it?"

"It was probably my fault. I shouldn't have threatened him." As per, the fight had come out of nothing. He'd made some belittling remark about her performance. She said he wouldn't have to suffer her singing much longer because as soon as this tour was over, she'd never sing in another of his bands and he might have to think about moving out of the marital home. He then objected to Jeannie having her dinner made as he was paying for the food. "I pay her enough to buy her own fucking grub." Although Jeannie said she wasn't "that hungry", T insisted on her eating the Bolognese she'd cooked for her. Colin tried to snatch the plate off T as she was handing it to Jeannie. They grappled. It was just as well Jeannie wasn't hungry because the dish crashed against the kitchen wall.

T was still unsure what would really happen when they got home. The threat to kick him out was only that – a threat. She couldn't imagine going through an actual divorce. Yet he was a pig. It would serve him right if he woke one day to find she *had* run off with someone else. Since meeting Colin, she'd never, ever thought about being with anyone else. She'd even repressed the odd sexual fantasy because that was almost like committing adultery. But that was before William. The man from Alabama was different, exciting. She'd never before been with anyone from outside Yorkshire, let alone an American Coloured.

Bloody hell Morgan, listen to you. You're getting as bad as Jeannie.

Jeannie was stroking her hand through Bobby's perm. Less than a week before, T had watched her promiscuous friend do something similar to the back of Lincoln's head. All these thoughts about being a rescued damsel, and being whisked off by William for a dragon slaying weekend, were getting out of hand. They were, after all, only in her head. And yet, she couldn't stop thinking about William saying they'd 'unfinished business', whatever that meant.

Theresa Morgan, don't you even dare think about that. You're just visiting a couple of friends.

She looked at the hessian box alongside her on the back seat, hoping, at least, she and Kim could again become friends. Happen, Kim would be cooking her Vietnamese version of American meatloaf to show there were no hard feelings. "Are we staying at Carter's for dinner," she asked.

"No man, we're going off to look at a castle in Wurzburg. You're welcome to join us," Bobby said.

"A castle?"

"It's very old. I think you'll enjoy it."

"I think Carter might want to entertain her himself," Jeannie said.

What the heck does that mean?

Jeannie turned to Bobby. They shared a grin.

And what the heck does that mean?

"Entertain me with what?"

"I just meant he was very excited about you coming. Isn't that right Bobby?"

Was this some sort of tease or something more? T tried to read Jeannie's expression for any sign of suspected conspiracy but her friend's eyes were now fixed on the Mustang emblem, rearing its forelegs on the tip of the car bonnet.

I wish I'd never mentioned anything about fancying William.

The approach to Schweinfurt Town Centre crept into view beyond the roadside fruit trees. The Mustang stumbled over the familiar cobbles that'd once housed some sort of rail lines, either for trains or trams, it was no longer obvious. First stop, Bobby's apartment, then on to the enclave of the US Army-housing estate and William's.

T had never been to Bobby's plush apartment but she'd heard many stories about the place from Jeannie and of course, Adam. It was as lavish as her colleagues had told her, much too large for a single couple, plus a bit messy following the divorce. The mess didn't prevent Bobby from showing T around. The kitchen was to die for.

That boy can't possibly be making proper use of all this new fangled kitchen stuff now that he's on his own.

That Boy showed her into the master bedroom.

I bet this place could tell a few tales.

T had always felt detached from the sexual shenanigans that went with being in a pop band. She thought herself every bit a musician but was only an interested observer when it came to the social pastimes of filling your life on the road. Still, she delighted in the exciting stories brought to her from the likes of Adam and Jeannie, even if she didn't feel part of it. Maybe it was time she lived up to her rock star title.

Where the hell do you buy those things? T's distraction had nothing to do with the handcuffs on the dresser; it centred on the circular bed. She'd never seen anywhere, sheets to fit such a bed, let alone in royal blue satin.

The Mustang didn't dwell long at Bobby's. T was soon on the back seat again, next to her Bird Gods. Soon they'd be hers no longer but if they did the job, it'd be worth it. The car left West Germany and entered the Military section of American Army houses.

"Welcome to the American Mid-West, girls," Bobby said. "There's a town in Pennsylvania just like this."

The Mustang pulled into Carter's street and parked in the space outside his apartment. They all got out. T manoeuvred the hessian box from the back. She turned and almost collided with a girl with long, dark hair.

"Signora Bone, how are you?" T recognised the accent.

"Oh hello, Emma, I was only talking about you this morning with Adam. He said to give you his regards if I saw you." T was unsure how much Emma would understand but she seemed to get the gist.

"How is Adam?"

Jeannie joined the conversation. "Still the same old Adam."

"Ah *si*, he has many girlfriends, yes?"

"No, actually, he does not have girlfriend since you," T said. "We're in a new place, called Wildflecken, not many girls around. And anyway, he still likes *you* very much." Jeannie's look of astonishment glanced off T. "He talks about you all the time."

"Me? He talk about me?"

"Yes, all the time." T guided Emma away from Jeannie. "He said if I see you, I must tell you how much he misses you. He is sorry for hurting you and he would really like to see you again."

"He say this? He really does not have girlfriend since me?"

"Not a one. I don't think he ever got over you. He's a changed man. You tamed him. Why don't you call him?"

Emma stroked a strand of hair away from her eyes. "Yes, perhaps I can do this but I do not have his telephone."

"Here, let me give you the number of our digs. Jeannie, have you got a pen?"

T juggled with her box. Bobby came to her rescue and wrote down the number for Emma.

T grinned. "He'll be chuffed to bits if you do call."

"*Scusi?*"

There was a gap in the conversation. Having performed her matchmaking skills, there was little else to say. "Your English is much better since we were at the Carters'."

"Carter? Ah *si*, you have come to visit, William?"

"And Kim: not just William."

"Kim is not here."

"What?" T's head tilted. "Where is she?"

"She is gone."

"Gone? What do you mean, gone? Gone where?"

"Gone to America."

"America?" T turned to Bobby. "What's going on? I thought Kim was expecting us?"

"Well I told Carter you'd be here Sunday, man, and Sunday it is."

T got a faint whiff of an ambush, a big, black, Carter-sized spider, spinning his fly-trapping web. Daydreams were one thing but if William's intentions were his 'unfinished business', she might have to temper her fantasy. "Didn't he say anything to you?"

"Maybe there was a family emergency or something," Jeannie said.

T turned back to Emma. "When did she go?"

"She go before Christmas."

"What's going on?" T appealed to both Bobby and Jeannie but they merely exchanged a shrug. This time, embarrassment lined the gap in the conversation. Had William set a trap? Had she been dumb enough to get caught in it? And did they all know about it? "Right Emma, I'll tell Adam to expect your call," she said.

"Ah *si. Ciao.*" Emma wiggled off down the street.

"What made you tell her all that rubbish about Adam?" Jeannie asked.

"Never mind rubbish." The only discussion T wanted was one about the spider's web notion but she was too late, Bobby had rung the Carters' doorbell.

His large, dark figure filled the rosewood frame of the door. "Hey, my babe, Happy New Year." William embraced T and without any shame, planted a sloppy kiss on her lips.

T's head was too befuddled to fit in any embarrassment. "Happy New Year, William," was all she managed.

He ushered them into the living room. "Sorry, Kim ain't here. She taken the kids to a festival in BK, man. She gonna be real sorry to have missed you guys."

"Really?" T looked at Bobby and Jeannie. Both looked away. "And what festival is that?" She put her hessian box on the table.

"Oh man, it some New Year toy festival. The kids been at her about going, since they got back from the States. I ain't sure, what time they coming back. They taking in a show up there, too."

"Sorry, big man." Bobby put a hand on William's arm. "We just bumped into Emma. She told Theresa that Kim's gone home."

William flopped on the couch. "Oh shucks." He preened his moustache. "I'm real sorry, Theresa. I didn't want to lie to you."

Jeannie stepped forward. "Sorry, T, this is my fault. I thought you might not come if you knew Kim wasn't here so I suggested saying she'd gone out for the day."

So, there was some deceitful scheming going on. Was it as innocent as they obviously wanted her to think or more sinister? She was reluctant to ask the obvious question, in case the answer was 'Actually, Theresa, this is all your fault' but she asked anyway. "So why has she gone?"

William stopped preening his moustache. "The kids gone back for their schooling. She thought she'd go back with them for a vacation."

"I see." T was still suspicious. She looked to the hessian box. "I brought my statues. I would've liked to have given them to her face to face but I suppose I'll just have to leave them." To be honest, she'd been worried about meeting Kim 'face to face'. There was a touch of relief at avoiding any confrontation, especially in front of Jeannie and Bobby.

William put a hand on her arm. "Anyway, I's glad you've come. I's looking forward to hearing what's been happening to y'all."

"I'm afraid we ain't staying around, man," Bobby said. "I promised to take the girls to Wurzburg Schloss."

"What! You all going?" William asked. "You too, Theresa? But I made dinner an' all."

"You're welcome to join us," Bobby said.

Jeannie laughed. "They don't want to be squashed in the back of the car, all the way to Wurzburg."

"You could sit in the back and William can sit in the front," T said.

Jeannie screwed up her nose. "I can't sit in the back of the Mustang. I get car sick."

"Since when?" T distinctly remembered seeing Jeannie's head being thrown across the rear window when Debbie had been driving.

"Wouldn't you rather stay here, T?" Jeannie asked. "It's got to be better than spending the day wandering around some crummy old castle."

"What? Bobby was telling me how great it was on the way here."

"And it sure is cold out there," William said.

"It's up to you Theresa," Bobby said. "I could pick you up on the way back, man, if that's what you want."

There was something going on. T checked all round for furtive winks. She was unbalanced. The castle was the perfect chance for escape. Then again, they were right, she wasn't that keen on old buildings and the weather wasn't exactly inviting. Yet the main reason she wasn't rushing out to jump back in the Mustang was a feeling that the Carter web was one of excitement. "I'm not sure." She returned a smile in exchange of William's pleading look. "I suppose if you've made dinner."

"Good, I'll pick you up around five, man." Bobby said. Jeannie nudged him in the ribs and presented a false smile to T. Bobby laughed. "Oh yeah man, I'll pick you up a bit later."

"Around nine." Jeannie said.

"Nine?" T said. It got dark around four o'clock.

"We'll probably call in at Bobby's place first." No wonder Jeannie was so concerned about T's welfare at the castle.

Just as well I'm not going along if they're going to be at it.

"Okay, see you guys later." Bobby led Jeannie out.

T was now alone with William and there were nine hours in front of them, nine hours, fending off a sex crazed Coloured man, ravenous for her body.

William took T's coat. He called from the hallway. "What time you wanna eat? I'm starving."

"What's for dinner? I expect it's chicken." She tried to disguise the awkwardness.

He returned. "Theresa."

"Yes?"

"It don't matter. We'll talk over dinner."

She was right about the chicken but she queried the unexpected spicy aroma of the dish.

"This is one of Kim's recipes," he said.

"It's delicious."

The forkful of food about to enter his mouth lowered back to his plate. "She ain't gone on vacation. She left me."

"Left you? What do you mean? You don't mean you've split up, do you?"

"The kids really have gone back to school but we had a ruckus. Bobby don't know. He think she really is on vacation."

"Bloody hell."

"I try to tell you at Christmas when I called but I couldn't."

"It's not because of me, is it?"

"You? Hell no, man. Why would you say that?" He put down his cutlery to take her hand in both of his. "Theresa, you ain't done nothing wrong. This been coming for a long time."

"But I thought you were the perfect couple. Everybody said you were."

"She was pretty good at pretending." Throughout the rest of dinner, T listened to the charade that was the Carters' marriage. The reason the children had been in the States when 'Images' had arrived was to prepare them for their change in schools so that Kim could return home. She'd hated Germany from the start. "I always loved her, but she never felt the same about me."

He started clearing up the dinner dishes. T naturally joined in and followed him into the kitchen. "Kim seemed so happy here."

"Hey, you don't want to be hearing all my troubles." He relieved her of the cruets and put them away. "So, tell me what's been happening to y'all since you left?"

He insisted on doing the washing-up himself while she simply stood there, recounting the legend of the Bird Gods, her story about what had happened to the van and how Colin had pretended to burn the statues, though for some reason she was unsure of, she omitted telling him they weren't together.

"Jeez," was William's only interruption.

She stroked his arm and continued her account of all the things that'd happened to Adam since coming into contact with the Bird Gods. William lapped it up, though it was very odd. "You shouldn't be letting me go on, like this." She enjoyed being the centre of attention but it was uncomfortable standing by while a man did the housework, especially a he-man like William. Colin had never washed a pot in his life.

The washing up completed, the spider led the fly back into the web of the living room. "How do you take your bourbon?"

"I don't think I've ever had it."

He brought out a bottle of 'Jim Beam' from the drinks cabinet and poured a large, neat measure.

She sipped. "Bloody hell, that's too strong for me. Are you trying to get me drunk?"

"Yep, dat's the general idea." He topped it with ginger ale. "Don't worry, I ain't gonna jump on you. I knowed that's the last thing you'd want."

She didn't correct him but she could think of many more things on her unwanted list below that. In fact, an undeniable tinge of disappointment buzzed around her.

He led her to the settee. The hessian box was on the table. He went to a drawer and brought out T's missing Bird God. "Sorry Theresa."

"Thanks." T kissed her and put her in the box alongside her sisters. She smiled to herself. There was one thing at least, if Kim wasn't coming back, she no longer needed to leave them.

He stroked a hand over the statue. "Kim almost took this with her but I stopped her. I wanted a reminder of you." The inward smile grew into a satisfactory grin. He moved the box to the dresser behind them then came and sat beside her. "Don't worry, you're safe," he said. "After what you been telling me about those things, I ain't gonna upset no African queen."

The tinge buzzed back. She swatted it. "Do you know what? When I found out that Kim had gone, I thought you'd tricked me into coming here so you could try and get me into bed." One of William's attractions was his smile, his pearly teeth contrasting against his ebony skin and the white in his eyes widening to twice their normal size. He was beaming at her now.

"Get you into bed?" He gave one of his familiar chuckles. "What made you think a thing like that?"

"You did. On the phone at Christmas, you said we had 'unfinished business'. I thought that's what you meant."

"Is that what I said? I guess I just meant we had a lot of catching up to do."

She clasped her glass with both hands and put it in front of her face, trying to hide behind it. "Oh God, how embarrassing. I feel so stupid, now."

He chuckled again. "I wouldn't even suggest such a thing to a fine lady like you. Wouldn't expect to get that lucky."

You silly mare, Theresa. Wait a minute, did he just say he'd be lucky to get me?

It appeared the fear she might have to spend the day fighting off uninvited sexual advances was wrong. But if sex wasn't on his agenda, what was? "What are we gonna do for the next seven hours?"

"We could go for a walk. I'd like to show you the parts of Schweinfurt you didn't see when you were here."

William was right; there were lots to see in the town. This was her first visit to the park. Colin wasn't one for taking walks. They walked arm in arm, the great trees shading the path. Some had mushrooms like warts, others, covered in ivy. One had even been struck by lightning but most stood there, majestically, like grand old men. William and T strolled past until they came to a park bench overlooking a still lake. More trees with bare winter branches reflected in the calm water. The air was cold and fresh.

She snuggled down into her warm coat then re-linked his forearm. "This is nice, really peaceful."

"I used to come here with Kim but we ain't been for some time, not since Will Junior was in his stroller."

"How did you two meet?"

"Who me and Kim? Oh man, are you ready for this? We met in a cat-house."

"What?" T took in the word. "In a what?" He didn't answer but she'd understood, she just needed more time. "Do you mean …" She wanted to confirm that he was referring to a brothel but William was almost three questions in front of her.

"Yeah that's right, Kim was a lady of the night."

"Bloody hell." She unlinked her arm from his.

He told Kim's story. During the Vietnam War, many of the female population turned to prostitution. It was the only thing left to sell. He'd been Kim's number one client. Even then, he'd fallen in love with her. When she became pregnant, he'd been only too glad to marry her and take her home.

"How did you know it was your baby?"

"At the time I didn't. But I do now. Will Junior look more like me than I do."

Bloody hell, Kim a prostitute: and fancy him taking someone like that back to the States and marrying her. *I wonder how Momma felt about that. Well, as Adam says*: '*It wouldn't do for us all to be alike*'. She tried to imagine herself in a royal blue circular satin bed with a pair of handcuffs on the pillow. No, it was no good. She'd have to give the rock star lifestyle a miss. It wasn't prudishness that led to her lack of adventure, more a lack of imagination. "Didn't it bother you that she'd been with so many other men?"

"Hell no man, she had to eat. She wasn't doing it 'cos she liked it. And what if she was? What do ya think I was doing in the cat-house in the first place?"

"Oh yeah, I never thought about that, you randy bugger."

Wow, who'd have thought it? You just don't know about anybody, these days. Another couple arrived at the edge of the lake. *I mean, look at them two.* They could be into all sorts of kinky goings-on. He could be wearing her bra and knickers under that overcoat. You hear about those kind of things. Happen they met in the launderette when she mistook his underclothes for hers.

T linked her arm back through William's. The kinky man picked up a stone and skimmed it over the lake, disturbing the calmness. *Still, as my mother used to say: 'They're not spoiling another couple'.* The couple left. T watched the ripples from the stone as they spread across the lake. A mini tide lapped up to the water's edge in front of the bench.

The arrival of the ripples triggered T. "Be dark soon."

William stared out over the lake. "Man, I miss her." A tear crept down his cheek. "I miss them all."

It was twilight when they left the park; completely dark by the time they reached the apartment. She declined the offer of yet more food but Jim Beam rejoined them on the settee.

William chinked his glass to hers. "Did you really think that's what I meant by unfinished business?"

"Yeah, I did."

"But you came, anyway."

"Yeah, I did."

From behind, Barry White whispered his baritone seductions. "Can't Get Enough of Your Love, Babe."

She gazed at William. Oh dear, this was the face of an aroused man and it was possible she'd put the thought in his head. The right thing to do would be to get up and leave before the situation got out of hand but Jeannie and Bobby weren't due back for some time. William, Barry and Jim Beam advanced. It was difficult to resist the male trio. She didn't resist when William kissed her. She didn't resist when he undid the top buttons of her dress and kissed her breast. She even granted him permission to progress when he asked: "Are you alright wid dis?"

Too bloody true I'm alright wid dis.

She blamed Barry White for the seductive atmosphere. She blamed Jim Beam for the fact that she was allowing William to go further than they'd ever gone before, though by this point with Colin, she'd be flat on her back with thoughts of the Union Jack fluttering. Strains of *God Save the Queen* would yet linger in the air but the trombonist would be stripping down his instrument. However, it appeared Old Glory required a little more wooing time before rousing *The Star Spangled Banner*. He nibbled her lobe.

Mm, that's new. Down to her neck: *Yeah, that's good, too.* She gripped his muscular arm and responded with a full-on kiss.

She didn't resist when he led her upstairs to the bedroom. The surroundings were so familiar. It was the same bedroom that she'd shared with Colin, the purple and lilac headboard imprinted on her mind from the couple of times she'd leant on it whilst … *Oh my God*! She faltered at the entrance to the web. "Erm, I need the bathroom."

In the bathroom she confronted the reflection in the mirror. "Theresa Morgan, you can't go through with this." Once again the young Miss Morgan was turning a deaf ear to the more experienced Mrs Bone. Mrs Bone continued the lecture. "And you're not as drunk as you're pretending to be, so don't give me that 'helpless little girl who couldn't protect herself' routine." Of course: Mrs Bone was right. God, what was she even thinking? Miss Morgan relented and signed the agreement. Now was the time to resist. She felt guilty about leading him on, but surely he'd understand. "Morgan, you're going to go straight in there and tell him you've changed your mind. You should never have let it get this far. You say thanks but no thanks."

She tidied her clothing and entered the bedroom. William was sitting up in the bed, naked as far as she could see. In his outstretched hand he offered a glass of Jim Beam. They'd left Barry White downstairs. He was no longer needed, he'd done his job.

Oh sod it.

Mrs Bone covered her eyes. Miss Morgan undressed to her underwear and climbed in next to the ebony hunk.

Bobby and Jeannie arrived back at twenty minutes before nine but T was sitting on the settee, ready.

"Have you had a good time," Jeannie asked, with yet another bloody wink.

"Actually, I've had a brilliant time."

"Oh yeah?" Bobby said. "What you guys been doing all day?"

"We've been to the park," William said.

"Yeah, we've spent the whole day eating, drinking and talking." T glared at Jeannie, defying her to show disbelief.

Jeannie's only reply was: "The park? Bloody hell, Carter, you took her to the park?" She sniggered. "That must've been novel, T; Colin wouldn't have walked you to the end of the street."

"Oh yeah, how is Colin?" William asked.

"Still the same old Colin," Jeannie said. "Still smashing her over the head with his caveman club."

"Jeannie, don't." T felt a stab of guilt at the mention of Colin. Jeannie smirked. William asking about him obviously showed he hadn't been the main topic of conversation. T wondered again why she hadn't said anything about them splitting up.

"We need to hit the road," Bobby said. He shook hands with William.

Strange, they didn't usually. Was this part of some done deal? Something made her feel uneasy about the exchange. She checked again for any furtive winks between the men. No, she was being silly. She dismissed her suspicion of a set up.

William gave her a kiss on the cheek, thanked her for coming and told her to call him, soon. No one could hear the implosions inside her head. It was just as well. She prayed for a last moment alone with William but no one heard that either.

"I'll call you tomorrow." She surreptitiously squeezed his hand. "Sorry about Kim."

"Thanks." He kissed her; again, on the cheek.

As the Mustang sped northwards, T manoeuvred her rotund shape into a comfortable position on the back seat. She kept her eyes closed; giving the impression that she was dozing. This left her alone with her thoughts.

Oh God, what have I done? Chimes of guilt pealed. *No use worrying about it now girl*, Miss Morgan said. *What's done is done and can't be undone. Besides it was done wonderfully.* She couldn't believe a man could be so gentle yet still be in forceful control. He was incredibly sensitive, something, up to now, she'd loathed in a man. Yet, you couldn't describe him as soft or wimpish. Mrs Bone swept aside the daydream. *Never mind all that, you dirty bugger. You've just slept with another man, and she might not have been there but he's still somebody else's husband. And you're somebody else's wife. What the hell made you go to Schweinfurt?*

Her eyes popped open. "Bobby, we have to go back."

"Say what?" Bobby didn't turn his head but Jeannie did.

"Are you okay, T?"

"I've forgotten my statues."

"It's too late to go back now, Theresa." Bobby said.

Jeannie turned again. "I thought you were leaving them for Kim."

"She's not coming back. She's left him"

Bobby and Jeannie exchanged a look. "No sweat, I'll bring them back for you, next time I'm up," was Bobby's only comment.

She settled back. "I suppose that'll be okay." *Bugger*! The chimes were back. She tried to muffle them with thoughts of self-pity. She'd been forced into it. Colin's behaviour had made her vulnerable. Jeannie and Bobby had tricked her into going. And bloody William himself probably wasn't as innocent as he made out. *Bugger*! Oh God, what had she done to poor Colin? First thing she'd have to do when she got back to Bahnhof Strasse would be to clean up that spaghetti Bolognese. She'd probably be paying for this, for some time, at least ninety years. Jeannie stroked a hand through Bobby's hair, a reminder that she'd be paying that night. Another night on the bloody couch.

When the Mustang party arrived, the Bolognese mess had gone.

"Steve, I told Adam that spaghetti hadn't to be touched," T said.

"Nothing to do with me," Steve said. "It was Colin. He cleaned it up before they went out."

"Before who went out where?"

"Colin and Jimmy have gone up to Fulda to check out this new all night casino."

"All night casino?"

"Yeah, they won't be back until tomorrow morning."

"There you are," Jeannie said. "You've got a bed for the night. You don't have to kip on the couch."

"So T, did you see Emma, at all?" Adam asked.

"What? Oh yeah, she's going to give you a call."

"Really? Aw brilliant. T, you're a star." He bounded over and kissed her cheek.

"Get off! Are you sure it was Colin and not Jimmy who cleaned up the mess?" T checked the tiles and floor. They were immaculate.

"Nope, it was definitely Colin." Steve put an Emerson, Lake and Palmer album on the turntable.

"When's she going to call, T?" Adam asked.

"I don't bloody know, Adam. She just said she would, okay?"

"We're going up." Jeannie ushered Bobby upstairs.

T shouted after them. "Chuck us down my continental quilt, will you?" She sat on the couch.

Adam produced a pack of cards and waved it at Steve. "Fancy a game of bastard brag?"

"Yeah, okay."

Adam waved the deck at T. "You playing, T?"

"Don't be soft. I don't play cards."

"We'll teach you," Adam said. "Don't worry; we're not going to steal all your money. We'll play for matches 'til you get the hang of it."

"No thanks." She looked toward the turntable. Progressive rock was alright but much too loud for this time of night.

The game got under way. "Bastard!" Steve said.

"Aren't you lads going to bed?"

"Are you joking?" Adam said. "Didn't get up 'til four after being out all night."

Wonderful!

She looked to the stairs. "What's she doing with that continental quilt?" She would've gone up for it herself but by now them randy buggers could be up to anything. If Colin's out all night, happen she *should* just go up and get in his bed. No, it was *his* bed. After what she'd done, she deserved nothing better than the couch.

"Was Emma happy to hear from me?"

"For God's sake, Adam, how the hell do I know if she was happy? I gave her your message, what more do you want?"

"She did say she'd call though, didn't she?"

"Good God! Yes, Adam she said she'd call." ELP got started on their version of 'The Eighteen-Twelve Overture'. The flicking of cards sounded even louder than the music. She let go of a sigh.

"I thought you were sleeping upstairs, T?" Steve said.

"Bastard!" Adam said.

"I think I might bloody have to. In fact …" She got up from the couch. "Good night."

"Bastard!"

On the bedroom floor, a pair of inside out jeans wore a pair of red and grey paisley underpants. She resisted the urge to put them in the laundry basket and stepped over. Chimes pealed again. She undressed, dropped her tainted clothing into the basket then climbed into Colin's empty bed. It didn't help. Whatever was going to happen after the tour, if Colin ever found out what she'd done, it'd kill her; and probably him, too. Happen by the morning, her feelings might be clearer. The red and grey paisleys were begging for the wash. She pulled the cover up over her shoulders.

She opened her eyes to Colin, standing over her. "What time is it?"

"Half twelve."

"Steve said you were out all night at some casino in Fulda."

"They shut early on Sunday. We had to get a taxi back."

"Bugger, I'll get up."

"It's alright; I'll kip downstairs."

"Thanks."

"How was old Kim and Carter?"

"Fine." She sat up and hoisted the cover up to her chin. "You cleaned up the Bolognese."

"Eh? Yeah. T, I'm really sorry about last night."

She resisted the urge to say: *And so you should be*. Provoking a fight would only compound her sin.

He sat on the bed. "Can we talk?"

"Talk? Talk about what?"

"Us."

"What about us?" The sin was there again, rising from her tainted clothing and poking its head out of the laundry basket.

"I really, really miss you. I never meant to do or say owt to hurt you."

"It don't matter, Colin. It was probably my fault as much as yours. I didn't feel too good, last night."

"I'm not just talking about last night. I think the world of you, Theresa Bone. Please, can't we just give it another go?"

"Give what a go, Colin?"

"I absolute promise, we can have as many kids as you want. I just want another chance. You won't be sorry."

"You said that last time. As soon as we get home and something bad happens, it'll be back to 'we're not having any kids, ever', the same old Colin."

"It won't. I've told you. I absolute promise it won't. Please, just give me a chance and I'll prove it. You can kick me out again any time you want if I do owt wrong."

"Okay, let me think about it."

"I mean it, you won't be sorry." He grabbed her by the shoulders and plonked a kiss on her lips.

"I said I'd think about it. I need a few days. You've been drinking."

"Just a bit." He took hold of her hand. "T, why wait a couple of days? Why wait 'til we get home to start a family?" He grabbed the back of her neck. "T, if it's what *you* want, it's what *I* want."

"You know it's what I want."

"Good, come here." She couldn't resist his kiss. He got up and undid the lace of his cowboy shirt. She'd never liked that thing. "I'm serious. I really do mean it." He threw his trousers to join the inside out jeans and pulled back the covers. "Budge up." He got into bed and kissed her properly, a big sloppy one. She reeled from the reek of whiskey but it didn't feel right to complain. The bristles of his Desperate Dan chin gouged her shoulder. For the following twenty minutes, a cocktail of whiskey, bourbon, euphoria, guilt and confusion saturated her brain.

With the Union Jack standing at half-mast and the trombonist packed up and gone home, Colin puffed on a post coital. "I really have missed you, you know." He kissed her cheek. "It's brilliant having you back in my bed."

"Listen, Col—"

"Things are going to be alright." He switched off the bedside lamp and cuddled her to him.

T stared up into the darkness. Colin's snoring filled the whole room.

15 Adam's Sexploits: Wildflecken. Jan '77:
Money, Money, Money.

"It's bloody rocking again in here today." Jeannie arrived with the drinks. Adam took note of the numerous empty leather-backed chairs but ignored her sarcasm. They were the only two customers, despite it being the sole pub within a five-mile radius. On a previous visit, Adam had laughed with Jimmy about what they'd deciphered as oompah band pennants surrounding the bar. The pennants were still there. Adam and Jeannie had arranged to meet Steve "for a quick drink in the local" before work. Steve was on an afternoon date. Since the recent orgy, he'd continued to see his newfound friend, Ulrike, on a regular basis. Adam had stayed clear of the mad Gabi on the assumption that you *can* have too much of a good thing. And anyway, the feeling was mutual. She'd misinterpreted his message on the pad outside her apartment. When he'd written '*I Have Shit Out Here*', she'd taken it literally and thought he'd actually defecated somewhere in the hallway.

On the far wall of the deserted pub, Adam noted another set of oompah triangles, strategically placed to hide a patch of damp, only they'd been there so long that the damp had taken hold of the pennants themselves.

"God, this is a miserable shit hole. Did you put this Abba shite on?" He sneered at the '*Mamma, Mia*' lyric coming from the speaker above their heads.

"No, she must've."

The girl under the pennants wiped the bar and dusted the optics for the third time before returning to her magazine.

"I think I'd rather have Boney M back," Adam said.

"Why aren't you out with your new girlfriend, Gabi?" Jeannie laughed. "Oh yeah, sorry, I forgot, Steve told me. She 'dumped' you. No, I'm wrong; it was you that took a dump."

"Very funny. Anyway, maybe I prefer a better class of bird, these days."

"Sounded like a doozy of a night: six tits? A doozy, even by your standard of orgy, or should that be substandard?"

"Why'd you keep having a go at me, Jeannie? Did you get out the wrong side of the bed, or something?"

"Wrong side of the bed? I don't even know which bed I *am* getting out of these days. I've had to swap bedrooms yet again."

"That's good isn't it? You've got a room to yourself. You can bring back who you like, when you like."

"I can't believe she's taken him back. She was free of him and she decides to take him back. She's mad, could've got rid of him forever."

"Maybe she didn't want rid of him. Even if she *wanted* to shag around, she's not going to be spoilt for choice, is she?" He turned in his seat to look her in the eyes. "Anyway, shagging around isn't all it's cracked up to be. Have you ever thought what a frigging debauched sordid life we lead?"

"You speak for yourself."

"No, seriously, Jeannie, wouldn't you just like to settle down with somebody? Come home from work at a proper hour, your tea waiting for you, then down to the local pub on the canal and finally, home for a nice relaxing shag before bed."

"Alright, you dirty alien bastard, get out of Adam's body and give us back the lovable, shag everything with a pulse, wassock we're all used to."

"Come on, Jeannie, we're not getting any younger. Even you must get fed up shagging around. Wouldn't you like to be with just one person?"

"My God, you have got it bad. Aw is lickle Adam missing his Emma Wemma angel?"

"This isn't down to Emma."

"Has she called yet?"

"No, still waiting."

"Then what? You take her back to the Halton Moor Housing Estate and bring up half a dozen Eyeties on the dole?" When T told Adam of Emma's mutual desire to meet up with him again, he'd been ecstatic but Jeannie's teasing had gone on since their return from Schweinfurt. It was no more than a minor irritant. The best thing to do was not to scratch.

"If you don't mind Jeannie, I'll forgo today's offer of sarcastic badinage."

"Ah, big words: I must've struck a chord, then?"

Adam still didn't scratch.

"Hey, are you gonna tell Emma about your six tits orgy? I bet she'll laugh about that, won't she? Or is she not just 'one of the lads'?"

"Bloody hell Jeannie, are you still bitching on about those French girls in Garmisch?"

"Bitching? Bitching? Oh yeah, that's me all over, Adam, just a moaning bitch."

"Sorry. I didn't realise I'd hurt you that much."

"Well, you did."

The irritation threatened to flare into something serious but some calamine lotion entered in the guise of Steve. His beaming brown face suggested he was bearing tidings.

"Guess what?" Something in that 'guess what', told Adam that these tidings were not of the glad variety. "We've got a buyer for the drugs."

Adam's intuition was bang on target. "You what?"

"Yeah, Ulrike has a contact at *The Pussy Kat Klub*. We've got to go and meet him tonight, after work. She's coming to pick us up."

"Wow! Are there no limits to the excitement in your lives? Things just get better and better for you: orgies, drug dealing, what next?"

Adam didn't quite agree with Jeannie's summing up. "Steve, is this wise? Your previous association with drugs hasn't exactly been good, has it?"

"It's all under control. Ulrike has sorted it. She says we'll get at least a thousand bucks for what we've got."

"Oh no, you haven't shown the stuff to Ulrike, have you?" Adam put his hand to his forehead. "I mean, who is this contact? He could be a copper, a nutter, or owt. How do you know we can trust him?"

"We don't. That's why we're going to meet him."

"Oh bloody cosmic. Why is it that I feel a need to acquire the taste for hospital food, all of a sudden?"

"Don't be silly, Ace, there's nothing dangerous about it. We just hand over the gear and he gives us a grand."

Another Abba came on the jukebox: *Money, Money, Money.*

"No mate, you hand over the gear. I'm not going anywhere near that club."

Adam wasn't too pleased to find the familiar penguin bookends of Big Henri and his pal ready to greet them at the door of the Pussy Kat.

I hope they don't realise it was us that sampled their breakfast before them.

And more worrying, did they realise the breakfast nibblers were carrying a cache of assorted illegal substances. Steve was transporting the ill-gotten commodity around in a bag from the American commissary. "Very inconspicuous, the ideal hiding place."

"You didn't have to come." Steve tucked the bag under his arm.

"Don't keep reminding me. I should've left you to get mashed up by some gangster or sommat."

"So why did you come?"

"I don't know, Steve. Maybe I was worried my best mate would do something stupid on his own. Or maybe I'm just nuts."

"Or maybe you wanted to make sure you got your share of the thousand bucks."

"I think me being nuts is nearer the mark." Adam turned on Ulrike. "So, Ms Cook, where's your mate?"

Under cross-examination, on the way to Fulda, Ulrike had given little away about the contact, saying it was a friend of Gabi's. They were to meet Gabi outside the club. "Ah yes, she is come." Ulrike welcomed the long-legged vixen.

"Just a minute, Gabi." Adam pressed a hand against her shoulder. "Before we go in this club, I want to know all about this friend of yours who's buying the drugs. Who is he? Where's he from?"

"He is from here." She pressed a hand against *his* shoulder. "Why do you shit at my apartment?"

"What?"

"And where did you do it? I look everywhere."

"What the hell do you take me for?"

"You are one dirty pig."

"Frigging hell, Steve, didn't you explain?"

"I tried, but then I thought, what's the point? It's funnier if she thinks you did it."

"Look, Gabi, I didn't shit outside your apartment. It's a Yorkshire expression: to 'shit-out'. I thought I was going to miss-out on a night of entertainment with your good self."

She didn't seem convinced. "Come we must go in." They walked to the entrance.

The bouncers didn't search Steve's bag but they did stop the girls to talk to them. Adam wondered if the tiny grunt of acknowledgement from Penguin No: 2 might be an invite into the alley for his turn of light-relief with Gabi. He was welcome to her.

They were eventually waved through, down the rabbit warren to the bar with the Roman Catholic, confessional style booths. A low-cut evening dress showed them the way. The hostess was not Gudrun. Again: less distraction. They filed along the red velvet bench around the table. Everything was so familiar yet different to the previous occasion, mainly because the club was virtually empty. The hostess returned with the order. This time the drinks weren't free, though Gabi took care of the bill. Another good thing, he wouldn't be getting pissed.

"Is that stuff safe?" Adam asked. The drugs were in Steve's lap.

"He's got the jitters." Steve said to the girls.

You've got that right. Adam looked to the entrance. "So where's this contact?"

"He will come soon," Gabi said. Ulrike had explained in the car that the club was a well-known haunt for drug trafficking. This made perfect sense to Adam. Both he and Steve had learned from past experiences, in any house of prostitution, drugs will be hiding in the wardrobe. And of course, this was where the girls must've met the infamous Merle.

Yes, it made perfect sense to Adam that anyone with a connection to drugs would frequent a place such as this. Therefore, it should've been no surprise to see the baldpate of Alan Tait come in, accompanied by his two soldier henchmen. Nonetheless, surprised Adam was. "Christ at the frigging ballet!" He grabbed the brown paper bag and pushed it under the table to the floor between Steve's legs. "It's the baldy bugger." Even Steve's dark face blanched visibly pinker under the red light. The two henchmen went to sit at the bar. Adam froze as the hostess led Tait towards their booth.

"He comes," Gabi said.

Adam turned on her. "I thought you said he was German?"

"No, I said he was from here. He is from the US base."

Yes, it all made perfect sense, especially given the Merle connection. So why hadn't Adam worked it out before? He probably would have if bloody Gabi hadn't distracted him with all that stuff about shitting outside her apartment. Best mate or not, why hadn't he heeded his instincts and stayed well out of it?

"Well, well, well," Tait said. "If it isn't two of my British friends. Man, this is a surprise."

"Ah yes, you all know each other from your party," Ulrike said.

"You're damn right we know each other." Tait closed the glass door of the booth. "When Gabi told me she'd met an English musician, interested in selling, I figured it might be you guys. You want to know what else I figured, man?"

Answer came there none.

The Stylistics smooched away on the dance floor outside the closed-door. Nevertheless, the deep voice of Tait continued, as if competing with a Led Zeppelin concert. It was not a happy tone. "I figured you guys found my stuff and brought me down here to buy back my own goddamn merchandise."

Adam waited, expecting Tait to click his fingers. The sound of the click would travel through the glass, above the music to the two goons at the bar who'd come over and do what heavies do.

Steve spoke before the click came. "This isn't the way you think it is."

"Oh really?" Tait said. "What way is it then?"

Oh really? To Adam it seemed exactly the way the bald man had described. *This better be good, Steve.*

"We didn't set out to rip you off," Steve said.

"Oh no?" Tait's voice was slightly calmer.

"We found the stuff after we talked to you."

Tait stroked a hand across the back of his head, causing Adam to flinch. "Really? You found the stuff after I came to your club? Then how comes when my friend Gabi here came to your place to retrieve the goods, they weren't there anymore?"

The sneaky cow. So that's why she brought the quilt back.

"When she looked under the bed and in the box where I left them, they were gone."

Dropped her contraceptive pill? How did I fall for that one?

Gabi smiled at Adam.

Ulrike smiled at Steve.

The Englishmen smiled at no one.

Tait wiped his head, again. "And not only was the merchandise gone, the things I took out of the box to put the merchandise in, hey presto, that stuff somehow jumped itself back in the box and back under the bed where it started." He mimed a little demonstration of the things jumping back into their box. "Ain't that right, Gabi?"

"Oh yeah, you mean, the statues?" Steve said. "You could be right. The statues might've been in the box."

"You know what? You're damn right they were. So if you didn't put them there and you didn't take out the merchandise, it seems what we got here is *magic* statues." Tait's smile suggested he was enjoying himself.

"It's funny you should say that," Steve said. "They are supposed to be magic."

"I don't think you're helping, Steve." Adam wiped the sweat from his neck.

"I'm just saying," Steve said. "They come from Africa."

Tait thumped the table. "Well you better get your magic statues to conjure up my merchandise or Africa won't be a big enough place for you two to hide."

The signal to the goons was imminent. Adam delved under the table, grabbed the commissary bag and placed it in front of Tait.

While the bald man was checking the contents, Steve glared at Adam. "Listen, I'm not stupid. I knew it was your gear." The scouser's poker face never flinched but he couldn't disguise the desperation in his voice. "I knew you and Merle were friends with Ulrike and Gabi, so who else could the goods belong to? The reason we came was because you said they were worth five grand. I reckoned you might consider a thousand to get them back on the cheap side."

Tait massaged his temples. "Oh that's what you thought, was it? Well you got some balls, I'll give you that. But I got to tell you—"

"Christ in a mangle; look!" Adam's attention was diverted to Herr Vogel.

"What's up?" Steve was the first to ask. Various international versions of 'what's up' followed.

Adam cleared his throat. "That's him." Herr Vogel's bank manager appearance looked even more imposing in these surroundings. "That's who threatened to deport me. He's Kraut police, Robinson's oppo." He stood and took hold of Steve's arm. "Come on, it's a set up."

"Hold up there, buddy," Tait said. "You saying that's Lieutenant Robinson's German partner?"

"Like you didn't know," Adam said. "It's a bit of a coincidence finding him in this place when you're here. And if you don't know him, he must've followed you. Come on Steve, let's bugger off. We don't want to get caught up in all this."

"Hang on." Steve pulled his arm loose from Adam. "He hasn't paid us our thousand bucks, yet."

Tait laughed and tapped the commissary bag. "Now, why would I want to do that?"

"Because if you don't know our German friend over there," Steve said, "we could always call him over and introduce you."

Oh shit, that's the goons back in the picture. Shut up, you Peruvian pillock; do you know what you're saying?

It appeared not. "They already know all about your organisation. Isn't that right, Adam?" Steve craned his neck as though needing a better look at Vogel.

"Is that a fact, Adam?" Tait said.

Adam's mouth had momentarily stopped working. Steve's hadn't.

"They've already suggested us trapping you into doing some sort o' drugs deal. We could say that's what we're doing here. He'd be very interested to see what you've got in that bag."

"Halt one moment, Alan," Gabi said. "That man is not here on an undercover drugs assignment. That is Crazy Karl. He comes here all the time. He likes to do strange things with the baby's diapers."

"What strange things?" Tait asked.

"Yeah, what strange things?" Adam said.

There was a collection of dropped jaws as Gabi divulged Herr Vogel's perverse sexual secrets.

"Chuffing hell!" Steve said.

Various international versions of 'Chuffing hell' followed the part about the cooking oil and the lavatory brush. The German drugs director stimulated their imagination by disappearing into a booth.

"So, Limey," Tait said, "you still want to go talk to him?"

"Maybe not," Steve said. "It was worth a try."

"I ought to bust your head for trying to shake me down, that's what I ought to do but I'm gonna cut you some slack – this time." Tait held up the commissary bag. "Thanks for returning my merchandise." The inevitable click of the fingers finally arrived but not until he was crossing the dance floor. The goons obeyed the command and the three Americans left.

Gabi got up and squeezed past Adam. "This is payback for you dirty pig. *Tcheuss.*" She wiggled across the dance floor after Tait.

"Yeah, nice one, Adam," Steve said. "You just managed to lose me a thousand bucks."

"Whoa, back up there, *compadre*," Adam said. "Your Kraut tart, here, just nearly got me annihilated. I think the word you're both looking for is sorry."

"I am sorry," Ulrike said. "I did not know the drugs belonged to Herr Tait."

"Piss off," Adam said. "A likely story."

"I only know he is a friend from Gabi. I am only meeting Herr Tait when I am in the ambulance."

"Bollocks, you must think I fell out of the idiot tree."

Steve put an arm around Ulrike. "If she says she didn't know Tait was the contact, then she didn't know he was the contact."

"Then she must be frigging brain-dead."

"You'll be fucking brain-dead when I've kicked your head in, you self-centred twat."

The festivities throughout the remainder of the evening remained a little constrained.

Between sets at the following night's gig, Adam sat alone, sipping his *apfelwein*. A bald shadow fell across his table.

"Okay if I sit?" It was Alan Tait.

Shit, I knew it. Steve's half inched some of the drugs. "Look mate, this has nothing to do with me." Adam instinctively stood and looked for the goons.

"Cool it man, I ain't come to cause no trouble. Sit, man."

"I'll get him to return your stuff."

"What stuff? Please, just sit a minute. I need to talk to you."

"About what?"

Tait looked around before continuing. "This trap your buddy was talking about."

"Trap? I don't know anything about any trap."

"He said the Germans had tried to set a trap for us."

"Oh that." Adam sat. "It wasn't the Germans exactly. It was Lt Robinson."

"Billy Whizz?"

263

"Yeah, him." Adam exposed the lieutenant's plan of setting him up. He saw no reason not to. Tait now knew he wasn't an 'English dealer', anyway. "He's going to contact me when he's ready to make the deal."

"Perfect," Tait said. "Billy Whizz: even better."

"What do you mean, perfect?"

"This thousand bucks your buddy asked for, how'd you like to make it two thousand?"

"For what?"

"I want you to help me turn the tables on Billy Whizz."

"How do I do that?"

"Tell him it's on. You've set up a deal and he can be there when it goes down."

"I don't understand."

"What we need is a diversion. This could be perfect." Tait explained his strange objective. This opportunity had come along at the ideal time for his organisation. A consignment of merchandise was due in from across the East German border and Tait's plan with Adam would be an excellent decoy to occupy the snooping Billy Whizz. Tait seemed to delight in explaining that Merle had always brought the drugs through the Eastern Block because the border guards were easier to bribe. There was a suspicion that the local authorities had recently got wind of what was known in the narcotics' world as the Red Route and a double set up would be the ideal distraction. "So there you go, Limey, now I've told you all this, you can think of yourself as one of the gang." Tait stood and held out a hand. "Okay, you need to tell him a mite soon 'cos the consignment's due any time."

"Er, can we just back up a bit?" Adam saw no inducement to hide his fear. "I haven't agreed to anything, yet."

"Listen Limey, the way I see it, Billy has you by the balls. You either come in with us: and make yourself a bit on the way, or you got to deal with him on your own. And he's going to be a mite pissed when you can't deliver."

"That's all well and good, but what happens to me when you don't show up with the gear?"

"You don't have to worry none about that. We'll be there." Tait held out his hand again. This time Adam shook it, albeit reluctantly. "We'll be in touch, soon," Tait said.

Adam didn't mention Tait's proposition to the others not even to Steve, especially not to Steve, who was still sulking over losing his thousand dollars. Of course there was the prospect of the prize money being doubled but Adam was sceptical about that. To tell Steve he was going to receive a huge payout and for it then not to come off could make things worse between them. And anyway, if he was taking all the risk, why should he share with the sulky pillock. Actually, Adam hoped the whole thing might not happen at all, money or no money. However, Alan Tait's 'soon' was sooner than expected and from a totally unexpected source. A couple of nights after Adam's meeting, Jeannie was conducting her nightly struggle into her boob tube.

"Billy Whizz has told Lincoln he's to keep an eye on you, make sure you do what he's told you to."

"Has he, now?"

"And he told him he has to help you set up the trap to get Tait."

"Cosmic."

"Lincoln's also been telling me all about your plan with Tait to double-cross Billy Whizz."

Adam stopped applying his eyeliner. "How the frigging hell does Lincoln know about that?"

"Tait told him."

"Tait told him? I don't get it; Lincoln's with the Military Police. Why would Tait talk to him about double-crossing Billy?"

"I keep telling you, he's not with the Military Police. What Billy doesn't know is that Lincoln made friends with Merle at the party."

"What! MP or not, why would any reasonable minded human being make friends with that tattooed twat? He's a drug peddling monster."

"When Billy first started in narcotics, the only people he could catch were young kids dealing in speed. That's how he got his nickname. Anyway, he blackmailed one of these kids into working for him. But when one of these deals went tits up, Billy sold him out to the dealers. They killed him."

"What's this got to do with Lincoln joining forces with Merle?"

"The young kid who got killed was Abie, Lincoln's brother."

"You're sending me dizzy, here, Jeannie."

"He's been waiting almost a year to get Billy back."

"Christ on a bike!"

"He told Billy that before he joined up, he used to be in a rival gang and he wants to get back at Merle and he told Merle that Billy once caught him with some drugs and is blackmailing him.

"Christ in a frigging helicopter."

"This decoy thingy, Tait promised it'll not only divert Billy's attention away from the shipment, it should put him out of operation all together. That should be good for you as well, shouldn't it?"

"Bloody hell, first Lincoln's a soldier; then he's a copper, now he's a double bloody agent."

"So Lincoln's gonna tell Billy you've made contact and you're ready to set up the deal. The excitement goes on."

"Don't tell me, you've become a gang member as well. Bloody cosmic, I can't wait."

At least with Lincoln on board, Adam wouldn't be undertaking the operation alone, though he was still unsure who to trust. The captain laid out Billy's plan, simple enough. Adam would pose as a buyer; then Billy would catch Tait red-handed when they made the exchange.

"Never mind how Billy intends to catch Tait, what is Tait doing to Billy?" Adam asked.

"Tait's got a plan to set him up," Lincoln said.

"What sort of plan?"

"You'll see when it happens."

Given what'd happened to his brother, it was clear why Lincoln would want to get back at Billy but why was he helping a bunch of thugs? Maybe he had been in a rival gang: maybe Billy was blackmailing him: or maybe he was also getting two thousand dollars.

So far, all arrangements had been made through Lincoln. There'd been no direct contact between Adam and Billy. However, it was now the night of the pick up and Billy had insisted on being in on the kill. Initially, in wishing to make the trap secure, he'd insisted that the exchange took place on US territory. That way, he'd have the support of a full complement of MPs. However, Tait said there was no reason to make a deal with a civilian on the base with a perfectly safe venue in the Pussy Kat Klub. Billy had reluctantly agreed that the meeting would take place on neutral grounds. He would've been more reluctant had he been aware that the owner of the Pussy Kat Klub was yet another recruit into Tait's 'gang'.

Herr Vogel, himself, would not be in on the operation but he'd assured Billy that there'd be plain-clothed German police at the club to assist with the arrest.

The other band members now knew of the escapade but Steve hadn't yet been told of the 'reward' money. This hadn't been a problem for Adam as he and the Peruvian pillock were still not on speaking terms.

After the gig, Adam came off stage to a waiting taxi. This was to take himself, Lincoln and Billy to Fulda. Both soldiers wore civilian clothing.

Billy sat in the front with a briefcase on his lap. They exchanged few pleasantries throughout the journey. The only conversation entailed Billy ensuring that Adam and Lincoln knew what they were doing. He also informed them, much to Adam's discomfort, he would be providing back up after all. They were to meet up with a group of other MPs in Fulda. Thankfully, Billy instructed his four colleagues to wait outside in their car. It was not feasible to storm team-handed with a bunch of American MPs into a German, civilian nightclub. Billy said it wouldn't be a problem. "Tait ain't likely to bring too much muscle to deal with Mr Fogerty."

Adam, Lincoln and Billy entered the club past the familiar bouncers. Gudrun met the trio in the tiny foyer and led them through the rabbit warren to the inevitable red-lit booths. To get himself in position, Billy made sure they arrived well before the appointed time. Then, on Tait's arrival, he'd be able to pounce before the bald man had a chance to dispose of the evidence. Should Tait make a run for it, the officers outside would be able to take care of him.

Gudrun housed them in one of the vacant booths and took a drinks order. "Hey, what the hell, we've got plenty o' time." Billy was obviously excited. "You guys have done a pretty good job here. I'm buying. What'll you have, sir?"

"Just a beer," Lincoln said.

Adam chanced his arm and ordered a whiskey. He felt he needed it.

Billy scanned the room. "Vogel's men will be here already, in these booths." He scanned the room again. A long nosed man was propping up the bar. Billy nodded and smiled. "When these guys arrive, no heroics. When the thing goes down, leave everything to us."

Oh what a shame. I was hoping to take them all on single-handed.

For the first time, Billy opened the briefcase. Adam peered around the lid. He wished he hadn't. He was expecting to see rows upon rows of Deutschmark bills but there was merely a bulky envelope. However, alongside the envelope was a pistol. Gudren arrived with the drinks. Adam took a large swig of whiskey.

"I need to check the john," Billy said. Gudrun pointed the way.

Lincoln touched Adam's arm. "Just sit tight and don't worry." Billy's absence might've been the first opportunity for the captain to put Adam at ease but if that was his intention, it wasn't quite working.

"In case you hadn't noticed, he's got a gun," Adam said.

Lincoln nodded. "Yeah, I seen it. It's a Beretta, nine-millimetre. You can tell a Beretta by its chequered handle."

"Chequered bloody handle? I don't care if it's sky-blue pink, with yellow bloody dots, it's a frigging gun."

"I promise, you're in no danger."

"Lincoln, Billy might not be intending to bump me off but this other lot happen to be vicious drug dealers." Lincoln put a finger to his lips. Adam ignored the advice. "For some reason, I've yet to understand, it doesn't seem to bother you that these bastards we're helping, are evil drug peddling—" Lincoln slapped a hand over Adam's mouth.

Billy was back before Adam could quiz Lincoln further. He placed the briefcase on the table.

Lincoln tapped it. "I take it you've got real money in there and not just pieces of blank paper?"

"Don't you worry, Captain, I've taken care of the money. Let's just hope that the merchandise in their case is the real McCoy." Billy took a large gulp of his beer. He was still enjoying himself. Lincoln appeared to sense Adam's unease and touched his thigh under the table.

"But I am worried," Lincoln said. "It is army money ain't it? I wouldn't want to see the Army lose that money."

"As a matter of fact, it ain't army money; it's my own money."

"Well lieutenant, you must be doing some pretty heavy moon-lighting to have that sort o' dough. I sure don't have that much spare from my captain's pay-check."

"When I say it's my own money, I mean it came from another source outside the Army."

"The Army do know about this little transaction, don't they?" Lincoln asked.

"What, do you think I'm dumb?" Billy said. "Course the Army knows about it. Where do you think the four guys outside are from?"

"Then why aren't you using army money?"

"Look, you don't need to worry." Billy clenched a fist. "You just got to help me nail these bastards."

"Lieutenant Robinson, what am I doing here?" Lincoln folded his arms. "What are we doing in a civilian night club, wearing civilian clothes, with a British musician, waiting to exchange fifty-thousand Deutschmarks for narcotics? Why aren't we meeting on the base?"

"What the hell are you talking about? You know goddamn well why we're here." He leaned across the table and spoke directly into Lincoln's face. "You ain't going funny on me, are you Captain? I've been waiting a long time for this. Just remember why *you're* here, Captain, sir." The two officers were less than six inches apart, eyeball-to-eyeball. Lincoln broke the silence.

"I apologise, lieutenant. I just wanted to clarify the situation. It's very clear now."

Billy backed off. "Good." He took another drink from his beer. From outside the booth, The Drifters filled the void with 'Under The Boardwalk'. Billy opened the case, took out the Beretta and cocked a bullet into the chamber.

Adam took another swig of whiskey. "I need the toilet." He stood and tried to get past Lincoln.

"Hold on there, boy." Billy reached across the table and grabbed Adam by the cuff. "We don't have time for that, now. You should have gone when we first got here." The last person to say that to him had been his father, when Adam was ten years old.

Adam sat again and downed the remainder of his whiskey.

Gudren came over and tapped on the glass.

Billy opened the door.

"Your guest is on his way, Herr Fogerty."

"What guest?"

"Thank you Miss," Billy said. Gudren left. Billy looked at his watch, finished his drink and said: "Okay, we're going into the john. When Mr Tait gets here, you bring him in." He was directing all this to Adam. "Tell him you've stashed the money in there. Try and get him in there alone, if you can. When he's in, knock on the door of the first cubicle: three knocks if he's alone, two quick sets of three if he isn't." He demonstrated the knocks on the table. "You got all that?"

"Right got it, three knocks then two, no two sets of three," Adam said. "Yeah, I've got it, really, I've got it."

"You better have." Billy motioned to Lincoln. "Captain, you come with me. Make sure no one comes into the john that shouldn't be there." The two soldiers crossed to the toilet.

Adam wasn't alone for very long. Into the club, came the familiar baldpate of Tait. He also had a briefcase. The equally familiar, pair of henchmen accompanied him, taking up their usual position at the bar. Tait crossed the dance floor and opened the door of Adam's booth.

"He's in the toilet," Adam said. "I'm supposed to take you in there. He's got a gun." Mentioning the pistol sent Adam's hand reaching for his whiskey but the glass was empty.

"Okay," Tait said. "Everything's looking good." Adam couldn't get up to show the bald man over to the toilet as Billy had told him. He was too frightened to move. He awaited instructions from Tait. None were forthcoming. Instead, Tait circled around the other side of the table and knocked on the door of the boudoir. It opened from inside, out squeezed Merle and yet more surprising, if that were possible, behind him, Herr Vogel.

"Man, we got some good stuff." Merle carried a tape recorder.

"Right on," Tait said. Adam didn't say anything. He was dumbstruck by the sudden appearance of the two men from the closet.

"So, how's the world been treating you?" The man from Iowa offered his hand to Adam. A neck brace, obviously covering his recent injury, poked from under Merle's shirt.

"Oh you know," Adam managed to say. Frigging hell, what was going on? At their last meeting, Adam had pronounced Merle dead. No, he wasn't dead. The cobra must've taken a bit of a battering, but Merle himself appeared to be alive and kicking and living in a prostitute's closet.

"*Hallo* Herr Fogerty, welcome to Espionage." Herr Vogel edged around Tait. Merle handed him the recorder, then Vogel left the party and crossed to the long nosed man at the bar. Vogel and the man entered the booth opposite. All the fear felt by Adam was leapfrogged by curiosity about Merle, the long nosed stranger and the German interrogator.

"Is Vogel behaving himself?" Tait asked.

"So far," Merle said; "but we gotta watch him. Billy says he's got men waiting outside, as back up, right?" Merle looked to Adam for confirmation.

"What?" Adam collected his scattered faculties. "Oh yeah: four of 'em, across the road in an American car."

"A brown Buick," Tait said. "I saw it on the way in."

"Okay," Merle said. "Tell Larry to take the boys out back. I'll get the cops to come round and meet them." Tait went over to the henchmen at the bar to relay the instructions. The henchmen took up the baton, crossed to another booth, from which four more men spilled out on the dance floor. The six-man reception team left the disco. Merle then summoned Gudrun over to the booth. "Go outside. Across the road is a brown Buick. Tell the men inside that Lieutenant Robinson needs help. Take them down the side alley. Larry will be waiting for them."

Oh the infamous alley. Adam's trepidation momentarily lapsed again, when an image of Gudrun frolicking down the alley with ten men flashed across his mind. Gudrun set off on her errand.

From the opposite booth emerged Herr Vogel, accompanied by the long-nosed stranger and three others. The contingent set up camp in the booth next to Adam's. It was all too hectic.

Tait had returned to the booth. "They're Kraut cops." Adam was grateful for any titbits of information but it explained nothing. Then it mattered little because anxiety returned when an American hand settled on the English shoulder.

"Now go in there and tell Billy: Tait won't play ball," Merle said. "Tell him: he's sent you to get the money."

"Bloody hell. He'll shoot me."

Merle laughed. "Man, this guy's so funny."

Adam didn't laugh.

"Go get the money." The American hand squeezed the English shoulder. "Unless you really object to working for: 'evil drug peddling bastards'."

Adam tried a smile but it got stuck at a grimace.

The hand squeezed a little harder. "That is what you called us, ain't it?"

Adam looked at the hand. His English shoulder resigned to undertake the mission.

Merle took away his hand. "And don't mention *me* being here."

Simple though Billy's instructions were; Adam went over them several times on the short journey to the toilet.

Knock three times on the ceiling if he's on his own, twice on the pipe if he isn't. Something like that. He didn't say how many times if I'm on my own.

Inside, Lincoln was sitting on an imitation brown marble shelf, alongside a beige sink. Adam shrugged, not knowing what to do or say. Lincoln nodded and pointed at the first cubicle. Adam said nothing, but knocked four straight raps. The door burst open, out jumped Billy, brandishing his Beretta.

"Okay you turkeys, on the goddamn floor …"

Adam's heart jumped into the beige sink but then the absurdity of the situation suddenly hit him.

Okay you turkeys?

"What the hell's going on here?" Billy's bellowing only added to the ludicrousness.

"Tait won't come in," Adam said. "He's sent me to fetch the money out."

"Damn." Billy slapped his palm against the cubicle door. "Has he brought the merchandise with him?"

"Well, he's carrying a briefcase."

"Good, how many of them are they?"

"He's on his own." Adam tried to field the questions without saying the wrong thing.

"He won't be on his own," Billy said, "He'll have somebody already in there. Where is he?"

"What?" Adam nearly missed a slip-catch.

"Where is he? Is he in the booth, at the bar, or doing a goddamn boogie on the dance floor?"

"He was in the booth, when I left him."

"Okay, I'll have to rush him. The Krauts can take care of his friends."

"If he sees your face, he's gonna make a run for it." Lincoln jumped down from his marble perch. "He'll be out o' this place quicker than you can spit."

"You got a better suggestion, Captain, sir?"

"Well yes I have," Lincoln said. "Give the money to the British kid. Adam can keep him occupied with the deal; then you can sneak up on him."

"Hey, hang on a minute," the British kid said.

"Okay," Billy said. "But you better take good care o' this money. You better guard it with your life 'cos that's what it'll cost if you lose it."

"I don't want to guard it. I don't want to take it."

Billy took the envelope from the briefcase and pressed it against Adam's chest. "You got two minutes; then we'll be out. Keep him talking as much as you can, especially if you see me coming."

"Frigging hell. Thanks a lot, mate," Adam said to Lincoln. "I'll do you a favour, sometime."

He set off back through the disco with the money. The hive of coming and going preceding Adam's visit to the toilet had settled. The lone figure of Tait occupied Adam's table. Merle was nowhere in sight. Adam took care not to close the door.

"Everything okay?" Tait was drumming his fingers on the briefcase.

"I've got the money." Adam brandished the envelope. "He's coming to get you, in two minutes. What happens now?"

"Just sit tight," Tait said. "Give me the money." He counted the contents. Though relieved to see that the envelope actually contained real Deutschmarks, Adam was unsure why he should feel any easier. Genuine money didn't necessary make the situation any less dangerous, but then fewer people would be annoyed when the big bang came.

"Where's Merle?" Adam looked towards the door of the boudoir.

"The boss ain't needed to take care of this."

The big bang was on its way. "Don't look now but Billy Whizz has come in." Adam took a gulp of air. "He's edging his way round to us. Keep your head down, please."

Tait didn't give any cause for alarm. Engrossed in the money, he faked his ignorance.

Billy slid through the open door into the booth. His Beretta was immediately at Tait's temple. "Hello Mr Tait. I'll take that." He took the money. "Leave your hands on the table where I can see them." Tait didn't speak. "You boy, open the case." Adam pulled Tait's briefcase to his side of the table and opened it. The case contained one large plastic package of clay brown powder.

Shit, I hate heroin.

Tait and co were the type of scum that used to feed Steve's habit. Never mind why Lincoln was helping them, why was he?

"Give it over," Billy said.

Adam pushed the open case across to Billy, who placed the money envelope alongside the plastic package and closed it. From behind Billy's head, coming out of the adjacent booth, were the long-nosed stranger and the three men, guns drawn. The Big Bang had definitely arrived in full make-up, wearing a brightly coloured party hat with streamers.

Long Nose shouted instructions in English. One of the other men gave a simultaneous German translation. "Everyone, stop what you are doing. Nobody move. This is a police raid. Put down your weapons and come out onto the dance floor with your hands above your head." From the booths and from behind the bar, seven people did as ordered.

"I've got this one covered," Billy called, his Biretta still aimed at Tait's head. "This one is mine."

Long Nose poked his gun into the booth at the lieutenant. "Put your weapon on the table."

Billy gave him a startled look but did so. "Hey boy, be careful with that thing. I'm on your side. I take it you're one of Vogel's men. I'm Robinson. I work with Karl, you dumb ass Kraut bastard."

Long Nose picked up the discarded Beretta. "*Raus hier.*" He signalled them to vacate the booth. They came out on the dance floor with their hands above their heads, Billy protesting all the way. Tait winked at Adam. "On the floor, hands behind your backs," the officer said. Adam and Tait joined the other clientele face down on the floor. Adam began to perspire when he felt the handcuffs click shut behind his back.

"What are you doing, boy?" Billy asked. "Don't you know who I am? I'm with the American Military Police. I'm on your side."

"You are a bad policeman," Long Nose said.

Before Billy had a chance to argue, Herr Vogel came from the adjacent booth.

Billy lowered his hands. "Karl. Where the Sam Hill did you spring from? This putz, here has just threatened me with his gun. Me! He threatened me."

"On the floor," Long Nose said.

"*Halt, ich kenne diesen Mann*," Herr Vogel said. Adam lay on the floor, totally bemused. He wondered when would be the right time to start protesting his own innocence. He knew that there was some sort of scam going on; yet the actions of Herr Vogel and his German colleagues surprised Adam, as much as it obviously surprised Billy. Herr Vogel had just told Long Nose that he knew the lieutenant. This was as expected; the following charade wasn't. "Lance, you surprise me," Herr Vogel said. "You appear to have been caught with your hands in the cookie jar."

"What?" Billy glared at Vogel. "Karl, what the hell are you talking about?"

Long Nose had entered the booth. "*Hier ist es*." With a strain of his eye, Adam saw the officer bring the briefcase from the booth.

"What the Sam Hill's going on here?" Billy said. The pistols of the other officers were all pointing in his direction. Herr Vogel said nothing. He opened the case and poked a finger into the bag of brown powder. He tasted his finger, gave a little spit, checked the contents of the money envelope and closed the briefcase. He then clicked a finger at one of the other officers. The officer went into his booth and brought out the tape recorder Merle had given Vogel.

Billy's ravings halted when the play button revealed his own voice saying: "*Don't you worry, Captain; I've taken care of the money. Let's just hope that the merchandise in their case is the real McCoy.*" The tape whirred on. "*Well, as a matter of fact, it ain't army money, it's my own money.*"

Billy aimed a visible lunge at Herr Vogel. "Hey Karl, what is this, some kind o' set up? You know damn well where the money came from. You provided it yourself."

"I can assure you, Lieutenant, I do not have access to that amount of money."

Adam turned his head toward Tait, who lay next to him on the floor.

"It's Merle's money," Tait whispered. "Don't worry; everything's fine." He gave Adam a soothing smile.

The tape button flicked again. Lincoln's voice turned Adam's not so soothed head back towards the action. "*Lieutenant Robinson, what am I doing here? What are we doing in a civilian night club, wearing civilian clothes, with a British musician, waiting to exchange fifty-thousand Deutschmarks for narcotics?*" Lincoln, himself, was mysteriously missing from the party.

Billy's frown showed as much disbelief as the realisation of betrayal. "Why, Karl? Why?"

Herr Vogel gave him no reason. Instead, he displayed what was obviously a warrant and said: "Lieutenant Lance Robinson, *Sie sind verhaftet.*"

"You can't arrest me, you dumb ass Kraut." The handcuffs were already on before Billy had finished speaking his first sentence. "You can't get away with this," he called, as he was led towards the door. "Everyone's gonna know they got you in their pocket." Billy's objections wound their way back through the rabbit warren. Adam cast his thoughts into the polished dance floor. If Merle's organisation was powerful enough to get the head of the American Military Police arrested then anything could happen. And of course, Tait wasn't exactly the most trustworthy. Adam himself could be bound for Billy's adjoining cell.

After Billy left, Vogel said something to Long Nose, who then relayed instructions. The officers helped up the prostrate clientele. The removal of their handcuffs washed more anguish over Adam. He and Tait remained handcuffed. Herr Vogel approached the shackled pair.

"Let the Limey go, he ain't part o' this," Tait said.

"Here, here." Adam waited in hope of his release.

"Of course he is part of it." Herr Vogel leaned his head between Tait and Adam. "I need to take you both to the police station in order to make the arrest look authentic." Vogel's grin brought out more beads of sweat on Adam's forehead and the German officer's instructions to his long-nosed colleague didn't help mop the worry from his brow. "Take these men to the police station. I will attend to them later." Adam assumed the English instructions were for the benefit of himself and Tait. "Take this, also." Vogel gave the briefcase, containing the drugs and money to his second in command. "Be certain to take good care of the evidence."

Long Nose took the case from his boss then he in turn, issued orders down the chain. Adam decided it was time to put in his six-penneth.

"Hey mate, I think this joke's gone far enough." His six-penneth met with total disregard from Vogel.

The handcuffed Adam and Tait were escorted outside and guided into the back of a waiting green Volkswagen. Long Nose carried the briefcase in the front seat, alongside his driver.

"I don't like this," Adam said. "I'm gonna end up getting stuffed. I can feel it."

"Don't worry, we ain't done nothing wrong." Tait smiled at Adam. Long Nose peered over his shoulder. He said nothing but raised an eyebrow.

"We don't even get to ride in a decent motor," Adam said. "It's like riding in the back of a washing machine. In England, the police have Jags." The effrontery went unheeded. The green Indesit hurtled along the streets of Fulda.

After stopping at some traffic lights, they set off slowly. From a side street, a large American car pulled out. The police car swerved, too late. The other car rammed into the front wing. Adam, still handcuffed, went sprawling across Tait's lap. The Volkswagen shunted into a post. The stunned police officers groaned. Adam sat up to see a balaclava-masked man at the window.

The man pulled open the passenger door and poked a pistol into the car. "Don't be a hero, just hand over the case." The accent was American. He reached in and grabbed the briefcase. He then stepped back and fired a pistol round into the tyre of the Volkswagen. The gunshot echoed through the empty Fulda streets. Adam wished he'd worn his brown trousers. The masked man leapt back into his car and the American monster sped off into the early morning.

Before the car was out of sight, Long Nose was on the car radio, gabbling some sort of German code into the mouthpiece.

"... *Braun Buick, Americanisch. Ludwig, Nordpole, Caesar, funf, acht, sechs.*"

Tait blew some invisible debris from his shoulder. "Those bastard MPs could've killed us."

Long Nose turned to Tait "What are you saying? Do you know *dieser* men?"

"I think you'll find those plates are assigned to the Military Police," Tait said. "They shouldn't be too hard to trace. Can't be too many brown Buicks around here this time of day."

"Hey, you're right. That was the same car that Billy's back-up team was in." Adam felt he should add to the information. "I don't frigging believe this. The Military Police have just tried to wipe us out."

"They were obviously desperate to get their money back," Tait said. "Now they've got the drugs as well. Are you okay?"

"Am I okay? What do you frigging think?"

Long Nose was back on his radio. For some inexplicable reason, Tait had a smug expression. He was still grinning twenty minutes later when two other green Volkswagens arrived to pick up the party and complete the journey to Fulda police station.

Inside, with handcuffs removed, Adam and Tait were led to a room where Herr Vogel and two other officers waited. It was the same room where Adam had had his last Fulda interrogation.

"Come in Gentlemen." Herr Vogel motioned them forward from behind his desk. "You will be pleased to know that I am releasing you without charge." Adam closed his eyes to get a better sense of relief. When he opened them, the German officer flashed a smile. "You may or may not have been complicit in these affairs. I give to you the benefit from the doubt." Vogel checked towards the other officers in the room. There was no reaction. He gave another smile. "If there was any evidence against you contained in the briefcase, this was stolen during the attack on the car bringing you here. Herr Fogerty, you have been very fortunate. I release you with a warning. I advise you to behave yourself for the short remaining time you have in our country. When do you return home?"

"Soon, in a couple of weeks," Adam said.

"If you must return to my country, do not return to Fulda or even Wildflecken. Do you understand?"

"Abso-frigging-lutely! Er, sorry, I mean yes, I understand."

Vogel came out from behind his desk. "Herr Tait, you are also very fortunate, this time." He emphasised the words "this time" directly at Tait's face, making him flinch on each syllable. "I know I will meet you and your American friends again. Next time I will be prepared. I will not, as you say, be caught with my trousers down." Vogel himself escorted them to the exit where he abandoned them to the early, winter morning of Fulda.

A sense of liberation mingled with the longing to discover who'd done what to whom but Adam's priority was: "How are we gonna get back to Wildflecken? Fulda, again, I keep ending up in this place."

"Don't worry, Limey, Merle ain't gonna let us down." Tait set off across the police station car park. Limey scampered behind, neither of them dressed against the cold. Before Adam had a chance to establish where they were going, he saw a welcome sight. Parked a hundred and fifty yards down the road was Merle's Oldsmobile, asleep on the back seat, Lincoln. Tait tried the locked door then tapped the window. Lincoln stirred and opened the door for the two freezing men.

"You guys been a long while." The captain clambered into the driver's seat.

"You might say we had a run in with Larry and the boys," Tait said.

"What kind o' run in?" Lincoln's question echoed Adam's thoughts.

And I was there.

Tait explained: Merle's henchman, Larry, drove the brown Buick that'd crashed into the police car.

Adam screwed up his eyes. "You mean they weren't Military Police?"

Tait continued: the four MPs stationed outside the club by Billy were high-jacked by Merle's henchmen. The brown Buick was then used to retrieve the merchandise plus the money from the possession of the German police. By using the American car, suspicion could be planted with Billy and the Military Police.

Adam felt like he'd been shooting the rapids and had just missed the waterfall. Fatigue and confusion began to weigh heavy in his head. "I can't take all this in." Any more and the raft would probably sink under the extra weight. He threw his head back on the seat. "Oh, there is one other thing you can tell me. How did you get Vogel to arrest Billy Whizz?"

"Man, we got some powerful weapons of persuasion in our arsenal," Tait said.

Adam was about to ask him to elaborate but Lincoln's question jumped the queue. "What will happen to him?"

"Who Billy? Ain't too sure what'll happen to him," Tait said. "Probably nothing."

"Nothing?" Lincoln almost swerved on to the pavement. "What do you mean nothing?"

"Vogel will just warn him away from our operations for a while. The Krauts ain't in a position to take any risks of prosecution."

"You mean I just went through all that for nothing? I thought you said this would get him off my back?" Lincoln glared at Tait.

"I said we'd make it impossible for him to operate. I think you'll find that's what we've done."

Bloody hell! Adam's raft was really rocking.

Lincoln banged the steering wheel. "This ain't gonna help with—"

"Hey, Captain, you came to us, remember?" Tait turned to the back. "You done a good job, Limey." He gave the top of the front seat a tap as though this would transfer back to Adam. "The boss is gonna be real pleased with you."

"Oh yeah: what happened to Merle?" Adam asked.

"Where do you think he is?" Tait gave a short laugh. "Why do you think we set up this operation, in the first place? As soon as we got Billy on tape, the boss went to the border to collect the shipment from the Reds."

So, hang on, I still don't know how they got Vogel to stitch up Billy? And I still don't know if that means I'm in the clear. Lincoln doesn't seem very happy. And I still ... What was the question again? Adam's fatigue began to get the upper hand in the fight with his confusion.

"Good, so long as y'all are happy," Lincoln said. "Don't worry none about me. You got what you wanted on tape and you collected your shipment."

"Hell, yeah." Tait laughed. "Merle would've been a mite pissed if we hadn't, spending all that time in the closet with Vogel, an' all."

"But that still leaves me with Billy. And now he knows it was me tricked him into saying what he did on the tape."

Adam tried to keep track of the conversation in the front so he could fill in his own missing details but the rapid-shooting ride kept veering off course.

"Come on, Captain, ain't nobody gonna take him serious after this." The raft changed into a roller coaster carriage. The impending waterfall turned into a deep plunge down the track. Adam hung on tight and tried to piece together the fragments of the previous six hours.

"We've come to the end of your ride." Lincoln's voice jolted Adam from his confused dream. The car pulled into Bahnhof Strasse.

"Well done," Tait said. "You did a good job. You'll get your money real soon."

Next night, Steve was sitting up in bed, doing his crossword. Due to his ongoing giant sulk, conversation from him had diminished to grunted responses. Adam was finding the curdled relationship depressing. Earlier, he'd thought maybe sharing the experiences of his Billy Whizz escapade might retrieve the situation. After a hairy night like that, not even Steve could say he was being "melodramatic". He wouldn't mention the money, though. If he did actually receive it, maybe then he'd think about giving him a few bob. That's providing he got an apology from the scouse git for being such a dick. However, so far, no apology had come. The inevitable bedroom rendezvous had arrived and the scouse git hadn't spoken a word. Adam wielded the icebreaker. "How long is this going to go on?"

"What?"

"You, staying out of my road all the time. Don't you want to know how it went last night?"

"I hear you were magnificent."

"Oh, you've heard about it, have you?" Adam awaited a response but Steve scrolled down his clues. "Was it Ulrike told you?" Answer came there none. This was obviously a difficult crossword because Adam was having trouble getting his attention. Why was Steve taking this so far? Perhaps now he and Ulrike were an item, there was a certain amount of regret and resentment that Adam had had sex with her. That's probably why he didn't like Merle, 'cos he'd shagged her, as well. "So, how's it going with you and Ulrike?"

"What the fuck has that got to do with anything?"

"Just asking."

"Why?"

"I envy you. I tried talking to Jeannie about *my* love life, the other day, but she just wanted to take the piss."

"Really? Not like her."

"I think it's good that you're with somebody." Adam unfastened the silver clasp of his jerkin. "It's about time you settled down, you old get." He stopped short of giving Steve's arm a friendly dig. "We need to think about where we're going in life. I mean we're not getting any younger; and some of us are not getting younger more than others."

Steve's pen went down. "Listen, Captain Marvel, I can take you on at anything you want."

"No, no, I'm not saying you can't. I'm trying to tell you something about me. I've changed."

"Yes, you have. You're a bigger arsehole than ever."

It didn't look like Adam was going to get his apology. "Anyway, I'm glad about you and Ulrike and if you're miffed 'cos—."

285

"For your information, it wasn't Ulrike who told me, it was Jeannie. Ulrike's moved out of Gabi's place; not that Gabi would've told her anything, anyway, her being too brain-dead to understand."

"Steve, this is daft. I'm sorry if I insulted your bird." Adam stopped undressing. "Okay, maybe she didn't know Tait was the contact."

"What do you mean, maybe?"

"She still dropped us in it."

"She didn't drop us in anything. You gave away my money. Speaking of which, when were you going to tell me about this two-thousand bucks you're getting for your heroic deeds?"

"What? Sorry, I was going to tell you after I'd got it."

"Yeah, course you were."

"I doubt I'll even get any money. They probably just said that to get me to help them. I'm not exactly in a position to sue them if I don't get paid, am I?" Adam sat on his bed. Steve was back doing his crossword. "Steve, they're a set of bloody thugs. I'm not sure I should even take their drug money."

"Yeah, must be such a struggle. Mm, let's see. Do I pocket two grand or not?"

"Hey, that was no picnic, last night. If I ever do get paid, I'll have earned every penny. "

"Should've been a piece of piss for a hot-shot drug dealer, like you."

Ah, maybe that was the problem. Steve resented the fact that Adam had become 'one of the gang' and he was missing out having access to all those drugs. "I promise you, mate; you're well out of it."

"Oh, that's why you shit on me, is it? You were looking out for me. Oh, thanks - 'mate'."

"What? I didn't shit on you. They didn't exactly give me any choice in the matter. And if I hadn't given Tait the gear, 'Gabi still knew we had it."

"*We* had it? As Tonto said to the Lone Ranger: 'What's this *we* shit?'"

Adam got his wash bag. "Tell you what, if I really do get paid, let's split it three ways, you, me and Ulrike. I mean, she did set the thing up in the first place."

"This has got fuck all to do with chuffing money. It's to do with you being a twat. You can stuff it right up your arse." Steve threw down the crossword and pulled his bedcovers over his head.

Adam went to the bathroom. *Yep, Adam, I'd say that went very well.* When he returned he got into bed.

Steve came out from under his covers. "Oy?"

"What?"

"The fucking light!"

The following morning, Steve was in the living room engrossed in a cup of coffee. Adam headed straight for the kitchen where T sipped at hers. "Morning, lover-boy, do you want a brew? Kettle's just boiled."

Adam tried to decipher why her grin was lighting up the room "Thanks."

T set about her task. "Well?"

"Well what?"

She broke off making the coffee and called into the living room. "Steve, didn't you give Adam the message?"

"What message?" Adam asked.

Steve called back. "Oh yeah, while you were out performing your heroic deeds the other night, your bird called."

Adam rushed into the living room. "My bird? You mean Emma?"

"Might've been Emma, then again, you've got so many birds you can't live without, it might've been anyone, Emma, June Roundhill, Gabi."

T came into the living room. "It was Emma."

"Emma?" Adam turned to Steve. "Why didn't you tell me?"

"Must've forgot, what with all the excitement."

"I've got her number upstairs if you want to call her back," T said.

"Thanks, T." Adam followed her up to the only telephone in the house.

"Colin's still in bed, though. I'll have to get him up, give you a bit of privacy."

Adam came down from his phone call to find Colin and T in the living room. He strode past them, heading straight for Steve, who'd gone into the kitchen. "Thanks a lot, you bastard."

Steve raised a fisted guard. "You asked for it, you conceited arsehole."

"You just couldn't stand to see me happy, could you? I've been waiting ages for her to get back to me."

"Yeah well, she deserves a better arsehole than you."

"I'll arsehole you, you black scouse get."

Colin came in the kitchen and rushed between them. "Hey, hey, hey, what's going on?"

"Emma phoned us while I was in Fulda," Adam said. "And this Peruvian twat told her I was out shagging."

"I didn't say you were shagging; I said you were at a night club, which you were." Steve leant back against the sink. "She asked if you were with a girl. I told her you were with two, which you were, Gabi and Gudren. And knowing you, you probably *were* shagging."

"I wasn't shagging Gabi, Gudren or any other fucker, you bastard."

"That's enough." Colin held up a hand. "Knock it on the head. We've got a gig to do tonight."

"Have you any idea what you've done?" Adam stabbed a finger in Steve's direction.

Colin brushed it aside. "Adam, I said that's enough."

Jeannie came in. "What's going on?"

"Nowt," Adam said.

Jeannie dropped some bread into the toaster. "You and me have got a party tonight."

"What?"

"Merle's throwing a party at Gabi's place to celebrate his success at the border. Lincoln's picking us up, after the gig. Merle's got some money for you."

"Well, isn't that cushty?" Steve said. "Looks like you'll be shagging Gabi and Gudren, after all."

"Fuck off," Adam said.

T picked up the coffee she'd made for Adam earlier. "It'll be cold, this. I'll make you another."

Lincoln picked up Adam and Jeannie in Merle's Oldsmobile. Adam was in the rear, still smarting from his encounter with Steve. "She hung up on me, thanks to that scouse get."

"Really sorry, Adam," Jeannie said.

"Thanks love." He patted her shoulder. "You know, you two make a good couple. You want to look after her, Lincoln. You've got yourself a nugget there."

"Bloody hell," Jeannie said. "Get me to a doctor. My ears have just gone. I thought I heard Adam pay me a compliment."

"Come on, Jeannie; you know I've always had a soft spot for you."

"Now I know there's an alien taken over his body."

"Did Jeannie give you the good news?" Lincoln asked.

"What good news?"

"Billy Whizz ain't going to be bothering us, no more." Despite the dark, Lincoln's grin registered through the rear view mirror. "Merle not only soured things real bad between him and the Germans, the Army decided to send his ass back home. They think they got enough evidence on the tape for a court martial. Ain't sure what'll happen about witnesses but can't see them inviting you over to the States."

"Cosmic."

"You don't sound too happy about getting him off your back."

"What? Yeah, course I am. Just wondering what tonight's all about. What is it you lot want me to do for you, now?"

"Me? I don't want you to do anything, Adam."

Jeannie turned to the rear. "I told you why Merle wants to see you. He's got some money for you."

"I'm sure he has."

"Hey listen, Adam." Lincoln's grin had turned to a questioning frown. "I ain't part of Merle's set up."

"Aren't you? So what are we doing here, then, in his car?"

"Goddamn, Adam, I hate those bastards more than you can know."

"So why are you still helping them? You've got rid of Billy so it's not him you're after. Or are you coming to this so-called party 'cos you've been promised a big pay-out, as well?"

Lincoln pulled the car into the kerbside and stopped. "Listen to me. The reason I came from Hanau is 'cos I owed Billy for what he did to my brother."

"I know, Jeannie told me he sold your brother out to some gang who killed him."

"That's right. And that gang was Merle's. They killed Abie. They killed my kid brother. I ain't gonna rest 'til every one of them murdering bastards is locked away."

Adam let the seriousness settle. "Sorry." *Fuck! Was Merle really a murderer?*

Lincoln drove off again. "You know, maybe you could help me, Adam."

"Help you? Help you with what?"

"It seems Merle kinda likes you. That might be useful."

"Useful as what?"

"You could maybe find out some things."

"I think you might be mixing me up with some sort of hero, or something."

"No, Adam, I ain't mixing you up with no hero. I ain't forgot who it was tried to sell me down the river."

"Hey look, Lincoln, I didn't have any choice with Billy—"

"I'm only joking."

Adam wasn't too sure whether he was or wasn't.

They arrived at the Fulda den of iniquity, 'House of the Six Tits'. "Whatever happens, I'm not leaving down the drainpipe," Adam said.

"You what?" Jeannie said.

"Aw nowt." It was a momentary reminder of Adam's lost camaraderie with Steve.

Drenched in a sense of curiosity, they were met at the apartment door by Gabi. After a scowl at Adam, she led them into the living room where they were greeted by Gudrun, Merle, Tait, and several members of the 'Larry and the Boys' entourage. The first thing Adam noticed was a screen and a film projector.

Still in his neck brace, Merle proffered an envelope to Adam. "Here, two-thousand, right. Well done boy, you earned it."

After the initial shock that he'd actually been paid and he wasn't asked to do anything more for it, a slight pang of regret that Steve wasn't there to receive his share of the reward sidled alongside Adam. *Nah, bollocks to him.* He brushed aside the pang and 'pocketed' the envelope. Ignoring the obvious questions about the screen, Adam involuntarily said to Merle: "I never got a chance to ask before but how's Jodie?"

Merle gave Adam a scary look but then went on to explain. In order to avoid any embarrassment with the German authorities, a week after the stabbing, Jodie had been shipped back to America. There'd be no trial. Though relieved to hear this news, Adam couldn't help feeling that the affair had left Merle sitting pretty, if you could call a face like that 'pretty'. The ugly bugger reinforced Adam's resentment. "I guess that's something else I've to thank you for. At least it got the bitch off my back and me and my girls can do what we like, when we like." His two girls were serving up drinks to the guests.

Tait stepped forward. "Okay we're ready." He plonked a chair in front of the screen. "Sit here, Limey. Now you'll see how we got Kinky Karl to play ball. After we showed him this, he'd have iced his own mother."

The guests readied themselves. Anticipation heightened with the switching out of the lights. The whirr of the projector started up and light from the screen spilled into the room.

On screen Herr Vogel, accompanied by Gudrun, entered into one of the boudoir closets of the Pussy Kat Klub. The film had a strange fish-eye effect. Aside the bed was a bowl of water and, what appeared to be, bathing accessories, a cucumber and an egg. Vogel began undressing, as did Gudrun, releasing her wonderful breasts into the already cramped space.

"Blessed be God." The entire personnel appeared to take an intake of breath to accompany Lincoln's seemingly inadvertent benediction.

"Yeah, you don't get many of them to the pound." Adam tried opening his eyes wider to absorb the whole vista. A fondling memory brought a smile. He peered behind him into the darkened section of the room but couldn't tell whether or not Gudrun was blushing.

The on-screen Gudrun was showing no signs of embarrassment. Kinky Karl was demonstrating how he'd acquired his nickname. Taking the egg from among the items next to the bed, he smashed it into his stomach and smeared the raw contents over his body. He showed particular relish when he rubbed the yokey gunge into his genitals. Gudrun took no part in this activity until suddenly screaming at him. The dialogue was all in German but it was obvious that she was chastising him for his actions. Vogel cowered from this admonishment. Gudrun then made him turn over on his front and to great whoops of delight and encouragement from the voyeurs watching the film; she lay into him with several whelps across his bottom. At the peak of his excitement, she stopped slapping him. She then massaged and bathed him. Although viewed with much interest and fascination, it was the finale of the film that Adam found most astonishing. After Gudrun had bathed and dried the police officer, she laid him out. He lifted his knees in the air. She then picked up the cucumber, smeared the end with a great dollop of Vaseline and rammed it hard into his anus. There were more whoops of delight from the onlookers but Vogel's screams could still be heard. Gudrun then covered his bottom with talcum powder, dressed him in an out-sized nappy and finally cradled him into her ample bosom where he suckled like an infant for the remainder of the film.

"Well fuck me wi' rough end of a rasp!" Jeannie said, as the lights came back on. There was little other comment needed.

16 T's Adventures: Wildflecken. Feb '77:

If A Picture Paints A Thousand Words.

T squared up to her image in the bathroom mirror and aimed the first verbal blow. "You ugly cow." She refused to back down from the stare of the Haggard Woman. "You must be at least three shovels, this morning." It was useless. The woman was immune to insults. T submitted and turned away from her challenger. The defeat reinforced her depression.

Five and a half weeks had passed since her encounter with Barry White, Jim Beam and William's web of ecstasy. Colin had repeated his promise to start a family as soon as they got home. In fact he'd been unbelievably nice since their reconciliation. If only he'd be horrible to her, it'd be fitting punishment for her adulterous deeds. But Colin didn't know of her deeds. If he had known, though he'd never raised a hand to her in the past, she was sure she'd now be dead, no more than she deserved. The nicer he was; the more chimes of guilt would peal like wedding bells. During the moments she didn't feel guilty, she felt guilty for not feeling guilty. She mentioned nothing of this to anyone, especially not Jeannie.

There was one tick in the plus box, in less than a week they'd be returning home to good old Yorkshire. But this carried a down side, home to no income. Also in the cheerless section it was unlikely she'd ever see William again. Even if they did come back for another tour, as Colin had promised, there was no guarantee they'd return to Schweinfurt.

No, that was probably a good thing. It was all so confusing. Should she even have gone back with Colin, promise or no promise? Having done so, what was she supposed to do with her feelings for William? But if she hadn't gone back, what would she do at the end of the tour and the rest of her life.

And, on top of all that, although finances, homesickness and even love-sickness might've been lead characters in her current depression, these cameos were downgraded to bit parts when compared to their roles in the Big Picture.

Stop it. Don't even think of the Big Picture.

The fact that she was almost two weeks overdue with her period was too horrendous to think about. And anyway, it was a bit early to dwell on that sort of catastrophe. Happen she'd miscalculated, things being thrown skew whiff lately. She'd messed up her pill since Frankfurt. Having said that, she hadn't worried enough about it to mention it to William. Contraception hadn't even been discussed. She drew the veil back across the Big Picture and left the bathroom.

Later that night, Colin came from the stage. "What's got into you now, you miserable bugger? What were you doing in 'Amorous'? You're singing like a plank."

"Sorry, I've been a bit pre-occupied." She certainly didn't give a stuff about Kiki Dee and her bloody love songs.

"Pre-occupied?" Colin said. "When you get home, you're not gonna be occupied at all, none of us are." He hurled his plectrum against the dressing room mirror. It bounced to the floor and disappeared behind the rubbish bin.

He'll be looking for that later.

"I don't even know yet, if we can do the next contract. Not one of those bastards has agreed to come back."

"Sorry."

He placed his hands on the dressing table. "No, I'm sorry." His sigh reflected through the dressing room mirror. "Look, we'll be out o' this place in a week." It suited her that Colin thought her troubles stemmed from homesickness. "I thought you'd be happy now that me and you are sorted."

"I said, I'm sorry."

"I know it's shite; but we just have to make the best of it. It's only for a few more days."

"Are you expecting *me* to come back for the next tour?"

"What do you mean?"

"I might get pregnant."

"It's not gonna happen straight away, is it? And if it did you'd still be okay for a few months, wouldn't you?"

"I'll look a right tit, singing with a bump."

"What fucking bump? You won't have no bump for months."

"I'll have morning sickness. Not that you'd care, so long as I'm not singing like a plank."

"Bloody hell, woman, there's no pleasing you, these days."

He glared at her. She glared at the bin hiding the plectrum.

"Sod it; I'm going for a pint." He left the dressing room.

Ah well, you said you wanted him to stop being nice.

Her thoughts wandered back to something she'd been thinking about that morning: contraception. Why hadn't she and William discussed it? He hadn't asked if she was on the pill. Happen he'd simply assumed. Happen he didn't care so long as he got what he wanted. Bloody men!

She didn't pick up the plectrum.

She was still sitting in front of the dressing room mirror when Jeannie came in. "Right that's it, the last I've seen of Bobby. He's gone back to Indiana."

"So, it's the last *I've* seen of my Bird Gods."

"Yeah, he said sorry about that." Bobby had only made one visit since T's return from Schweinfurt and he'd forgotten to bring the statues.

"I knew this was going to happen." *Serves you bloody well right, Morgan.*

Jeannie touched up her make-up. "Why can't you just ask Carter to send them on? Why haven't you even been in touch with him?"

"Jeannie, I haven't forgiven you, yet, for tricking me into going to Schweinfurt."

"I didn't trick you." She turned to face T. "Carter told us Kim had gone home for a holiday. He never said owt about 'em splitting up. He's the one who tricked you." She went back to her make-up.

Happen she had a point. T would never have gone to Schweinfurt if she'd known they *had* split up.

Jeannie raised an eyebrow. "Maybe your dreamboat isn't the Mr Perfect you keep making him out to be."

"God, don't you think I'm aware of that, Jeannie? I don't need you to tell me."

Jeannie stopped again. "Why? What did he do?"

"What? He didn't do anything. I don't mean that."

"He must've done something. You can't just drop something like that into the conversation and leave it there." She waited. "He tried it on with you, didn't he?"

"No. he didn't try anything on."

"Yes he did. And then he got funny with you when you said no. The bastard! I should've known he was too good to be true."

Bloody hell Morgan, why can't you just keep these things to yourself?

"Nothing happened." T went back to the mirror but Jeannie folded her arms and kept waiting. T fished through her make-up bag for more blusher. "Look, I don't want to talk about it, okay?"

Before T had to give away anything further, Colin returned with the others to prepare for the final set. He gathered his troops. "Okay, let's stop all this fannying about. Got that Adam?"

Adam looked around the room as though there might be another Adam. "Me? What have I done?"

T looked away, embarrassed that someone else was taking her flack.

Colin seemed unaware of any injustice. "I suggest we stop playing like pillocks and really sock it to 'em this set. Are you all with me?" No one disagreed with the strategy. "Right, let's get on stage."

Before starting the set, Colin put his arm around T's shoulder. He guided her to the back of the stage and whispered: "Are you okay?"

"Course I am." There was a 'rat-a-tat-tat' from Mr Guilt. T ignored the knocking.

No time for that.

He gave her a peck. "Right then, 'The Boys Are Back In Town', count it in, Fogerty."

Everyone got to their microphones and Adam set the tempo. "One, two, three—"

"Wait, hold on." Colin held up a hand to intercept Adam's drum fill. "Sorry about this, Ladies and Gentlemen. We've got a slight technical hitch." He turned upstage. "Anybody seen my plectrum? I definitely left it here, on top of my amp."

At the end of the gig, as the band made ready for the long trudge to the digs, a young crew-cut stepped in their path.

"Which one of you ladies is Jeannie?"

"Me, I'm Jeannie,"

"Captain Thomas asked me to give you this." The soldier handed her a note. "He's had to go away. Thanks ma'am." He left.

Jeannie opened her note and read it to the others. "*Won't be around for a couple of days, called away on army business but I've arranged a going away party for your band. I also think I've fixed you a ride home through Merle. See you, Lincoln.*" She waved the note at T. "Short and sweet, not even any kisses."

"What does he mean, he's fixed us a ride home," Colin asked.

"No idea." Jeannie stared at her note. "He knows what a mess we're in without the van."

Because of the problems getting home, Colin wasn't the only interested band member. They'd tried to hire another van but the cost was far too much.

Colin had considered going on the train and coming back for the others in his cousin Len's van, but the van needed some work and they had to vacate Bahnhof Strasse for the next band, so that wouldn't do either. The cheapest option left was for them all to go home by train, then Colin and Steve would come back for the equipment after they repaired Len's van. It was far from ideal but maybe Lincoln had somehow sorted something. "You never know; maybe he's performed a miracle and fixed us up with an army van," Colin said.

The night following the missing plectrum, Merle and Tait visited the band's venue. Merle and Colin slapped palms in what could only be a ritualistic country & western handshake. "Hey, how's it going my country pardner?"

"Could be better, man. Things could be better." Colin repeated himself as though it might improve matters. Merle acknowledged everyone except the two girls.

T didn't like Merle. She couldn't imagine any woman putting up with someone who mistreated them as badly as he'd mistreated his wife.

Colin motioned the two Americans. "Sit down, lads. Jeannie's had a note from Lincoln."

"That's why we're here, man," Merle said.

"Where is Lincoln?" Jeannie asked.

Merle shrugged. "Not sure, we were supposed to meet up with him yesterday but he didn't show."

"Must've been called away on army business," Tait said.

Colin turned to Merle. "What's this about a ride home?"

"Lincoln told me y'all are going home on the train then coming back later for your stuff."

"Best option we've got, up to now," Colin said.

"So how 'bout ya take my car?"

Colin cleared his gullet. "What?"

"Yeah, why not go in the car? Come back when you're ready."

"What, your precious Oldsmobile?" Colin put down his glass.

"Hell, sure."

"Why?"

"Lincoln says you guys are in a real jam."

"Yeah, he said you were real desperate," Tait said.

Colin frowned. "Well, we are but—"

"I ain't gonna need the car for a while."

"This is all a bit above and beyond, isn't it?" The band members all looked at Steve. "You've only known us a few weeks."

"Are you kidding?" Merle put a hand on Adam's shoulder. "You guys are practically family since this guy got Billy Whizz off our asses, man."

"We now got ourselves an open road," Tait said. "We're set to make a heap o' dough, thanks to Adam."

Steve looked skyward.

Merle took his hand from Adam's shoulder and put it on Colin's. "The least we can do is make sure you guys get back home safe."

"Well I'm flabbergasted," Colin said. "In fact, my flabber has never been so gasted."

T's flabber was in a similar condition. She reeled off a series of queries. "How can you trust us? How will you get it back? How do you know we won't just disappear with it?"

Tait gave a scoffing snigger that suggested: 'Double-cross the Boss? Are you for real?'

"You ain't gonna disappear," Merle said. "All your stuff's here." This made sense. "Plus, I got a friend who lives in England. He'll pick the car up for me. You only got to drive back with your truck."

"You what, you've got a friend that lives in Leeds?" Steve said. "That's a bit of a coincidence, isn't it?"

"Hell no, man." Merle gave one of his creepy laughs. "Deke lives in London. He owes me a few favours and he don't mind travelling anywhere. Hell, your whole country ain't but half the size of Iowa. He'd be happy to make your acquaintance."

"Absolutely, no problem, man," Colin said. "He's more than welcome wherever he's from. We'll give you our address and he can pop round for dinner. I still can't believe you'd do that for us? What a mate!"

"And what about this party?" Steve gave a huge smirk. "I expect you think you're holding it at our digs, again, so you can flog some more of your gear."

"The party ain't our doing," Tait said. "Lincoln fixed it. Set it up in the officer's mess."

"Oh ye of little faith!" Adam said.

Steve looked around for somewhere to stub out his discomfort.

T held out an ashtray of support with a smile.

Merle's sneer passed from Steve to T. "So, if that's okay with y'all, we have the party Sunday then you take the car on Monday."

"You bet it's okay." Colin checked his watch. "Sorry lads, I'm gonna have to get you a pint in later. We're due back on stage. Come on, you lot, we're bloody late, again."

"Now, are you sure you've got your plectrum?" Adam asked.

"Piss off," Colin said.

On the morning of their final gig, T was the first person to arrive downstairs. She'd already made her pilgrimage to the bathroom, where she remained in conflict with the Haggard Woman hiding in the mirror. Once again, she'd backed down from the confrontation. She was still trying to keep the veil firmly over the Big Picture but the problem hadn't yet been sorted. Nothing could stop it from poking its nose through the chink in the curtain.

Jimmy joined her in the kitchen. "Hey up, T, you're up early."

I haven't been sleeping too well, lately." She sipped her coffee. "Anyway, what are *you* doing out of your pit at this time o' day?"

"Oh, I'm not really up yet. I just came down to make some toast then I'm off back to bed." He poured some of T's coffee for himself and dropped the bread into the toaster. "Me and Jeannie were chatting with Colin last night. Looks like were gonna come back and do the next tour."

"That's, brilliant. I think the others have said yes, as well."

"Mind you, I won't be sorry to see the back of Wildflecken. And I'm well ready for home."

"Oh yes, there's a letter for you." She indicated the windowsill. "Who's writing to you now? We're going home in two days."

He checked the envelope. "It's from Marie."

"She was lucky to catch you. Must be love, the amount of letters she sends you."

"Yeah, something like that, silly cow." He buttered his toast, tucked the letter under his plate and went back upstairs to enjoy his love dispatch with breakfast.

T checked the belt fastening of her dressing gown before sitting down with her coffee and Catherine Cookson. Unable to find her favourite author in West Germany, she was reading the book for the third time. As she delved into the description of Geordie's terraced house, a cry of pain interrupted.

"Aargh no. Fucking hell, no." Unusual, Jimmy didn't generally swear.

She went half way up the stairway and called. "Are you okay, Jimmy?"

"Yeah, sorry T." He mumbled something else but she couldn't work out the words. Then he added, "I just had a bit of a shock. I er, spilt my coffee. It's nothing."

She momentarily thought of taking up a cloth but the tone in his voice suggested he didn't want any help. She returned to Geordie's terraced house.

Later that night at their finale, T noticed Jimmy's mood. "What's up? You seem down."

"Oh you know, end of the tour and all that, not knowing what's round the corner."

You don't know you're born, lad. Some of us have real worries.

She kept her thoughts to herself, no point taking things out on him.

Despite the sombre clouds, the evening was a success. With the final performance in the bag, she was ready to meet her final days in West Germany in a hopeful frame of mind. Next morning, she made her way to the bathroom, for one last tilt at the Haggard Woman. The reflection struck the first and only blow. Coming face to face with the green hue sent her hurtling towards the toilet.

"Oh shit!" She closed her eyes to block out the bowl. "Please God, no. Please don't let this happen to me."

The curtain fell away from the Big Picture to reveal an ebony baby in a chef's hat.

17 Jimmy's Journey: Wildflecken. Feb '77.

Baby Love.

Jimmy took out Marie's letter again but no matter how many times he looked at it, he still couldn't make the word 'pregnant' disappear. "Shit." He downed the last of his lager. Abortion wasn't an option. Marie had said so in the letter. This was no surprise. Marie was a Roman Catholic, her God didn't allow it. He no longer approved of any religion. *Superstitious claptrap.* And he'd never been fond of Catholics. *I ask you.* If they really wanted you to believe in miracles, why didn't the Angel Gabriel make Joseph pregnant? Jimmy sent a smirk across the table to Jeannie. "Maybe it's an Immaculate Conception."

"Can I have a look?" He handed her the letter.

On the pub wall, the oompah band pennants totally ignored the gust of wind, without so much as a flutter, as two locals entered the bar. Jimmy scratched the nape of his neck, ever careful not to disturb his recently blow-dried hair.

"It's a lot busier than the last time I was in here," Jeannie had said, when they arrived twenty minutes earlier. "And at least they're not playing Abba, or Boney M."

He'd scowled at the jukebox, playing The Supremes' "Baby Love".

Jeannie's eyes absorbed the contents off the yellow notepaper. He was always asking her to read his letters. She'd been a good mate away from home and had listened at length to the trials of his postal relationship with Marie. Jeannie was also a decent keyboard player. He'd often enjoyed telling her how much her left hand complimented his bass. Of course, he didn't find her as attractive as Marie but he liked her. She was fun and there was something special between them. When they'd shared a room together in Garmisch, he'd once sneaked a peak at her undressing. She'd obviously known he was watching but didn't object.

She handed back the letter. "I don't know what to suggest. At the end of the day, it's her choice."

"Exactly, her choice, not mine. I'm not ready for kids yet. Bloody Catholics."

"Sounds like her mother that's convinced her to keep it." She pointed to a page of the letter. "You can't blame it on her being Catholic. I doubt she's doing it to please God."

"That's someone I wouldn't mind kicking in the slats."

Jeannie laughed. "Who's that, God or her mother?"

He caught a waft of the humour. "Same thing, her mother 'personifies Catholicism'."

"You don't want to be kicking God in the slats, all that Devine retribution." She laughed again.

He knew she was trying to cheer him up and not merely making light of his problem. And perhaps she had a point: offending other people's beliefs wasn't such a good idea, having no longer any protection of a god, himself.

"What are you going to do?" She asked

He watched her down the contents of her stein. "Dunno. My life's knackered. We've only been together two minutes."

"It only takes two minutes, less than that with some blokes."

"You know what I mean."

"I thought you really liked her?"

"I do like her but we only met six months before I came here. That's hardly a basis for having kids and spending your life together."

"Well, I think she's lovely and she obviously thinks a lot about *you*."

He wasn't doing very well getting Jeannie on side as an ally. But then, while Marie had been in West Germany, she and Jeannie had become great friends. He gave up on her. "God, this is crap." From behind the oompah band pennants, the damp patch had definitely grown since the band's arrival. The premises typified the rest of the village. "Do you know something? Even though this place makes you feel as welcome as a fart in a crowded room, I'd still rather do a six-month residency here than come back and face what's at home."

"Nice to have the choice. What about Marie? It's her who's actually going through it. What exactly have *you* got to face?"

"Her brothers for one thing, Kevin and Shane. They already hate me. Kevin on his own's bad enough. They're both over six-foot tall and six-foot wide."

"Well, you've got to come home; the job's finished, thank God." She picked up his empty glass. "I'll get another couple in." She chinked together the glasses. "I have got one suggestion. Start drowning your sorrows early, then we'll both get well and truly blottoed tonight at this shindig." She left for the bar.

The shindig signalled the band's farewell to West Germany. A few days earlier, before Marie's letter, he'd felt so relieved to be leaving. He looked out of the window.

Snowing again.

He took a final look at the letter before burying it deep into his stylish jacket, yet the pocket would never be deep enough to obliterate his worries. It wasn't only Marie's brothers that were making home so unattractive. The fear of fatherhood was even more terrifying than Big Kevin.

Jeannie returned with a tray of four steins. "Here, get one of these down your neck."

"Are you stocking up?"

"No, I've just made two friends. They bought these. They're in the bog." She sent a nod toward the gents'.

"I saw them come in." He looked to the space at the bar, where he'd last seen the locals. "I've been thinking, do you reckon I could get into an outfit over here? In Germany, I mean, not Wildflecken."

"Jimbo, you'd hate being stuck here on your own." She unloaded the four lagers from the tray to the table. "Besides, you don't speak any other languages, you stupid wazzock."

He didn't like being called stupid, especially by Jeannie. But she was right. He wasn't equipped to live and work in a foreign country on his own. He deflected to the drinks. "Who are these friends you've met?"

"They're friends of Merle and they're coming to the party. I invited them to join us. Is that okay?"

"Okay by me but aren't they civilians? They won't be allowed on the base."

"Merle's apparently got special permission."

Her newfound friends arrived at the table. She introduced them as "Brn and Giorgio." Giorgio was your typical 'tall, dark and handsome', in a quirky sort of way. Brn looked like a weasel. Jimmy knew which one she had designs on.

"They're Austrian." Her chair shifted round the table to the athletic dial.

It wasn't that Jimmy was jealous. For a start, there were five and a half years between him and Jeannie. Giorgio, possibly in his early thirties, was more suitable. Jimmy watched, fascinated. It was the first time he'd actually seen her pulling-power in action. He'd often observed Adam's technique, even picked up one or two of his little tricks, though he couldn't foresee when, if ever, he'd get a chance to use them. But she was different, subtler, probably because she was a girl.

There was nothing particularly seductive in the conversation. It was all in the alluring grin, along with the widening of her eyes, the odd touch of his arm in response to something he said. "You can't get round me with flattery, just 'cos you're foreign," she said. At one point her little finger rested on his. "That's why I gave up my stamp collection, philately gets you nowhere." She slapped Jimmy on the arm. "Do you get it, Jimmy? Philately gets you nowhere."

Giorgio smiled. "Excuse me?"

"Never mind," Jeannie said. "I'll explain over breakfast."

Jeannie and Adam were the most sexually active people he'd ever met. She flitted like an unscathed bee from one dog rose to another. Adam stood there like a sticky-bud plant, making no effort at all, just waiting while the various creatures went out of their way to pick him up. And yet poor Jimmy, less than a handful of sexual relationships but caught in this Venus flytrap of Marie's pregnancy. The jukebox broke into his plant life pondering.

"Oh no," Jeannie said. "Boney M's back. Listen, why don't we get out of this dump and go back to our place? We need to get this party going."

On the way out of the pub, the swarthy dog rose stroked the back of the unscathed bee. Jimmy whispered in her ear. "What about Lincoln? Isn't he coming to the party?"

"He won't be at the digs though, will he?"

Jeannie took Giorgio upstairs, maybe to show off her stamp collection. Jimmy was left to keep Brn amused. Although only a couple of inches shorter, Brn was nothing like his compatriot. Athletic wasn't the immediate description that jumped to mind though he was wiry. 'Swarthy' was another adjective you wouldn't attribute. In fact, underneath the grease, his hair was possibly as blond as Jimmy's. It was probably the only thing they had in common. Accommodating him was never going to be easy. Doling out the last of the coffee was the height of Jimmy's entertainment skills. He cursed the other Bahnhof Strasse residents for being out and leaving him alone, having to make conversation with the laconic weasel.

"So, what brings you to Wildflecken?"

"We have a car, an Opel Rekord."

"No, you don't understand. Why are you here?"

"We come here for our work."

"Oh, what do you do?"

"Do?"

"What work do you do? Who do you work for?"

"We are working for no one but ourselves."

"Jeannie says you're friends of Merle. How do you come to know him? You haven't come to buy some of his drugs, have you?" Jimmy added a light-hearted laugh to show that he was okay with that.

"Drugs? Why do you speak to me of drugs?"

"Sorry, nothing; it was just a joke." Brn didn't seem to get it. "Yeah, it's good to be self-employed, innit?" Jimmy was eager not to leave any more gaps in the conversation. "I don't like bosses breathing down the back of my neck."

Brn blinked at him throughout the following lengthy silence. Then he asked: "Why does your boss breath on your neck?"

Oh bloody hell. I could spend the rest of my life having this conversation. Jimmy looked longingly at the stairway. *Come on Jeannie, show him your Penny Black and get me out of this.*

Brn took a sip of coffee then stared into the cup.

Jimmy sipped his own. "Sorry, I didn't ask, do you take sugar?"

"Yes please."

"Sorry, we're out."

"We are out where?"

Jesus, Mary and Joseph!

Thirty-seven and a half minutes later, the power of wishful thinking worked its magic and the casual couple came downstairs, Jeannie leading him by the hand.

"We must return to the army base to complete our business." Giorgio put on his coat and gave Jeannie a peck on the cheek. "I will see you at your party in the officers' mess, yes?"

"Be there or be square," she said.

Jimmy closed the door after the boys had left. "I don't care what you say, if Lincoln is at the party, he's not going to be very happy when you turn up wi' those two hanging from your shirt tail."

"I think you might be mixing me up with someone who gives a stuff. He didn't care about me when he just buggered off, the other night, did he? He's probably off on another drugs assignment, making some other stupid bitch think he's come just to see her."

"I don't know how you come out of all these casual relationships so unscathed."

"Casual relationships? Are you calling me a slag?"

"No, I'm just saying, I'd never get away with it."

"Bloody hell, I even had Adam commenting on my 'debauched life' the other day. I ask you, Adam?" She checked herself in the mirror and ran her fingers through her ruffled hair. "You might have a point. I need to get out of this place, get back to leading a normal life."

"Does that mean you're not coming back? You told Colin you would."

"You told him *you* were coming back but you might not be in a position to. You've got to think about supporting a family, now."

"What do you mean?"

"You might have to get a proper job, as my old mother used to say."

"What, you mean, give up music?"

"You might."

"Jesus, Mary and Joseph, you could have a point. Bloody hell, I've got to find a way out of this." He took Brn's cup into the kitchen. The weasel hadn't even touched his coffee. "I'd never be in a position to do owt, stuck with a kid," he called.

She called back: "What about Marie's position?"

He returned. "What do you mean?"

"Jimbo, I got to really like Marie. I wouldn't want to see her get hurt."

"I think you're being a tad unsympathetic to my situation, here, Jeannie."

"Unsympathetic to *your* situation? Jimmy, that girl has stuck by you, all the time you've been out here."

"I've stuck by her, as well, haven't I? I've not been near another girl since we left home."

"That's no excuse to drop her in the shit and dump her."

"I'm not dropping anybody in the shit. Anyway, I don't know if she's been faithful to me, do I? It might not even be my kid for all I know."

"Fucking typical. I thought you were different, Jimmy, but no. Bloody men, you make me sick. You're all as bad as each other." The front door opened and in walked Adam. "Oh look, right on cue; here comes another bastard. The ego has landed."

Adam didn't even flinch at the insult. "Lincoln's in hospital in Fulda. He's in intensive care."

Jeannie jumped up from her chair. "He's what?"

"He's been beaten senseless. They think it was a revenge attack from some of Billy Whizz's mates. I could be next."

At the party, Jimmy wallowed alone in a corner of the room with a drink, enjoying his melancholy. Jeannie had gone to visit Lincoln in the hospital. Jimmy looked around the room. T was busy keeping a boisterous Colin out of everyone's way, until she lighted on the melancholy corner.

Shit. He massaged his chin.

"What you doing sitting over here, all on your own, again? You should be partying," she said. "You're going home tomorrow. Aren't you excited?"

"Not really." He didn't feel he could confide in her about Marie's pregnancy. Only moments before, he'd been contemplating over all the things Jeannie had said to him. He feared more recriminations from T, so he opted for diversion. "Marie's chucked me." The lie slipped from his mouth. "She's gone off with someone else." His regret was immediate but it was too late, the words were already out there.

"Oh you poor soul. Is that what was in your letter yesterday morning?"

He nodded. His frown took his gaze down into his beer. He fidgeted with his hair and scanned the room in search of an escape but there was no one around apart from Colin, who was welcoming Jeannie's Austrian friends to the party. "What's Colin up to?"

"Oh bugger," T said. "Now what?"

It wasn't only curiosity that sent Jimmy over with T. Jeannie had asked him to explain to Giorgio why she wasn't at the party. They arrived as Colin was complimenting his newfound friend. "I'll knock that ugly head off your scrawny shoulders, you skinny little twat."

The weasel poised in readiness, undaunted by their difference in size. Giorgio stood apart, suggesting his compatriot was capable of handling the situation.

"Colin." T snapped into Headmistress Bone mode. "Drop it, now."

Colin cowered, proving he was very, very drunk. It was the only time he behaved this way with his wife. "This skinny little twat started it. He called me sommat."

"Called you what?"

"I don't know. I don't speak Russian, do I?"

"I'm really sorry, love." T said to the skinny little twat. "He's had a bit too much to drink." The afore-mentioned didn't flinch but continued his attempt to out-stare his oversized opponent. She gave up on the weasel. "Come on Col; let's go get you another beer." The staring competition continued for a good ten yards while she weaved her husband away from the danger zone, leaving Jimmy to clean up the dregs.

He took up T's apology baton. "Sorry, he's just a yob." He aimed his atonement at Giorgio for fear of yet another failed communication with the terse Brn.

"It is of no matter, merely a misunderstanding," Giorgio said.

It was hardly surprising that there was a blip in détente between Colin and the weasel.

Jimmy followed the Austrians over to the free bar. "Oh, by the way, Giorgio, I'm afraid Jeannie's had to go visit a friend in Fulda. She said to say sorry but she's not going to make the party."

"Ah yes, I am wondering of this."

Jimmy put his empty glass before the barman. "Another beer, please." He turned back to Giorgio. "I bet you wish you hadn't come, now."

"It is of no matter. There is nothing else to do, here."

"No, you've got that right, Wildflecken on a Sunday night. I still don't understand what you two are doing in this dump. What brings a couple of Austrians to a US Army base?"

"We come to collect supplies."

The DJ's selection caused Jimmy an aural distraction. "Bloody hell, that's all I need, Thin bloody Lizzy."

"You do not like this music?"

"It's not their music, it's 'cos they're Irish. I hate the bloody Irish. My girlfriend's mother, she's Irish, you see and it's because of her, I'm in a right pickle."

"She gives to you a pickle?"

With a drop more lubrication, he explained his plight over the pregnancy. The Austrians appeared to understand. "You see, I'm only twenty-three, that's miles too young to give up the road and settle down."

"Yes, a bad situation," Giorgio said.

This was Jimmy's first tour abroad. He'd expected to be making records before now but it hadn't yet happened. He scanned the room to check that Colin was out of earshot. "It's not that I want to shit on T and the others but if I could find another band and stay over here, then I wouldn't have to go home to God knows what." Brn laughed, showing a frightening set of yellow teeth. "It's not bloody funny," Jimmy said.

"How you boys doing? Having a good time?"

Jimmy turned. "Hey, Merle, great party." He put out an arm to steady himself on the corporal. "I was just asking Brn, before, how do you lot know each other?"

"These guys are business associates of mine," Merle said.

"What sort of business?"

"Blue jeans."

"What?"

Merle explained that buyers came from all over Europe, craving American Levis. Naturally, Merle was a supplier.

"Bloody hell, is there anything you don't sell?" Jimmy said.

"No, I can get you pretty much anything you need?"

"Don't suppose you do cheap abortions?"

"Say what?"

Jimmy repeated his tale.

"Man, that's some bad shit," Merle said.

"I wish to make solution." Giorgio snapped his fingers. "I am thinking perhaps you can join us." The Austrians were in transit to Zurich. Giorgio's suggestion was that Jimmy could accompany them. There were many foreign bands in Switzerland and he could try to find a new job. Also, in a month's time, Giorgio would be travelling to London. If things didn't work out, Jimmy could return with him and then come back to West Germany with the band if he wished. "You would be most welcome to our trip," Giorgio said. "We must make many foreign contacts. A British would be most helpful to our business in Zurich."

Brn agreed, again flashing his yellow teeth.

"It's a great idea," Jimmy said. "It would give me a bit of thinking time but I can't afford a months' holiday in Switzerland. I'll only just be able to exist, as it is, when I go home."

Merle tossed another suggestion on the pile. "If you needed to increase your funds, I'm sure these boys will let you invest in their blue jean franchise."

"What do you mean?"

"Yes, we can support you," Giorgio said.

When the proposals added together they began to make a viable solution. Jimmy could invest his savings in the Austrians' jean business. They'd pay for his keep over the next month and as soon as they completed the business in Zurich, he could repay them from a handsome return on his investment. He could expect at least four hundred percent.

"If you make a cent less than that, I'll give you the difference when you pick up your stuff," Merle said.

"I've only got about hundred quid, that's a hundred pounds."

"Okay, so you'll want four hundred pounds in a month's time."

Brilliant. Winner!

Jimmy's excitement hurtled him across the room until tripping on the sobering realisation he now had to tell the others. He looked around until he found T. Fortunately she was alone, Colin obviously having gone off in search of someone else to insult.

Straight out with it, that was best. "Listen, T, I'm not coming back to England with you."

"What are you going on about, you pissed up bugger?"

He relayed Giorgio's plan for him to go with them for a month. "Now that Marie's chucked me, I've nowt to come back for."

"Don't talk daft. You don't even know them. And if it's owt to do with that Merle, you should stay well clear."

"It's okay, T. I'll be back in plenty of time for the next tour."

"I think you're being really silly."

"Don't worry." He left to pass on his news to Adam but he was not around. He'd have to be told tomorrow.

'Tomorrow' found Jimmy saying goodbye as the others loaded up Merle's Oldsmobile for the return to England. "How d'ya get on in Fulda?" He asked Jeannie.

"He's in a right mess, tubes coming out of everywhere. Billy's mates have given him a right going over."

"Yeah, can we get out of here before they turn up for me?" Adam said.

She shook her head at Adam. "He couldn't even talk. I've to call the hospital later."

Brn and Giorgio's Opel Rekord pulled up alongside them. Jimmy threw his bag on top of the piles of jeans lining the floor of the boot.

"Are you sure about this?" T asked.

In the alcohol free light of day, he wasn't a hundred percent sure but he felt he'd committed to the plan and so had to go through with it. Besides, he'd given Merle the money for his investment.

"Don't worry, he'll be alright," Adam said.

"Course I will," Jimmy said. "Anyway, I've got nowhere to stay. My auntie's moved to Coventry."

"Why aren't you staying with your bird?" Colin asked.

"I don't really get on with her mother. Anyway, I think her brothers might be staying there."

"I told you yesterday, you can stay at the Passion Pad. There's plenty of room." Adam smiled at Steve, who returned an uncharacteristic smirk.

"Thanks but I've already said I'm going, now," Jimmy said. "I'll definitely take you up on it at the end of the month when I get back from Zurich."

Jeannie turned from her handshake with Giorgio. "Since when were Marie's brothers staying with her? Have you even phoned her and told her you're just buggering off to Switzerland?"

"No," Jimmy said, "I didn't see any point in upsetting her. I don't suppose you'd call her for me? It'll sound better coming from you. You've got her number, haven't you?"

"You've got a bloody nerve. Yeah, I'll tell her what a wazzock you are."

"I promise, I'll ring her on the way when I know what I'm doing." He caught T looking askance from himself to Jeannie. "Stop worrying," he said to Mother Hen. "Like I told you last night, I'll be back in plenty of time for the next stint."

So it was after five months he said goodbye to 'Images' and disappeared from the Wildflecken landscape, confirming the end of the tour.

18 T's Adventures: Wildflecken. Feb '77:
Homeward Bound.

The Austrian kidnappers melted into the ether, Jimmy's face peering through the back window of their Opel Rekord. The members of the depleted band watched the car get swallowed by a curve of the mountain road before they also prepared to escape their desolate confinement. The last conversation between Jimmy and Jeannie puzzled T. Why should the lad be contacting Marie when *she'd* dumped *him*? "Are you sure he'll be alright?" T's concern aimed at no one in particular.

"Well it's given us a bit more room in the car." The ever-thoughtful Adam found something positive about Jimmy's decision not to come home with them. "It would've been a right nightmare with six of us squashed in here." The Oldsmobile was a large vehicle but no one was going to dispute this. The back seat trio of Adam, Jeannie and Steve spread their limbs. Adam delved into the bag between his legs. "Look what I blagged from the party." He produced a six-pack of Budweiser and passed them around.

"I don't think so," Steve said.

"Please yourself." Adam offered one to Colin.

"Not for me, neither," Colin said. "I'd be just topping up the skinful I had last night."

"Oh great, we're being driven seven-hundred miles by a pissed up wazzock," Jeannie said.

"What's up with you, Moaner Lisa?" Colin looked over his shoulder. "The rest of us are happy to be going home, if you're not."

"That's if we ever get there."

The homeward bound excitement was obviously putting everyone in a good mood. T snapped back the ring-pull on her can and tried to distract the banter. "Hey, Jeannie, what were you and Jimmy going on about?"

"Me and Jimmy?"

"The soft bugger should be telling that Marie where to get off instead of ringing her up to see how she is." T took a swig of beer. "I thought when I first met her there was something suspect about the girl. She was obviously just out to use him."

"T, what the fuck are you on?"

The shock of Jeannie's attack turned T to face her colleague. She responded slowly and deliberately. "I beg your pardon?"

"You never cease to amaze me, T."

T poised in readiness for a verbal catfight. "You what?"

Jeannie pressed home the first strike. "Have you any idea what that poor girl must be going through?"

T parried "Poor girl? What poor girl?"

"What poor girl? What poor girl do you think?"

"Oh, is that the same poor girl that's just crapped on poor Jimmy."

"Crapped on poor Jimmy?" Each of the lads had that look of feigned deafness to the friendly female banter cross-firing the front and back seats. Jeannie unsheathed her indignation. "How the fuck has she crapped on him? Oh don't tell me, the conniving bitch got herself pregnant to trap him. No wonder your husband's the chauvinist wazzock that he is."

A spray of Budweiser peppered the right hand side of the dashboard as Jeannie hit her target. "Pregnant? Did you say pregnant? Marie's pregnant?"

"Yeah, she's pregnant."

T's shield dropped. Naturally, she had to keep her confused thoughts silent but the words "I'm sorry," needed saying. "I didn't know. Jimmy told me he wasn't coming home because Marie had run off with someone else."

"Run off with someone else? The bastard."

"Okay, you two, fucking can it." Colin kindly offered his services as referee.

"It's alright Col," T said. "It's my fault."

"I don't care whose fault it is. I said: that's enough." He pressed the start button on the cartridge player. The Eagles swooned their "Lying Eyes" between the women.

T was glad of the intervention. "Sorry," she said again.

"I can't believe this of Jimmy." Jeannie let go of a sigh. "It's not enough that he's dumped her. If anybody's being shit on, it's that 'poor girl'."

"You're right, she is a poor girl." T tussled with the mixed emotions induced by the exchange. She turned away from the rear and looked out to the road. The Oldsmobile bounded along, the unusual suspension causing a rocking that wasn't the best antidote to morning sickness.

She might be a poor girl but at least she knows who the father is. She's not likely to wake up with a Coloured baby suckling on her breast.

She sank lower into the brown and beige upholstery as the depressions stacked. Depression Number One: The Big Picture had just been revealed again and she'd have to stare at it alone for at least the next twelve hours. Depression Number Two: the misunderstanding had upset the only female ear within seven hundred miles. Depression Number Three: she couldn't even take out her frustrations on Colin because she felt so guilty about Depression Number One. "Can you pull over Col? I don't feel too good." She got out of the car and dispensed her Budweiser on the grass verge.

"Are you alright, love?" Colin asked when she got back in the car.

"I shouldn't be drinking in the morning, especially when I drank so much last night."

Possessing only the one cartridge for the eight-track, the merry band had passed 'Hotel California' three times by the time they cruised into Belgium, albeit without any other technical hitches. It was much easier crossing borders by car than having to deal with custom officers, checking carnets, searching vans and having to unload then reload the equipment.

"We've got Merle to thank for this." Colin lovingly stroked the steering wheel.

"Yeah, thanks Merle for lending us your gas-guzzling heap of shit," Steve said.

Colin looked over his shoulder. "Listen, Gunga Din, if it wasn't for this heap of—"

"For God's sake, will you all please just shut up?" All eyes descend on T.

"What's up with you, now?" Colin was his ever-supportive self.

"Sorry," she said. "I just can't take all this bickering."

"Yeah, maybe it is time for a pit stop." Colin's hand left the gear stick to touch her thigh. "I think we could all do with a leg stretch."

The services' café was busy. Despondent T took her frikadellan and looked around for a quiet spot. She didn't want her emotional dam to burst and have her blubbering in front of all and sundry. The first tear reached her cheek.

"I've just tried to phone the hospital but it only takes francs." Jeannie put down her tray on the opposite side of the table. "I'll have to wait 'till we— T? What is it? What's wrong?"

"Nothing, I'm just a bit hormonal, end of the tour and all that." T wiped her eyes with the palm of her hand. "Can't believe we're actually going home."

"You shouldn't be crying over that. You should be leaping up and down and cheering." Jeannie popped a chip in her mouth.

T put down her cutlery. "Jeannie, I'm really sorry about earlier."

"It's not your fault. Jimmy shouldn't have said that about Marie."

"He was probably embarrassed."

"He should be embarrassed for what he's doing."

"You're right. If Col had left *me* because I was pregnant, I'd be devastated."

"Well, you know what I feel about that." Jeannie gave a sneer. "I think it'd be worth putting it to the test."

T shielded her eyes trying to hide the crack in the dam but a tear dripped on her Dutch burger.

"T?" Jeannie gently pulled T's hand away from her face. "What's up, love? Hey, you're not really pregnant, are you?" She let go of her hand "That's why you were sick, isn't it?"

"Look, Jeannie—"

"Budge up, T. It's chocka in here." Steve edged her along the seat.

She was unsure if his timing was perfect or if he'd just spoiled her chance to unload. She shielded her eyes again.

Steve cut into his own frikadellan. "What's going on here? Has someone died?"

Through her fingers, she saw Jeannie shush Steve with a shake of her head.

T picked up her cutlery. "Sorry Steve, I'm a bit hormonal. I was just saying to Jeannie, can't believe we're actually going home."

He patted her arm. "Yeah, you got through it. You did good, girl."

"Anyway, Steve, what's going on with you and Adam?" Jeannie touched T's knee under the table. "It's like sitting between a pair of rabid dogs, snarling at each other."

"He's an arsehole."

"He's always been an arsehole," Jeannie said. "Didn't stop you being friends, before."

"Well now he's a bigger arsehole, a deceitful arsehole at that."

"Actually, he isn't," Jeannie said.

"What?"

"He's not a bigger arsehole now than he used to be." Jeannie gobbled up more chips. "In fact, recently he's been anything but an arsehole. He's been really sweet."

"Sweet? Yeah, the Sweet Assassin."

"You shouldn't have spoiled things between him and Emma," T said.

He scowled. "I couldn't stomach him running round like a love-sick dingo, any more. He's in love with a different woman every other day."

"Well I like the new Adam." Jeannie started on T's abandoned chips. "Do you know what's weird, T? He changed after you left your statues in Schweinfurt."

"My statues?"

"I think you might've been right about them. Maybe they are magic. As soon as they'd made Adam see the error of *his* ways, it's like they weren't needed any more, so they decided to go off and find *another* male chauvinist arsehole to put on the right track." Jeannie made her familiar spooky voice and hand wave to accompany her rendition of the 'Twilight Zone' theme. "Da-dee, da-da. Da-dee, da-da. They're probably on the lookout for 'Mr Perfect.'" This was obviously another dig at William. Jeannie had been fishing, ever since their conversation in the dressing room. It wasn't the first time since, that Jeannie had made some quip about him.

"You're bloody nuts." It also wasn't the first time that T wished she'd never gone anywhere near William Carter. "I'm sorry I took the bloody things to Schweinfurt." Jeannie's eyes opened as though expectant of an explanation. T grasped one out of the air. "Well Kim wasn't even there, was she? And Bobby didn't bring them back for me, as he promised."

"Well, he can't do owt about that now, can he? He's back in Indiana."

Steve joined in with the chip stealing. "Maybe we could make a detour when we go to pick up the gear and I could bring them back for you."

"Oh great idea," Jeannie said. "You're going to drive miles out of your way to bring back the dreaded Juju Birds. I don't think Colin will be very happy about that, do you?"

"I won't be very happy about what?" Colin and Adam were at the table.

"We were just talking about Jimmy," Steve said. "Just saying you won't be very happy if he doesn't make it back for the next tour."

"Come on, we need to get back on the road," Colin said.

On the way back to the car, Jeannie grabbed T's arm. "Okay T, what's going on? And don't give me any of that hormonal bollocks."

"Please, don't say anything." T kept her voice low. "I'm just a bit late. I don't know owt for definite, yet."

"I thought this was what you'd always wanted." Jeannie stroked T's arm. "Silly bugger. Colin's not gonna walk out on you. And if he does, it'd only prove I was right, all along. You're better off without him."

Colin called across the car park. "For God's sake, will you two get in the pissing car? You've got hours to do your gassing, bloody women."

Colin was back in the driving seat. Only he had the honour or the credentials to be in charge of Merle's precious Oldsmobile, which he never tired of telling them. T had no interest in her husband's driving ability or for that matter in the car, luxurious though it was. Yet his going-on about "Six litre, V8 auto, Super 88, Holiday Sedan" still managed to crash into her thoughts. She tried to mull over what they'd been talking about in the café. Happen 'Mr Perfect' did deserve some sort of retribution for his part in her predicament. Though, finding out he was going to become a father again would probably be retribution enough. "You only get fins and the optional air suspension on the Fifty-eight." Her brain melded into the Belgian countryside.

"Aren't we the lucky ones?" Steve yawned from the back seat.

Fortunately for him, Colin's eyes focused on the road. "Yeah, she's an absolute cracker."

"It's a female then is it?" Steve asked.

"Course she is," Colin said. "Merle's like me; he'd want a car that looks after him."

"Well I hope he treats her better than he treated his wife." It seemed they'd finally hit on a subject to which Jeannie could contribute.

"Haven't we had this conversation once before?" Adam asked.

"I won't hear a word against Merle. He's a diamond, an absolute diamond." Colin nodded toward the overhead sign, indicating the ferry port. "See, she's got us here in one piece."

"Stop the car." Steve almost jumped into the front seat.

"What?" Colin looked over his shoulder.

"I've worked out why he loaned us his car," Steve said. "Stop. We need to check the doors and sills."

"Check the doors and sills? Check them for what?" Colin asked. "Have you lost your bleeding marbles?"

"I don't know. We'll see when we have a look in the doors and sills." While they unloaded the tools from the boot to set about the task, Steve shared his musings. All the 'anthropomorphic talk' about female vehicles made him consider what Jeannie had said about Merle and his wife. "See, some people not only abuse women, they use them, as well."

"Just piss off, Steve," Adam said.

"What? I'm just saying: didn't Merle use his wife, asking you to shag her, just so he could sell his drugs at our place? Maybe he's using Ms Oldsmobile here in the same way."

A brief examination of the screws securing the sills suggested there might be something in Steve's theories.

"These are normally welded," Steve said. The experienced mechanic removed the plates.

"Shitting Nora, how did you know?" Colin asked.

"Doors and sills, obvious hiding places." Steve estimated the cocaine had a street value of over a hundred thousand pounds.

Colin punched his fist into his palm. "I'll kill the bastard."

"An absolute diamond," Jeannie said.

"It don't make any sense." T couldn't understand how Merle could profit from smuggling drugs into England. How could he access them from Germany?

"Maybe you should ask his mate when he pops round for dinner to pick up the car," Steve said.

"Deke!" Colin said. "Don't you worry; I'll bloody ask him." The right fist clenched in the left hand was a hint to what he might use as a questionnaire.

T had another consideration. "What if we'd been stopped? He'd have lost his car."

"Maybe he thinks it's worth a risk for a hundred grand," Steve said. "Worst scenario, he'd have all your gear as compensation."

"That won't be much use to him after I've ripped his arms out of their sockets," Colin said.

Steve put the bags of white powder on the bonnet of the car and scrambled his Head-bag from the rear shelf. "I'll take care of all this."

"And do what with it?" Colin pulled him away from the car.

"What do you think I'm going to do with it?" Steve asked.

Colin turned the volume of his bellowing switch. "I know damn well what you're going to do with it. You're going to dump it."

"Come on Col," Steve said. "We can't just dump it. We can't just dump a hundred grand."

"You're not dumping hundred grand." Colin gathered up the drugs and thrusts them at Steve. "You're dumping ten years in nick."

Steve began packing his Head-bag with the contraband. "I'll keep it with me. You can say you didn't know I had it."

"Are you off your bleeding chump?" Colin asked. "You're more likely to get searched than any of us."

"You're spot on there, Col." Adam said. "He always gets stopped. I've lost count the number of times I've seen him in his undies at borders."

Steve scowled at Adam. "Who asked for your opinion, Captain Marvel? This is all down to you."

"Me? How do you work that one out?"

"You introduced us to Merle in the first place. I suppose this is all part of your new, hotshot drugs dealer image."

T stepped between the warring friends. "Give up, you two. We've found the stuff now. We can just dump it in the sea."

"We're not taking any of that shit on that boat." Colin looked at T as though she'd just suggested having a cocaine party, right there on the quayside. "They're gonna be checking passports and God knows what else."

Steve held up a hand. "Yeah, you're right, sorry Col, I wasn't thinking straight." He scanned the car park. "I'll get rid somewhere in the terminal. Get in the queue. I'll see you on there. I'll board as a foot passenger."

"Hang on, I'll come with you," Jeannie said. "I need the loo."

Colin pointed an accusing finger. "Don't you dare take that gear on that boat."

Steve and Jeannie scooted off and disappeared into the terminal.

"That could've been fucking disastrous," Colin said.

"What if they'd searched us at the Belgian border?" T said.

"We'd all be having waffles for breakfast for the next hundred years," Adam said.

"I just want to get home to my little house. I'm not even sure if I ever want to come back." T got back in the car. Mrs Bone whispered into Ms Morgan's inner ear. *Oh I don't think you've got any worries there, young lady. You can't go gadding about the Continent with a child, whatever colour it is.*

19 Adam's Exploits. Zebrugge Feb '77:

Dream Lover.

A lone seagull balanced precariously on the ship's funnel, oblivious to the smoke billowing around its tail. Adam huddled into his coat, shielding his face against the wind. He watched the ferry slice its path through the sea, sending a chevron of spray back toward the Belgian coastline. He sent the gull a contented smile as it flew off, and not merely because he was going home. Before the farewell party, the previous evening, he'd made his weekly call to his brother to find out how his dog and his flat were faring. Adam was ecstatic. Weeks before he'd written to the one time love of his life, June Roundhill, in the hope of rekindling their relationship. Until now, there'd been no reply. He thought he'd blown it but he hadn't. She'd only been round to his flat to see him. She'd left him a message. This was exactly what he'd been waiting for. He'd come to West Germany with the sole aim of nailing every fraulein in Bavaria. But he'd made a right idiot of himself on this tour. Now he realised, albeit as a result of some bizarre experiences, what he really needed was a chance to settle down with someone he cared for, someone who cared for *him*.

Jeannie appeared, linked his arm and snuggled into his shoulder. "Are you glad to be going home?"

"Not many, Benny."

"Me too." She gave him an extra snuggle. "I've just been telling Steve how sweet you've been, recently."

"Have you, really?" He didn't disguise his cynicism. "I bet he agreed wholeheartedly with you on that one."

"You shouldn't take any notice of him. I think he's just a bit jealous. Probably why he tried to ruin things between you and Emma."

"I'm not bothered about any of that."

"You don't have to pretend with me, Adam. I know how close you and him were."

"Nah, he's probably done me a favour. Don't get me wrong. I really liked Emma, a lot, but he's right. I was an idiot. It was never going anywhere. I was never going to move to Krautland and I couldn't see her coming to Leeds."

"They wouldn't have let her anyway, unless you got married."

"Yeah, okay now, let's not get silly."

"Wasn't she the one, then, the real deal?"

"No, there's only one who's ever been the real deal for me."

"Aw Adam, I never realised. What a lovely thing—"

"Not you, you prannock, I'm talking about June, my ex."

She relaxed her grip on his arm. "Your ex?" She gave a mocking laugh. "Ex what?"

"I'm serious, Jeannie. For your information, June and me were together for over two years."

"Two years? I thought a week was a long-term relationship for you."

"She left me. Walked out, left a note on the telly saying: 'I'm leaving you. It's not working.' I couldn't understand it—"

"Did you try switching it on?"

"Bastard."

The Belgian coastline had vanished beyond the horizon. There was no reason to remain outside on the cold deck. They found a quiet corner in the ship's bar.

Jeannie transferred her small bottle of wine into a glass. "Did you know this Simon?"

"Course I knew him. He was the sax player for the Dawnbreakers, our biggest rivals."

"I remember them. They could've been quite big."

"Alright, don't rub it in."

"Don't remember the saxophonist, though."

"Frigging Pied Piper; running round with his sax, enticing other blokes' women to run off with him." Adam took a sip of his beer. "He's probably blagged half the population of Leeds since June."

"Good God, Adam Fogerty in a relationship. I'm very impressed."

"I'm not going to do my usual trick of messing things up."

"Not sure I can get used to that settling down image, though."

"Why not?"

"Why not? Because the Adam I know goes round humping the world and her dog. I don't think even her pet gerbil would be safe."

"Not any more. I'm finished with all that notches on my bedpost shite."

"Don't you mean your weapon?"

"Yeah well, I seem to have been missing the target a bit, lately. It's probably a good time to stick it back in its holster." Without thinking, he put his hand inside his belt and adjusted his dress.

She picked at the label of the empty wine bottle. "See? I was right, you have changed but you haven't suddenly become a deceitful arsehole, like Steve said. You've always been one of them."

"Is that what he said?"

"Among other things. He called you a lovesick dingo."

Adam gave no reply. He swallowed his hurt with a gulp of beer. Thirteen years, he and Steve had known each other. He couldn't remember a falling out as bad as this.

The boat sailed on as they chatted. She'd finished picking the label from the bottle and had started destroying a beer-mat. "So what was in the message, this June sent you?"

"Dunno, our kid said she just left me a card."

"Didn't you get him to read it?"

"Our kid? Not likely, don't want him nosing through my love letters."

"If it was me, I'd want to know."

"It's probably a Valentine's card. It'll wait 'til I get back."

She smirked. "Roses are red, violets are blue. I love you so much, I can't do a pooh. I wouldn't be able to wait that long. To read the card, I mean, not to do a pooh."

"Maybe you're right. I'll give Paul a ring when we get off the boat."

"Yeah, I've got to call and see how Lincoln's doing, as well."

"Sorry yeah, it's a bugger about all that. Are you really worried?"

"Ah, there you are." T had found them. "Look!" She pointed out of the porthole at the familiar white cliffs. "Come on; Col and Steve's waiting." The three stragglers joined the duo and skipped below to the car decks.

Between a Ford Anglia and an Austin 1100, the Oldsmobile trundled down the ramp into the port of Dover. Colin posed nonchalantly behind his left-hand-drive steering wheel, ready to take his trophy on to British Terra-firma. In just over five hours, Adam would be cradling his dog's mangy head and rubbing noses with the mutt.

"Can you pull in to the left, sir?" The voice crept into Adam's daydream. The conspicuous car had attracted the unwanted attention of the customs. "What have we got here, then?" the officer asked, after hearing Colin's accent.

Colin explained the circumstances.

"A pop group, eh?" was the officer's assessment. "Have you anything to declare?"

"Nothing but our genius," Adam said.

"Oh sorry, Mr Wilde, didn't recognise you, there." The officer had obviously heard Oscar's quip before. "Could you all please step out of the car?" Within seconds white shirts, epaulettes and navy coloured trousers surrounded them.

Adam left them to it and set off to call his brother but Jeannie had reached the sole working telephone before him. He went back to the car.

"Good old British hospitality," Colin said. Everyone's bag was receiving equal rifling. The navy and white brigade gave everything a thorough going over. "Come back Fritz, all is forgiven." Colin and Adam shared a confident smile in the knowledge that every crevice had already been searched.

Jeannie returned from her phone call. "I've just spoken to the hospital. Lincoln's okay. He's out of danger."

"That's brilliant," T said.

"I spoke to this sister I met yesterday. She says the police think he was beaten-up by a drugs gang." Jeannie looked at Adam. "I knew that note was suspect, no kisses."

"Yeah, I wonder who'd send us a note, offering us a car full of drugs?" Steve sarcastically stroked his chin. "Mm?"

"It wasn't Merle beat up Lincoln," Adam said. "It was Billy Whizz's mates."

"Now let me guess. I wonder who told you this." Steve gave his chin another stroke. "Wouldn't be some tattooed bastard by any chance?"

Adam felt his tail droop between his legs. "Shit!"

Steve's smirk grew. "And that concludes the case for the prosecution."

Adam turned to Jeannie. "I'm sorry."

Jeannie patted his arm. "It's hardly your fault."

"I meant I'm sorry your bloke got roughed up." Of course he wasn't to blame. He hadn't wanted anything to do with Merle and his bastard drugs. Then again, he had been handsomely paid. The two thousand dollars in his suitcase began to feel a little bloody. No, it was Lincoln's own fault. He knew the risk when he decided to infiltrate Merle's gang. If anything, the stupid black bugger should be apologising to Adam for getting *him* involved. And now look, what's going to happen when they come looking for their drugs? Adam, himself, could end up in hospital, or worse, if Lincoln's brother was anything to go by. Except, he wouldn't, 'cos he'd make sure he wasn't around when they turned up.

"Over here, sir." A white shirt and epaulette calling from the car trampled Adam's thoughts just as he was about to return to the telephone.

Shit, the spare tyre. Colin and Adam exchanged another look but this time there were no confident smiles involved.

The epaulettes scampered between the tyre and the tampered sills like excited jackals. There was a five-minute discussion between the group about Wormwood Scrubs and other holiday resorts of delight while the tyre was taken away and deflated. However, after the final screw went back in the sill housing and the drug free spare tyre was replaced, the officer slumped away, tie askew. The musicians were allowed to go on their way without blemish, albeit an hour late.

Back on the road, Merle bore the brunt of recriminations though several "what ifs?" and I-told-you-so looks headed in Steve's direction.

"Come on, lads, if it wasn't for Steve, we could've all been locked up for ten years." Not for the first time on tour, T was jumping to the roadie's defence.

"Anyway, soft arse," Colin turned to Steve. "Where's your green bag?"

"My bag? It's in the boot, isn't it?"

"No it isn't. I was checking when they searched 'cos I thought what would've happened if you'd brought that shit with you."

"Well I didn't bring it with me, did I? I must've left my bag in the toilet when I was flushing the stuff down the bog." Steve avoided Adam's frown. "Must've been the panic. It's no big deal. I'll check lost property when we come back for the gear." He and Colin would be returning through Zeebrugge in Colin's cousin's van. But Adam wasn't having it. Steve never let that bag out of his sight and he didn't seem as distressed about losing it, as he should've been.

A suspicion developed. Maybe Steve was expecting to pick up a lot more from 'lost property' than just his bag. The greedy Peruvian pillock had put them all in danger, in particular, Adam, himself. "So, Steve, when exactly did you realise about the drugs?"

"What are you on about?"

"I just thought maybe you might've had a suspicion straight away, when Merle offered us the car."

"What exactly are you trying to say?"

"Maybe you were hoping to keep the drugs for yourself."

"Piss off."

"Hey Adam." Jeannie grabbed his arm. "You didn't call your brother."

"What?"

"You wanted to find out what was in that card from your girlfriend."

"It's probably just a silly Valentine's Day card, like I said." Adam wanted to keep the pressure on Steve. "So—"

She tugged at his arm again. "You still need to find out."

"What? Yeah, I'll call him later."

"She might've left an urgent message, asking you to call as soon as you get back to England."

"What?" He turned from Steve's glower. "Hey Col can you stop at next services? I need to call our kid." He went back to the glower. "So, when you said you were going to check the lost property, did you mean that or did you really mean the left-luggage?"

There was another tug at his arm. "Look, Stour Services, half a mile." What the hell was Jeannie playing at? Oh, of course, whatever Steve was up to with the drugs, she was obviously in on it. This would continue after the services.

334

Shit, shit, shit! Frigging hell, why me? When Adam did telephone home, his brother, Paul, gave him the news. He hung up and went to find the others. "Have you got a minute, Steve?"

Steve had the same glower that he'd had in the car. "Why, what do you want?"

"It's your mum, she's ill." Adam relayed Paul's message. She'd been taken into hospital. Steve was to go straight back to Liverpool on his return to England.

"We'll have to drop him off at nearest train station?" T said.

Colin nodded. "Better if we take him straight to Euston."

"Sorry," Steve said.

"Don't be daft." Colin put a hand on Steve's shoulder. "It can't be helped."

Steve tapped a thank you on Colin's hand. "It'll be her heart, again."

"Paul didn't know," Adam said. "Sorry, mate."

"It's not your fault. Thanks for letting me know."

Steve closed the car door, trapping the sombre mood inside the Oldsmobile. Adam had exchanged places with Jeannie, putting himself as the divider in the back seat sandwich. Exposing Steve's subterfuge over the drugs, now felt inappropriate. "Hope she's okay. I like your mum."

"Thanks, she'd appreciate that. She likes you."

Adam lowered his voice. "I really am sorry."

"Cheers," Steve said.

"I don't just mean about your mum. I'm talking about all that crap over Ulrike."

"She really didn't know that Tait was picking up the gear. Gabi conned her."

"Yeah, I realise that, now. I'm sorry. She's a really nice girl."

"Gabi only set up the scene in the first place to find out if we had the stuff."

"Shit, really? What a pair of mugs." Adam laughed. "Devious cow. I wish I had shat in her hallway."

"I'm glad she did set us up. I wouldn't have met Ulrike, otherwise."

"I'm sorry for not trusting her. And, I'm sorry if I've become a deceitful arsehole and a lovesick dingo."

Steve leaned forward. "Thanks Jeannie."

"What for?" She appeared oblivious to the reconciliation happening on her right shoulder.

Adam raised his eyebrows and nodded at Steve. "See what I mean? You're always saying that me and Womankind don't see eye to eye but then look at the Womankind I've had to put up with." He waited for the usual riposte from Jeannie but she simply smiled and patted his bicep. She then leant forward and winked at Steve. There was definitely something going on between them. Not wishing to spoil the moment, Adam suppressed all suspicions. "I'm getting back with June."

"June?" Steve screwed up his nose. "As in June Roundhill, June?"

"It's all down to you, actually. You suggested I should write to her. She's been round to my pad to see me."

Jeannie touched Adam's arm. "What was your message?"

"What message?"

"From June. That's why you were phoning."

"Oh yeah, I forgot all about that 'cos of Steve's mum. It'll have to wait 'til I get back, now. Like I said, it's probably nowt."

"June?" Steve's sternness turned Adam's head. "I hope you know what you're doing. You know what she's like."

Adam laughed. "She was like that 'cos I was an arsehole, remember? Maybe I should've behaved more like a lovesick dingo."

The Oldsmobile weaved through the London traffic to Euston. Colin pulled on the handbrake. "Your stop, Steve. You'll probably be home before us."

Steve got out of the car. "Thanks guys. Sorry again about this."

"Don't be soft," Colin said.

Adam got out. There was an awkward gap prior to their hug. "You're still welcome to half this money."

"No, it's yours, you earned it." Steve collected his suitcase from the car boot. "I'll give you a bell tonight and tell you what's what."

Adam whispered. "I take it you've stashed the gear in Zeebrugge."

Steve smiled. "Good luck with June. I'm glad you're happy."

Adam smiled. "Give my love to your mum." They hugged again. "For fuck's sake, watch what you're doing."

It took another hour to clear London. The Dream Lover settled back into the hum of the car and the motorway traffic. It'd been a long time since he'd thought about plans for the future. Of course he wasn't talking about kids and stuff. No, they'd have enough with Ralph. He was, after all, originally June's dog.

Yeah, Ralph: can't wait to see Ralph.

Well within the allotted hours, the dog's front paws were bouncing a welcome off Adam's chest. "Hey, you mangy bugger, Daddy's home." The mongrel panted and bounded around his feet. "Calm down, you daft mutt. What you been feeding him, our kid? He's like a demented witchdoctor." The bounding continued as Adam explored his home. The flat was in good nick. "Have you been behaving yourself? I hope you haven't been messing the place up for Uncle Paul. Where's this Valentine's card from June, our kid?"

"Is that what it is? It's in there with the rest of your post." Paul opened the top drawer in the ebony cupboard. Adam had asked his brother to forward anything that looked important, so the stuff in the drawer was five months' miscellaneous junk mail.

"Couldn't you have kept it separate?"

"It should be near the top. She only came, yesterday. There, that's it." Paul pulled out the epistle and handed it to his beaming brother. The envelope was a bit fancy for a Valentine's card.

Adam opened it. The beam disappeared. "Oh shit."

"What is it?"

"I don't frigging believe this."

"What?"

"Mr and Mrs Roundhill have cordially invited me to Our Lady of Lourdes Roman Catholic Church to see their daughter get married to Simon the frigging saxophonist."

20 T's Adventures: Leeds. Feb '77:
Stand By Your Man.

T stood in her beloved kitchen, hot beverage in hand. The blanket of contentment she should've been wrapped in still hung by the door, the clammy sweat of anxiety stopped her wearing it. The previous conversations with Jeannie about the 'not so Mr Perfect' kept reverberating. Was the Big Picture their punishment for what they'd done? First thing tomorrow, she'd make an appointment with her doctor. Happen there's no picture at all. Any number of things can cause a late period. But happen she should've warned William. No, no sense in that until confirmation. Then again, what if it was his baby? After Colin had kicked her out, that's if he hadn't killed her first, she might be begging William to take her in.

Oh shut up, Morgan, that's ridiculous. For a start, Colin wouldn't lay a finger on her no matter how much she deserved it and he'd leave home himself before he'd kick anybody out. *Why can't you just enjoy being home?*

The sound of a steel guitar penetrated the kitchen from the living room, Colin going through his own homecoming ritual with one of his country & western albums.

She looked toward the drone. *If that's Merle bloody Haggard, I'm going to go in there and smash it over his bloody head.* It wasn't, it was Tammy Wynette, revving herself up to stand by some bloke or other.

Daft cow.

T closed the door.

With each sip of tea, she tried to imbibe something positive. True, in the debit column, the Big Picture hadn't changed, money prospects still didn't look too bright and not even a good pot of English would have any effect on her gestation. All the same, collating the credit page did give her a lift. She'd just completed a European tour as lead singer of a rock band. Alright, perhaps 'rock band' was pushing it but still, as Steve said: 'You did good, girl'. And now, she was home in her beautiful, two up, two down with extended kitchen, ex council house with a man who deep down loved her, even if he did have a funny way of showing it. Since their reconciliation, he *had* made more effort, which was enough. She didn't even deserve that. And then there was his promise they'd try for a baby as soon as they got home. Well, they *were* home and though, given her predicament, the promise might've been a bit redundant, it was a promise, nonetheless.

Besides, you never know, Theresa, the baby could be Colin's. Wow, wouldn't that be good?

In the living room, the phone rang. She waited. It continued. She went in to find Tammy had come to her senses. She'd given up standing by her man and got herself a D.I.V.O.R.C.E. Some Coal Miner's Daughter had taken over the turntable. Colin was asleep.

"Colin!"

He jumped and immediately grabbed the phone. "Hello? Oh, hiya Adam." He turned to T. "I wasn't asleep, I was just listening with my eyes closed." She returned to her kitchen. After a few minutes, Colin came in. "That was Adam."

"Gerraway!"

"You know he was supposed to be getting back with his ex?"

"Course I do, he never shut up about it all the way up the motorway."

"Make us a cup of tea, love."

She switched on the kettle.

"Well apparently, it's all gone tits up." He sat at the breakfast bar. "Also, Steve's called him and said he doesn't know when he's going to make it back to Leeds. He's asked Adam to help me fix up Len's van and even come back to Germany for the gear if needs be." She got the milk from the fridge. Colin continued. "Adam says he has no problem with any of that but he wants you to fix him up with some digs at Carter's."

She almost dropped Colin's pint pot. "What do you mean; fix him up with digs at Carter's?"

"He wants to go down to Schweinfurt and try and sort things out with that Italian piece. If he stays at Carter's, he can visit his bird. She only lives upstairs."

"I know where bloody Emma lives, I mean why can't Adam call himself?"

"Kim won't say no if you ask."

"What the hell's Adam doing ringing at this time? It's too late to phone the Carters, now." She undid the packet of biscuits and piled them high on Colin's plate. "I've no idea where the number is. I'll have to unpack all the cases to look for it."

"There's no rush."

Just a minute, Morgan, this could be the chance to get it over with. "Erm, maybe I *should* call now. They're both in and out during the day so this is probably the best time to catch them. William will just be getting in from the club."

"Like I said: no rush."

Of course she knew where William's number was. It wasn't in any of the suitcases, which had already been unpacked, it was in her handbag. She'd put it there when she'd contemplated calling him to explain the situation but chickened out. Colin took his tea and biscuits back to the living room. She took her handbag upstairs.

She sat on the bed, diary in hand, staring at the telephone. "Come on, Morgan, just get on with it." If she did pre-warn him, then it wouldn't be such a blow if the worst happened. And if it *was* a false alarm, as it surely would be, then he'd be as relieved as her. She unfolded the conversation plan. She could hardly open with 'Hello William, I'm pregnant'. Start with Adam's request to stay. Better not mention Kim or the children. He probably wouldn't appreciate that, having been on his own all these weeks. Desperation scanned her mind in search of a hopeful straw to grasp: yes, the statues. She could say how she'd forgotten them, and then perhaps mention the curse. She reached for the thought dangling before her. Yes, the bloody curse had struck again. She might, only might, mind you, be slightly pregnant.

She rehearsed the conversation with herself throughout the dialling.

Come on, Theresa, you can do this.

William's voice interrupted her self-encouragement. "Hello?"

Her left hand lowered the receiver but stopped an inch short of cutting off the call. She brought the telephone back to her ear.

"Hello? Who is dat?"

"Hello, William? This is Theresa from 'Images'. I'm calling from England."

"Well my, oh my, Theresa. How you doing?"

"I'm doing okay, thanks. How are you?"

"My, oh my, this is a real surprise."

If you think this is a surprise . . .

She decided to discard the preliminaries. "William, I forgot my statues."

"Say Kim; er, guess who I got on the phone from London."

Kim? Did he say Kim? What's she doing there?

"I'm not calling from London. I'm at home in Yorkshire."

"Oh, sorry, ain't that in London?"

"William, I thought Kim had gone back to America."

"Yeah, Kim and the boys been home for a few weeks, but they back now." The desperation in his voice had no trouble making it through the wire. "Everything's real good, here."

She floundered. "Er, listen, William, the reason I'm ringing, er, do you remember Adam, our drummer?"

"Oh, right on. How is Adam?"

"He's okay. He's more than okay but the thing is: he's coming to Schweinfurt. He's coming to visit your cleaner, Emma. Anyway, he needs somewhere to stay."

"Hell yeah, he can stay with us, no problem, man. Say Kim is it okay if Adam stays with us. He wants to visit Emma?"

T was sure she heard Kim mention something about a 'bad woman'.

"When he coming?" William asked.

"It'll be a few weeks off yet."

"Yeah, Kim says it's okay. He can stay for sure."

"Thanks. That's brilliant. He'll be dead chuffed." She waited for him to fill the silence. He said nothing. "I'm glad to hear Kim's back. I take it you two have sorted yourselves out."

"Say listen; Theresa, about them things you just mentioned."

"Things? What things?"

"Them things you left at the club."

"At the club? I never left anything at the club. You mean our equipment in Wildflecken?"

"No, not that. Them things: Bobby was supposed to pick them up but he forgot."

"You mean my Bird God statues?"

"Yeah: now you on it. I kept them for you. I'll give them to Adam when he come to stay."

"Er, yeah, course, that'll be good. Give them to Adam." Her mind raced through the silence. Had she been tricked? Maybe Kim hadn't left him. Maybe she'd only been visiting the States. "I forgot to tell you, me and Colin are back together."

"Yeah? I didn't know you stopped being together."

"Eh? Oh yeah, we split up for a bit."

"You did? I didn't know. How's Colin doing? He treating you good?"

"Yeah, he's okay."

"Fine. He give you a baby yet?"

"Listen, William, this call is costing me a fortune. I'd better go." She hung up, her head ready to explode. *I can't believe he said that about a baby.* And Kim was there.

Back in the living room, Brenda Lee was whispering Sweet Nothings in Colin's ear. He looked up from his empty biscuit plate. "That was quick, for you. Thought we'd have to take out a second mortgage once you and Kim got gassing?"

"Sorry." She headed for the solitude of her kitchen but Colin's voice stopped her.

"Well?"

What did he want, more biscuits? "Well what?"

"What do you mean, well what? What did they say?"

"What did who say?"

"What did who say? Who the bloody hell do you think? The Carters."

"What did they say about what?"

"What the hell's got into you: you gormless bugger? What did they say about Adam staying?"

"Oh that. They said okay, no problem." She escaped.

Back in the kitchen, as if by osmosis, another cup of PG Tips appeared in her hand. She couldn't even remember switching on the kettle.

So now what?

Actually, so now nothing! Kim's return made very little difference to the Big Picture, unless the baby was Coloured, of course. There was nothing she could do about that, other than wait. It was all in the hands of the Gods, as Steve would say. Hopefully, it was in the hands of female Gods and they'd treat her kindly.

Bloody hell, how did you get yourself in this mess, you silly mare?

Colin's appearance stopped her self-chastisement. "Oh, nice one, Cyril. I see you've made yourself a cuppa. Where's mine?"

"Sorry." She set about making the tea and opened another packet of biscuits.

"What the hell were you chatting to Kim about? It's sent you doolally tap."

"What?"

"You were away with the fairies."

"Sorry. I forgot why I'd telephoned."

"Honestly, T, you're so bloody stupid, sometimes."

No matter what happened to her, if both her arms dropped off or if one day she woke to find she'd been crowned Queen of England, always remaining, as her constant would be Colin, telling her she was a 'stupid mare' or a 'silly cow' or some other gormless female animal. She wished it *was* in the hands of the Gods to make someone change and treat her with respect. If Adam did bring back her Bird Gods, happen they would make Colin 'see the error of *his* ways', as Jeannie suggested.

Ah, some hope.

He shoved two Jammy Dodgers in his mouth and then washed them down with a large gulp from his pint pot. He put down the tea, came behind her and wrapped his huge arms around her waist. She closed her eyes, blotting out the Big Picture. Could this be just what she needed? He kissed her neck. "I bet you're glad to be home in your own little house."

She momentarily thought of making a sarcastic comment about stating the bloody obvious but decided against it. "I certainly am." She turned to face him. "Colin, do you love me?"

"What sort of a question is that?"

"A reasonable one. Well, do you?"

"Course I bloody do, you silly cow."

"How come you never tell me?"

"I thought it was obvious."

"No Colin, it's not obvious. Far from it."

"Okay, then: I love you."

"I love you too."

He took another biscuit and drained his pint pot. "Well come on girl, get upstairs and get your keks off. We get to shag in our own bed tonight."

What were you saying about respect, Theresa? The sooner those Juju Birds are back, the better.

"Come on, then." He pushed her toward the door. "We better get trying for that sprog."

Mm, I wonder what the chances are of him seeing the error of his ways. Happen!

EPILOGUE

London – 2019

Do you frigging love me? What does that even mean? It's like asking someone if they believe in God. God means different things to different people. It's subjective, same with 'love'. Adam hung his coat in the hotel wardrobe then looked at his watch. "Where the hell is she?" He looked down at the Knightsbridge traffic, still at a standstill. He sat on the bed, waiting.

At last! Jeannie finally arrived. She ushered in two porters, laden with bags and parcels. "Shift your arse, Adam." He jumped up. "Just put them on the bed, fellas" she said.

Adam tried to take some of the parcels. "Let me get those."

She pulled him away. "For God's sake, leave them alone. Let them do their job." He stepped aside while the porters made a show of unburdening their load. Jeannie took off her coat. "There's loads more downstairs in reception. Could hardly fit them in the taxi." The porters left. "How did the screening go?"

"That's a lot of shopping. Glad to see you've had a nice time." He switched on the kettle and threw a teabag and two sachets of sugar into a cup.

She got going on the unpacking. "Is that for me?"

"Yeah."

"What's got into *you*?"

"What do you mean?"

"Being a bit nice, aren't we? When do you ever make me a cuppa?"

"I'm always making you tea."

"You don't even make your own. When your Evie made you a cup, she asked if you take sugar. You said 'I don't know; you'll have to ask Jeannie'."

"That was a joke."

She picked up the empty sugar sachets and threw them in the bin. "I take it the screening went well. Is it good? I can't wait."

The porters arrived with the rest of the shopping. Adam looked into the corridor. "Christ stuck in a lift, is there any more coming?"

She rolled her eyes. "Shut up and give the lads some money."

He took some coins from his pocket and gave them to the porters. "Cheers."

She shook her head. "For God's sake, Adam, give them a proper tip." She went to her handbag, took out her purse and pulled out a wad. She peeled off two ten-pound notes and handed them to the porters.

Adam's eyes popped. "Oy, do you mind not being so frigging generous with the hard-earned?"

"Thank you very much, madam." They'd gone.

"Cheeky young buggers." No, this wasn't going to spoil his plans. He closed the door. "You haven't eaten have you? I've booked the restaurant downstairs for tonight." He finished making her tea then stopped her unpacking. "Leave them a minute. Sit down."

"What is it?"

He took some of the parcels off the bed to make room. "Sit down."

She sat. "What's happened? What have you done? Oh no, you've messed up haven't you? Did you fall out with Marshall?"

"What? Are you psychic or what, woman? How did you know that?"

"You and him are always falling out. He can't stop them making the series, can he?"

"No, I've sorted it." He put a finger over her lips. "Jeannie, shut up a minute. I've been shopping, as well. I've got something for you." He went to the wardrobe and put his hand into his coat pocket. "I was going to wait 'til we got to the restaurant to give you this but you may as well have it now." He knelt before her. "This'll save me making a will, if nothing else." He opened the box in his hand and presented a diamond ring. "Jeannie Hay, will you do me the honour of becoming my wife?"

She exploded into laughter and fell back into the parcels.

"What?" He was still kneeling, holding forth the ring. "What's so frigging funny?"

The laughter continued. She sat up and composed herself to a state of tittering. "Get up, you stupid wazzock."

He slowly got to his feet. "Bastard. I think the answer you're looking for is, yes."

She got up and kissed his cheek. "You daft arse. You didn't really think I was serious, did you?"

"What? Yeah, I thought this was what you wanted."

"No, Adam, it's the last thing I want."

"Bloody women, you can't frigging win." He sat on the bed.

She sat next to him. "I was just making you aware of my situation." She stroked his cheek. "What brought this on, anyway?"

"I don't know. I thought about what you were saying, this morning." He looked at the ring, still in his hand. "And then I watched Carmel's film." He put the ring on the bedside cabinet. "It's nowt like my book. She's made me out to be a right sexist tosser."

"Well, you are a sexist tosser. You were a sexist tosser when we were together in Germany and then I didn't see you for twenty-five years and you were still a sexist tosser when we met up again."

"Twenty-five years, was it really? Bloody hell, we're getting old, girl."

"You speak for yourself."

"Life's like a toilet roll."

"Yeah, I know, the nearer you get to the end, the quicker it goes."

"Bastard, couldn't you, just once, pretend you don't know the punch-line?"

"Your jokes are even older than you."

He passed her the tea. "Don't let it go cold." He went to look out of the window. "Something else she goes on about in this film, those frigging juju statues."

"You mean T's Bird Gods?"

"That Surround Vision thing is dead weird. It's like you're right in the film. At one bit, I was right there, in the room with the frigging juju bastards, even the spirits themselves at one point."

"Ah, I see it all, now." She got up and carried on with her unpacking. "That's what's got into you. I always said those Bird Gods could make men do strange things."

"It's no joke. I was terrified. You don't know what those things did to me."

"No, 'cos you won't tell me."

"I don't want to tell anyone, ever." He picked up the ring and held it in the flat of his palm. The diamond glistened. "What am I supposed to do with this? It cost me a frigging fortune."

She closed the box and then closed his fingers into a fist around it. "Why don't you bring it to the restaurant? You can ask me again."

"What, so you can knock me back and give me another kick in the bollocks? No thanks. You must think I'm stupid."

"I know you're stupid. What time have you booked the meal for?"

"Not 'til half-eight." He went to the wardrobe and put the ring back in his coat pocket. "If you shift that shite off the bed, we've time for a quickie, if you fancy."

"If I thought you could manage it at your age, I might be tempted."

"I could still keep you up all night, young lady."

"What, with your snoring?"

He took her around the waist and gave her a lingering kiss. "Do you know something Jeannie Hay?"

"What's that?"

"I fucking love you."

She cleared the parcels off the bed.

CHAPTER HEADING GLOSSARY

Chapter 1: Why Y'all Play No ZZ Top? **"ZZ Top's First Album"**: released 1971 by blues trio ZZ Top.

Chapter 2: **"Long Tall Sally"**: 1956 rock & roll single by Little Richard and later EP by the Beatles.

Chapter 3: Play That Funky Music White Boy. **"Play That Funky Music"**: funk rock song by Wild Cherry 1976.

Chapter 4: Sweet Home Alibami. **"Sweet Home Alabama"**: by rock band Lynyrd Skynyrd 1974.

Chapter 5: **"The First Time Ever I Saw Your Face"**: 1957 folk song written by Ewan MacColl, recorded by Peggy Seeger, Also by Roberta Flack soul ballad version 1972.

Chapter 6: **"Young Hearts Run Free"**: a disco song by Candi Staton 1976.

Chapter 7: **"By The Rivers Of Babylon"**: written and recorded by the Melodians in 1972: made famous 1977 by West German band Boney M (1976 in West Germany).

Chapter 8: **"Wipe Out"**: surfing song by the Surfaris 1962: cover versions by The Ventures, the Beach Boys and many others.

Chapter 9: **"Let There Be Drums"**: instrumental by Sandy Nelson 1961.

Chapter 10: **Down Town** on the piste: "**Downtown**": pop song written by Tony Hatch recorded by Petula Clark 1964.

Chapter 11: "**Blue Suede Shoes**" written and recorded by Carl Perkins 1956: covered and made famous by Elvis Presley same year.

Chapter 12: "**I Wish It Could Be Christmas Every Day**": pop song by Wizzard 1973.

Chapter 13: "**Four Seasons**": a set of four violin concertos by Antonio Vivaldi, 1723 and also Frankie Valli's Jersey Boys pop group **The Four Seasons.**

Chapter 14: "**Can't Get Enough of Your Love Babe**": soul song by Barry White 1974.

Chapter 15: "**Money, Money, Money**": pop song 1976 by Abba.

Chapter 16: If A Picture Paints A Thousand Words: Opening line of "**If**": Ballad by David Gates of Bread. Covered in 1975 by Telly Savalas.

Chapter 17: "**Baby Love**": Holland Dozier Holland Motown song for The Supremes. 1964.

Chapter 18: "**Homeward Bound**": Simon & Garfunkel pop song 1966.

Chapter 19: "**Dream Lover**": pop song, written and recorded by Bobby Darin 1959.

Chapter 20: "**Stand By Your Man**": country song by Tammy Wynette 1968.

LEGEND TWO
THE WRATH OF MARIE'S GOD ALMIGHTY

In the beginning there was the word; and the word was God. God made Heaven and Earth and sent His Only Son down to Earth to give Man the Word. But Man rejected the Word and put God's Only Son to death. On the third day, God's Only Son rose from the dead and ascended into Heaven. Here, he will sit on the right hand side of the Father, on the Day of Judgement.

Beware Vengeful Deities.

LEGEND THREE
ATAHUALPA: GOD OF FATE

Atahualpa was Chief of the Inca civilization. The Inca Indians believed that the Sun was God and Atahualpa was the Son of God, sent down to Earth. The Sun God provided everything for the Inca. He controlled their fate. The Inca worshipped their God of Destiny until the Spaniard Pizarro executed Atahualpa.

Beware Vengeful Deities.

Lightning Source UK Ltd.
Milton Keynes UK
UKOW04f1856230115

245036UK00004B/202/P